A Good Time for Goodbye

A Jake Horn Mystery

Gregory Payette

8 FLAGS PUBLISHING

CHAPTER 1

I HURRIED TO MY desk, knocking a can to the floor with the cord as I lifted the phone off the hook. With warm beer soaking through my socks, I cleared my throat and answered. "Horn Investigations."

"Jake?"

A chill ran up my spine. And it wasn't from the cold in my office.

I sat at my desk and ran my free hand down my face as if to stretch the skin right off of it. "Something I can help you with?" I looked to my left, the morning light working its way through the blinds on the window at the front of my office.

"Don't sound so excited to hear from me," she said.

"I was asleep."

"At your office?"

"Didn't you just call me here?" I got up and carried the base of the phone around to the other side of the partition behind my desk and back to the couch in the so-called client area. I kicked over another can, although it was empty.

The last person I wanted to hear from was Lily Dempsey.

With the phone between my ear and shoulder, I pulled on my boots. "You've got ten seconds to tell me why you're bothering me this early." I looked at my watch. "Eight seconds."

"Jake, please," Lily said. "I need your help."

It crossed my mind to hang up, but I knew she'd only call back until I answered. Or worse, she'd be at my door. "What makes you think I'd help you?"

There was a brief pause on the other end of the line. "Jake, please. I'm serious."

"Did it sound like I was joking?"

"I... I was hoping I could see you."

I laughed. "*See* me?"

"To talk." She paused again. "Can I come by your office?"

The only light in the place was the two lamps: one at my desk and the other next to the couch. The florescent lights on the ceiling flickered, and needed to be replaced, so I usually left them off. And with the heat down low, it was always cold in the office.

We were five years past the energy crisis of '73; my landlord—a friend of mine—predicted energy prices were going to shoot up again. Although he knew he couldn't, he always joked he'd raise my rent if I used too much heat.

The office was one big space: a couch on the far right, my desk in the middle, with a wood-paneled partition behind it, and a folding table and cabinets on the far left. I had a coffee maker, a mini fridge, and a bathroom down the short hall toward the back.

Horn Investigations was different back when my Uncle Pat was still alive, with five employees, including me. Six, with our secretary.

I said to Lily, "Why can't you just tell me over the phone?"

"I'd like to discuss it face-to-face. Is that too much to ask?" She paused with a sigh into the phone. "I hoped you'd gotten over your little grudge."

"My 'little grudge'?" I laughed. Not that it was funny.

2

"It's about Michael," she said.

I leaned back on the couch and waited to hear more, although I wasn't sure I wanted to.

She continued, "I know this might sound strange, but I... I'd like to hire you."

I got up off the couch and stretched the phone's cord so I could look out the window. I spread the horizontal blinds with my fingers and looked out at my grandmother's yellow Chevy Nova still covered in frost on East Broadway.

"I'm not accepting new clients right now," I said.

The sun was working its way up, but it wouldn't be warm enough to even make a dent in the snow the blizzard dumped on us a few weeks earlier in February. There were piles of snow everywhere in Boston and throughout New England. It was bad enough the Saint Patrick's Day parade had been postponed until April.

Not that I was big on parades.

The only time I remember close to the same amount of snow was during the 100-Hour Storm, nine years earlier, in '69.

I dragged the cord around the partition and back to my desk. I kept the phone against my ear, opened my drawer, and pulled out my appointment book. The ribbon was still on the first week of February. I flipped to March even though I knew without having to look, my days were empty. "I'm very busy, you know."

She said, "Really?"

I could tell she didn't believe me.

I looked down at the blank pages in my book. "I'm sorry. I just don't have any free time for a new client."

She paused on the other end. "Jake," she said. "People talk, you know."

Yeah, no kidding.

"What's that supposed to mean?" I said. Although it was no secret the business had been slow.

"Please, Jake. I'm right around the corner from your office. I can be there in ten minutes, if you'll just give me a chance to explain."

I walked over and grabbed the glass carafe from the coffee maker. I'd left it on the day before, an inch of burnt muck glued to the bottom. "All right," I said. "But give me at least a half hour before you show up. I have a couple things to take care of."

***

Lily walked into my office like a cliché. A beautiful, confident woman looking for a private investigator she could trust to make things right. She wore a long powder-blue wool coat with brown fur that ran around the edge of the hood, which was pulled up over her head, and down the front over the buttons. Her spicy perfume filled the office. I guess I can admit I knew it was Cinnabar. But that's only because I'd given it to her as a gift more than once. I remember the lady at the Filene's counter describing the scent as "mysterious."

I still don't know what that meant.

But I knew the smell. It gave me a quick flashback and a hint that letting her step inside my office was a mistake.

I helped her with her coat and looked it over. "How many animals had to be killed for this thing?" I hung it on the rack near the door and walked to my desk.

Lily followed me over and sat across from me. "It's faux."

"Faux?" I laughed. "Why bother with the French?" I said. "Can't you just say it's *fake*. Although I assume they charge more for *faux*."

Her eyes moved along the floor and over the thin, stained green carpet under her feet, then at the framed photos hung on the brown-paneled wall at the back of the office. "I thought when Nick bought this building, he promised to clean this place up for you?"

I shrugged, looking up at the stain on the drop-tile ceiling above my desk. "I'm just lucky the building hasn't been condemned."

Lily crossed her legs and placed her purse on my desk in front of her, her hands rested on her lap. "Before I tell you what this is all about, can you promise me you'll listen? Without the hostility?"

I looked down into my mug of coffee. "Why don't you just get on with it." I glanced at the clock on the wall. "I don't have all day."

"I just want you to know, I'm not here looking for a deal, Jake. I'll pay you your full rate." She gave a quick swipe of her hand across my desk as if clearing dust or some crumbs. "Couldn't you use the work?"

I leaned forward on my desk, my hands clasped in front of me. "I don't need you to do me any favors, Lily."

"That's not what I meant," she said, brushing a strand of hair from her face, her big brown eyes coming back at me. "I believe Michael's been cheating on me."

I almost spit out my coffee. And not because I was surprised. "What goes around comes around," I said.

"This is different," she said.

"Is it?"

We both sat quiet.

"You and I were never in a good place," she said. "You know that. There was never going to be enough room in your heart for me." She looked at the partition wall behind me, at the framed photo of my wife with me and my daughter, Nancy, as a baby.

"So what do you want me to do? Prove he's cheating?"

She nodded, her lips pressed together.

I got up from the desk with my Red Sox mug and walked to the coffee maker. I filled my mug and took a sip. "It's not what someone like you would consider good coffee, but it's not bad, if you want a cup?"

"No, thank you. I think I'll pass."

I went back to the desk and sat down across from her in the old, cracked leather chair. It squeaked as I leaned back. "So, what makes you believe he's cheating?"

She pulled a small round mirror and lipstick from her purse and covered her lips in a glossy shade of red. "I have my suspicions."

"Ah," I said, and thought for a moment. "Can I ask you why you'd come to *me*? There are a few hundred private investigators in Massachusetts. And I'm guessing most of them don't despise you as much as I do."

She seemed to force a small grin, closing her eyes for a handful of seconds.

That looked like it stung. "I'm sorry," I said. "I mean, I *do* despise you. I'm not even sure hate's too strong a word. But I probably didn't need to say it out loud, with you sitting across from me."

"Thanks, Jake." She shifted in her seat. "Would you believe me if I said I've never stopped feeling bad about—"

I put up my hand. "Please. Let's not go down that road. Okay? I'd appreciate it."

She nodded. "You're the one person I can trust," she said. "I don't want to have to ask some stranger to help me."

I stood up and walked toward the front of the office, pulling the string to open the blinds to let the sun in from the three windows facing East Broadway. "Why do I get the feeling there's something you're not telling me?" I waited for an answer.

She stared back at me and cleared her throat. "I thought you'd jump at the chance to prove Michael was—"

"I don't need to follow a guy around for cheating on his wife to make myself feel better," I said. I went back to my desk and sat down, swiveled in the chair to my right and looked at the framed photos on the back wall. My favorite was the one with my uncle and Tony Conagliaro at Fenway Park. The photo was taken in July 1967, a month before Tony C. was struck in the face with a Jack Hamilton fastball.

"All I need is proof he's cheating," she said, shifting in her seat. "But it can't be just a picture of him out to dinner or anything like that. He'll just deny it, say was a work thing."

"He must've learned that from you?" I said.

Lily threw up her hands with a sigh. "Didn't you just tell me to let it go?"

I turned my chair to face her. "Are you asking me to catch him in the act?"

She swallowed hard, paused a moment before finally nodding.

I rubbed the stubbled three days of growth on my face with both hands and leaned with my elbows on the desk. "Why don't you just confront him?"

"Well, there are some legal things I need to worry about. I've actually already met with a divorce attorney."

"Oh," I said, picking up my coffee. I took a sip. It was barely warm. "You don't have any proof he's cheating, but you've already hired a lawyer?" I still had to decide if I wanted the case but opened the middle drawer of the desk and took out a lined yellow legal pad. "Give me the woman's name." I kept my eyes on the pad, the pen ready.

Lily said, "Angela."

I wrote it down: A-N-G-E-L-A. "Last name?" I looked up when she didn't respond, but she wasn't looking back at me. I said, "Hello? Can you tell me her last name?"

She looked up, and in a quiet voice, one she didn't use very often, said, "Gautieri. Angela Gautieri."

I placed the pen on top of the pad and leaned back in the chair. "You're joking, right? Gautieri? *Gautieri?* Are you telling me your husband is sleeping with Mayor Gautieri's daughter?" I thought for a moment. "Isn't she engaged to Lawrence Martin?"

"The football player?" She nodded. "Apparently, they broke it off."

I pushed the pad to the side, got up from the desk, and walked to the door. "Sorry," I said. "You're going to have to find someone else foolish enough to help you."

She picked up her purse and stood. "It's not like you to be afraid," Lily said.

"Oh, I wouldn't say I'm *afraid*. I'm just not *stupid*."

"Nobody has to know it's you," she said, stepping toward me. "Isn't that part of what you do? Work undercover?"

I grabbed her coat from the rack and held it out to her. "We're done here," I said.

"I'll pay you whatever you want," she said, reaching for her coat.

I pulled open the door, the frigid air pouring in from outside. "How many times do I have to tell you? It's *never* about the money."

CHAPTER 2

I WALKED OUT OF the First Street Diner and unbuttoned my pea-coat, the sun shining with warmth I hadn't felt in months. I thought I'd enjoy it while I could, knowing the weather in Boston, especially in March, swung both ways.

I hadn't thought much of Lily since she left my office, although I wondered if maybe it was time I considered allowing money to be more of a motivating factor for me than it had been in the past. I realized a new client wouldn't be a bad thing.

I waved through the window at Mr. Lyle, the owner of the laundromat a couple of doors down from my office, and continued to my door. I slid the key into the lock and felt the presence of someone behind me.

When I looked, it was Nick Sullivan, a friend of mine, who also happened to be my landlord. He owned the building once owned by my Uncle Pat and where Horn Investigations was located. As the person who inherited Horn Investigations, I had no interest in taking on the debt that came with the building. So I worked out a deal with Nick.

I wasn't much of a businessman or very good with money. But I trusted my friend. He claimed the deal was good for both of us. At the very least, I wouldn't be forced to run Horn Investigations from my Chevy Nova.

"Everything all right?" Nick said, asking in a way like he had his doubts.

I unlocked the door and held it open for him to go in ahead of me. "Oh, you know how it is." I stepped in behind him and hung my coat on the rack. The smell of perfume still hung in the air.

I walked past my desk, situated in the very center of the office with a wood-paneled partition behind it, and headed over to the coffee machine. I noticed I'd left it on, but asked Nick if he wanted a cup anyway.

Nick sniffed, with a sneer. "How old is it?"

I grabbed the carafe and walked down the hall at the back of the office and into the bathroom. "I'll make more." I dumped the black sludge into the sink and rinsed the carafe, then filled it from the tap. The glass was stained black from all the times I'd left it on.

Nick hadn't moved from the door, watching me as I walked back to the Mr. Coffee.

I knew his visit wasn't social.

"Jake, listen," he said. "I know business has been slow. But it's, you know, it's been over three months. I don't want to make this weird between us, but"—he rubbed the back of his neck—"the space upstairs has been vacant for a long time. Nobody's even looked at it. So, I'm just being honest with you. When I don't get paid, I can't pay the bank. I can't even pay the utility company. I'm sure you don't want them to come turn off the power."

I dumped a scoop of ground coffee from the yellow Chock Full o' Nuts can into the machine and dumped the tap water from the carafe, then walked over to the thermostat by the door and lowered it. It was always cold in the office, although I'd raised it a few degrees before my ex showed up out of the blue.

"I only had the heat up because someone, well, a potential client came in earlier." I pointed toward the ceiling. "I don't even use the overhead lights." I grinned. "Just trying to save you some money."

"I never suggested you shouldn't use the heat," Nick said. "But that's good news, right? A client?"

"Oh yeah, no. I mean, I don't know yet. Maybe." I wasn't about to get into the details. He didn't know Lily but had heard enough to know she was trouble. "Listen," I said. "I should have things straightened out soon. I'm sorry I had to do this to you, but if you can just give me until the end of the month, I'll—"

"Two weeks?" Nick nodded. "We can make that work." He looked around the office, then shifted his eyes up toward the stains on the ceiling over my desk. "When you pay up, maybe we can make some repairs to the place."

I poured myself a coffee and asked him again, "You want a cup?"

Nick stepped toward the door, and we both stood quiet until he finally pulled it open and looked back at me. "Two weeks?"

I nodded, giving him a thumbs-up. "You have my word."

***

Raymond was out on the top step of his porch reading the *Boston Globe* with a mug next to him. He raised his eyes from the newspaper as I stepped out into the warm sun from the Nova, gave me a nod, then went right back to reading.

I continued up the walkway cut between shrinking piles of snow on either side. At least you could finally see the bricks with the way the sun was beating down on them. I stood at the bottom step looking up at Raymond still reading the paper as if I weren't there. I could see it was the sports section.

He finally closed the newspaper and placed it down next to him on the step. "Did you see that game last night?"

"Bruins?"

Raymond nodded. "Canadiens will be tough, but I think that's who it'll be in the end. Canadiens and Bruins."

"I think I'm ready for baseball," I said. "Sox should be all right this year."

Raymond shrugged. "I like some of the moves they've made. Jerry Remy's a nice pickup at second. It's only spring training, but with Tiant and Lee... I don't know. This could be the year."

I laughed. "You say that every spring."

Raymond shrugged and sipped from his cup.

"So, you want to guess who came by my office yesterday?" I said.

"Not really."

I sat down on the bottom step. "Lily."

"Lily? Borden?"

"Well, she's Lily Dempsey," I said. "At least for now." I looked up at his surprised expression. "She thinks her husband's cheating on her."

Raymond grunted. "Well, what goes around comes around."

I glanced up at him and smiled. "That's exactly what I said to her."

I already knew what Raymond was going to say before I even explained my situation. But I couldn't help but turn to him for advice. I always did. I said, "She wants to hire me, to help prove he's cheating. Funny thing is, she's already got a lawyer lined up."

"A lawyer?"

"She's filing for divorce. So she wants me to catch him cheating, give her some ammunition in a settlement."

Raymond laughed, shaking his head. But then his expression turned serious. "Please tell me you said *no*," he said. "You don't need that back in your life. You know how I feel about her."

I paused, thinking. "I told her I couldn't do it. But, I don't know, the more I think about it... business has been slow. I might have to just tuck my tail between my legs and take her on as a client. Do it for the money, you know?"

"You sure she's not looking for a freebie?" he said, lifting his mug to take a sip.

I cracked a smile. "She's not like that. I could probably double my rate and she'd pay it."

Raymond stood up and tossed what was left of his coffee cup into the shrubs next to the stairs. "You do what you gotta do, cuz. Maybe it's what you need, get things moving for you again. A few quick photos... Be an easy one, *no*?"

"Well, I thought so too. But there are a couple of pretty good reasons I told her no." I stood from the step and squinted, looking up toward the clear blue sky. "For one, she wants me to catch them in the act."

"In the *act*?"

"Which you would think a mature private investigator like myself wouldn't have a problem with. The problem is the young woman he's allegedly sleeping with is... you know Tony Gautieri, right?"

"Mayor Gautieri? In Providence?" He nodded. "Of course I do."

"It's his daughter. Angela Gautieri."

Raymond raised his eyebrows high on his head. "He's got a young daughter, doesn't he?"

I nodded. "Twenty-three."

"And how old is Lily's husband?"

"Michael's thirty-seven."

Raymond walked down the steps from the porch and onto the walkway. "I think I read something in the *Globe* about Lawrence Martin dating Gautieri's daughter. Could that be right?"

"That's accurate," I said.

"Martin single-handedly helped keep the Patriots' record respectable last season," Raymond said. "Before he got hurt, the man was a monster. Lily's husband must have a death wish, sleeping with a woman whose father's got alleged mob connections and a boyfriend who crushes people for a living. I know you need to put food on your table, Jake. But I'm not sure I'd go near this one."

"Well, like I said, I already told her I couldn't do it."

"Yeah, I can tell you're still thinking about it."

I looked at the water dripping down from the gutters. "I've turned my back on a lot of potential clients over the last couple of years. Maybe I have to face the fact the big cases aren't going to land in my lap the way they did when your dad was still around."

Raymond shrugged. "It doesn't mean you have to be foolish either," he said. "I'm not sure you've considered the fact it's Lily we're talking about. I don't know anyone who is as manipulative." He picked up a shovel leaned against the porch and jammed the blade into a mound of snow along the walkway, tossing it out into the yard. "My advice, again, is not to touch it."

I reached down and picked up a handful of wet snow, shaped it into a ball and threw it across the yard at the Japanese maple. I hit it dead center on the lower part of the trunk. "I guess you're right. But I need to get some work. I haven't paid Nick rent in a couple of months."

The front door opened, and Raymond's wife, Beth, stuck her head outside. "Hi, Jake," she said. "You guys want a couple of beers?"

I looked at my watch. "Thanks, Beth. I think I'll hold off for now."

Raymond gave me a look like something was wrong with me. "You on the wagon?"

I let out a laugh. "I need to go out for a run when I get home, clear my head. I have a beer, all I'll do is hit the couch and take a nap."

Raymond rolled his eyes. "I wish I had the discipline like you," he said. "I guess that's why you're all muscle and I've got this." He rubbed his own stomach hanging a bit over the belt. "This is what happens when you retire and have nothing to do but drink beer." He looked up toward Beth, shaking his head. "I guess not right now, hon."

She was on the top step, her hands out in front of her. "Nice to have some warm sun," she said, then walked back to the door. "You guys change your mind, give me a yell."

I leaned against the post at the bottom of the stairs and said to Raymond, "So even if you needed the money, like I do, you still wouldn't do it?"

He took a moment to answer and jammed the shovel into the snow. "I'm in a different situation. Beth works. And I got a pension. You know, I never even thought about going into business for myself. Or to work with my father. You were more like him than I was: independent minded. Neither of you showed much respect for authority. But I did everything by the book. I still do. So it's going to be something you'll need to decide for yourself.

***

The sun had disappeared behind thick, gray clouds by the time I got to my grandmother's house in Milton. I went inside and changed into my gray sweat suit and headed back outside, walking down the driveway where I stopped and looked up at the darkening sky. A drop of cold rain hit my face.

I took off down Pagoda Street, jogging down the same street where I'd spent most of my days as a kid. After my father left us high and dry when I was seven, Mom and I went to live with my grandmother.

It had only been over a year since my grandmother died and left me that same house. For some reason, I still considered it *her* house. I guess because it was.

I ran hard, my breathing heavy and labored with the cold air filling my lungs. The warmth earlier in the day had shifted to cold, like somebody flipped a switch.

I turned down Lafayette Street and continued toward the entrance for Popes Pond, dropping on the cold and wet sidewalk to get in at least thirty push-ups. But I stopped at twenty-three when a car pulled up next to me. I stood and leaned with my hands on my knees, looking up as Raymond rolled down the driver's-side window of his brand new Chrysler LeBaron

Billy Joel, "Just the Way You Are," played on the radio. I could smell Raymond's cigar, although he didn't appear to have one lit. He reached to his right and turned off the music. "I thought I might find you out here. I called Grandma's house a few times but you didn't answer."

"Just trying to clear my head."

Raymond nodded, looking out toward the park. "You haven't talked to Lily by any chance?"

"I'm not sure I *will* talk to her. The more I thought about it, I—"

"A man who works for Mayor Bedford's office was found dead this morning, at the Morrissey Motel."

"Are you serious?"

Raymond nodded. "Heard it on the news. Made me wonder if Lily's husband still works for the mayor?"

I started to understand why Raymond drove down to Milton just to tell me about it. "He's not the only employee at the mayor's office," I said.

"Of course not. Could be someone else entirely. But I thought I'd let you know in case you wanted to look into it. I can make some calls, if you want? Maybe call Maggie, see what she knows?"

I didn't answer. "They say what happened? Or when? I mean..." I looked down toward the ground. "I was wondering why Lily showed up at my office so early."

"No need to jump to any conclusions just yet," Raymond said. "Lily's a lot of things, but I'm not sure she has it in her to kill someone."

I nodded. "Yeah, no... I was just thinking; if he was—"

"It may not even be Michael," Raymond said. "I just thought you should know, before you rack your brain trying to make a decision."

"You said something about calling Maggie?" I said. "When was the last time you talked to her?"

Raymond shrugged. "I don't know. We keep in touch." He stared back at me through the window. "You all right?"

I nodded.

"You want a ride back to the house?"

I thought about it for a second. "No. But call me as soon as you hear something."

Raymond gave a nod and started to crank up the window.

"You think I should call her?" I said.

He rolled the window back down. "Lily?" He looked toward the windshield, his wrist hanging over the steering wheel. "If I were you," he said, "I'd stay clear of her. At least until we know if it was him or not."

CHAPTER 3

IT WAS GOOD TO wake up in my own bed. And I do mean my *own*, because the only thing I replaced when I moved into my grandmother's house was the mattress she'd slept on with my grandfather for sixty-four years.

Although other than the glow from my clock radio telling me it was 5:58, it was still dark in the bedroom. I'd gotten a few hours sleep, one or two of the hours solid, although I hadn't gotten word on the name of the victim found at the Morrissey Motel. And it kept my mind racing, especially with all that had happened between me and Lily.

I put my feet down on the cold hardwoods and walked to the window, looking out toward Pagoda Street. A car drove by, its headlights shining around a neighbor walking his dog. I could see their breaths in the glow of the headlights.

The house phone rang, breaking the quiet in the bedroom.

Calls before sunrise were never good.

I hurried around the foot of the bed and picked up the phone from the side table. "Hello?"

There was a brief pause on the other end, although I could hear slight breathing. "Jake?"

It was Lily. And I had a bad feeling as soon as I picked up the phone.

"Lily? Yeah, it's me. Who else would it be."

Another few seconds of silence. I realized the breathing sounds I thought I'd heard may have been Lily crying. "It's Michael. He's... Michael's dead."

I sat down on the edge of the bed and rested the base of the phone on my lap. "At the Morrissey Motel?"

Her voice was weak and shaky, absent of her confident tone. "You knew?"

"No. I mean, I'd heard... I saw it on the news, but he hadn't been identified. I guess I don't know many other people who worked for Mayor Bedford's office. I didn't know if I should have called you, or..." I wasn't exactly sure what to say. "I'm sorry, Lily."

No matter how I felt about her husband, Michael—and how I felt about Lily, for that matter—I knew too well what it was like to lose someone. "Do they know what happened?"

Lily sniffled into the phone. "I... I don't know. They're not saying anything."

I thought for a moment, wondering what I should say or do. "Do you want to... do you want me to come over?"

"I'm leaving," she said.

"You're *leaving*? Leaving for *where*?"

"I don't know. I need to get out of here. I can't stay around while—"

"Lily, you can't just take off. The cops are going to want to talk to you. You know how it's going to look if they can't find you?"

"I was there," she said, her voice quiet and soft.

"You were *where*?"

"At the motel."

I gave myself a minute to take that in and stood from the bed, walking with the phone in my hand to the window. "I don't understand. Were you with him? Do the cops know?"

"No. They probably would've arrested me on the spot."

I stared out the window. The sky had already brightened, and some of my neighbors were outside scraping the frost from their car windows. "Okay, Lily. I think you know what I'm about to say. But this isn't going to look good. Seriously. I know you're hurt right now and probably not thinking very clearly. But you can't take off."

"I... I followed him there," she said as if she hadn't heard a word.

I guess she'd decided to take things into her own hands. "Did anybody see you?"

It took her a few seconds to answer. "Well, I got the key from the woman at the front desk. I showed the young woman my license and told her he was my husband."

"She gave you a key? Just like *that*? So did you walk in on him?"

"No."

"He wasn't there?"

"His car was. His keys were in the room, but nothing else."

"You didn't touch anything, *did you*?"

"I took his keys. I just wanted to leave him stranded. I knew he'd have to make up some lie about where his car was when he came home."

I knew once Lily had her mind set on something, she was going to do it. And it would take more than me trying to convince her over the phone not to take off and disappear. Even if it was for a short time.

I put my hand up against the cold, wet window, turning back to my bed. I placed the base of the phone back on the nightstand. "Give me a half hour; I'll come out to see you. You need to make sure you have your story straight, then you have to go to the cops."

She broke out into a cry. "I'm scared, Jake."

"Just tell me what you did after you left the room. What else did you see? Were there any other cars in the parking lot?"

"Why are you asking me so many questions?" she said, her voice raised. "I didn't do it."

"I'm not trying to say you did."

Her early morning call wasn't Jake Horn the private investigator. I realized she was looking for someone to talk to and maybe comfort her, to help alleviate the brutal sting of what had happened.

"Just tell me what you want from me," I said. "Whatever you want, I'll help. It's just... I don't know what to say right now. I'm sorry for what happened to Michael. I mean that. But what you just told me—that you were at that motel—is something you need to take seriously. Especially if you haven't told the police. They think you're trying to hide something, you'll—"

"That's why I just told you I'm getting out of here. I'll come back in a couple of days."

"What about his family? Won't you need to make plans?"

"Plans?" she said, crying through her words. "Will you please just give me a chance to catch my breath? I... I haven't called anyone. And I barely know his parents. They didn't even come to our wedding."

There was nothing more I could say. Lily was the type to ask for advice but do whatever she wanted to, regardless. That might've been one of the few things we had in common.

"Lily, if the woman at the motel knows you were there, you're not going to be able to just make that go away. I have no doubt the cops already spoke to her."

The phone went quiet.

"Lily?"

"I'm here."

"Was there anyone else who might've seen you there?" I said.

She blew her nose on the other end. "I went to the bar across the street. I'm not sure what it was called. Freeman's, I think? It's a dive bar. A real hole-in-the-wall."

"Why'd you go there?" I said. "It doesn't sound like your kind of place."

"Well, it's not. *You'd* like it though. I went there looking for Michael and had a drink at the bar. I showed the bartender a photo. And he recognized him. But he didn't know his name, or the last time he'd been in there."

I said, "Did he say if he'd been in there alone?"

"He didn't know. He didn't seem like he wanted to say much more than he already had."

As much as I knew I shouldn't get involved, I had no doubt Lily was going to need my help. Sadly, she didn't have a lot of friends around Boston. She was a New York girl and, for one reason or another, never seemed to want to go out of her way to fit in. I knew she didn't have many others to turn to. And it wasn't in my nature to leave someone in the lurch.

"Lily," I said. "Listen to me. Don't take off. If what you've told me is all there is to it, then you have to go to the police and just be honest. Tell them everything, even that he may have been cheating on you. If you don't, it's going to come back to bite you."

***

I pulled into a parking space at the back of the rest stop off the Mass Pike, a few miles past Route 128, and watched through the passenger-side window as Lily pulled in behind me, driving her Saab into the parking space to the right of me.

She wore the same long powder-blue coat with the fake fur collar, the hood pulled up over her head, and a pair of dark, round sunglasses over her eyes. She opened the passenger-side door and slipped into the seat next to me, looking around at the brown interior as she removed her hood. "Your grandmother loved this car."

I nodded with a small grin. "She barely drove it. Had just over six thousand miles on it when she died." I had my eyes on Lily looking straight ahead, toward the bare trees in the wooded area in front of us. "You okay?" I said.

She pulled a tissue from her pocket and dabbed the corners of her eyes behind her dark sunglasses. She didn't give an answer.

I don't think she had one. "I *am* sorry," I said, like I had to keep telling her because she knew it was hard to believe.

She turned to me, but it was hard to tell where her eyes were focused. "Am I supposed to pretend I didn't come to your office yesterday morning and tell you my marriage to Michael was over?"

I knew where she was going. "Like I said on the phone, the best thing you can do is come clean about everything. You also said you spoke with an attorney. I don't know if you've spoken to him yet, but—"

"*Her*," she said. "Why would I hire a *man* to represent me in a divorce?" She turned her body in the seat to face me. "Jake, I... I want to tell you how sorry I am about everything that happened between us. I guess I didn't understand what you were going through. I didn't know where you were coming from, how important it was for you to keep Barbara in your heart. I was..." She pulled off her sunglasses but had her eyes toward the seat between us. "I was selfish." She reached out and grabbed my hand. "I'm sorry."

But I pulled my hand away from her. "What the hell are you doing?" I said, shaking my head. "I didn't come here to get into any of the past with you, Lily. I thought you needed my help."

She straightened out in her seat and looked out the passenger window. "I just thought you should know how much I've always regretted what happened between me and you. How much I regret leaving you for Michael."

I laughed. "Lily? What the hell are you doing? Why are you telling me this? What happened between us... it's over. *Waaay* over. If you didn't cheat on me with Michael, it would've been with someone else. I'm sorry to admit that now, but..." I didn't know where she was going or why she was trying to make up with an old boyfriend on the day her husband was found dead. "You don't have to apologize to make sure I won't leave you hanging. I told you I'd help."

She looked me in the eye. "You're such a good person, Jake. It's why I've never stopped loving you, even if—"

"Jesus Christ, Lily. Will you knock it off? Can we talk about your present situation?" I said. "If you're not careful, you're going to end up a prime suspect. But, as difficult as it can be for you, you're going to have to be honest with me for once."

"Do you think I *killed* him?" she said.

I looked straight ahead through the windshield, thinking for a moment. "No. No, I don't. But there are pieces of this story so far that don't look very good for you. Had I known when I told you I couldn't help you, that you'd turn around and take things into your own hands, following him to that motel..." I thought for a moment. "Wait a second, you said you followed him, right? Then didn't you see him get out of the car? Or see who he went in with? If anyone?"

"You think I was just going to pull in the parking lot behind him? Blow my horn, let him know I was watching?"

"Well, no," I said. "Then what'd you do?"

"I kept driving, went another mile before I could find a place to turn around. You know how hard it is trying to make a U-turn off Morrissey Boulevard?"

"So you went back and he was—"

"Why are you making me feel like I'm under interrogation?"

"My questions are the least of your worries," I said. "They're going to want answers, and running away so you don't have to answer them isn't going to do you an ounce of good. It's going to be important that you have your story straight."

She closed her eyes, nodding. "I'm sorry. I'm just so goddamn nervous, I could throw up."

I cracked the window to let some cold, fresh air inside the car.

"So what happened when you turned around, pulled into the parking lot? You saw his car?"

She nodded. "Yes, but I didn't know what room he was in. And I didn't want to start knocking on doors."

"So you somehow convinced the woman at the desk to give you a key? Then what—you let yourself in, and he wasn't in the room? But his keys were there?"

She nodded, reached into the pocket of her coat, and came out with a set of keys. "They're right here," she said.

I stared at the keys, knowing she wasn't making things easy. "Don't you think the police are wondering where they are?"

She slipped them back into her pocket. "I'd assume so. But, Jake, you have to believe me. I didn't do anything. They still haven't told me the cause of death."

"If I don't believe you, you'll be the first to know," I said, thinking. "So, whatever happened to him, he didn't have much time to go inside the room. And he left his keys? It doesn't make much sense. You sure he wasn't in the bathroom, or—"

"I'm not an idiot," she said. "I looked in the bathroom. I even looked under the bed. Unless... unless he saw me in the office and took off. That's the only thing that makes sense."

"Why would he leave his keys? I assume the door was locked when you went in? You used the key, so..."

She shrugged. "I assumed it was locked. I slid the key in and opened the door. Maybe it wasn't."

I said, "You went right over to that bar? As soon as you left the room?"

"I drove."

"Did you talk to anyone else? Other than the bartender?"

She shook her head. "No. I had one drink and left."

"Didn't you go back to his room? See if he was there?"

"I had already given back the key, before I drove over to the bar. I did ask if she had seen him…"

"She hadn't?"

She shook her head. "I wish you'd just agreed to help me. You would've been there. Then we would have—"

"Please don't try to put this on me," I said. "I'll be honest, Lily. If I was ever there, and he was killed, you know how that would look?"

Lily, still facing the other way, pushed open the door, and stepped out of the car.

"Where are you going?" I said.

She stood outside, holding the door open, and looked back at me. "I told you already. I need to get away from here."

"But what about talking to the police?" I said. "The longer you wait, the worse it's going to look for you."

She slipped her sunglasses over her eyes and shrugged. "Like you said, at least it wasn't you who was there." She slammed the door closed and stepped into her Saab without another word, tires spinning on the sand and salt covering the asphalt, as she took off for the exit.

I looked over the back seat out the rear window as she merged into traffic on the Pike and disappeared.

CHAPTER 4

I PULLED OFF ROUTE 1 heading south, looking for a pay phone to call my daughter, Nancy. She'd left a message on my answering machine while I was in the shower and said she'd call me back after her next class. But I was anxious to talk to her—I always was—and knew I wouldn't be home to catch her call.

It was hard on both of us when she left for college. She leaned on me for all the years after her mother died. But I leaned on her just as much. Maybe more. Some parents are happy to see their kids leave for college. But that wasn't me. It was the second hardest day of my life when I dropped her off.

Nancy had a pay phone in the hall of her dormitory at Plymouth State, but it wasn't always easy getting in touch with her. I was happy when one of the girls in her dorm answered and said Nancy was in her dorm room. I waited, and Nancy finally picked up.

"Good morning!" I said, doing my best to put a little more energy into my voice than I had.

"Hi, Dad," Nancy said. "Why do you sound so weird?"

She could see right through me. In fact, she could see right through just about anyone.

"Me? Why? I sound *weird*?" I said.

She laughed. "I don't know. You do that when you don't want me to know something's wrong."

"Oh yeah, no... everything's good. How about you? Are you okay?"

"Yeah, I guess so."

"You *guess* so?"

"It's good. Why?"

I looked at my watch. "I saw you left a message on the machine. You normally don't call early in the morning, so I just thought I'd call, make sure you were okay?"

Nancy laughed again. "Can't I just call you to say hello without something being wrong?"

She'd told me more than once I worried about her too much. But what was I supposed to do? *She's my little girl.* "I actually thought about calling you last night," I said. "But I know you're busy with school, don't need your old man bothering you."

Nancy paused. "Well, you're not an old man. And I told you before you don't ever have to worry about bothering me," she said. "You can call me whenever you want. As long as you can get through. There's always someone on this phone."

Nancy was a lot like her mother, although there was more to it. She had her mother's smarts, her mother's independence, and her outspokenness. Not to mention, she had my wife Barbara's good looks. But she picked a few things up from me too. Although I wasn't sure they were any of my good qualities, if I had any to begin with.

"Any new cases you're working on?" she said, sounding excited as always to talk about crime.

In fact, she loved that I was a private investigator. She enjoyed hearing the details about my cases. Even the boring ones. I tended to spare her the tough aspects of running the business, and how it was often a struggle just to keep my head above water with clients who seemed harder to find than they used to be. The other problem was half the people who'd call me were as broke as I was. They wanted me to work for free, as if Horn Investigations was some kind of volunteer agency.

"I'm working on something right now," I said, although as soon as I said it, I wished I'd kept my mouth shut.

"Oh cool. Anything exciting?"

"Have you been following the news?"

"I don't watch much TV around here. The only one's down in the sitting room. But I go to the library and read the *Globe* whenever I can."

Before I could say anything else, the operator came on the line:

"Please add eighty-five cents for the next three minutes."

"Shit," I said, reaching into my pocket. I only had one quarter and two pennies. "Hang on, Nancy. Let me get some change from the car."

"That's all right. I have to get to my next class. It's all the way on the other side of the campus, so I should probably head out."

"You sure? There's change in the car if you—"

"I'll try to call you tonight," she said.

"Oh, okay. If you can," I said. "Otherwise, I know you're busy."

I hated having to hang up. Even though she was only a couple of hours away in New Hampshire, a day didn't go by that I didn't miss her. "I'm sorry, Nance. We'll talk more later. Oh, and make sure you call collect."

Nancy took a moment before she responded. "Bye, Dad. I love you."

She hung up, and I stood with the handset against my ear, my forehead rested against the top of the pay phone. I looked when I heard a voice behind me.

"Sir?" a young man said, holding up his dime. "May I use the phone?"

***

I stepped past the counter inside the First Street Diner and headed toward the last booth on the left.

Maggie Donovan was already sitting, waiting for me. She watched me walk toward her, then slid out from the red vinyl booth. She was dressed nice, not in uniform, wearing multicolored plaid pants and a cranberry blazer over her pink-collared shirt. She stretched her arms out and gave me a hug, placing a gentle kiss on my cheek. "It's good to see you, Jake."

We both sat down on either side of the booth, facing each other.

"You look great," I said, staring back at her, wondering why she looked different from the last time I saw her. Maybe it was because she was more dressed-up than I'd remembered her being. I thought maybe her red hair was shorter. "Thanks for meeting me," I said.

She picked up her cup, the string from the Lipton tea bag hanging over her finger. She nodded, holding the cup in front of her mouth. "Almost two years." She took a sip and looked back at me over the rim. "So how have you been?"

I shrugged. "You know how it is…"

She placed her cup down in front of her but kept her hands wrapped around it. "Nance tries to keep me up to date."

I nodded and looked down into my cup. "Oh," I said. "You've been in touch with her?"

Maggie had a slight grin on her face, appearing like she was con-fused why I'd asked. "Of course," she said.

"I'm sorry it's been so long," I said. "I've thought about calling you. More than once. But, you know how it is. And I'm sure you've been busy."

She shrugged, nodding. "You know what they say: crime doesn't sleep."

I waved for the waitress, Rhonda, and asked her for coffee.

Maggie and I sat quiet for a moment, almost uncomfortable at first, like neither knew what to say. So much time had gone by since we'd even spoken to each other.

"So, what's new in your life?" I said, hoping to get something going.

She smiled, lifting her cup toward her mouth. "I got a cat. Name's Max."

"Max? That's a good name for a cat," I said.

"He's big and kind of fat." She stared back at me, sipping her tea. She placed the cup down, pushing it off to the side, then leaning forward with her hands in front of her on the table. "We don't have to do the small-talk thing," she said. "Or pretend this is a social visit."

Maggie was always one to tell it like it is.

I shifted in the seat and cleared my throat.

She said, "I knew as soon as I heard your voice it had something to do with Michael Dempsey. You're not the type to call without having a reason."

"Is that a bad thing?" I said.

Maggie gave me a smile. "I wish we'd kept in touch more over the past couple of years. It got to a point where it felt weird if I picked up the phone and called you."

I swallowed hard. I knew what she meant. And she was right. The thing is it was mostly my fault we stopped talking. I was the one who went cold over the way she treated Lily. Both Maggie and Nancy seemed to feel the same way about her and never warmed up to the idea of me dating someone after Barbara. But there was more to it. In hindsight, it turned out I was the only one who didn't see it.

"I spoke to Lily," I said. "She's scared. Confused. She's afraid of what could happen, especially if it turns out she's viewed as a suspect."

Maggie said, "Does she have a *reason* to believe she could end up a suspect?"

"I don't know. I don't think so." I wasn't in a position to tell Maggie what I knew. And, although I considered her a friend, she was an officer with the Boston Police Department. It was for her own good I kept things to myself, or at least between me and Lily, for the time being.

"I don't have a lot of information to share right now," she said. "If that's what you were hoping for?"

I felt like an ass: Maggie, for the most part, calling me out, knowing full well there was a reason I asked her to meet with me. "I'm sorry," I said. "I don't want you to think I'm... I don't want you to think this... getting together, is only to—"

"If there's something I can do to help, Jake. I'll help. You don't have to pretend this is anything more than what it is." She picked up her tea and took a sip.

"I know how you feel about Lily," I said. "But I can't turn my back on her right now. And I'm just afraid she's going to get dragged into something she may not deserve."

Maggie nodded, her eyes narrowed. "It sounds to me there's something you know? But you're not going to tell me?" She stared, waiting for my answer.

"No. I mean, I don't know. But she did call me. Like I said, she's scared. I'm not sure she knows which end is up right now."

"That's to be expected, of course," Maggie said. She rubbed the back of her neck, looking down toward the table for a moment before raising her eyes. "You're a good guy, Jake. All she did to you, and there you are, first one in line to help when she comes calling."

I wasn't sure if that was much of a compliment. A backhanded one, to say the least. *You're a good guy, but maybe a little weak,* is how it came across.

"I'm not a victim," I said. "I just want to make sure she gets a fair shake. You know how much I trust that bureaucracy you work for over there on Berkeley."

"You don't have to remind me how much you despise those of us who wear the blue."

"Oh, it's not just the uniform," I said. "And you know I don't have anything against you or any other of the hundreds of men and women who serve and protect this great city. But to say I don't trust the Boston Police would be an understatement."

Rhonda walked over to our table and filled my cup with more coffee. "Either of you want to order some food?"

Maggie opened the menu and glanced over it, closing it a moment later. "Can I get a turkey sandwich? To go? No mayo." She looked at her watch and picked up her empty cup. "I'll have another tea."

Rhonda walked away as I pulled my coffee toward me. I said to Maggie, "So, there's nothing you can tell me?"

"About Michael Dempsey?" She shook her head. "Nothing you haven't seen on the news. Investigation's just getting started."

I hesitated a moment, wanting to gather my thoughts before I said something I didn't want to. "So, would you tell me if Lily was a suspect?"

Maggie looked down toward her cup, taking a moment before glancing at me across the table. She had a look on her face telling me there was something she wanted to say.

"What is it?" I said.

"No, nothing. Jake, I..."

"Come on, Maggie." I leaned on the table, trying to make eye contact, but she wasn't making it easy the way her eyes drifted toward the counter. "What is it?" I said.

She sighed, leaning on the table. "Well, from what I'm hearing, she's not being cooperative. As far as I know, the detective on the case is having a hard time getting her to return his calls. I'm sure you know how that'll look."

"They said the same thing about me," I said. "Remember?"

"This is different," Maggie said. "You answered the questions. At least, early in the investigation. But, the fact is, a woman's husband is dead. And she won't answer basic questions? Wrong or not, it's going to raise suspicions."

Rhonda brought over another tea bag for Maggie and filled her cup with steaming water.

Maggie waited for her to walk from the table before continuing. She leaned forward, her eyes right on mine. "The best thing you can do for Lily is get her to tell the truth. I know that's not easy for her. But, otherwise, she tries to twist things around, as we both know she has a habit of doing, it's not going to be pleasant for her."

CHAPTER 5

AFTER A SHORT EVENING run around the neighborhood, I sat down to eat the turkey club I'd brought home earlier from the diner. I turned the TV dial to channel five and adjusted the rabbit ears on top to watch the six o'clock news. I hadn't heard from Maggie after we'd left the diner, and Lily wasn't answering the phone at her apartment. I called the ad agency where she worked, at least last I knew, but was told she hadn't been there in over six months.

The phone rang in the kitchen, but I didn't want to miss any mention of Michael on the news. Reaching my arm around the doorway for the phone hanging on the other side of the wall, I lifted it off the hook, keeping my eyes toward the TV.

"Hello?" I could hear loud music coming through the phone. "Hello?" I said again.

"Dad? It's me."

"Nancy? I can hardly hear you." I had to raise my voice. "Can you turn down the music?"

The line became muffled, and I heard Nancy yell for someone to turn down the music. "Sorry," she said, the music quiet. "We were listening to this new band, Van Halen. You should hear them."

"What're they called?" I said.

"Van Halen. You'd like them," she said. "You should hear the guitar."

I had stopped paying attention to the news, but it caught my ear when Michael Dempsey's name had been mentioned. "Nancy, give me one second, all right? There's something on the news. I gotta hear it." I stretched the cord as far as it would go so I could get in front of the TV, turning the volume up with the knob:

"Michael Dempsey, a member of Mayor Bedford's staff who had played a critical role in the mayor's reelection campaign, has died of an apparent gunshot wound. His body was found earlier this morning behind the Morrissey Motel. Police are still investigating, and at this time there are no suspects. Mr. Dempsey was thirty-eight years old and leaves behind his wife, who police have not been able to locate since the death was first reported."

"I'm sorry about that," I said into the phone. "I was listening to something on the—"

"Was that the news about Michael Dempsey?" Nancy said.

"Oh," I said. "You heard?"

"They had it on the news up here. I guess it's a big deal, since he worked for the mayor's office."

"I guess so," I said.

"You think Lily did it?" Nancy said, with a slight chuckle in her voice.

"Are you serious? Of course I don't think she—"

"Relax, Dad. I was just kidding. Lily's a lot of things, but I can't see a killer being one of them."

"I know. I'm sorry, I—"

"Are you okay?" she said.

I could hear the concern in her voice. I hated that she worried about me. But she did.

"Yes, everything's fine." I thought for a moment. "I actually spoke with her."

"Lily?"

"Yes," I said. "And I'm not going to lie to you, Nance. I'm worried about her."

"You're worried about Lily? Why? She's never worried about you or another person. Why should anyone worry about her?"

"That's not true," I said. "She's not—"

"Of course it's true," she said. "And why would you... after what she did to you? Please, Dad. Don't get involved with her. Please."

"Oh, come on, Nance. You really think you need to say that?" I stepped in front of the TV and hit the knob to shut it off.

"Just promise me you'll stay clear of her."

I didn't want to go into too much detail with her, but Nancy always had a way of figuring out when I had something to hide. "I did speak to her," I said. "And I promised her I'd help, if she wanted me to. But she hasn't called."

"And you're going to tell me that doesn't sound suspicious?" Nancy said.

"Of course it does. But I'm not going to make any assumptions." I tried to reach for my can of 'Gansett beer on the coffee table, but the phone's cord was stretched from the kitchen as far as it would go. I held the phone in one hand, reaching for the can with the other, but I still couldn't get to it. "I met Maggie earlier. She sounds just like you when it comes to Lily."

"Yeah, because Maggie and I actually care about you."

I let that sink in for a moment.

Nancy was quiet for a moment on the other end. "Sometimes I wish you didn't care so much."

"What's that supposed to mean?" I said.

"That you shouldn't get so wrapped up helping people who put you in a bad position."

I smiled. "You sound like your mother. And as I told her, it's my job. I don't always get to choose who I help."

"Is that really true?" she said.

"Sometimes I think I liked it better when I could tell you anything I wanted, and you'd believe me. Without questions."

"Yeah, when I was two," she said, laughing.

I said, "How about if I promise I won't get involved more than I have to? But I need you to understand, I'm going to do what I feel is right. But unless I can find her, there's not much I can do right now."

"You're sure she's not at home?"

"I've called a half dozen times. The police have been there looking for her."

"What about work? Is she still at the same ad agency?"

"No. I called there. She left six months ago. I'm not sure where she's working right now. If anywhere. Her mother's in a nursing home. I guess it's possible she drove out to New York."

The line was quiet. Nancy said, "What about her cousin Jill's house? That's where I'd go if I needed to get away from the city."

***

I got up early, filled the Nova with gas and grabbed a coffee for my ride back onto the Mass Pike, heading west. Lily's cousin Jill lived in Woodstock, Connecticut, just over the border in an area known as the Quiet Corner. I wasn't sure how often Lily had kept in touch with her, but it was worth a shot. A phone call, of course, would've been easier. But lying over the phone was too easy for most people. And a drive out to the country wasn't a bad way to spend a morning.

Jill lived with her husband, who spent his life on the road as a tractor-trailer truck driver. I knew Jill but only met Pete a handful of times when Lily and I were together.

I took 290 all the way down to 395 South, turning west on 197. The narrow, wooded roads were a different world from the busy Boston streets I was used to.

There was very little development in Woodstock. Mostly residential houses built on land with plenty of space. Nobody had to worry about fighting for a parking space.

I turned into the dirt driveway and pulled up toward the white Cape Cod-style home with the two dormer windows. A barn bigger than the house was set back in the woods. I parked behind a black Ford pickup, with fresh snow covering the truck's bed and hood. I didn't realize it had snowed again.

I didn't see Lily's Saab or even see tire tracks going across the yard toward the barn, as I might've expected. I also didn't want to walk around their yard and raise any alarm before I knocked on the door.

I was almost certain Pete was a hunter and, therefore, most likely armed.

I walked up the walkway mostly cleared of snow, past at least a dozen bird feeders hanging from various trees, including a large oak and a couple of pines in the yard. A bird bath in the middle of the yard appeared to be cleared of snow, although the water inside it was frozen.

I knocked on the glass storm door rather than ring the doorbell, and within a moment or two, the red interior door opened.

Jill stood on the other side of the glass looking out at me as if she already knew I was there. Pushing open the door, she wore a thick white sweater with a green turtleneck underneath. She stepped outside and pulled the interior door closed behind her, letting the storm door close on its own. She crossed her arms and squeezed her shoulders inward as if feeling a chill from the cold. "It's been a long time," she said.

"It has," I said.

She cleared her throat, her eyes looking out toward the road. "She's not here," she said.

I didn't even have to ask. But the way she offered it so fast, I knew she wasn't being straight with me.

"Am I supposed to believe you?"

She grinned, lips tight, nodding. "She didn't tell me where she was going. But I know she just wanted to get away for a little while."

"Well," I said. "The cops are looking for her. And all I'm trying to do is help her. But she's not making it easy."

Jill didn't seem interested in looking me in the eye. She was the quiet one, almost shy but likely more an introvert than anything, living out in the middle of nowhere to avoid conversation those of us in a city were forced to have.

"It's cold out again," I said, looking at the smoke pouring out from the chimney. "Do you mind if I come inside?"

She still hadn't looked at me. "You should have called first, Jake. Instead of driving all the way out here."

"Well," I said. "That doesn't usually work. Most people have a lot easier time lying on the phone than they do face-to-face with someone." I kept watching her, waiting for her to give me a look. "You know what I mean?"

She finally gave me a quick look in the eye but then back out toward the street.

"Are you expecting someone?" I said, looking out in the same direction. "She's got to get back to Boston, Jill, I know she's hurting. And I know she's scared. But staying away like this isn't going to make it any easier for her."

Jill looked back at me, this time with a blank stare. She opened her mouth like she had something to say but stopped, shaking her head. "I don't know what to tell you. She's not here." She reached for the door's handle and started to pull it open. "I'm sorry, Jake."

I looked toward the road as a small blue Datsun pickup pulled into the driveway, drove around my Nova, and parked next to the pickup truck a few feet away from where we stood.

"Pete's got to leave soon for work," she said. "And I have to drive him up to the storage facility where his trailer's parked. So if you don't mind..."

She watched her husband, Pete, step from the truck and walk toward us.

He had a tray in both hands with three to-go coffees tucked inside it, a look on his face like he'd seen a ghost.

Jill said, "Pete, you remember Jake, don't you?"

He nodded without saying a word, like thoughts were racing through his mind about what he was supposed to say. His eyes went from me to Jill and back to me. He balanced the tray with one hand and finally reached out to shake my hand. "Sorry, Jake. I didn't recognize you at first. It's been a long time." He again looked at Jill, and I caught his heavy swallow.

I looked at the three coffees in the tray, then at Pete. "Do I remember correctly, you have three kids?"

Pete and Jill both nodded.

"They must be getting big. They were little when I last—"

"Joey'll be eleven next month," Pete said. "The girls are eight and nine."

I looked over toward the tall oak trees with the bird feeders hanging on one side, but on the other was a rope and a tire swing tied up around a thick, low branch. "So which kid's old enough to drink coffee?" I turned back to Pete and Jill, eyeing the three coffees in

Pete's hand. "Or do one of you need a second large coffee, just to get your wheels turning?"

Pete started to speak. "Listen, Jake, I know you must've driven all the way out here looking for Lily, but..." His gaze moved past me.

I heard the crack of the interior door opening, seeing Lily looking out at me from behind the glass. She pushed open the storm door and stepped outside. "Jake, you shouldn't have come here."

***

Lily and I sat alone at the kitchen table after Jill had left to drive Pete to where his tractor trailer was parked out in Thompson.

I sipped the coffee Jill had made for me before she left and gazed at Lily. "You don't have a choice," I said. "I spoke with Maggie, and she agreed the only thing you can do right now is drive back to Boston," I said, looking out the window into the side of their yard, toward the barn. "Where'd you park your car?"

She looked up from the table. "Down the street, at a neighbor's. Friends of Pete and Jill's." She stood and walked across the kitchen. "Did you tell Maggie anything I told you?"

"No. But I'm telling you right now, I'm not going to lie for you. I'm sorry, Lily, but—"

"Does she know I'm out here?"

"No. But she knew I was going to try to find you. Nancy was the one who thought you'd be out here."

Lily cracked a smile. "How's she doing?"

"Nancy?" I said.

Lily nodded. "She's in college?"

"She is," I said. But I wasn't in the mood to get into more of my personal life than I had to with Lily.

She looked out the window toward the front yard. "What if they don't believe me?" she said.

"Tell the truth, Lily," I said. "That's where it all starts."

CHAPTER 6

LILY DROVE HERSELF TO the police headquarters on Berkley Street, and I went straight to my office. I'd just sat down at my desk when the phone rang. I paused a moment before I answered, just to catch my breath.

"Horn Investigations," I said, the chair squeaking as I leaned back and put my feet up on the desk.

"Jake, it's me." Maggie was on the other end, her voice hushed.

"Is everything all right?"

Maggie was quiet for a moment. "Jake, listen. Before I say a word, you have to promise me that if anyone asks, you didn't hear this from me."

I leaned forward on the desk. "Yeah, of course. What... what is it?"

"They're bringing you in for questioning..."

I wish I hadn't heard her right. "Questioning about what?" I said. "About Lily?"

"Michael Dempsey's death. It's a murder investigation."

"Well, no shit it's a murder investigation. This is what I mean about red tape. The man's body's found in a dumpster, and it takes how many hours to finally make it official, whatever that means, he was murdered?" I laughed, but it wasn't that I found anything to be funny. "Tell me you're kidding."

"I *wish* I *was*," Maggie said. "I think it's just... they want to ask you more about what happened between you and Michael."

"Christ, they think I killed him now?" I stood up from my desk but leaned against the edge, looking out toward Broadway.

"I'll see what else I can find out. But I just thought I should at least give you a heads-up. Just, please, Jake, do your best to act surprised."

"Why wouldn't I be surprised? This is ridiculous. I got in a little scuffle with him, how long's it been? If I wanted to kill him, I would've done it then."

"I know, Jake. Just, I don't think you should worry about it. Hopefully it's nothing."

"Christ," I said, thinking through how quickly I could end up in a mess without even trying. "Clearly, they have no leads?" I said. "What about Lily? You see her down there?"

"I saw her with Moriarty."

"Detective Moriarty?" I said. "Is that who's on this case? He's that pretty-looking one, right?"

She let out a slight laugh. "You mean, is he the good-looking one? Yes, that's him."

"So he's the one who wants to talk to me?"

"Most likely. I don't know if he's planning to call you, have you come down, or if he'll just show up at your door. But as soon as I hear anything, I'll call you. Just don't worry, Jake. I'm sure it's nothing. I'm so sorry."

"I'm the one who should be sorry," I said.

***

48

A couple of hours had gone by, and I was hungry, ready to go out and get something to eat but didn't want to miss Detective Moriarty if he stopped by to see me. I was anxious to get it over with, see what was in his head and where it placed me on his list of suspects, if that were even the case.

But the phone finally rang, and I cleared my throat, putting on my most professional voice. "Horn Investigations."

The truth was it was better when my uncle was running the show and we had a receptionist who sat by the front door and answered the calls.

A male voice was on the other end. "Is this Jake Horn?"

I'd never spoken to Moriarty, but I was fairly certain it was him. "This is Jake. How may I help you?"

"This is Jeffrey Moriarty. I'm a detective with the Boston Police Department. Have you got a few minutes to talk?"

"Uh, sure," I said, not sure how I should play my cards, whether I should've played dumb... or played it cool. "How can I help you, Detective?"

"Well, I'm working on a case right now, I believe you're familiar with at this point."

"I'll take a wild guess and say you're calling about Michael Dempsey," I said. "Did I get it right?"

Moriarty was quiet for a moment. "Well," he said, "I'm not at a point I can force you to come down to the station, but I'd really appreciate it if you would."

"Uh, what kind of questions?" I said.

"Well, I'd rather discuss things face-to-face, if you'd be all right with that. Would you rather me come out to your office? You're on Broadway. Is that correct?"

"I am, yes. But, I'll tell you what, Detective. I'd be happy to come down, see what I can do to help. But if I may ask, just so I'm clear... you don't happen to believe I had something to do with Mr. Dempsey's death, do you?"

Moriarty was quiet. I didn't think he'd want to answer. "We don't have any clear suspects right now. We're just doing some preliminary work in the investigation, trying to get our ducks in a row. I'm sure you understand."

I didn't want to drag it out longer than I had to. "How about I take a ride over right now; would that work?"

***

I parked a block away from 154 Berkeley Street and didn't mind the walk, with the warmer afternoon sun still trying to melt the hard, dirty piles of snow left behind from the blizzard. I had to dance around the puddles and mud-filled holes after the long, cold winter. The springlike air felt good, although I'd been in New England my whole life, knowing snow in March or April was always a possibility.

There was a dramatic drop in temperature when I stepped into the shadows stretching from the tall buildings. A transit bus pulled from the curb, filling the spring air with the strong odor from its exhaust.

I walked into police headquarters and stopped before the desk just inside the entrance. I looked at the rows of chairs lined up behind me. Some of the seats were occupied, but most were empty. A bored-looking young man with his hat on backward and his chin resting in his hand glanced back at me but looked away.

The cop behind the desk was an older man, an officer with white hair and an unlit cigarette in the ashtray in front of him. He was on the phone and didn't look at me until he hung up a couple of moments later, picking up a stack of papers, tamping them down, then moving them to a tray on a table behind him. He finally looked up at me. "Can I help you, buddy?"

"I'm here for Detective Moriarty. He's expecting me."

The officer turned a clipboard with a pen and paper in front of me and tapped the top sheet. "Fill this out," he said.

There was a space for *Person You Are Visiting* and another for *Purpose of Your Visit.* At the end on the right was a line for *Full Name* and *Signature.* I filled it out and signed my name. I wrote *Michael Dempsey (Murder)* in the space for *Purpose of Your Visit.*

The officer took the clipboard and looked it over, gave me a quick glance with a raised eyebrow, and picked up the phone. He mumbled something I couldn't quite make out, then hung up and stood from his desk. "Come with me," he said.

I followed him through a heavy wood door he unlocked with a key.

The older cop was short and round; I guessed he hadn't worked the streets in twenty years. He didn't say a word as he walked a few steps ahead of me at a good pace without looking back.

He stopped at an open doorway. "Go in there and sit down. The detective will be with you shortly." He started to walk away but stopped. "You want a coffee?"

"No, thanks," I said.

He turned and walked away without another word.

The room was small, maybe eight feet wide by ten feet long. The radiator on the far side of the room hissed, the smell of a commercial-grade cleaning solution so overwhelming, it burned the inside of my nose. Other than the long table with a chair on one side and two on the other, the room was empty. No windows. The walls were gray and the concrete floor painted the same color. There was a drain in the middle of the room a few feet from the table. The single chair on the side of the table closest to the door had a cuff bar welded to it.

I sat on the single chair with my back to the door and turned to look behind me when I heard someone walk in and close the door.

"Jake? Thank you for coming down." He reached out and shook my hand. "Jeffrey Moriarty." He walked around to the other side of the table and sat down, his concentration on the opened folder in his hands. He wore a light-blue turtleneck with colorful plaid pants. Funny, they were similar to the pants Maggie was wearing at lunch. I wanted to ask him if they shopped together but didn't think it was the right time or place.

Moriarty dropped the folder on the table. "So you're the private investigator, huh?"

I stared back at him. "*The?*" I shrugged, shaking my head. "I'm *a* private investigator. Yes. There are others."

He had a confused look, but maybe it was more because he knew I wasn't going to make this easy on him. He sat down and looked inside the folder, flipping through the papers. "I've heard a little about your uncle, Pat. Long before my time, but I understand he was a good cop."

I nodded. "My Uncle Pat's the 'Horn' in Horn Investigations."

"Lost his leg, huh?"

"They didn't want a one-legged cop at the time," I said.

Moriarty didn't have much of an expression on his face, nodding after I spoke but looked to be drifting away from the small talk.

"You must've worked with his son, my cousin Raymond?"

Moriarty shrugged, looking across the table at me with a look like he was done with the subject and uninterested in my law enforcement connections. His eyes shifted back to the folder. "I never got to know him very well before he retired."

I didn't know how old Moriarty was, but my guess was maybe still in his twenties. Thirty, at most. He had a cockiness about him, with his blond hair and blue-eyed baby face. I guess you had to have confidence to dress the way he did.

The detective leaned back in the chair, one leg over the other with his ankle resting over his knee. He held the folder open on his lap. "So, you want to tell me how much you know about the Michael Dempsey case?"

"How much?" I shrugged. "Only what I saw on the news."

He stared back at me, his eyes squinted. "Is that it?"

I nodded but kept quiet.

"But you've discussed the situation with Mr. Dempsey's widow. Isn't that correct?"

I paused and stared back at him. "Discussed the situation? You could say that. It doesn't mean I know anything about what happened. Neither does she, as far as I know."

"She was in here a little while ago. Did you know that?"

"Yeah, I knew that." I left it at that.

"I'd like to be very clear," Moriarty said. "We're in the very early phases of this investigation. You're not a suspect. And right now, neither is Mrs. Dempsey. But I'm sure you understand, as a so-called investigator yourself, you know a good detective leaves no stone unturned."

"So-called?" I said, cracking a grin. "Does that make you feel better?"

"Excuse me?"

"So-called detective? You think you're better than me, because you get your checks signed by the governor? Or whoever the hell signs them."

Moriarty had a dumb look on his face, shaking his head. "I'm so sorry. I did not say 'so-called?' Did I? I believe you may have misheard me." He looked down at the folder again. "So, let's see here. You were charged with assaulting Mr. Michael Dempsey two years ago." He raised his eyes to mine. "You want to explain that?"

"No. I don't have to. The charges were dropped."

A cocky grin covered Moriarty's face. "I assume that's where it pays to have a relative who's a cop." He closed the folder. "So you're not going to deny there was an altercation, are you? And how you had *attacked* Mr. Dempsey?"

"Attacked? I hit him. But barely. I slap myself harder to wake up in the morning." I looked away, shaking my head. "It's not my fault the guy had a glass jaw."

Moriarty stared back at me. "I understand. But the fact remains there was physical aggression toward him on your part. Is that correct?"

"The charges were dropped. You can't—"

"I just want to make sure it's clear whatever ill will you had toward him didn't continue after that particular incident."

"Is that a *question*?" I said.

Moriarty tossed the folder on the table and slid the chair closer to it, leaning forward with his hands clasped together in front of him. "You and Lily Dempsey still have a relationship. Is that correct?"

"A relationship? No, I don't think I'd call it that at all." I took a deep breath and tried to keep my composure. But it wasn't easy. I didn't like this guy at all. His tactics were way off base. "Listen. She was my girlfriend. My fiancée. We were engaged for a short time. But then I was hired to do some work with the mayor's office. Michael Dempsey was in charge of his reelection campaign. He's the one who hired me."

"He was your client?"

"Well, he wasn't the one who paid me. But yeah, he was my direct contact. A real pain in the ass too. Well, long story short, Lily ended up sleeping with the guy. And as any *real* man would understand, I was a little upset." I stared the detective right in the eye. "Wouldn't *you* be?"

He didn't answer. "So your relationship with Mrs. Dempsey ended at that point?"

"She slept with another man. Of course it was over. Then she married the guy." I leaned back in the chair and looked around the room. "I hope you know this is a joke that you're even asking these questions. Whatever happened between me and Michael is off my record. You can't—"

"So you never again engaged in any romantic activity with Lily Dempsey *after* she married Michael Dempsey?"

I leaned forward on the table and tapped my fingers on the laminate top. I thought for a moment before I spoke and wondered how this guy knew what he was trying to get me to admit. Something didn't add up. "Did she tell you?" I said, knowing it made no sense for me to try and lie my way out of it. I held up my index finger and looked Moriarty right in the eye. "I went home with her *one* time. Once. It was a mistake. But I'd had a few drinks, and she showed up at the bar I was hanging out at, and—"

"Hawkers?" he said.

I nodded. "Yeah. Hawkers. I had a lot to drink. I can admit that. All she said was she'd give me a ride home. But I passed out in the passenger seat and woke up in her car outside her apartment. She tells me Michael's out of town and I can crash on her couch."

"So you slept with her?"

"No way! Are you serious?" I looked toward the door. "I hadn't talked to her since. Not until she showed up at my office Thursday morning." I thought for a moment, unsure how much I should tell him. "I assume she told you he was cheating on her? Or so she believed?"

Detective Moriarty leaned back in the chair, not saying a word.

"Did she not tell you that part?" I said.

He waited a moment before he answered. "No, she did *not* mention he was cheating on her. Or that she suspected he was."

I wondered, if Lily left that part out, then what *did* she tell the detective. Clearly, her struggles with the truth weren't behind her.

I knew I had to shut my mouth and stood up from the chair. "I think I'm done here," I said. I slid the chair back under the table and stepped toward the door. I tried the knob, but it was locked. And you needed a key to open it. I turned to Detective Moriarty. "Can you please let me out?"

"I thought we were just getting started," Moriarty said. "Perhaps if you stay, we can—"

"You'll have to arrest me," I said. "Otherwise, I'm sorry. We're done."

Moriarty stepped to the door and slid his key in the knob. He unlocked it and opened the door, nodding with his chin toward the hall. "You walking out of here right now doesn't mean this is over for you, Jake. I hope you understand that."

CHAPTER 7

I SAT IN NEAR darkness, the only light in the office coming from the thirteen-inch black-and-white TV on top of the refrigerator and the lamp in front of me on my desk. Johnny Carson was on the TV, but the volume was down. I sipped from a can of 'Gansett and stared at the phone. It was almost midnight.

I had a pen in my hand resting on top of my yellow legal pad but hadn't written anything down. I tried to think through what I knew about Michael Dempsey's case but little came to mind. The only thing written on the sheet of paper was *Angela*. I hadn't even written down her last name, once Lily made it clear Angela was Tony Gautieri's daughter. I could've only wished at that point, when Lily walked out, I was done with her for good.

Clearly, I couldn't have been so lucky.

I picked up the phone and dialed Maggie's number, letting it ring five times until I was about to hang up.

But Maggie answered. "Hello?"

I could hear it in her voice I'd woken her up.

"Oh... I'm sorry. I thought maybe you'd be awake."

"Jake?"

"Yeah, it's me. Sorry. Are you asleep?"

"No. I mean, yeah. It's all right. I was... I'm on the couch." The phone became muffled for a moment, like she'd put it down. "You there?" she said. "What time is it?"

I looked at my watch, holding it under the lamp. "Eleven fifty-three."

"What's up?" she said. "Are you all right?"

"Yeah, I'm all right. I just, I don't know what to make of Moriarty. The questions he was asking me. And I thought I would've heard from you earlier, after I met with him, but—"

"I'm sorry, Jake. I was going to call you. But I hadn't heard anything. I was out on a call when you were meeting with him. And I got back late; he wasn't there. I actually drove down to Milton to see if you were home. Your car wasn't there so I left. Are you there now?"

"The house? No. No, I'm at the office. I went to Hawkers and had a drink." I looked over at the TV but could hardly see what was going on. It looked like there was a monkey climbing on Johnny Carson's back. "I'm at the desk, to be honest."

"You're working?"

"Not really," I said. "I didn't like Moriarty's approach. He asked me about the fight with Michael, a charge he knows was dropped. But he made a point to say it was only dropped because of Raymond."

"You can't take it personally, Jake. Jeffrey's just doing his job."

"Well, I walked out. I didn't like where he was heading. It made me think of everything I'd been through with Barbara's case. I'm not going to go through any of that shit again."

"You can't compare the two," Maggie said.

"I know I can't. But I... I know how you feel about Lily. But I'm not going to let them do to her what they did to me. I won't sit back, wait to see what happens. That was my mistake."

The line was quiet.

I hesitated to go on. "They did everything they could to keep me from trying to find Barbara's killer. And here we are, eleven years later... not one suspect?"

"It was different back then, Jake."

I sipped my beer. "I'm sorry," I said. "I didn't mean to wake you with all of this. I'm just frustrated. Thanks for listening."

Maggie paused on the other end. "I miss Barbara, too, you know. But this case has nothing to do with her. Don't try to tie them together; you'll make yourself crazy."

I leaned back in the chair, finished what was in the can, and tossed it in the basket next to my desk.

"I'm glad you called," she said. "I just wish it was under different circumstances you finally reached out."

***

I was on the couch with the wool blanket over me, remembering my uncle and the things he used to say. One thing was "innocent until proven guilty." He said it was pretty much bullshit when it came to the cops. At the time, I saw him as the ex-cop with a chip on his shoulder for the way he was treated after his accident.

But when Barbara was killed, and they tried to go after a kid I knew hadn't committed the crime, I learned firsthand exactly what it was my uncle meant.

I tried to close my eyes but had that eerie feeling you get when you think someone's watching you. I got up when I caught a glimpse of a shadow through the blinds, walked to the window, and opened them to look outside.

Someone was standing outside on the sidewalk under the streetlight, a few feet from my door. It only took a moment to realize it was Lily, dressed in her long powder-blue winter coat with the faux fur, the hood pulled up tight over her head.

I turned the lock on the door and pulled it open, a blast of cold air coming in at me. "Lily?" I said. "What the hell are you doing out there?"

She stepped toward the door, and I could see she had tears coming down what little I could see of her face inside the hood.

I helped her inside, slamming the door closed behind her before too much heat escaped out onto East Broadway. As warm as it had gotten during the day, we were back into the twenties at night.

Lily stumbled as she took a step and fell right into my arms. The smell of booze on her breath was so strong, I swear it gave me a buzz.

"Guess you've had a few?" I said as if it took a detective to figure it out. I flipped on the overhead lights and put my arm around her, walking her over to the couch.

I eased her down and sat next to her. "What the hell are you doing out there so late?" I said, looking at my watch. It was a few minutes after one o'clock.

Lily pushed the hood back from her head and wiped the tears from her face with both hands. Her makeup had run in black streaks from her eyes. "I'm sorry," she said. "I didn't think you'd be here." She looked back toward the street. "I... I was going to take a cab to my apartment. But I don't... I can't be there right now."

"Where have you been?" I said. I was going to take her coat, but the office had enough of a chill, she was better off with it on.

She stared back at me without an answer. "Jake, the detective, he—"

"Moriarty?"

She nodded. "He came across like he already thinks I'm guilty. I mean, he was nice at first. But the way he asked me questions, I couldn't even think straight. I'm not even sure exactly what I said."

"Did you tell him the truth? About going to the motel?"

She looked me in the eye, then tilted her head, looking down at her hands. She wore gloves but removed them, tucking them into her coat pockets. "I was afraid to tell him anything." She sniffled a bit through her nose, then looked around the dark office. "Do you have a tissue?"

I got up from the couch and walked to the bathroom, came out with a roll of toilet paper and handed it to her. "Sorry, it's all I've got."

I sat back down next to her and leaned forward. "So what *did* you tell Moriarty?"

She shrugged. "That I was scared. That I was worried whoever killed Michael would come after me."

"Do you really believe that?" I said. "You think you're in danger?"

She sniffled, wiping her nose with the paper she tore from the roll. She looked up at me. "Shouldn't I be? I have no idea who—"

"Is there something you're not telling me, Lily? You must have a reason to believe you have to worry about someone coming after you?"

She unbuttoned her coat but didn't remove it. She wore white nylons over her long legs pressed together, coming out from under a blue pin-striped skirt that stopped at her knees. "He asked me about my relationship with you," she said. "And about what happened between you and Michael."

I nodded. "They pulled me in for questioning, you know. I met with Detective Moriarty, probably soon after you did. Sounds like he asked me the same things." I thought for a moment. "But, Lily, why didn't you tell him you suspected Michael was having an affair?"

She stared back at me, her eyes wider than they'd been since she walked through the door. "Did you tell him about that?" she said.

I hesitated but had to be straight with her. "I wasn't going to lie," I said, "put myself in a bad situation. I was under the impression you'd gone in there and actually told the truth for once. Like we talked about. But it didn't take me long to realize you didn't tell him much of anything. I got up and walked out."

"You walked out? You can do that?"

One of her eyes was half closed, a sure sign the booze was in control of her face. "They have you in for questioning, you're under no obligation. Unless you're under arrest, of course. Although even then..."

She wiped a tear from her cheek, nodding.

I stood up. "You could use a coffee," I said.

"You have cream?"

"Cream? Sorry, no. You'll have to drink it black." I started toward the other side of the office. "It'll put hair on your chest."

She didn't laugh.

I took the carafe into the bathroom and rinsed it out, filling it with fresh water from the tap. When I walked out, Lily had lain down on the couch.

"I can give you a ride, wherever you need to go," I said. "Not all the way out to Connecticut at this time of night, but..."

She was stretched out along the couch, her eyes closed now. She mumbled, "I can't go home."

I was going to suggest a hotel but didn't want to push it. The truth was, I didn't want her sleeping on my couch. For more than one reason. Mainly, I didn't think it would be good if she was spotted leaving my office once the sun was up. I didn't like how it would look to the cops, or anybody else out there either.

I reached on top of the refrigerator and turned off the TV, made a half pot of coffee and listened to the Mr. Coffee machine cough and sputter until the dark liquid started to drip into the carafe. The smell of the coffee smelled all right, almost woke me up a bit, but I wasn't going to have any. Caffeine didn't normally keep me awake, but I needed to get some sleep, even if just for a few hours. I put the can of Chock Full o' Nuts away, and the jingle popped into my head:

"That heavenly coffee…"

I removed the carafe and stuck a cup underneath to let the coffee drip straight into it. It was stronger coffee this way, but I figured Lily could use it. Carrying it past my desk and around to the other side of the partition, I looked at Lily, flat out on the couch.

She appeared to be asleep.

"Hey," I said, giving her shoulder an easy nudge. "Are you awake?"

Lily didn't move.

"Hey," I said again. "Lily, wake up. Come on."

She opened her eyes and popped up like a spring, staring at me as if she didn't know where she was. She brushed a few strands of hair back from her face and looked straight ahead.

I sat down next to her and held the cup out for her. "Here, drink this. It'll help you wake up."

"I don't want to wake up." But she took the cup from me and took a sip, making a face as soon as she did. She held the back of her hand in front of her mouth. "How do you drink this stuff? I think I'm going to be sick."

"It's just coffee," I said. "You can handle it. Go on."

She looked down into the cup and slowly raised it up to her mouth with both hands. Taking another sip, she held the cup toward me. "Here. No. I can't drink this."

I took the cup and reached past her, placing it on the side table next to the couch.

"Are you sober enough to have an adult conversation?" I said. "I know it's late, but we really need to talk."

Lily leaned back on the couch and stretched her legs out straight in front of her. She rolled the back of her head on the cushion and looked up at me, lifting one of her legs. "Can you take off my boots?"

I looked her over. "Are you serious?"

She rolled her eyes and sat up, leaned forward, and took the boots off herself. She tossed one at a time on the floor, toward the other end of the couch. She took off her coat. "Why's it so cold in here?" she said, folding her arms, rubbing her hands up and down her arms.

I got up and grabbed the coffee cup from the table and sat down next to her. "Just drink this," I said. "It'll at least warm you up." I handed her the cup and she took it from my hand.

"Now, again, are you sober enough to talk?" I said.

She sipped the coffee, maybe got used to the taste, then nodded as she rested the cup down on her thigh. "I only had a few drinks."

"You look like you had *more* than just a few."

She smiled, her eyelids heavy, and handed me the cup. "I need to sleep." She started to lie down in the other direction and put her legs up across my thighs.

I pushed her off me and stood up. "I'm sorry, but no!" I said, like I was speaking to a dog.

Her eyes were already closed again.

I walked into the bathroom and dumped her coffee down the sink. I stepped out and said, "What I don't get is, if you didn't tell Moriarty much of anything, why did you bring up that night you took me back to your apartment, when Michael was out of town?"

Her eyes shot open, and she lifted her head, sitting upright, and staring back. She paused. "The detective was the one who asked me about it," she said. "I didn't tell him anything. Why would I?" She shrugged. "It's not like there was anything to tell."

I stared down at her. "Then who did you tell? Because someone told him. The only person who might've known was Reggie, just because he was behind the bar that night. But Reggie knew nothing happened... and he would've never said a word if anything did."

She shook her head. "I never told anyone about it."

"So what'd you say when he asked about it?"

I watched her try to fight back a swallow. Her eyes were down for a moment before she raised them back to mine. "I told him the truth. Nothing happened."

I wasn't sure I was buying it. "Then how would he know about it? It doesn't look good for either of us, you know. Even giving him the slightest idea the two of us were—"

She shrugged. "I swear, Jake. I told him it was nothing... that you were heartbroken and we just—"

"You told him *what*? You made it sound like it was *me*? That's not even close to the truth, Lily. You know that. You were the one who..."

"Maybe I should go," she said, standing up from the couch.

"Listen to me," I said. I could feel my voice grow louder. "Don't you understand how it would look the way you said it? Like I'm this broken-hearted madman out to settle a score with Michael?"

Lily said, "That's not what I said. It didn't come across like that at all."

I put my hands up and covered my face. I wanted to scream. I wanted to throw Lily out into the cold, dark street.

"I never meant to drag you into this," she said.

I stared back at her, doing my best not to lose my cool. "You know what? You *did* drag me into this. And I'm starting to wonder if this is, I don't know, some kind of wacky plan of yours."

She sat back down, pulled on her boots, threw her jacket on, and stormed toward the door. "You know what, Jake? This is exactly what your problem is. You don't trust me. You don't trust—"

"Why *would* I trust you?" I said.

She started to open the door, but I stepped toward her, putting my hand out and pushing it closed. "As much as I'd like you to leave," I said, shaking my head, my voice calm, "you can't go out there. It's the middle of the night. And you'll freeze to death. And, from what I can tell, you're in no condition to drive."

She tried to shove me out of the way and open the door.

But I held it closed. "Lily, stop," I said. I grabbed her arm, nodding toward the couch. "You can sleep there."

She kept her eyes on me as I stepped past her to the thermostat and turned it up a few degrees. "I'll even keep it warm, while you're here."

I looked at her and saw the tears coming down her face.

"Go ahead," I said. "Sit down."

She nodded, stepping toward the couch. She picked up the roll of toilet paper and tore off a piece, wiping her eyes.

I walked down the short hall past the bathroom door and opened the closet, pulling down a pillow and two blankets from the top shelf.

She sat on the couch, breaking into a smile. "Do you have anything to drink besides that sludge you call coffee?"

I handed her the pillow and the heavier of the two blankets. "Water, from the tap," I said.

"I mean, something with alcohol in it?" she said.

I had four 'Gansetts left from the six-pack in the fridge. "No," I said. I walked into the bathroom and poured her a glass of water and handed it to her. "You want an aspirin?"

She took the glass from me and took a sip.

I turned out the overhead lights, and the place got dark, other than the lamp on my desk and the city lights outside, slipping through the spaces in the blinds.

I watched Lily rest her head on the pillow and pulled the blanket up over her, then walked back to my desk, and sat down in the chair.

I unlaced my boots and pulled them off, covered myself with the blanket, and leaned back in the chair with my feet up on my desk. I reached for the lamp and turned it off, and within a handful of seconds, heard a snore from the other side of the partition behind me.

CHAPTER 8

I DIPPED THE CORNER of my toast into the yolk of my fried egg, the *Boston Globe* folded over in front of me on the table at the First Street Diner. I was there early enough to beat the church rush, although I'd expected at that point I'd be having a conversation with a more sober Lily. Problem with that was she snuck out the door before the sun had even come up. I was awake when I heard her get up. I decided not to stop her, letting her believe I was asleep as she tiptoed out the door.

The truth was, I hadn't slept at all. Not in an old desk chair barely comfortable enough for sitting, never mind trying to get a good night's sleep. I let her get out of there before the rest of the city was awake, thinking at the time it was best if she hadn't been seen leaving my office. I certainly didn't want more seeds planted about our so-called relationship. And I had a pretty good feeling the cops would be keeping an eye on both of us for the foreseeable future.

I sipped my coffee and came to the realization the only way to clear my own name—and help Lily in the process—was to try and figure out what really happened to Michael. Anything I could do to cut off further accusations would be worth my time. And I wasn't going to sit around and wait for Moriarty to drag me, or Lily, through the mud.

The problem was, I had no idea where to start. Of course, I realized, then, I probably should have talked to her when she sobered up. And before I'd finished my last piece of toast, I knew I'd made a mistake letting her leave my office.

***

I walked along Emerson, the sidewalks busier than they'd been since before the storm, mostly families dressed in church clothes heading toward Gate of Heaven Church for Sunday morning Mass. I continued alone and cut over to First toward East Broadway.

Maggie walked toward me, wearing her unzipped ski jacket and mirrored sunglasses over her eyes. Her red hair glowed in the sun, although I remembered Barbara correcting me that Maggie's hair was strawberry blonde, not red. I guess I wasn't clear on the difference.

The smell of fresh-baked bread from Gino's Bakery, a few doors down from my office, floated over the sidewalk. Gino was one of the handful of Italians who ended up in Southie, instead of the North End.

"Are you looking for me?" I said as Maggie approached, shading my eyes with my hand. I'd forgotten my sunglasses in my car, parked in front of my office.

"I called your house and the office, stopped here first and saw your car. I assumed you were somewhere in the area."

"If you showed up a little earlier, you could have joined me for breakfast." But as soon as I said it, my next thought was how thankful I was that she *hadn't* shown up earlier. She didn't need to know

Lily was there. Even though Maggie was a friend, and I trusted her as much as anyone, she was a good cop who did just about everything by the book. That's what made her different from a majority of officers in that department. Other than, of course, she was one of just a few females.

I unlocked my office door, held it open, and let Maggie walk in ahead of me. I tossed my keys on my desk and looked over at the couch; the blanket and pillow Lily used were still there. The blanket I used was on my chair. I wasn't sure if Maggie would pick up on the scent of Lily's perfume or notice the cup left on the side table.

I grabbed the pillow and blankets and tossed them in the closet. "So," I said. "You're being quiet, and I'd have to guess it means you've got something maybe you want to tell me?"

Maggie looked around the office, almost like she was looking for something.

"You shouldn't have walked out on Moriarty," she said.

I opened all the blinds to let some of the sun in, then lowered the thermostat. "I didn't like where it was going," I said. "And I'm not going to let him push me around just for..."

"That's how he works, Jake. He likes to get under people's skin. I'm sure you figured that out."

"He has nothing on me." I thought for a moment, assuming Maggie must've known most of what was discussed. "He tried to say I slept with Lily while she was married to Michael."

"Is that true?" she said.

"No. It was one night. I'd had a few drinks, and she drove me back to her apartment. I slept on the couch."

Maggie stared back at me, like she wasn't buying it.

"Nothing happened," I said. "What I don't understand is where he would've heard it. Lily claims she didn't tell him."

Maggie looked toward the couch, her eyes going to the half-full glass of water on the side table, but she said nothing about it. "I think

Jeffrey's just interested in the relationship between the three of you. Of course, between the fight you had with him, and if somebody told him you and Lily hooked up while she was married"—she removed her jacket and tossed it on the couch—"I'm sure you understand how it looks to someone who doesn't know you."

"If this is all he's got, then we're all in trouble. You ask me, the guy's a clown. I don't even understand how he's a detective. He looks like he's barely old enough to drink." I sat down on the couch, my elbows on my knees, my head resting in both hands.

Maggie said, "Jeffrey's been a member of the Boston PD for ten years. And his track record speaks for itself." She walked around the paneled-wall partition, came around with one of the chairs from in front of my desk, dragged it over, and sat down across from me. "I will admit, he seems a little fixated on Lily."

"And me," I said, looking up at her.

"I don't think so," Maggie said. "If you ask me, I think the question he has about you is whether or not you're hiding something, maybe trying to protect Lily. If you'd only stayed, talked to him instead of walking out..."

"He wanted cooperation, he could have asked for it." I stood up from the couch and ran my hands through my hair. "He called me a 'so-called' private investigator? What kind of detective insults another detective like that? Just because I'm not employed by the big bureaucracy?"

Maggie let out a small laugh. "You're really going to let something like that bother you? Like I said, he likes to get under people's skin."

"He's a jerk."

"I'm not sure I can argue with that. But it doesn't mean he's not good at what he does," she said.

I walked to the front door and looked out toward the street. "Lily thinks Michael was cheating on her."

"She *thinks*?"

I turned from the door. "She didn't mention it to Moriarty. But I did, just because I assumed she came clean with him. Clearly, she had not. And once I realized she hadn't, I got out of there. I knew she hadn't been straight with him about the whole thing and didn't want to be the one to open the can of worms."

"You'll get yourself in trouble trying to protect her," Maggie said.

"I'm not protecting her. I didn't want him to know what I knew. Especially since she tried to hire me to follow Michael."

"She tried to hire you?"

"*Tried*," I said. "But I didn't take the job. Luckily. I walked out before I had to answer any more questions."

Maggie sighed, shaking her head. "Do you have a name?"

"A name?"

"Who Dempsey might've been cheating with?"

"Oh yeah. But this is the other part I didn't tell Moriarty. So, if I tell you..."

"I'm an officer of the law, Jake. I can't—"

"Well, I have no proof. It's all speculation. So even if you told him..." I paused a moment. "It's Tony Gautieri's daughter."

"The mayor of Providence?"

I nodded and walked around the partition to my desk.

Maggie followed me over, dragging the chair behind her. She took a seat across from me.

I pulled the pad from the middle drawer and looked over the only thing I'd written when Lily first came to see me. "She's twenty-three, works for her father at the mayor's office, of course. Apparently, Michael and Angela—"

"Angela's the daughter?"

"Yes. They might've had some kind of work relationship. So, again, it's all speculation on Lily's part."

"You know the mayor down there allegedly has ties to the New England Mafia, don't you?" Maggie said.

"Of course I know that. That was a big part of why I turned Lily down. On top of the fact I can't stand her."

"For someone who despises her, you're putting your neck on the line lying to a detective, just to protect her."

"I didn't lie," I said. "I just got out of there before I went into any further detail."

"To protect a woman you claim to despise?"

I rolled my eyes, looking down at the pad.

Maggie leaned forward in the chair. "I think you should let me tell Jeffrey about the mayor's daughter."

"Like I said, there's no proof. That's what she wanted me to do for her. Prove he was cheating."

Maggie leaned back in the chair. "You never know, maybe Gautieri got wind of his daughter messing around with an older, married man."

"You think that's a serious motive?" I said.

"What would you do if you found out Nancy was messing around with a man ten years older, who was married?"

I shrugged, nodding. "Yeah, I'd kill him." I smiled.

"Did she say anything else?" Maggie said.

"Not really. But there's more to it: from what I understand, Angela Gautieri was engaged to Lawrence Martin. You know who he is?"

"Should I?" Maggie said.

"Offensive lineman for the Patriots. At least he was. There were rumors he was done."

"Done?"

"Yeah, released. Or, not re-signed by the team. He's only twenty-eight, but he's got a bad knee."

"Does he still live around here?" she said.

"Sounds like he does, at least for now."

Maggie had a look on her face like she was trying to process all I was giving her. "Are you okay if I share this information with Jeffrey?"

I was hesitant. I knew how it would look, especially for Lily. And I worried it was only going to drag me in deeper, just for trying to help her. I got up from my desk without answering Maggie's question, walking over to the coffee machine. "You want a coffee?"

"Do you have any tea?"

I opened the freestanding cabinet in the corner next to the refrigerator near the coffee machine and took out a box of Lipton tea bags. I walked into the bathroom and filled a mug with water, went back out and stuck the mug of cold water in the Radarange.

The bell rang a minute later, and I pulled out the mug of hot, steaming water. I carried it to my desk where Maggie had switched sides and sat in my chair behind the desk. I placed the mug in front of her with the tea bag inside, then stepped around and sat down in the chair across from her.

"If you think you should tell Moriarty, then I think you have to do what you feel is right," I said.

She picked up the mug, holding it with both hands, her lips pursed as she blew into the steam coming off the top. "You know what? Jeffrey reminds me a lot of you, when you were younger."

I gave her a look like she was crazy. "I was never that pretty. And I certainly wouldn't leave the house dressed the way he does."

She sipped her tea and looked back at me over the rim. "Another option is for you to go back to the station in the morning and sit down with him yourself? Let him see you're on his side. I think it would go a long way. I'm just afraid if I tell him, he's not going to like the idea you came to me, when you could have come clean when you met with him."

I thought for a moment. "But I don't know if we *are* on the same side. That's certainly not how it felt when I left that station. And I still don't like the idea he brought up that night I went home with Lily."

"But you said nothing happened," Maggie said.

"That's the truth. But I don't like what he tried to imply, like he's trying to make me out to be the jealous ex-lover."

Maggie looked down into the cup of tea. "Jake, I don't believe you're a suspect. And I'm not sure Jeffrey does either." She was quiet, looking to her left toward the window. "Okay, then I'm going to have to tell him, Jake. Are you going to be okay with that?"

I shrugged. "It doesn't sound like I have much of a choice."

The phone rang, and I stood up to reach for the phone in front of Maggie. "Horn Investigations."

I could hear someone on the other end, but whoever it was didn't say a word.

"Hello?" I said. "Are you going to talk?"

The caller hung up.

I placed the handset down on the base and sat back down in the chair.

"What is it?" Maggie said.

I looked at the phone, shaking my head with a slight shrug. "Nobody there."

Maggie took another sip of tea and stood up from my desk. "I have to go." She stepped around to my side and put her hand on my shoulder, looking me in the eye. "Let me talk to him. He knows you and I are friends, so... I'll just tell him I beat it out of you." She smiled, looking at her watch as she started toward the door. "My shift starts in twenty minutes," she said. "I'm off by ten. I'll try to call before then, once I've had a chance to talk to him. I'm not even sure he'll be in, seeing it's Sunday."

CHAPTER 9

IT WAS LATE SUNDAY; *The Carol Burnett Show* was on but I wasn't paying much attention. James Garner was a guest, and I tried to remember the last time I'd watched *The Rockford Files*. I liked James Garner, but it was like an ER doctor watching *Emergency!*

I hurried into the kitchen when I heard the phone ring, grabbing the receiver off the wall before the second ring.

I answered, "Hello?"

"Jake? It's Maggie. I'm sorry I didn't call you sooner, I—"

"I figured you had a busy day."

"I did. But I wanted to wait until I got home to call you. I have something to tell you, but you just have to promise me you won't tell anyone, not even Raymond, you heard it from me."

"You have my word," I said.

"Well, you're not going to like this, Jake. But I'm afraid Moriarty's not ready to let you off the hook. I'm sorry. Same with Lily. There's something he knows, something she might've said to him that's made him suspicious."

"Like what?" I said, walking with the phone to the table.

"I don't know."

"Did you tell him about Angela Gautieri?"

"He wasn't very receptive," she said. "Like he didn't believe it."

"Are you serious?" I said. "A fellow officer gives him a piece of information and he blows it off?"

"He doesn't see me as his fellow officer. He's a detective. I'm on patrol. That's just how he is."

I got up and walked to the refrigerator, reaching in for a can of beer. "Are you telling me Lily and I are the only two people he's questioned so far? And now he wants to come down on us? Is he really that desperate?" I cracked the top on the can and sat back down at the table.

"I'm not sure he's desperate, but yeah, he doesn't seem to have much else right now."

"So he didn't even flinch when you mentioned Angela Gautieri?"

"He said he'd need a lot more if he's going to go knocking on the mayor's daughter's door."

"Then what about Lawrence Martin? Did you mention him?"

"I did. That caught his ear, but he seemed preoccupied. Like I said, I don't know what it is; he's got his eyes on you and Lily right now."

"This is why I said I can't just sit around, wait for him to do something foolish that puts me in a bad spot, Maggie. You know what I'm saying?"

She was quiet on the other line. "I did try to locate Lawrence Martin. He had a home in North Attleboro that's listed for sale. I made a call down there, spoke with a friend of mine who's an officer there, said the place has been empty for a couple of weeks."

I sipped my 'Gansett. "What about the woman who was working at the Morrissey Motel? Any word on her?"

"Well, I don't believe she's a suspect, if that's what you're—"

"No more than I am," I said. "But I've got a hard-up detective up my ass now. And I have nothing to do with any of this."

"I'm not sure that's completely true," Maggie said. "You got yourself involved."

"I'm guessing she had to give a statement, right?"

"Who? The woman from the motel?"

"Yes. Did you see it?"

"There's not a lot to it. She went out back to toss the trash around three a.m. and saw his body in the dumpster."

"Do you have her name?" I stood from the table to look outside, toward the street, moving the curtain to the side. A car drove slowly by the house but seemed to speed up, disappearing into the darkness.

"Her name's Nora Hayden," Maggie said. "She's been an employee at the motel for a little more than six months."

I grabbed a piece of paper from the drawer and dug around for a pencil. "Nora Hayden, you said?"

"Yes. H-A-Y-D-E-N. Hayden."

"You have a number? Or an address?"

Maggie was quiet on the other end. "Actually, I don't. But, Jake, promise me this is between me and you. Whatever I share with you didn't come from me. You got it? You start knocking on people's doors and—"

"You have my word." I stepped to the window again and pulled the curtain aside, looking out at the glow of the lamp on the street. "Is there anything else? At this point, any good detective would've spoken to at *least* a dozen people, no?"

"Moriarty's the type who likes to hold his cards close to his chest. He's actually been reprimanded for it in the past, but they usually let it slide because, in the end, he always seems to solve the case."

***

I saw the sign for Morrissey Motel on the left side of Morrissey Boulevard, having to drive up another half mile to bang a uey and come back down Morrissey from the other direction. I pulled into the parking lot of the motel that appeared slightly run-down, somewhere I'd describe as a place a man would go when he didn't want his wife to know he was up to no good.

I parked the Nova in front of the motel's office and walked in the front door where a No Vacancy sign hung on the other side of the glass.

A man behind the service desk looked up from a newspaper opened flat in front of him. He sipped his coffee, the cup tucked under his dark, thick mustache. "Can I help you?" The look on his face said I'd disturbed his morning routine.

I leaned with one arm on the counter between us and looked at the keys hung on a pegboard behind him. "I'm looking for Nora?"

"It's just me." He scratched his balding head.

"Well, can you tell me when she works here?"

"It is just me."

"Just you? You mean, you're the only employee who works here?"

He tucked the paper under the counter. "I am the owner, sir." He looked past me toward the parking lot. "If you're looking for a room..."

"No, I'm not. But, like I said, I'm looking for the woman who works here, or at least used to. From what I understand, Ms. Hayden was behind this desk the other night when one of your guests was found shot dead in the dumpster."

The man removed the glasses from his face and tucked them into his shirt pocket. "We already told you people, we don't know what happened. "

"You *people*?" I said.

He nodded. "You are a policeman, no?"

"Do I look like a policeman?"

He looked me up and down, nodding. "Yes."

I pulled out my wallet and removed a business card, placing it in front of him on the counter.

He picked it up and looked it over. "A private investigator?"

I glanced over my shoulder toward the door. "As it says there on the card, my name's Jake Horn." I gave him a nod and read the plastic name tag pinned to his chest. I reached out and shook his hand, which happened to be limp and sweaty. "Adesh? So, you own this place?"

"I do."

"So, again, can you tell me when Nora will be back?"

"She doesn't work here anymore."

I paused. "But she was here that night, was she not?"

He shifted his eyes to the counter before he answered. "Nora wouldn't work late at night anymore. She said she was scared, after what had happened." He shrugged. "I had to let her go."

"You fired her? Because she was scared to work nights after a man was murdered? That's a little cold, no?"

"I even told her she could bring a gun to work, but she—"

"Wasn't she the one who found the body?" I said.

Adesh nodded. "Yes, sir."

I turned and stepped to the door, put my hand on the metal bar, and looked through the glass toward the parking lot. "Was Michael Dempsey, by any chance, a regular customer?"

I could see Adesh was thinking before he answered. "He has been a guest here before. I would not consider him a 'regular.'"

"You ever see him with a woman?"

"I don't get into my guests' personal business. As long as they pay me, what they do behind closed doors is none of my business."

I looked around the small office, the same brown paneling on the walls as what was in my office. There was a small TV facing Adesh from the far end of the counter, but I couldn't see what was on the screen. The sound on it was turned low.

"You happen to know how I can get in touch with her?" I said.

He picked up my card from the counter and held it up in front of him, shaking his head. "What I will do for you, sir, is give her your information. I will tell her to call you. Is that all right?" He put his hands down on the counter, spread wide from his shoulders. "I do not know you. I would not feel safe giving a stranger her personal information."

"I just had a few questions, but whatever you can do, I'd appreciate it." I glanced once again at the keys hung on the pegboard on the wall behind Adesh. "Would you mind if I took a look around the place?"

"I'm sorry," he said. "The rooms are all occupied."

The parking lot was empty. "Are you sure?"

Adesh stared back at me without a response.

I didn't want to push him any further. "Are you okay if I just poke around outside?"

Adesh nodded once. "But please, Mr..." he looked at my business card. "Mr. Horn. Please try not to bother the guests. I don't need any trouble, or any more bad publicity than I already have."

I gave him a slight smile. "You know what they say—there's no such thing as *bad* publicity."

He didn't seem to find it amusing.

I left the office, headed outside, and walked around the side of the building. As soon as I turned the corner to the back, I saw the dumpster with three plastic garbage cans lined up next to it. It was on the smaller side with doors on the front, low enough that anyone of average size and strength could easily manage to reach the opening to dump the trash.

Or... a body.

I didn't expect to find much behind the motel. The police had already combed the place, although even a small clue could easily be overlooked.

I opened the doors on the dumpster and looked inside. I hadn't seen the police photos of Michael and didn't have much detail on his condition other than he'd been shot. I didn't see any bloodstains, either, on the dumpster or the concrete, assuming it had either been cleaned up or the body was disposed of in a way that there would be no signs. At least not until someone looked in the dumpster.

Other than a few bags inside it, the dumpster appeared to have been recently emptied.

I walked into the small, narrow parking lot at the back of the motel, with enough room for maybe five or six cars. Behind the lot were trees, but I could see a building on the other side.

The back of the motel was without any windows, and only one door with Not an Entrance painted on it.

I walked to the far end of the parking lot and around the corner, where a handful of cars were parked on the side. They weren't visible from Morrissey Boulevard, the way the trees and shrubs blocked the view. I kept walking until I was again out at the front of the building but the opposite side from where the office was. Including the rooms on the side of the building, there were sixteen total. Each steel door was painted black and had a white metal lawn chair out front with a tall ashtray beside each one. Most looked to be filled with old cigarette butts.

I walked along the building and stopped at room number eight. That was the room Michael Dempsey had checked into the night he was killed.

I looked toward the office at the far end of the building and spotted Adesh's big eyes looking out at me through the open blinds on the window on my side of his office.

He moved away as soon as I caught his eye.

I continued and walked into his office; Adesh looked down when I walked in as if he was too busy to look up.

But I knew better. "I'm going to run over to Freeman's and grab something to eat," I said. "You mind if I leave my car?"

Freeman's was the bar Lily said she'd gone into the evening before Michael was killed. For all the times I'd been on Morrissey Boulevard, I'd either never noticed the place or just hadn't paid much attention to it, especially with the way it was set back from the boulevard, with the entrance on Conley Street, facing the motel parking lot fifty yards from the entrance.

Adesh looked out the window toward the Nova, nodding. "Yes, that is okay."

But I wasn't sure he meant it.

"You sure? I can drive over. I just thought..."

He brushed his hand backward through the air. "Go. You can leave it here." He turned from me with a piece of paper in his hand, looking over the reading glasses seated at the end of his nose, not saying another word.

Chapter 10

FREEMAN'S SIGN OUT FRONT on the corner of the parking lot was as faded as the green awning hanging over the front entrance.

Two men stood just outside the front door smoking cigarettes and stopped talking when I walked past them. I gave them a nod, pulling on the heavy wood door with a single pane of glass at eye level, to see inside. But the door seemed to stick, so I yanked on it and it opened.

The inside was full of cigarette smoke with the smell of stale beer. The small bar had three sides with green-and-yellow stained-glass light fixtures hanging over the bar every few feet from the ceiling. The sound from the small TV on a shelf on the back wall mixed with the loud chatter from the patrons at the bar and tables along the wall. It was mostly a male crowd, from what I could tell, although I did notice two older women smoking cigarettes, leaning on the table laughing with each other. One of them broke into a cough from perhaps laughing too hard, holding the cigarette in her hand.

I had the feeling all eyes were on me when I stepped to the bar and pulled up a stool to the far right. There were two empty stools next to me, but the rest looked to be occupied.

The bartender was down at the other end of the bar, not paying enough attention to notice I'd walked in. He smoked a cigarette, his foot up on a cooler, his arm resting on his raised knee.

I sat down, waiting. I wanted to call out for the bartender but figured he'd have had to've been blind not to notice when I walked in.

He finally looked toward me, giving me a nod. "You all set, buddy?"

"Can I get a menu?"

The bartender wiped his hands on a towel hung over his shoulder and reached under the bar. He walked to my side of the bar and handed me a paper menu that looked like it'd been handwritten by a child. "You want a drink?" he said.

"Can of Narragansett," I said.

He grabbed my beer from the cooler and popped off the top, placing it down in front of me. The phone on the back wall rang before he said anything else and he turned to answer it. With his back to me, I watched him nodding as he spoke to the caller. "Yeah," he said. He was quiet, listening. He glanced back at me over his shoulder and continued to nod. "Yeah, no problem. I'll take care of it." He hung up the phone and walked through the swinging door to the kitchen.

I looked over the menu I had in front of me. From what I could decipher, they had clam chowder as the soup of the day, a turkey club sandwich, a pastrami sandwich, grilled ham and cheese, and a hot dog. *Chef's Special: Shepherd's Pie*, was written in big letters at the bottom of the page.

The bartender walked back through the swinging door, and I said, "Sir?" I held up the menu and pointed to it as if he could see from ten feet away. "You make the chowder right here?"

He grabbed a beer glass from the red rubber mat near the tap in the middle of the bar and filled it with Miller High Life. "The chowder?" His eyes stayed on the glass under the tap in front of him until the glass was filled. He flipped the handle up on the tap and delivered the beer to one of the older gentlemen at the other end. He wiped his hands on the towel and walked toward me again. "Sorry," he said, "but we ship the chowder up from Florida." He cracked a slight smile and looked toward the older crowd at the other end of the bar. One man, the only one who seemed to be listening to him, laughed.

I realized the bartender was being a smart-ass.

He stood in front of me, pulled a cigarette from his shirt pocket and stuck it in his mouth. "Of *course* we make it here. What kind of question is that?"

I couldn't tell if he was pissed I asked a question or just being a typical Boston bartender: your best friend as long as you don't ask any dumb questions.

He took a drag from his cigarette and reached under the bar for an ashtray, putting it down in front of him to flick the ash. He gave a quick nod toward the swinging door. "Bruce is the cook. Everything he makes is fresh. You wouldn't think a place like this would have good food, right?" He looked around the bar at his customers. "Ask anyone. We got the best chowder in Boston."

"Okay," I said. "I'll have a bowl." I finished my beer before he'd even placed the order.

"Another one?" the man said, nodding toward my beer.

"Please."

He put another 'Gansett in front of me, then walked away.

"Hey," I said. "What's your name?"

He stopped and looked back at me, like he wondered why I was asking. "Sean." He didn't seem to care enough to ask for mine.

Saved me from making one up.

He continued through the swinging door and took a couple of minutes to come back out. When he did, he grabbed two more empty beer glasses, flipped upside down on the red rubber mat next to the tap, and filled them both with beer. He carried the beers to the other end of the bar, then walked back over my way, picking up his burning cigarette from the ashtray. He took a drag. "You live around here?"

"Sort of," I said but left it at that.

He stared back at me, squinting his eyes with the cigarette's smoke rising toward his face. "Are you a guest at the motel?"

"No." I glanced to my left toward the door. "I heard someone was killed over there."

Sean looked up at the small TV, nodding as he scratched the side of his head, the cigarette between his fingers. "Lots of crazy things happen over there. Guests usually end up over here, half of 'em, I swear, just looking for trouble."

"What kind of trouble?" I said.

He drew from his cigarette and shrugged. "I don't know. Just stirring things up. Mostly regulars here, so..."

I sipped my beer, thinking about a way to get some answers without coming across as too nosy. "You know what happened?"

Sean took one more drag of his cigarette and blew a double-stream of smoke out his nostrils. "What happened to what?"

"The guy killed over there."

He crushed the butt in the ashtray, shaking his head. "I don't know a thing about it. Just try to mind my own business, if you know what I'm saying?"

I sipped my beer, watching him over the top. "Any chance you happened to be working Thursday night?"

He turned and looked down the rest of the bar, a handful of the patrons watching us, like they had nothing better to do but listen in.

"The night of the murder?"

"Before. From what I've heard, it was sometime Friday morning. But yeah, middle of the night. Same difference."

Sean leaned on the bar with his hands out wide, looking over his shoulder. "You got something you want to ask me?"

I knew I should probably play it cool with this guy. I sipped my beer and placed it down, leaning on the bar. "Okay," I said. "A friend of mine told me she was in here that night. Thursday evening. She might've talked to you, so I'm just trying to see if I can get some things straight."

He stared back at me, then reached under the bar, coming up with a towel, wiping down the bar a few spaces down from me. "If she was in here looking for a man, I'm sure I would have told her the same thing I tell the rest of 'em: 'Sorry, haven't seen him.'" He grinned. "I don't get involved. And don't want to be involved. Not my business to—"

"You'd remember this one if you saw her." I looked around the place at what looked like a crowd of losers. I like a good dive bar as much as the next guy, but sometimes I gotta draw the line. "I gotta imagine she'd stick out like a sore thumb in this place." I looked along the others at the bar. There was less chatter than when I'd first walked in, half the eyes focused on me.

The kitchen door swung open, and a large, bearded man wearing a white smock and a belly you could rest a tray on, stepped behind the bar. He held out a bowl toward Sean. "Who's got the chowdah?"

Sean reached for the bowl and placed it down in front of me with silverware wrapped tight in a paper napkin. He put two bags of oyster crackers beside the bowl and walked away, following Bruce back into the kitchen.

Steam came off the chowder. It smelled good, and I was starved. I unrolled the spoon from the napkin and skimmed it over the top, blowing on it before I got a taste. I stuck it in my mouth and sure enough, knew the guy wasn't kidding.

The chowder was good.

I reached inside my coat hung on the backrest of my stool and took out the Polaroid I had of Lily. I put it down next to me on the bar and sipped my soup.

Sean walked out from the kitchen but in the opposite direction from me. He moved along the bar and grabbed any glass that needed to be refilled.

I waved him over as soon as he made eye contact, holding up the photo of Lily. "You mind taking a look at this?"

He finished filling the glasses with beer, walked back over, and took the Polaroid from my hand.

"This is her," I said. "Recognize her?"

He looked the photo over, studied it, shook his head, then put the Polaroid down in front of me. "Sorry."

I wasn't sure I believed him. "Come on, man." I held up the photo. "You sure?"

"I don't get involved." He looked down at my chowder, then walked down the other end of the bar.

He had his back to me, facing the men at the far end from where I sat. One of them leaned so he could get a look at me, staring for a moment as if he wanted to let me know it wasn't my place.

I sipped my chowder from the spoon, hunched over the bowl, looking back at the man watching me.

Sean walked toward me, then started through the swinging door.

"Hey, Sean," I said. I reached for my wallet and pulled out a twenty. I put it down flat and slid it across the bar, holding my hand on top of it. I tapped on the photo. "You sure you don't recognize her?"

He eyeballed the twenty. "I told you, buddy. I've never seen her before in my life. I'm not going to tell you again." He walked through the door and into the kitchen.

The man down the other end was still staring at me. I'm not sure there was a point he actually looked away.

I gave him a nod.

"Why don't you finish up and get lost," the man said, his big hand gripping the short glass of beer in front of him. He straightened up from a somewhat hunched position, folding his tattoo-covered arms in front of his chest. The other men sitting next to him all stared back at me, with him.

I looked toward the kitchen door, but Sean hadn't come back out. I wondered if he asked his buddy to get rid of me. And I didn't need the trouble.

I threw back what was left in my beer and picked up the twenty and the photo of Lily. I got up, tucked a handful of bills under the half-eaten bowl of chowder and headed out the door.

I walked across the street to the motel parking lot. Gray clouds had covered the sky, and the temperature felt like it had dropped. I might've felt a drop of rain.

I walked past the Nova and toward the office. But when I pulled on the door, it was locked. I knocked on the plate glass and waited, but nobody answered. I looked at my watch. Maybe the owner, Adesh, had gone out for lunch. But why would he close with nobody else there to watch the place?

I looked around the parking lot. It was mostly empty. Perhaps all the guests had checked out when I was over at Freeman's.

I started toward my car, and reached into my pocket for my keys, but stopped when I saw the man from the bar coming toward me across the parking lot. I tucked my keys back in my pocket. "Can I help you?" I said.

I realized the man was bigger than he looked seated at the bar, with a thick neck and mountain-like biceps practically bursting out of the fabric of his short sleeves. He stepped around from the back end of the Nova and came straight at me without a word, throwing a wild punch I'd admit I wasn't exactly ready for.

It sent me stumbling back, but I steadied myself just in time to take another punch to the side of my head, his left hand connecting like a horse's kick, sending me into the driver's-side door. I dropped to one knee but came up fast with an uppercut, catching him under the jaw with as much as I could bring.

He fell back, and his big body dropped down to the asphalt. Before he could get up, I jumped on top of him and threw another punch, sending his head back to the ground.

I reached into my pocket for my keys, trying to hurry before this guy was back on his feet. And just as I slid the key into the lock, I saw his reflection in the glass and ducked, his fist connecting with the top of the car door.

He hit it so hard, he left a dent, screaming in pain and holding his hand, blood coming off his knuckles.

But I wasn't going to give him another chance. And I wasn't afraid to play dirty, especially when I felt I was somewhat over-matched. I charged after him, wrapped my arms around his shoulders, and drove my knee square into his crotch.

He dropped like a bag of cement, his hands between his legs, toppling to the ground with deep moans coming from somewhere inside him.

I stood over him, about to drop a round-ending punch on him when a gunshot was fired. I ducked, unsure where it had come from but stayed low, turning the key in the door and sliding inside the Nova.

I stayed slouched in the driver's seat, turned the ignition and slapped it into reverse without even looking back. I slammed my foot down on the gas, tires squealing. The 350 engine roared and I spun the car around, headed for Morrissey Boulevard. I straightened up in my seat and looked out the rearview at the man, coming to his feet. I took a quick look toward Freeman's. There was nobody else anywhere outside.

I cut the wheel and took off, fishtailing into moving traffic on Morrissey Boulevard. Horns blew and tires squealed as I straightened the wheel and looked to my right at the man standing at the edge of the motel parking lot, watching me.

CHAPTER 11

LITTLE HOUSE ON THE Prairie was on TV, but I wasn't paying much attention to it, laying flat on my couch with a bag of frozen peas pressed against my head. But I jumped up and hurried into the kitchen when the phone rang, reaching around the wall as I stepped through the doorway to answer it.

I got to it by the second ring. "Hello?"

"Dad? It's me."

Nancy was on the other end. And I was happy to hear her voice.

"Hey" I said, feeling pain in my jaw as soon as I opened my mouth. "What are you doing?" I could hear music in the background.

"We're all just hanging out, listening to records."

"Van Halen?" I said.

"38 Special."

"Good band," I said. "The new album?"

"Uh-huh," she said, and I could tell in her voice she'd called for a reason.

"I was thinking about coming home for a couple of days, through next weekend," she said. "I wanted to make sure you'd be all right if—"

"Of course it's all right," I said. "Why would you think you'd even have to ask," I said. "This is your home too."

"Well, I know you're busy with work, so I just wanted to make sure."

That was true. I was busy, and I knew my life was about to get even more complicated. But I would never let anything get in the way of seeing Nancy. "Do you need a ride down?" I said.

"I have a ride." Other than the music in the background, the line went quiet for a moment. "Um, I wanted to ask you something else," she said. "I was hoping, well, would it be all right if I brought a friend with me?"

My first thought was how I knew right then I wouldn't be spending as much time alone with Nancy as I'd hoped. She wasn't a little girl anymore. Even when she came home, she'd run out to see her old friends. It was selfish of me to think she'd sit and watch *Little House on the Prairie* with me, like we did when she was younger. "Of course you can bring a friend." I looked around the house, which wasn't exactly a mess but not what you'd consider presentable. "Who is she? A friend from the dorm?"

There was more silence.

"Actually, um, my friend's not a *she*. It's a... his name is Corey."

"Corey?" I had the bag of peas in my hand but stretched the phone's cord across the kitchen, opening the freezer door so I could toss them back in. "I guess I wasn't expecting you to say you were bringing a boy home," I said, knowing too well a college-aged male was likely no longer, technically, a boy.

"We're just friends," she said.

"Friends?" I opened the refrigerator and pulled out a can of beer, cracking the top with the phone pressed against my ear with my shoulder. "Are you just saying you're 'just friends' to make me feel better about bringing this person home with you?"

She laughed. "Trust me, Dad. He's just a friend. I swear."

I held my hand flat on the left side of my head as pain shot from my jaw into my skull. "So you're saying you like him, but you don't—"

"He plays lacrosse."

"An athlete, huh? Although, that's a rich kid's sport, isn't it?"

"I don't know. I guess. He's nice. You'll like him."

I felt a twinge in my stomach. "I probably won't. Just so you know that ahead of time."

She laughed. "So is it okay with you?" She had a touch of excitement in her voice I wasn't sure I liked. Not when it had to do with bringing a boy home to meet her old man. "So this kid has his own car?"

"Yes, he has his own car."

I had to think for a moment. "I guess this means you and I won't be able to spend time together. I mean, without the boyfriend?"

"He's not a boyfriend," she said. "I'm serious. But we will, because he's going into Boston one night to stay with another friend."

"All right," I said. "Just make sure he knows I own a gun."

It'd been a tough road raising Nancy alone, at least when she was younger. But there was a point—maybe when she was in high school—when she took over taking care of herself. She matured fast. Maybe faster than most kids, and maybe more than I wanted her to. She was just a little girl when she lost her mother. And one thing it did was force her at an early age to deal with things most kids never have to.

It was never easy for her. It wasn't easy for either of us. But we always had each other. And we had friends and family to help out. Raymond and his wife, Beth, were there for Nancy. My grandmother was still alive at the time, and Maggie was always there for Nancy. At least until I started dating Lily.

***

Raymond was in the back clearing what was left of the snow off his deck. With the warmer weather during the day, the snow was finally starting to disappear, although leaving behind a lot of mud and pools of water everywhere you turned.

He leaned the shovel up against the house and narrowed his eyes, looking at my face when I walked onto the deck. "What the hell happened?"

I touched my jaw, still tight but thankfully feeling better. "Someone apparently didn't like me asking questions."

"You got in a fight?" he said. "What the hell happened?"

"I went to the Morrissey Motel and the bar across the street to ask some questions."

"They take anything?" he said. "Your money?"

I cracked a slight smile. "*What* money?"

Raymond grabbed the shovel and slid it under the hard snow, throwing a chunk over the deck's railing. He looked up at the sky. "You want a beer?" He put the shovel down again and grabbed two lawn chairs he had folded up and leaning against the house, next to the door. "Took these out, thought I'd pretend spring is here." He took his winter hat off his head. "I'm sweating."

I took one of the chairs and opened it where he'd cleared the space on his deck down to the bare wood. I looked up at the gray sky. "I wouldn't be surprised if we got another storm."

Raymond clasped his hands together and held them under his chin, his eyes up toward the sky. "Please, Lord, no. I beg you. No more snow."

I sat down in the chair, and Raymond went inside, came back out with two bottles of Black Label.

"Here," he said, giving me one of the beers, cracking open the top on the other. He opened the other chair next to me and sat down, looking me over. "You need some ice for that ugly face?"

I took a sip of beer and looked off the deck into the yard. "No, it's fine. Happened yesterday."

"*Yesterday?* Why didn't you call me?"

I sipped the beer and put my other hand at the base of my aching skull. "Guy came out looking for a fight right after I left Freeman's. But I got a piece of him... actually had him down until someone fired a gunshot."

"Someone fired a shot at you?" Raymond said, his eyes opened wide. He turned to me in his chair.

"Honestly? I don't think anyone shot at either of us. Maybe into the air. But I didn't see anyone. I'm not even sure where it was fired from."

"You didn't see who it was?"

"No. I was more interested in getting out of there. He was a big bastard."

Raymond sipped from the bottle, both of us quiet for a few moments.

"So are you going to tell me what you were doing over at the motel?" he said.

"Well, I wanted to talk to the woman who found Michael Dempsey's body. See what else she knew."

"But why?" he said. "Why can't you just leave it alone? Let the police handle it?"

99

"They've already dragged me into it. I'm a suspect right now. Even if I'm barely on their list, I'm not going to wait around to see what happens."

Raymond stared back at me. "From what I've heard, they don't have any leads. All they're doing is starting with the low-hanging fruit." He faced straight ahead, looking into his backyard. "I still think you're better off keeping your hands clean," he said.

"That's pretty much what Maggie said." I leaned my head back and finished off what was left in the bottle. "You're both loyal to a fault."

Raymond laughed. "Law enforcement exists for a reason. You think we'd be in a better world if all we had were private investigators to solve crimes? Go private? Maybe go big, let the corporations take over law enforcement?" He laughed. "How do you think that would work out?"

"I'm not even sure what that's supposed to mean," I said.

"You've never believed in the system we have in place," he said. "That's why you and my dad got along so well." He put his big hand on my shoulder. "You've got a good heart, Jake. This woman cheats on you and marries the man she slept with. And now you're trying to help her?" He sipped his beer. "Most men would tell her where to go."

"The important fact is I'm already involved. The detective on the case—"

"Jeffrey Moriarty?" Raymond said.

"Yeah," I said. "You know him?"

"I know *of* him. Rubs a lot of guys the wrong way, from what I hear. But he does good work, and that's usually all that matters."

"Yeah, well, he was hoping he could say I had an affair with Lily, painting the picture like I'm the jealous ex."

"They've got nothing on you," Raymond said. "You have nothing to worry about. Lily might be another story." He tapped the side of his head. "That one... she's not all there. You know that."

"It doesn't make her a killer," I said.

Raymond shrugged and stood up from the chair. "Are you sure you believe that?" He walked in the house and came back out with two more beers, sitting back down in the chair. He handed one to me. "I hate to say it, but the way you're putting yourself out... If I were you, I'd let it play out. I don't mean you shouldn't take care of yourself, do all you can to keep your hands clean, and maybe make sure your name is clear. But as for Lily..." He shook his head. "I'm not sure you really know what she's capable of, Jake."

I got up from the chair and walked to the edge of the deck, leaning forward on the railing and looking down into the yard. "I haven't even talked to her. I've called her apartment and she doesn't answer. I left her a couple of messages."

Raymond said, "Did you find anything at the motel?"

I thought for a moment. "I talked to the owner. But, like I said, I went hoping to talk to the woman who found Michael in the dumpster."

"For what?"

"What do you mean 'for what'? To see what she knows. What she saw."

"So, did you talk to her?"

"No," I said. "She doesn't work there anymore. Owner said she refused to work late nights anymore, so he fired her."

"He fired her, after she found a body in the trash?" Raymond sipped his beer. "Sounds like a great guy." He stood up from his chair and leaned on the railing next to me. "So what's the story with the fight? Was it at the motel? Or the bar?"

"The motel parking lot. Guy came out of Freeman's though."

Raymond nodded. "Place is wicked shady. Used to get calls every other night when I worked that area. Would have to go in, break up fights and whatever else was going on in there. Used to have drug problems. Probably still does. Point is, I'm not surprised you ran into trouble after going in there."

I smiled. "I did have a good bowl of chowder though."

Raymond made a face, like his beer was sour. "You went in there to eat? Of all the places around you'd—"

"I only went in because Lily said she'd gone looking for Michael."

Raymond's eyes widened. "Lily was there? At the motel? Or the bar? When was this?"

"The evening before Michael was killed."

Raymond put his hand on his forehead. "Jesus, Jake. She was at the motel the night her husband was killed? No wonder she's a suspect. Does Moriarty know this?"

"I'm not sure," I said. "I told her to come clean, tell the cops when she was being interviewed."

"Did she?"

I said, "Doesn't sound like it."

Raymond looked out into the yard. "You tell Maggie?"

"No. Not yet. I don't want to get Maggie caught in the middle or put her in a bad position."

"Well, it's going to come down on you if they see you're holding critical information from a murder investigation. I'm not telling you anything you don't already know, but—"

"That's why I wanted to go over to the motel, at least make sure Lily was telling me the truth. She said the woman who worked there gave her the keys to go into Michael's room."

"Seriously? She had keys to the place? Christ, Jake. And you still believe she had nothing to do with it?"

CHAPTER 12

I HAD JUST UNLOCKED the door to my office and glanced over my shoulder when I heard a car pulling up along the curb. A white, unmarked Dodge Monaco was backing into a tight parking space two spots behind where I'd parked the Nova. I did a double take and realized it was Detective Jeffrey Moriarty behind the wheel.

I opened the office door and hurried inside, pretending I didn't know he was there. As I closed the door behind me, I heard him call my name, but I locked it and walked toward the back of the office and into the bathroom. I closed the door and listened, hoping he'd just go away.

I could hear him knocking and knew I was acting like a fool. The chance was good, knowing he saw me, he'd wait outside until I opened it. So I walked back out through the office and unlocked the door. "Hey, Detective," I said. "What a surprise."

He stepped through the door and past me, loosening the plaid scarf from around his neck. He wore a long black trench coat but didn't take it off. "Didn't you hear me out there?" he said. "You looked right at me."

I closed the door. "Sorry, I wasn't paying attention."

He had his eyes fixed on my face. "You look like someone got the best of you," he said in what sounded like a condescending tone.

I touched the bruise over my cheek. "I slipped on the ice." I sat down at my desk and leaned back in the chair. "So, to what do I owe this pleasure?"

Moriarty sat down across from me. "Do we really need to play these games?"

I stared back. "Who's playing games?"

He shifted in the chair as if trying to get comfortable, then crossed his leg over his knee, leaning back. "Are you going to tell me where she is?" he said.

I knew who he meant but went ahead with the game he didn't want me to play. "Where *who* is?"

"This is what I mean about playing games," he said. "Lily Dempsey. We can't find her. And this doesn't look good for her... slipping away once again while we're trying to solve her husband's murder." He narrowed his eyes—some kind of tough-guy look—and stared back at me. "I hope you're not the one helping her to hide." He looked around the office as if she could've been there. "Because it won't be a good look for either of you."

"Is there really something wrong with a woman needing to get away after losing a loved one?" I said.

"Give me a break," Moriarty said. He stood up and walked over to the coffee machine, appearing to study it for a moment. "This thing work?"

"The coffee machine?" I laughed. "Are you really going to ask me to make you coffee?"

He shrugged. "I'd appreciate it if you would. You know, I had a very long night. My brain could use the caffeine."

"Christ," I said, getting up from the desk and over to the coffee maker. I walked into the bathroom to fill the carafe. He was watching me as I walked back toward the Mr. Coffee.

"Did you just fill that carafe from your bathroom?" he said, making a face like he was disgusted.

"It's the only running water in the office." I dumped the water through the top of the machine and looked at him. "What's the difference?"

He didn't answer, going over to my desk. He leaned back against it, folding his arms in front of his chest. "I want you to understand something, Jake. I don't believe you killed Michael Dempsey. I just thought I should get that out in the open. I'm not saying you're free and clear. Rather, I'm letting you know what my gut is telling me."

"Your gut?" I said. "It should be more than just your gut. You don't have an ounce of evidence that even comes close to me being a suspect. And knocking a guy out who slept with my fiancée is not a motive for murdering the man. You know that."

The detective looked down toward the floor, rubbing his chin as he raised his eyes. "However, I can't say the same goes for Mrs. Dempsey."

"Lily didn't do it," I said, flipping the switch on the coffee maker.

"Would you tell me if you knew she *did*?" he said. "I'm going to guess the answer to that is *no*."

The Mr. Coffee coughed and sputtered, the drip starting into the carafe.

He continued, "I know you've had a relationship with Officer Maggie Donovan, going back quite a few years."

"She was my wife's best friend."

He nodded. "Right. Well, I don't know if she wants you to know this or not, but she came to me this morning."

I braced myself, wondering where he was about to go.

"She tells me I can trust you. That apparently, you know what you're doing." He let out a small laugh. "I haven't met many private investigators who do. Especially those who weren't formally trained in law enforcement."

I stared back at him without making a comment. I knew whatever I said to defend myself, not that I felt I had to, would come out the wrong way. I grabbed the carafe and poured a cup of coffee into a white Styrofoam cup, carrying it to Moriarty. I placed it next to him on my desk.

He picked it up and looked inside. "Haven't you got any cream?"

I sat back down at my desk. "What's this look like, a coffee shop?"

He grinned and sat in the chair across from me.

I looked at my watch. "Listen, I don't have much time, so if you've got something else you'd like to ask me... unless you came by for the coffee?"

He took a sip and got up from the chair, placed the cup down on my desk and walked to one of the windows, twisting the wand to adjust the horizontal blinds.

The sun's rays shot through the slits, sunshine brightening the office. As much as I liked seeing the sun, especially after a long winter, there were days I just wasn't in the mood. This happened to be one of them.

Moriarty faced the window, looking out toward East Broadway. "Of the few private investigators I have met, I've found, at least in my experience, they tend to show a little more respect to people like, well... to those of us who are in legitimate law enforcement positions."

"Legitimate law enforcement positions?" I laughed. "You ever think maybe respect goes both ways?"

Moriarty opened his trench coat, put his hands on his hips. He wore his badge on his belt, a revolver holstered on his right side. Standing wide-legged, his stance was that of a cowboy.

We didn't have cowboys in Boston.

"I asked you when I walked in here if we could go without the games," he said. "So how about we give that a try."

I said, "Sure."

He stepped toward me and picked up the coffee from the desk. He took a sip, taking his time like it was all part of his act. He sat back down in the chair. "Are you aware Lily was at that motel the evening before her husband was murdered?"

I tried to hide my swallow. I was usually pretty good at holding a straight face, but I had a pretty good feeling he knew what I knew, without really having to ask. "I might've known something about that," I said. "Did Lily tell you that?"

Moriarty shook his head. "No. She did not." He sipped his coffee and didn't appear he'd bother telling me how he knew.

I could only assume it was the woman, Nora, who worked at the motel. Or perhaps the owner, Adesh. But I knew it didn't look good for Lily. And I was starting to see how her lies, or secrets, were coming back to bite her.

"I know how it looks," I said. "But Lily was... she was scared. All I tried to tell her was to tell the truth. Apparently, she wasn't willing to do that." I looked him in the eye. "You know what?" I said. "I don't know where you learned your interviewing tactics, but I can tell you whatever you said to her, you scared her enough that she was afraid to tell you anything. So, maybe you think the tough-guy act works in some cases... I think this time it might've backfired."

"Oh, I'm sorry," Moriarty said, looking around the office. "I'll have to schedule some time to come by, get a few pointers from you. Hopefully, next time, I'll know what I'm doing." He rolled his eyes, leaning forward to place the cup down on the desk.

I didn't respond. I had no interest in continuing the back-and-forth with the guy. "What is it you want from me," I said.

"I don't know where she is. And that's the truth." I got up and went over to the coffee machine, pouring myself a cup.

"I know you want to protect her," Moriarty said. "But you're not going to do her any good."

I said, "How many times do I have to tell you? I *don't know where she is*. I haven't heard from her. I haven't even seen her."

He stared back at me, a smirk on his face like he was holding something back. "So when she left your office early Sunday... are you telling me you weren't in here with her?"

I lifted up my mug to take a sip of coffee as if I could hide behind it. I looked toward the floor, thinking about exactly what I should say. "She showed up. She'd been drinking, so I let her crash on the couch." I stared back at him. "Why? Were you watching me?"

"We weren't. We were watching Lily. We followed her all night, until she ended up here."

"Then why don't you know where she went, after she left?"

Moriarty cleared his throat. "Well, we lost her."

I cracked a slight smile. "Boston's finest, huh?" I walked to the window and looked outside, my back to Moriarty. I could feel him watching me.

"There was blood in that motel room. But it didn't match Michael Dempsey's."

I said, "I don't believe it's the cleanest motel in Boston. How do you know the blood wasn't already there?"

"It was fresh," Moriarty said. "There wasn't much of it, but somebody else was in that room, bleeding." He sipped from the cup. "You notice any cuts or abrasions on Lily? Her arms or—"

"No," I said.

Moriarty scratched the side of his neck, nodding in a way he'd accepted what I told him. "I understand Lily wanted to hire you, to catch her husband cheating?"

I hesitated a moment, assuming Maggie had told him as she said she was going to.

"And I told her I wouldn't do it," I said. "I wanted nothing to do with it."

"Why not?" He looked around the office. "From what I hear, you could use the work."

"You're a condescending bastard, you know that?" I said.

Moriarty looked like his head was going to explode. "Did she happen to tell you who she believed her husband was having an affair with?"

I nodded. "I'm surprised you don't know the answer." I cracked a slight smile. "If you're such a great detective, how come you don't seem to be able to get the information without asking me?"

Moriarty cleared his throat. "If Mrs. Dempsey would cooperate..."

"Well, apparently, according to Lily, Michael was having an affair with Angela Gautieri. You know who that is?"

He nodded. "Mayor Gautieri's daughter." He didn't seem surprised.

***

After Moriarty finally left the office, I was sure I hadn't made matters any better for Lily. Although she could just as easily be blamed for not only withholding information from the detective, but disappearing once again without a trace.

So I told him most of what I already knew, although it still wasn't much. The one thing I held back was I hadn't mentioned anything about Lily's cousin Jill. I knew there was a chance Lily had gone back there, although it was also possible she had gone somewhere else.

It was getting late, and I wasn't about to drive out to Connecticut, not with Nancy coming home. There was no way I could spend an hour plus, each way, driving to Jill and Peter's house.

So instead, I dialed the phone and it let it ring at least a half-dozen times.

On the seventh ring, Jill finally answered. "Hello?" she said in her soft, timid voice.

"Jill? It's Jake."

She paused before responding. "Oh, uh... Jake. Hi." I wouldn't say she was being cold, but she didn't sound very happy to hear from me.

"I know you're going to tell me Lily's not there, but I'm going to ask you to be honest with your answer. She's digging herself into a deep hole she won't be able to get out of if she doesn't get back to Boston. So if she's there, the best thing you can do for her is put her on the phone. I'd—"

Jill sneezed. The phone became muffled, like she'd covered the mouthpiece so I couldn't hear. She sneezed again and came back on the line. "Excuse me," she said. "I think I'm coming down with a cold."

"Will you just tell me if she's there?" I said, probably sounding a bit impatient.

She paused on the other end. "She's not, Jake. She's not here. That's the truth. I haven't seen her."

I didn't want to believe her, but something in her voice told me she was telling the truth. "Then when was the last time you saw her?" I said.

"Not since she left with you."

"You mean the first time you tried to tell me she wasn't there?" I said.

There was silence on the line, although I could hear quiet music in the background.

"I'm sorry about that," she said. "We were just trying to protect her."

I leaned forward with my elbow on the desk, my chin resting on one hand, the phone in the other. "If she's not there, can you at least tell me where she could be?"

Jill took her time answering, like she was being careful with every word she chose. "She called me from a pay phone that evening, after she went to the police station. She'd been drinking, and was pretty upset. She said she'd call me the next day, but she didn't."

I hesitated to tell Jill too much, but I also didn't want her to be worried. But by the sound of her voice, I had a feeling she was. And I realized, right then, my mistake was letting Lily leave my office without stopping her.

CHAPTER 13

I DROVE PAST THE clock tower on the S.S. Pierce Building at the corner of Beacon and Harvard Street in Coolidge Corner. It was the fifth or sixth time I'd driven past it, trying to find a place to park. I finally found a space three blocks from Lily's apartment and dug for change in my pocket for the meter. I was a nickel short of covering an hour and looked at my watch, making sure I knew what time I had to be back. One minute late, I'd have a ticket tucked under my wiper blade.

Lily had lived in the same apartment in Brookline since before I met her. And although I'd spent plenty of time there when we were together, I rarely stayed over. Not unless Nancy happened to sleep over at a friend's house, which wasn't very often. Lily never really understood.

It felt a bit strange walking along Beacon Street on the way to Lily's, my walk through Coolidge Corner stirring up memories. Some of them were good.

I looked up at the building to Lily's seventh-floor apartment window, then walked up to the locked entrance. I looked through the glass-paned door into the tiny lobby; the elevator was no more than ten feet from the door with a cluster of mailboxes to the right of it.

I pushed the buzzer for Lily's apartment, number 731, even though I was certain she wasn't there. But even if she was, there was a slim chance she'd answer. I waited, pressed the button one more time, then looked behind me, toward the street. The sidewalk was somewhat busy with people strolling in both directions. I hoped maybe someone would show up and let me in, perhaps if I lied and said I forgot my key.

I looked toward the lobby again, and this time a young man and woman, both dressed in matching blue Adidas jogging suits zipped up tight under their chins, stepped off the elevator and walked toward the door. The man pushed it open, held it for his female friend, then held it for me without a second thought.

I stepped inside and watched the two break into a jog along the sidewalk, disappearing around the corner. Heading straight for the elevator, I pushed the button with the up arrow, waited thirty seconds, then stepped on when the door finally opened.

The ride up felt strange. It had been a long time. Although it also felt like a week ago.

I stepped off onto the seventh floor and took a left down the hall.

Not much had changed. The overhead lights were as dim as I remembered, and the red-patterned carpet was the same. The walls had the same flowered wallpaper on them; the smell of food being cooked was familiar. I walked past each apartment and took another left at the end of the hall, stopping at Lily's door. Hers was the second to the last one on the right.

I stared at the peephole on her door and wondered if Lily was on the other side of it. I didn't think it was likely.

I looked right, then left at the neighbor's doors, removing my lockpick set from my coat pocket. I kneeled down on one knee with my eye level with the doorknob, glancing left and right one more time, listening for the neighbors.

But all was quiet in the halls as it had always been.

I removed the rake from my lockpick set and stuck it into the keyhole. It didn't take me more than three seconds to feel the single pin. I stuck the tension wrench in the hole, being careful as I turned it. The lock clicked, and I used the small screwdriver from my pocket to turn the lock, and the doorknob, the rest of the way. I stood and pushed open the door.

I was about to step through when the door to my left opened. An older woman with gray hair and a housedress stepped into the hallway, looking at me.

"Oh, hello," I said, forcing a smile.

"Is Lily home yet?"

I hid my lockpick set behind my back and hesitated a moment before I answered. "Um, actually... she's not home now. Not yet. But she—"

"I remember you," she said, staring back at me until her face broke into a smile. "You're Jake, aren't you?"

I nodded. "I remember you too," I said.

The woman's eyes followed my hand as I slipped the lockpick case into my coat pocket. She didn't ask what it was.

She pointed to herself. "I'm Marie."

"Marie? Yes, I remember. It's been a long time."

Her expression changed to one of confusion. "What are you doing here now? I'm sure you know Lily lost her husband?"

I nodded. "Yes. Very sad." I cleared my throat.

She looked me up and down. "Does she know you're here?"

"Lily? Yes, of course. She'll, uh, she should be here a little later. I'm just helping her with some things. Actually, with Michael's things. She asked me to help her clean out some of his belongings. That's why she hasn't been home. She's having a tough time with it all, as you'd expect. She just doesn't have the heart to clean up." I pointed with my thumb into Lily's apartment. "Too many memories," I said.

"It's nice the two of you remained friends," Marie said.

"It is, yes. The three of us—me, Lily, and Michael—we remained close." I shrugged. "That's just the way things should be, right?" I gave her a nod. "Okay, well, Marie... I guess I'll get inside and get started, see if I can clean up. It was good seeing you again." I started into Lily's apartment.

But Marie stepped in behind me, trying to look past me down the narrow hall into Lily's apartment. She had her hands on her hips. "I'm sure she's upset with what's happened, but..." She raised her eyes to mine. "I don't believe they had a very good marriage, to be honest. It's not really my place to say so, but she hadn't seemed very happy lately." She smiled at me. "I know you and I never got to know each other very well, but you were always so polite and nice when I saw you in the hall." She lowered her voice. "Not many of us really liked Michael very much."

I wondered if she'd dropped that piece of information on the police, assuming they'd already talked to her and most of Lily and Michael's neighbors. I leaned against the door between Marie and Lily's apartment behind me. "Did you speak with the police?"

"They spoke with most of us," she said. "Mostly basic questions, like if we noticed anyone suspicious being around, or heard anything out of the ordinary."

"What did you tell them?"

She shrugged. "Well, I try to mind my own business around here." She looked into Lily's apartment.

I got the feeling she wanted to tell me something but for some reason was holding back.

"So, was there anything you saw or heard?" I said. "Whether between Lily and Michael, or—"

"I used to hear them fighting," she said, her voice hushed. "I would just try to turn the TV up a little louder so I didn't hear it."

"Yelling?" I said.

Marie shrugged. "Like I said, I never got the feeling those two kids had a very good relationship. I was married for forty-three years before my husband passed. I don't think we ever yelled at each other. Not the way those two did."

I wasn't surprised to hear Lily and Michael were at each other's throats. Especially in a tiny apartment the size of Lily's. In Brookline—like most areas in and around Boston—the premium you paid for an apartment was for the location. You didn't get excessive space or privacy.

"Did you tell the cops?" I said.

"That they fought?" She shook her head. "I didn't want to look like a snitch. And, I'll be honest… I was afraid it would put Lily in a bad position. It wouldn't look good for her, if you know what I mean?"

I nodded, watching Marie step back out into the hall.

"I'll let you do whatever it is you're supposed to be doing." She looked up at me, smiling. "A pretty girl like Lily, she never has a hard time finding someone to help her out."

"I guess not," I said, stepping out into the hall. "Marie?"

She had her hand on the knob, about to open her door. "Yes?"

"You don't have to tell me this if you don't want to, but did you ever see Michael here with anyone else?"

"You mean, another woman?"

"Another woman, or—"

"Not that I recall."

I thought for a moment. "What about Lily? Did she ever have anyone over?"

Marie gave me a funny look, like she might not have liked my inquiry. "I don't think so. I guess the only time I can recall seeing anyone else here was just a couple of weekends ago. Lily said he was installing some shelves for her."

"Like, a handyman?" I said.

Marie shrugged. "I got the feeling she knew him." She turned the knob and started into her apartment. "Well, nice seeing you. Please tell Lily if she needs anything, she can always knock on my door."

I stood in the doorway as Marie closed her door behind her.

I stepped back into Lily's apartment and closed the door. The sun had gone down by the time I was done talking to Marie, the whole apartment dark now. I had a flashlight, and used it instead of turning on the lights, just in case there was someone watching from outside. Looking around the apartment, it had an almost sterile feeling to it as it did back when we were dating. The same couch I remembered was pushed up against the wall across from the full-size console TV. The small maple table with four matching chairs was still there in the adjoining kitchen.

The only difference, from what I could remember, were the shelves in the corner near the windows overlooking Beacon Street. I thought about what Marie had said about the man who installed them and wondered if he really was someone Lily knew.

The shelves had mostly framed photos, with plenty of Lily and Michael. There was a framed photo of Lily when she was much younger, with her mother. I took a photo of Lily and Jill from the shelf, realizing how much they looked alike. There was another small framed photo of Jill posing with her husband, Pete.

I opened the drawers in the kitchen but found nothing out of the ordinary. It wasn't like the kitchen was a place where Lily spent much time. She could barely make a grilled cheese sandwich.

I walked into the bedroom and felt a sense of discomfort standing there, looking at the bed with the same spread she had when we were together. Other than the bed and two nightstands, there was also a tall dresser in the corner and a small desk under the window.

Lily wasn't the kind of person to spend a lot of time in her apartment. She never seemed to feel at home, no matter where she was. Anxiety seemed to take over whenever she tried to relax. So she rarely relaxed, choosing to instead work and stay busy, squeezing in what little time was left for anything else... such as relationships with other people.

I opened the top dresser drawer. It appeared to be filled with men's socks and underwear. I moved them around, looking for any sort of clue but found nothing. I moved down to the next drawer and found more of Michael's things. The lower four drawers were filled with Lily's clothes. I didn't find anything else inside.

The small closet was packed tight with more clothes, including what looked like mostly Lily's dresses and a handful of Michael's suits.

I remembered living in a one bedroom with Barbara when we lived in Boston, having to deal with the tight space of a one bedroom.

I walked over to the desk under the window, pulling open the wide middle drawer. I was sure the police had likely already gone through the place but hoped maybe there'd be something they could have overlooked.

The drawer was mostly empty, other than a couple of pens and a small yellow pad. The pens had Boston Mayor Bedford's election slogan printed on them. I pulled the whole drawer out and placed it on top of the desk, crouching down to look inside the opening. I noticed a piece of paper that appeared to be stuck toward the back. I reached my hand in and pulled it out, looking it over. It was a phone bill, or at least a *page* from a phone bill, dated February 28.

It didn't even have a name or address on the page I was looking at but listed what looked like out-of-state toll calls. I recognized most of the area codes, including some to Connecticut. I assumed they were calls made to Jill. Other calls listed were different, including the 212 area code in New York and a handful to 603 in New Hampshire.

I recognized the 215 area code in Pennsylvania—a call lasting thirty-eight minutes—and one to the 301 area code in Maryland. There were thirteen calls made to 401 in Rhode Island.

I stuck the phone bill in my pocket, then slid the drawer back into the opening.

CHAPTER 14

I PULLED INTO THE driveway of my grandmother's house and parked behind the green Plymouth Scamp, stepping out from the Nova as the Scamp's interior light turned on.

Maggie got out from the driver's side and gave me a wave.

"How long've you been here?" I said, walking toward her.

She straightened out her knitted winter hat. "I passed you on Blue Hill Ave." She laughed. "You were driving like an old lady."

I jiggled the keys in the palm of my hand looking for the house key in the darkness outside. I didn't know how late I'd be and walked ahead of Maggie to the front door. "I wish I'd left some lights on."

I slid the key in the lock and opened the door, letting Maggie step into the house ahead of me.

"I hope you don't mind me showing up like this," she said.

I reached for the switch and flipped on the lights. "Not at all," I said. "Why would I?"

She unzipped her jacket and pulled her hat from her head, pushing her hair back from her face. "I wanted to let you know: Jeffrey spoke to the captain, recommended I stay clear of the Michael Dempsey case. Apparently, Jeffrey sees a conflict of interest."

"A conflict of interest?" I said. "Is he serious?"

She hung her jacket on the coat rack next to the door and folded her arms, running her hands up and down her arms. "It's *cold* in here."

I hung my coat on the rack and looked at the thermostat. "Just trying to conserve a little energy." I adjusted it and turned the heat up a couple of degrees. The furnace kicked on with a slight bang. The sound of it running meant money out the door. That's why, when it was just me, I dressed warm indoors with the heat low.

"I can just wear my coat," she said, reaching toward the rack.

I laughed. "Give it a few minutes, it'll warm up." I glanced at the fireplace. "I didn't light the fireplace all winter. No wood."

"I think we'll be out of it in a couple of weeks."

"The cold? I'm not too sure about that. I heard there could be another storm."

"Snow?"

I nodded and headed into the kitchen. I opened the refrigerator and reached in for two cans of beer, turning to Maggie, leaning against the doorway. I held one out to her. "You're off duty, right?"

"Got the next two days off."

I ripped the tab off one of the cans and handed it to her. "So, what exactly are they considering a conflict of interest?" I said. "Because you're a friend of mine?"

She took a sip of beer and pulled out a chair at the kitchen table. She sat down and looked to her left out the window into the night. "I think you need to be careful, Jake."

I sat down across from her and pulled the tab off my beer. "When am I not careful?" I grinned.

"I just mean, I know you want to help Lily. But she's put you in a bad position. And, I'll be honest, the way Moriarty's fixated on

Lily... I have a feeling he's got something. Something he's holding on to."

I drank some of my beer. "He stopped by my office. Did you know that?"

"When?"

"This morning. Just showed up. He was hoping to get something out of me, as if I knew something."

"I spoke to him earlier, must've been before he showed up. He didn't say anything about going to talk to you. But I'm not surprised he didn't say anything. I have a feeling he's not going to be telling me much of anything going forward."

"Because he's afraid it'll get back to me?"

Maggie shrugged, leaned back, and looked to finish half her beer.

"He did say he didn't feel I was a suspect. But in the same breath, he told me I wasn't completely in the clear."

"He plays games like that," she said. "That's what I mean by you needing to be careful."

"He seems like the type, he'll do what he can to make sure he's never wrong," I said.

Maggie looked down at the can of 'Gansett in her hand, turning it as if she were studying the label. "He's not going to cross any lines to prove what's not true. But he doesn't like to be wrong. That's a fact."

I got up from the table and leaned against the counter in front of the sink. "I know you're telling me to be careful. But I'll say what I've been saying all along: I'm not going to sit around and wait to see what happens."

Maggie smiled, her lips tight. "I know you're not, Jake."

I pulled the page from Lily's phone bill from my pocket and unfolded it, handing it to her. "Check this out," I said.

She took it from me and looked it over, raising her eyes to mine, holding the paper up in front of her. "A phone bill?"

"A piece of one," I said. "It was stuck up inside the drawer of a desk in Lily's apartment."

"You were in her apartment?"

I nodded. "Uh-huh."

"Please tell me you didn't break in."

"I didn't *break* in. I picked the lock."

Maggie rolled her eyes. "This is what I mean, Jake. You can't just—"

"Let's not make a big deal of it. All right? But look at those numbers. Rhode Island, Connecticut, Maryland... New Hampshire. I don't know how much either Michael or Lily had been traveling in February. And it's not like any of these locations are winter getaways."

"But what's your goal here, Jake? To find Lily? Do you really think it's necessary you're involved, trying to solve her husband's murder? Because I don't see what you gain from doing that."

"Well," I said, resting my can of beer on the counter. "I don't know. Lily's missing right now. And she seems to be a suspect. Do you really think I should just leave her hanging?"

Maggie looked out the window, shaking her head. "No, I don't."

We were both quiet.

She looked over the phone bill, front and back, and stood from her chair. "If you really believe she had nothing to do with his murder, then give me one good reason why she's hiding." She held up her finger. "Just one. And I don't want to hear that she's scared to talk to the police. What is she, twelve?"

Maggie was normally the one who was cool and calm. Nothing seemed to bother her. But she appeared to be more agitated than usual.

"How do we know she's hiding?" I said.

Maggie stared back at me, shaking her head. "I... I guess I don't. But I just thought—"

"I'm not saying something else happened to her. But, let's just think about this. What if, by chance, Michael was into something? What if Lily knew what it was? Or whoever killed him thinks she knows something. Or they're looking for something."

"Is there something you're not telling me?" Maggie said.

"Not at all," I said. "I hate to sound like a broken record, but I can't just sit around, pretend it'll soon all get wrapped up, with a nice red bow on top."

Maggie picked up the phone bill from the table. "So what do you want to do?"

I stood next to her and pointed to the calls made to the 401 area code. "Well, I'm curious about this number, in Rhode Island. I wonder if it's Angela Gautieri. Quite a few calls were made to it, and it'd give us something, if it turns out it's her." I pointed to the 215 number. This one here's made to Pennsylvania, a call lasting thirty-eight minutes. There were a few other calls, but they were only charged one minute. So I'm just guessing it's someone that one of them—Lily or Michael—knew well enough to talk to for that long."

Maggie said, "I'm surprised you didn't call any of the numbers."

I took the paper from her hand. "I haven't had a chance." I reached for the phone on the wall, put the paper down on the table, and dialed the Pennsylvania number. I looked at my watch and realized it was kind of late.

A man answered on the second ring. "Turnpike Inn, may I help you?"

"Hi," I said. "Where are you located?"

"Harrisburg, just off Eighty-One."

"Okay, thank you." I said and hung up.

"Who was it?" Maggie said.

"A place called the Turnpike Inn, in Harrisburg, Pennsylvania." I thought for a moment. "It could've been Michael traveling. The bill was from February. I guess Lily could've called him, right?"

Maggie took the paper from my hand, grabbed the phone and put it up to her ear. She was quiet, leaning against the doorway, listening. A few moments went by, and she hung the phone up on the wall. "No answer," she said.

"What number was that?"

"The one in Rhode Island."

"I bet it's the mayor's daughter," I said. I looked over the bill and saw two numbers. I got up and walked into the other room, taking my small leather-covered phone book from my coat pocket. I opened to Jill and Pete's number, went back into the kitchen, and sure enough, the numbers matched. "One of these Connecticut numbers is Lily's cousin." I pointed at the other, the same 203 area code. "This one, though, I'm not sure of."

I dialed the number and it rang six times. Just as I was about to hang up, a man answered. "Hello?"

I said, "Who's this?"

The man on the other end said, "Who're you looking for?"

"I'm looking for Pete. Any chance he's there?"

"Pete?" the man said. "I have no idea. This is a pay phone."

"A payphone? A payphone *where*?" I said.

"Outside the Fuzzy Grape. In Killingly."

"Mind if I ask what exactly is the Fuzzy Grape?"

"A strip joint," he said, like I was asking a stupid question. "Next to Cumberland Farms, off Route One oh One."

"Killingly? That near Woodstock?"

"Couple towns away, yeah. But listen, buddy, I'm not the answering service." The man hung up.

I made a note on the bill next to the phone number:

Fuzzy Grape, Killingly, Connecticut.

Maggie looked over my shoulder as I made the note. "What's the Fuzzy Grape?"

"A strip club, apparently," I said.

I reached for my beer and took a sip, staring at the roosters on the wallpaper on the kitchen wall. The chalkboard my grandfather had put up long ago was still next to where the phone hung, as were the words my grandmother had written in chalk some time before she died.

"Maybe Jill or her husband can tell me why Lily or Michael would've called a pay phone outside a strip joint." I dialed Jill's number, and the phone rang three times until someone finally answered.

"Hello?"

"Pete?" I said.

"Who's this?"

"It's Jake Horn."

The line went quiet.

"It's kind of late, isn't it?" Pete said.

I looked at my watch. "But you weren't asleep this early, were you?"

"No. But I'm kind of in a hurry, Jake. Something I can help you with?"

"Maybe," I said. "Have you ever been to the Fuzzy Grape?"

The phone was quiet. "Uh, maybe once when I was a little younger. Not really my kind of place, but... listen, Jake, I don't have time to chit chat right now. I gotta be out on the road."

"This late?" I said.

"I get a lot of miles in the truck when the amateurs are off the road."

"What about Jill? Is she available?"

He was quiet. "I'm sorry, she's not," Pete said. "She's in the shower."

"The shower, huh? Okay, then I'll just call back in a few minutes?"

"She doesn't know anything about Lily. Neither of us do. I wish... I wish I could help, but like I just said, I gotta get on the road. And Jill's taking me out to my truck. So, she won't be available tonight."

"It's for Lily's own good, you know. I'm just trying to help her. And if the cops show up over there looking for her..."

"They already did," Pete said.

"Who, the police? Boston?"

"Yeah, showed up earlier today with a couple of deputies from Windham County. Did as much looking as they could without a warrant, although said they could get one. We just don't want any trouble, Jake. We live out here in the country for a reason."

I glanced at Maggie, watching me from the table. "I don't know if Lily trusts anyone else the way she trusts Jill. There aren't many other people in her life she'd turn to. So, again, for her sake... if Jill knows anything, will you at least have her call me?" I gave him both phone numbers, although I was sure she already had them.

I wasn't sure he even wrote them down.

I heard a female voice in the background. "Is that Jill?"

"It's the TV," Pete said. "I gotta go."

"Hey, before you hang up," I said. "Have you ever stayed anywhere in Pennsylvania?"

"I stay all over the place," he said. "Up and down the coast."

"What about a place called the Turnpike Inn?"

Pete was quiet on the other end, although I could still hear whatever was in the background.

"I'm not sure I've heard of it. But, listen Jake. I told you I gotta go. I'm hanging up."

Next thing I heard was a dial tone.

CHAPTER 15

IT WAS 3:18 WHEN I rolled over and looked at the clock. I hadn't slept a wink. Nancy would be home later in the day and the stress of it—the boy she'd be bringing with her—rattled around inside my head.

But on top of it was knowing I'd have to put some things on hold. And it wasn't ideal, when every minute counted.

I tried to fall asleep, but with all the thoughts in my head, it wasn't much of an option. I grabbed an Elmore Leonard book that belonged to my grandmother—*Split Images*—and read a couple of chapters until my eyes were so tired, my mind finally gave up.

I woke up a few hours later to the noise of the trash cans banging and the rumbling sound of the garbage truck. I jumped from the bed in shorts and a sweatshirt and hurried down the stairs in my bare feet, ran through the kitchen and into the garage. I grabbed the garbage can and lifted the garage door. But by the time I made it outside, all I could see were the red taillights in the darkness, coming from the back of the garbage truck. Empty barrels were tossed on lawns and littered the sidewalk on both sides of the street.

It was the second week in a row I'd forgotten to put out the garbage the night before. But at least it wasn't the heat of the summer, when the putrid odor from the trash would be unbearable sitting in the garage.

I dragged the barrels back into the garage and pulled the door closed, heading back into the kitchen. I'd just started to make a pot of coffee when the phone rang. I grabbed it off the wall. "Hello?"

Maggie was on the other end, her voice quiet. "I had my friend pull that number. It turns out you were right. It's Angela Gautieri's."

"I appreciate it," I said.

"I took it another step for you, so just promise me you won't tell anyone where you got it from."

"You know I won't say a word," I said.

There was a brief pause. "She lives on Spruce Street in Providence. Her father owns the building; she lives in the apartment on the third floor."

"You have a number?" I grabbed a pen from the drawer and pulled out a matchbook.

"Sixteen Spruce Street."

I wrote it down on the inside of the matchbook. "And you said she's on the third floor?"

"Yes."

"Thank you, Maggie."

"Jake?"

"Yeah?"

"Will you please just be careful?"

***

I was in Providence by eight thirty, parked on the corner of Spruce and Atwells Avenue. I looked up at the brown three-story tenement house with a VW Scirocco parked in the driveway. The Rhode Island plate was DDYSGRL.

Daddy's Girl?

I stopped, with hesitation, thinking maybe it would be smart to get right back in my car and head back to Massachusetts. Because it was Angela's "Daddy" who'd served three years in the Rhode Island State Prison eight years earlier, following his term with a winning bid for mayor of Providence.

I walked up the brick steps and pushed the third-floor button with GAUTIERI typed in white embossed letters on a black plastic label, next to the name.

A voice came from somewhere behind me. "Who's down there?"

I looked around, went down the steps, and looked up at a young woman sticking her head out from a third-floor window.

"Who are *you*?" she said, gazing down at me.

"Are you Angela?"

She stared back at me as if hesitant to answer. With a nod, she said, "Who's asking?" She had a toughness to her voice.

"I'm here to talk to you about Michael Dempsey."

She stared down at me without a word, then pulled her head back inside, and slammed the window closed.

I had my eyes on the window for a few moments until a lock clicked at the top of the stairs. The door opened, and Angela Gautieri stood on the other side looking out at me. "Are you with the police?"

"Actually, no."

She wore wide-bottomed jeans pulled up high on her waist with a short-sleeved shirt that looked like an American flag, tucked into the pants. "You still haven't told me your name," she said.

"It's Jake. Jake Horn."

131

"Jake?" She looked out toward the street where I'd parked the Nova. "So what's your deal?"

"My deal?" I said.

"You knew Michael?"

I nodded. "You could say that."

She snapped gum between her teeth, staring out at me for a moment. "I'm sorry, but I can't let you in just because you knew Michael." She narrowed her eyes like she was thinking, then wagged her finger at me. "Wait a minute. Jake Horn? Are you the one who used to date Michael's wife?"

"How'd you know that?" I said.

She shrugged. "Michael mentioned you before. He said you broke his jaw."

"Well, I don't think it was technically *broken*, but..."

"You're a private investigator. Is that right?" She looked me up and down. "Is that what you're doing here? Investigating what happened to him?"

I nodded with a slight shrug. "You could say that." I looked past her, toward the stairs. "Would you mind if I came in? I hate to have you keep the door open like this, all your heat escaping outside."

Angela shrugged. "I don't pay for it." She stepped back from the door. "I have to get to work in a little while, so I don't have a lot of time." She nodded for me to follow, and I stepped inside as she closed the door behind me. I followed her up the narrow stairs, and she looked back at me over her shoulder. "I already told the police the rumors about me and Michael aren't true, if that's what you're here to ask about."

The door on the third floor was already open, and I followed her inside.

"I don't know much about that," I said, leaving it at that.

The first room we entered was warm. Almost *too* warm. I unbuttoned my coat, smelling the moist steam from the radiator. The walls were white with dark wood trim on the doors and windows.

Angela nodded toward the yellow leather couch with a framed painting of what looked to me like Venice, hanging on the wall over it. "Have a seat," she said.

The morning sun glared through the tall windows and filled the room. A hiss came from the radiator.

Angela sat across from me in a green leather chair.

"You mentioned rumors about you and Michael," I said. "You mind telling me what you meant by that?"

She had a lazy look to her face, her eyelids appearing heavy as she stared back at me. "Don't patronize me. I'm not a fool."

"I'll be honest," I said, shaking my head. "I'm here because your phone number was on Michael and Lily's phone bill. Someone from their apartment had called you quite a few times last month."

She shifted in her chair and cleared her throat. "Like I told the police, Michael and I had a working relationship. We were friends. He worked for Mayor Bedford in Boston, and I work for my father here in Providence, so..."

"What do you do, exactly?" I said. "For your father?"

"I'm in communications. I do some community outreach... public relations..."

"So you must've known Lily too? That's her specialty, marketing and PR. That's how she met Michael."

Angela nodded. "Yes, I know the whole story."

"Oh, right. Okay, so then, if this was just business between you and Michael, then why was he calling you from the apartment? Some of the calls were late at night. Are you telling me it was all work related?"

She stared back at me and didn't seem to have an answer right away. She crossed one leg over the other, her eyes toward the floor. "He was a hard worker. He was always working."

I didn't respond.

She said, "The past few months Michael and I had been working hard on a cross-city campaign, between Providence and Boston, to reduce the trafficking of illegal firearms."

"Illegal firearms?" I said. "Really?"

She looked up and nodded. "It's a big problem."

I knew it was. I knew *all* about illegal firearm trafficking. But I found it funny that her father, Tony Gautieri, would be the one allegedly trying to reduce it. Maybe it was just to stop his competition. Because the mob connections he had throughout New England, as far as I knew, were usually the people *involved* in the illegal firearm trade.

She picked at her fingernails. "I can't tell you about those calls with Michael, or why he'd call so late sometimes." She shrugged, nodding. "But, yeah, he'd call me at home sometimes if he had an idea or he just wanted to talk something through. He was very passionate about his job."

I didn't buy it, but wasn't going to push her that hard just yet.

Her eyes moved toward the window to her right, with a decent view of downtown Providence. "We were still just friends. But you know how people are... they can't help but talk. That's how the rumors got started."

I knew exactly what she meant.

Angela turned from the window. "I'm sorry, but I'm a little confused why you're asking these questions. Who hired you? Lily?"

"Not exactly," I said. "You could say I'm trying to help her, make sure the cops have all the facts straight before they go after the wrong person for Michael's murder."

Angela raised both eyebrows, her eyes opened wide. "Is Lily a suspect?"

I hesitated a moment, not sure if I should get into it. I was having a hard time getting a read on the mayor's daughter, who seemed to be trained in how to answer questions without saying much. "Everyone's a suspect until the police have something solid to hold on to. Right now, there's a body with bullet holes and..."

Angela closed her eyes and covered her face with her hands.

"I'm sorry," I said. I probably didn't need to get into the visuals. "I'm just saying, right now they have nothing. And that means none of us, me and you included, are in the clear."

"Well, the police told me I had nothing to worry about. The man who was here said I'm not a suspect."

"Is that right?" I said.

She wiped her eyes with her hands, but there didn't appear to be any tears. "I wish there was something I could do to help find who did it. I can't imagine who would kill him. Michael was a nice man."

I wasn't sure I agreed with her assessment. But Angela had a father who'd likely done a lot worse than Michael ever did, so her opinion of what makes a man a "nice" man was relative.

"Listen," I said. "Let me be honest with you. What I said earlier, about not knowing of any rumors about Michael." I paused. "Lily believed he *was* having an affair. She's afraid that's what got him killed."

Angela froze for a moment. "Did she think it was me?"

"She wasn't sure who it could've been," I said, which, of course, wasn't true. But I didn't want to create friction with Angela by making accusations I couldn't back up with solid proof.

"I was engaged, you know," she said. "But we broke it off in January."

I nodded. "To Lawrence Martin?"

She gave me a small grin. "I guess you've done your homework."

"Did it have anything to do with the rumors?" I said.

"No, not exactly. But they didn't help. Really, after he was released by the Patriots, right after the season ended, things got, well... it was really hard for him. He was angry after it happened, and not much fun to be around."

"So who broke it off? You?"

Angela took a moment before she answered. "We just agreed to take a break, put things on hold."

We both sat quiet.

A tear came down her cheek.

"Do you still talk to him?"

She took a moment before she answered. "I honestly don't even know where he is." She took a deep breath, looking toward the floor. "He put his house up for sale a couple weeks ago. He didn't even tell me he was selling it. And now... I don't even know where he is."

"Doesn't he have family you can call? Talk to him?"

"They're down in Florida. Jacksonville. Nobody knows where he went. At least from what they've told me. His mother didn't sound very concerned. I don't think she ever liked me very much."

"You think she knows where he is?"

She shrugged. "If she does, she's not telling me."

She started to cry, beyond just tears. And I realized if she loved him, Lawrence Martin, as much as it appeared, then there was a chance the rumors about her and Michael were just that: rumors.

"I'm sorry," I said. "I didn't mean to—"

"No, it's all right." She ran the back of her hand over her cheeks. "I think the rumors about me and Michael, on top of everything else, sent him off the deep end."

"The deep end?" I said, curious as if she was trying to suggest something or hadn't carefully chosen her words. "Do you think he could have—"

"What? No! Lawrence? He's a sweet man. He looks scary—six six, two ninety—but he's a teddy bear. I promise you, he didn't kill Michael, if that's what you're trying to say." Her voice had gone from quiet and sad to loud and angry.

I'd known enough Italians in my life to know the range of emotions swung wild.

"I'm sorry," I said. "But, I imagine the police asked about him too, no?"

"I just tried to answer their questions. The detective who was here, it was only ten minutes or so. He was nice."

"But if Lawrence believed you were cheating on him, don't you have to wonder if—"

"I don't like what you're trying to insinuate, Mr. Horn." She got up and walked toward the door, pulling it open. "I'm sorry... I'd like you to leave." She wouldn't look me in the eye.

I walked toward her and stepped through the open door. "I didn't mean to—"

"You know what's funny?" She cleared her throat. "Michael was the one who thought Lily was cheating on *him*. And the only reason I know your name, why he brought it up, is because *you're* the one he thought she might've been sleeping with."

CHAPTER 16

I WALKED OUT OF Barbato's Bakery, sipping my black coffee, the salt and sand on the sidewalk crunching under my feet. I had a Danish in the white paper bag, was about to reach in and take a bite but stopped when I saw two men standing next to the Nova.

I continued along Atwells Avenue toward my car, watching the two men, both in long, dark coats, looking back and forth. The shorter of the two noticed me first, slapping the other one's arm with the back of his hand.

They both looked my way.

I didn't like how things looked, tossing my fresh coffee and Danish into a trash barrel on the sidewalk, just in case I needed both hands. The shorter one was stocky without much of a neck, not much taller than a twelve-year-old. He pulled his sunglasses from his eyes as I got closer.

The taller one, more my size or around six feet, looked like the older of the two, with jet-black hair greased back and streaks of gray coming through.

"You Jake?" the shorter one said. His shoulders were hunched, his long arms hanging by his sides with his knuckles turned forward, like he hadn't fully evolved.

"Who's asking?" I said.

The short one took a step toward me, pointing his finger in his chest. "*I'm* asking," he said. "And I'd suggest you knock off the wisecracks." The man shifted his stance and pulled his long wool coat back from his waist, making sure I saw the gun tucked in the front of his pants.

"Okay, so good for you," I said. "You know my name. So why don't you tell me what you want."

The older and taller one stepped around his friend and grabbed my arm, sticking a revolver in my ribs. He looked around. "Whattaya say we go for a walk, uh?"

I ripped my arm from his grasp, but he still had the muzzle pressed into my ribs. "I'm a big boy," I said. "I know how to walk."

The shorter of the two stepped ahead of us and turned down a walkway between tall, colorful apartment buildings on either side.

"Either of you going to tell me what this is all about?" I said. "I can make a guess but—"

The older one with the gun in my ribs pushed the gun's muzzle a little harder. "How about you keep your mouth shut."

We followed the shorter one, and I watched him with his funny walk, taking long steps with his arms swinging back and forth by his sides.

A black Cadillac was double-parked on Spruce Street, five cars down from another bakery I could smell as soon as we took the corner.

We got to the car and the short, stocky one pulled his gun from his pants and pointed it at me as he opened the rear passenger-side door. "Go 'head," he said, gesturing with his gun. "Get in the car."

I ducked into the back and slid across the seat.

The older one with the slicked-back gray hair walked around to the driver's side and got in. His stocky friend kept the gun pointed at me but got into the front passenger side. He turned around in the seat and faced me, had the gun pointed over the backrest.

The driver had his eyes in the rearview, watching me. "You behave, and nobody gets hurt."

I looked around the car. "Nobody? Does that go for all three of us? Or just me?"

The shorter one of the two reached his hand over the seat and moved the gun closer to my face. "Shut your mouth, or I'll shut it for you!"

"I'm going to make an educated guess here, based on the timing of this... and considering I haven't been to Providence in a couple of years." I looked out the window toward the bakery, but nobody looked to be paying attention to the man—that would be *me*—being abducted by the two gangsters driving the black Cadillac. I had a feeling even if anyone had noticed, it wouldn't have made a difference. Not in Providence. "Any chance this has something to do with me going to see Angela Gautieri this morning?"

The driver straightened out his hair in the mirror before shifting the car into drive. I had a better look at him and guessed he was at least somewhere in his sixties, with the pasty-white skin that didn't quite fit the obvious shoe-polish dye job.

He glanced at me over his shoulder. "Why don't you just shut your mouth and relax, huh?"

We continued down Spruce Street, tires splashing with each puddle-filled pothole the car hit.

I don't know which of the two had bathed in a bottle of cheap cologne, but I rolled down the window to let out the odor.

"What are you doin'?" said the one in the passenger seat. "Close that window. It's cold out there!"

I knew a little bit about Providence—a city with a heavy Italian population. The two men in the front seat were clearly of that heritage. What I liked about Providence, other than having plenty of restaurants, was that it was fairly easy to get around, being such a small city. I glanced at the one in the passenger seat, facing me with the gun still pointed my way. I had my eyes on the street sign as the driver drove onto Empire Street and continued for half a block past the Biltmore Hotel. He drove around the back of it, past the entrance to the parking lot, into the service entrance, and down the ramp below the building.

He proceeded past a box truck backed up to an elevator door, with two men loading corrugated boxes onto a dolly. Once we were around the corner, the driver stopped at a chain hung from one side of the wall to the other. He got out, removed the chain from one side and got back in, driving forward until we stopped in a dim area of the parking lot, enclosed on three sides with solid concrete walls. Other than a closed steel door, there appeared to be only one way in and one way out. Making a run for it didn't seem to be an option anyway.

I looked out the rear window down a long stretch of parking lot. There was nobody else around, and for the moment, I kept my mouth shut.

The two clowns stepped from the Cadillac, the one in the passenger seat opening my door. "Let's go," he said, his .38 in his hand, but he tucked it in the waist of his pants. "Don't try anything stupid," he said.

I slid out from the back seat, my hands up so he could see them. I looked around and wondered if this was going to be it, where I'd be left for dead on the cold concrete in the garage below the Biltmore Hotel.

They led me through the steel door and to an elevator with a sign that read Not for Guest Use.

The three of us stepped on and faced the door as it closed. I stared straight ahead at the broken reflections in the brass finish surrounding us, on the door and walls. I tried to think through my options, which were limited, of course, considering both men were armed. I looked them both over, guessing I could probably take them both in a fair fight. But the key word was *fair*. I looked at the older one to my left, the other to my right. "Either of you going to tell me why we're at a hotel?"

Neither responded nor gave me a look.

The bell dinged at the thirteenth floor. The older one stepped off first, but I didn't move. I kept my knees slightly bent and my weight centered, the way I'd learned playing hockey so nobody'd knock me off my skates. And when the shorter one tried to shove me toward the open door, I didn't budge.

"Ayyyy," the man said. "Come on, you gonna play games now?" He pulled out his gun and shoved it into my side. "The preference would be to not have to spend the morning cleaning up your blood."

The older one stepped back onto the elevator, his feet spread shoulder width and a slight tilt to his head. "Come on, buddy. This'll be painless, if you just come along without any problems. Capisce?"

"Capisce? Well, I'm not sure. The thing here is I've been abducted against my will," I said. "And nobody's told me why. So, no, I don't 'capisce.'"

The shorter one pointed his .38 toward my leg. "Look at the thick thighs on this guy. Let me just shoot him, Sal, see if it'll go through."

The tall one with the gray hair slapped his friend in the head. "I told you not to use my name. And how many times I gotta tell you, put the goddamn gun away when we're in here." He, the man whose name apparently was Sal, gave me a nod. "Mr. Horn. Somebody wants to have a word with you. I assure you, your full cooperation will be appreciated."

"Somebody? Should I guess who 'somebody' might be?" I stepped off the elevator. "I'd be happy to talk to *somebody*," I said. "I'm going to assume *somebody* didn't like me talking to *somebody's* daughter a little while ago this morning. Is that what this is all about?"

I followed Sal down a hall, the stocky, short one behind me, until we got to a set of double doors. A gold plaque on the wall was engraved with the number 1308.

The older one gently knocked his knuckles on the door with the backside of his hand. He stepped back as the locks clicked on the other side. It opened, and the man I recognized as Tony Gautieri stood in the doorway, hair greased back on his head, like Sal's.

Tony wore dark suit pants and red suspenders over his white dress shirt and a matching red tie. "You must be Mr. Horn."

I didn't answer but felt a nudge from behind me. I stepped through the doorway without resistance into a room that was more than just your basic hotel room. It was a suite with a wet bar and more than a few bottles of liquor on a shelf. There was a kitchen adjacent to a room I'd just walked into, two leather couches and a matching chair in front of what looked to be a gas fireplace, unlit. A large window took up a good part of the wall, street side, and overlooked downtown Providence.

"Djeat?" he said, pointing toward a plate of muffins and a silver carafe on the glass coffee table between the two black leather couches.

I wasn't sure exactly what he'd said. "Excuse me?"

"Djeat?"

I stared back at him. "Duh jeat? I'm not sure what you're saying."

"Did you eat!" he snapped, shaking his head, pointing at me with his thumb with his eyes on the others. "This guy deaf?"

Sal and his sidekick both shrugged, like they weren't following.

I'm not going to claim we don't have what some might consider a unique accent in Massachusetts, but Rhode Island was in a world of its own when it came to the way they spoke. Letters were dropped and moved around and words came out that made it hard for anyone outside of their tiny state to understand their native language.

"I'm good," I said.

Gautieri gestured toward the couch facing the window. "Sit down." He sat across from me on the other couch. "You wanna coffee?" He leaned forward and grabbed the carafe, poured coffee into a small, flowered china cup without waiting for my answer. He pushed it toward me. "You like espresso?"

I sat down, nodding, and reached for the cup, glancing over my shoulder at the two goons standing in front of the double doors. "You have these two well trained," I said. "They roll over? Play dead?"

Tony Gautieri laughed, looking past me at his friends. "You hear this guy?" He nodded at me with his chin. "You're a smart-ass, uh?" He leaned back on the black leather couch, relaxed, his arm straight out over the top of the cushion, one leg crossed over his other knee. He picked something from his polished, pointy shoe, reached for a cocktail napkin from the glass table and wiped whatever it was from his finger. He leaned back again, ran his tongue around his gums, and stuck his pinkie inside his mouth, picking at his teeth. "So," he said. "What do you want with my daughter?"

"What do I want with your daughter?" I looked back at him. "What gives you the idea I want something with your daughter?"

He raised both eyebrows. "Let's not play games, Mr. Horn. Okay?" He nodded toward his men at the door. "They saw you leaving her apartment this morning. And when I called her to ask who you were, she told me you're some kind of private detective? Is that right?"

I nodded. "I'm a private investigator."

"Same difference," he said. "So why don't you go ahead and explain to me why you were bothering my little girl this morning."

"Why was I bothering her?" I shrugged. "She must've told you why I was there, no?"

He narrowed his eyes. "I thought I'd give you the opportunity to explain yourself."

I said, "How about you tell me what your daughter told you, and I'll tell you if she's accurate or not."

He cleared his throat and glanced over at his boys, still standing at the front door. "Mr. Horn, I think we'd both be better off if you knocked off your wise-guy act."

"Wise guy?" I said and cracked a grin. I pointed to myself. "You're calling *me* a wise guy?" I could tell I was quickly getting under Gautieri's skin and started to wonder if it might be foolish for me to keep it up. "I wanted to talk to her because I had questions about her relationship with Michael Dempsey."

Gautieri kept his eyes on me, quiet for a few moments. "I'm not sure why you'd come all the way down here to Providence to ask my daughter about a man she hardly knew?"

"A man she hardly knew?" I said. "Michael Dempsey was not a man she hardly knew. I know they worked together. And Angela admitted they were, at the very least, friends."

"That's just Angela. She gets along with everyone. She's a friendly kid. But it certainly doesn't mean she had a relationship with the man outside the office."

I stared back at him, then looked around the room. "Can you tell me why are we in a hotel room? Do you live here or something?"

"Hotel room? Does this look like a 'hotel room' to you?" He stood up and walked past me toward the window, kept his back to me, looking outside. "Yes, I do live here. Mainly because it's one of the best views of downtown you'll find in Providence. It allows me to keep my eye on my beautiful city." He straightened his tie, walking toward me. "So, why don't you tell me what business you have regarding Michael Dempsey," he said. "Someone hire you to find out who plugged him?"

"Nobody hired me," I said.

"So, what, you're just sticking your head where it don't belong for shits and giggles?"

"Shits and giggles?" I said. "No."

He gave me a look. "Why do you do that?"

"Do what?"

"You repeat things, like what the other person says. It's annoying."

I stood up from the couch, and the two men took a step toward me from the door. The shorter one pulled his .38 from the waist of his pants.

"Take it easy," I said to the two goons. "I'm just stretching my legs."

Gautieri put up his hand, palm toward the two. "Relax, gentlemen." He rubbed his hands together, watching me for a moment. "Listen," he said. "There's no need to have any trouble between us. So I'm going to ask you—just once—to leave Angela out of whatever it is you're doing. She's had a hard enough time these past few months."

"Oh yeah?" I said. "That's too bad."

Gautieri stared back at me. "I thought she was done with it, after a Boston detective and another uniformed officer showed up down here. My lawyer made a few calls, and we've been assured Angela will no longer be bothered. I hadn't expected some Jim Rockford wannabe would show up after. So now, I'd like to request you leave her alone. It would be in your best interest you do."

"Is that a threat?" I said.

Gautieri shrugged. "You wanna call it a threat? You call it what you want. I'm simply making a request. It doesn't have to be anything more than that. Unless you'd like it to be." He sat back down on the couch and poured himself an espresso. "Do we have an understanding?"

I hesitated, knowing my only option was to tell him I'd leave her alone. It didn't mean I would.

Gautieri stood, extending his hand to me. "We got a deal? Or what?"

I nodded, looked at his hand, and walked toward the door without shaking it. "I'll show myself out."

"Would you like a ride back to your car, Mr. Horn?" Gautieri said.

I stepped past the two men at the door, gave them each a nod, and turned the knob, shaking my head as I looked back at the mayor. "I'll grab a cab."

CHAPTER 17

I SPENT A GOOD part of the afternoon cleaning the house. At least as best I could. There were a hundred other things I could've been doing, but Nancy had called and would be showing up with her so-called friend later in the day.

I sat at the table once I was done and flipped through the *Globe* looking for an article I'd heard about, regarding the rising crime in the area around Morrissey Boulevard. Michael Dempsey's death was mentioned as one of more than a few over the past six months. The Morrissey Motel was also mentioned, as was Nora Hayden, the woman from the motel who found Michael's body.

I hadn't gotten a call from her, as I'd hoped, and wondered if the motel's owner, Adesh, had even given her my number as he'd promised he would. I grabbed the white pages from the cabinet under the counter and sat back down at the table, flipping through the pages. I stopped at H and ran my finger down through the first names until I got to Lauren... Mary... Nathan... until I came to Nora Hayden.

However, I was surprised to see there were *two* Nora Haydens listed. One had an address out in Western Massachusetts, in the Berkshires. I couldn't imagine anyone would commute all the way to Boston to work in a motel. I was left with the second Nora Hayden in the book, apparently a resident of Quincy, just a few minutes from Milton, where I lived.

I got up from the table and grabbed the handset off the wall and pulled the card from my pocket with the number to the Morrissey Motel. I dialed, and the call was answered on the first ring. "Morrissey Motel. This is Adesh. How may I help you?"

"Adesh? This is Jake Horn."

"The private detective?" he said.

"Yeah, uh... hey, listen, I missed you the other day after I left Freeman's. I don't know where you disappeared to, but I had a little run-in outside your office. You happen to hear anything about it?"

"A run-in?" he said. "What does that mean, a 'run-in'?"

"It's a kinder way of saying, *I was jumped*. A man followed me out of the bar and wanted to fight. Actually, we did fight. I only got out of there because someone fired a gun. Luckily, it wasn't fired at me."

"A gunshot?" Adesh was quiet on the other end. "Are you sure it was a gunshot?"

"I know what a gun sounds like," I said.

"Well, I am sorry, Mr. Horn. I did not hear anything. I'm sorry that happened to you, but I must not have been there when it happened. I had to go out and buy soda for my machine. You know that Morrissey Boulevard can be very noisy. Perhaps you are mistaken that—"

"I told you, I know a gunshot when I hear one. It wasn't the damn traffic. I'm surprised nobody else said anything to you. None of your guests heard it?"

It was hard to say if Adesh was lying. It could've been that he *had* heard about it but didn't want any more bad publicity than he already had. Word was already out his motel was in a troubled area. Not to mention a man's body being pulled from the dumpster behind the place.

I could hear Adesh talking to somebody else. "I'm sorry, Mr. Horn," he said, "but I am very busy. I have guests who need my help. Is there something I can help you with?"

"Well, you told me you'd have Nora Hayden call me. But I haven't heard from either of you."

"Well, I am sorry, Mr. Horn. I called her two times but she didn't answer."

"No answering machine?" I said.

"I did not leave a message."

The line went quiet again, but I could hear someone in the background.

Adesh said, "Mr. Horn, I have to help my guests. I will have to hang up now." Before I could say another word, he hung up.

I looked at the white pages and Nora Hayden's phone number in Quincy and dialed the phone. But before it even rang, a blue BMW pulled into the driveway. I hung the phone up on the wall and went to the front door.

I'm six three, two twenty-eight. It takes a lot to scare me. But meeting a boy my only daughter was bringing home from college gave me a nervous feeling I didn't like.

I had my hand on the doorknob, took a deep breath, and put on a smile as I opened the door.

Nancy was already on the top step with a bag over her shoulder. She looked different. Even though it had only been a few weeks since I last saw her, something about her looked older.

She gave me a hug, and we held each other, my eyes going to the young man coming up behind her.

My first thought was why wasn't this kid carrying her bag for her? Although I knew even if he had offered, Nancy would tell him no.

I let go of Nancy and reached out my hand for the young man behind her. I say *young man*, but he really was a boy. Tall and thin, maybe one fifty soaking wet.

He was a good-looking kid. Maybe a little *too* good looking.

I took Nancy's bag and threw it over my shoulder, reaching my hand out to shake the boy's hand.

"Jake Horn," I said.

Nancy introduced him before he could speak. "Dad, this is Corey. Corey, this is my dad."

Corey and I shook hands, and I looked him in the eye, giving him a good squeeze before I let go of his hand. "Nice to meet you, Corey."

He looked nervous. "Nice to meet you, Mr. Horn."

I didn't like the sound of that. I never did. "Just call me Jake," I said.

He nodded, with a look like he was unsure I meant it. "Okay."

I opened the door. "Welcome to Milton."

Nancy walked in ahead of us and looked around the house like she'd never seen it before. "I love what you've done with the place." She smiled at me. She knew I hadn't done a thing since my grandmother—her great-grandmother—had passed away at eighty-six, leaving me and Nancy her house.

I nodded toward the stairs. "Corey, if you want to go up and put your bag away, your bedroom's up the stairs. First door to the right." I felt Nancy watching me.

The room I was referring to was my mother's—Nancy's grandmother's—as a little girl. Nobody'd ever slept in there. After my mother died at twenty-nine years old, my grandmother wouldn't let anyone ever step in there.

Funny that my mother was the same age as my wife, Barbara, when she died.

Corey stood still just inside the door. He looked like he wasn't sure what to do.

"Go ahead," I said. "Go up and put your stuff down. You'll see the bathroom up there, too, if you need to powder your nose." Nancy started to walk behind him, but I put my hand on her shoulder to stop her, then waited for Corey to make it to the top of the stairs. "Listen, I don't want you two sneaking around at night or anything like that. I see anything I don't like, Corey'll have to sleep out in the garage."

I was half kidding. But not really.

She stepped back and slipped out from under my hands.

"I told you already," she said, smiling. "We're just friends."

I looked out the window at the fancy BMW in the driveway. With my voice in almost a whisper, I said, "A *rich* friend."

She rolled her eyes and grabbed her bag by the door. "He's not *that* rich. His father owns a car dealership." She walked away from me toward the stairs. "You shouldn't judge, Dad."

"Sorry," I said, laughing. "But that's kind of my thing."

She stopped at the first step. "We haven't eaten."

I looked at my watch. "I was going to order from Regino's."

She nodded with a big smile on her face, then headed up the stairs.

I went into the kitchen and called my friend Paulie, the owner of Regino's, and ordered pizzas.

Nancy stood at the top of the stairs and yelled down to me, "Dad, Corey needs to use the phone."

"Go ahead, I'm off," I said. "He can use the one in the room."

I went up to grab my wallet and stopped on the top step. I heard Corey on the phone. Maybe it was rude of me, but I heard his voice, almost in a whisper, and couldn't help but be a little suspicious. It was just my nature.

"You know I love you," he said. "I told you, I'm at Jeremy's." He was quiet for a few moments. "Yeah, up the North End."

Jeremy's? I knew I couldn't stand there and continue listening. So I walked into my room and grabbed my wallet, then poked my head in Nancy's room. She had her back to the door. "I'm going to pick up the pizza. I assume you two'll be all right here, alone?"

She rolled her eyes. "You already ordered? What kind?"

"I ordered two. One plain and a special."

She scrunched her face. "Oh, I forgot to tell you. Corey doesn't eat meat or cheese."

I kept my voice low. "He doesn't eat meat or cheese?" I said. "Then what's he *eat*?"

She shrugged. "He just doesn't eat cheese or meat. He'll eat whatever else."

"What's a pizza without meat or cheese?" I said.

"Da-ad," she said, like she'd reverted to being ten.

I went into my bedroom and picked up the phone to make sure Corey was off, then called Paulie back to change the order. I headed for the stairs and stopped in the hall.

Corey walked out of the bedroom.

"Oh," he said, "Hi," looking somewhat startled.

I gave him a nod. "Are you allergic to cheese?" I said. "And meat?"

His face turned red. "Me? No, I just—"

"No need to explain," I said. "I ordered a pizza with your name on it, just sauce and vegetables.

He swallowed, nodding. "I hope it's not a problem, Mr. Horn. I, uh…"

"I'll be right back," I said, my voice raised, heading down the stairs. "Oh, sorry Corey, you'll have to move that Beemer so I can get out."

He hurried down the stairs past me. "I'm sorry about that." He went out the front door.

I laughed. I liked that the kid seemed a little scared of me. I looked up at Nancy, standing at the top of the stairs looking down at me. "What's Corey doing?" she said.

"Moving his car." I smiled. "Is he always this nervous?" I said.

Nancy shrugged. "I told you. He's just a nice guy."

"Okay. I'll be back." I went outside and closed the front door behind me, buttoning my coat when I felt the cold air.

Corey walked up the driveway and pointed at his car parked on the street. "Is it all right I parked out there?"

"You mean, is anybody going to steal it?" I said.

"No, I meant, is it all right to leave it there? Are the neighbors okay that I parked on the street?"

I laughed. "The neighbors? They're fine." I nodded to the driveway. "You can pull it in the driveway when I pull out, if you want. As long as you're not trying to sneak out in the middle of the night."

He stood in the walkway looking up at me, scratching his head. "No, we're not going anywhere. Not until tomorrow."

"I was kidding," I said, walking toward my car. I slid behind the wheel, the seat cold, like ice. It was officially the time of year where days warmed up, but nights didn't let us forget winter wasn't over.

I revved the engine and cranked the heat, although nothing but cold air came out from the vents. I backed down the driveway and gave Corey a wave as he stepped into his car.

***

I sat at the bar at Regino's and ordered a beer, drank half, and got up to use the pay phone around the corner, near the restroom.

I set the beer on top of the phone booth and pulled out the card from the Morrissey Motel. I'd written Nora Hayden's number on the back of it. I dropped a dime in the phone and dialed her number. It rang six times before somebody finally answered.

Her voice was slow and quiet and seemed somewhat hoarse. She sounded like an old woman. "Hello?"

"Hi, is this Nora?"

"Yes, it is," she said without hesitation.

"My name's Jake Horn. Are you the same Nora Hayden who worked at the Morrissey Motel?"

There was silence.

"I'm sorry, I think you have the wrong number."

"So you're not the Nora Hayden who worked at the Morrissey Motel?"

There was quiet on the other end. "I'm sorry, you have the wrong Nora Hayden." She let out a slight laugh. "I'm retired, my dear. I haven't worked in twenty years."

"Do you happen to know the Nora Hayden who worked at the motel?" I said.

There was a brief pause. "No, I don't. I'm sorry."

The phone disconnected.

I took another dime from my pocket and dropped it in the slot. This time I dialed Raymond's house.

His wife, Beth, answered.

"Beth, it's Jake," I said. "He around?"

"No. I was hoping you were with him. He went out to pick up fish and chips an hour ago."

"From where?"

"McShawn's."

I laughed. "I'm sure he's having a couple beers."

"Yeah, but I'm hungry." She didn't seem overly upset or worried. Just hungry.

"Did you call over there?" I said.

"You know me, Jake. I'm not one of those wives... nagging their husbands for having a couple drinks."

I laughed. "I know you're not. But if you want, I'll call over there and tell him to get his ass home."

"Oh, you don't have to..."

"Give me a minute. I'll call you right back."

"Oh, okay, Jake. Thank you."

I hung up and dialed McShawn's. I knew the number because Raymond had been hanging out there for as long as I could remember. If I couldn't find him at the house, I'd find him at McShawn's. A lot of cops hung out there too. Which meant they never had much trouble.

The phone rang five times before the bartender finally picked up. "McShawn's." The background noise just about drowned out his voice.

"This Eddie?"

"Who's askin'?"

"Eddie, it's Jake Horn. My cousin there?"

"Raymond? I don't know, let me ask him."

The background noise was muffled with a sound like Eddie's hand covering the mouthpiece on the phone. But I could still hear him when he said, "Hey, Raymond, are you here? It's Jake."

Raymond came on the phone. "Hey, what's up?"

"What's up?" I said. "Your wife is hungry."

"Beth?"

"You have another wife?"

"No, I mean. What'd she say?"

"Does Beth ever get mad? I called her looking for you; she said you left for fish and chips an hour ago."

Raymond went quiet. "Shit, has it been that long?" With the background noise muffled again, I heard him say, "Eddie, my fish and chips ready yet?" He came back on the line. "Was she mad?"

"Beth? Does she ever get mad?"

Raymond laughed. "You don't see her behind closed doors."

I grabbed my beer from the top of the phone and took a sip. "Listen, I'm trying to track down a woman, and—"

"You mean, someone besides Lily?"

"Yeah. She's the woman who found Michael Dempsey, behind the motel. So, I was just hoping you might be able to help me track her down."

"Track her down?"

"I mean, call your friend at the phone company."

The background noise was loud, but with Raymond's deep voice, I could still hear him all right. "You talk to Maggie?" he said.

"She already did me a favor, got me an address down in Providence. The mayor's daughter."

"You went down to Providence?"

"I'll tell you all about it when I see you."

The phone and Raymond's voice got muffled. He said, "Hey, Eddie, you got a pen? Thanks." The sound was clear again. "I'll see what I can do," he said. "Give me the woman's name. I'll see what I can find out."

CHAPTER 18

I WAS IN THE middle of flipping over the eggs in the cast-iron pan over the stove when Nancy walked into the kitchen, already dressed, and pulled down a coffee cup from the cabinet. "Morning," I said. "Did you sleep okay?"

She yawned and nodded, pouring coffee from the coffee maker into her cup. "The mattress is so much more comfortable than the one in my dorm."

I looked toward the doorway leading to the living room. "Your friend's still in bed?"

"He's going to take a shower. He's one of those people who likes to get dressed and ready before he does anything else."

I placed two fried eggs onto a plate. "He's wound a little tight," I said, wanting to ask how she knew his morning routine but preferred not to think about it. I handed her the plate. "There's toast."

She took the two pieces of toast from the toaster and dropped them on her plate. "I think you're making him nervous," she said.

"I'm making him *nervous*?"

She sat at the table and took a bite of her toast, nodding. "You've always made my friends nervous. At least until they get to know you and realize you're all bark."

"All bark, huh?" I said, dropping two more pieces of white bread in the toaster. I flipped two eggs onto another plate and looked down at the last two in the pan. "He doesn't eat cheese or meat. Are you going to tell me he doesn't eat eggs?"

She nodded, smiling. "Don't worry about him."

I sat across from Nancy at the table. "I don't know how old they are, but there's a box of Cheerios in the pantry."

She grabbed the *Boston Globe* I'd left on the table and turned it toward her. She ran her finger over the article I'd read about Boston's growing crime problem. She looked up at me. "Is this about Lily's husband?"

I nodded.

"Where's Lily?" Nancy said.

I wiped my mouth with my napkin and took a sip of coffee. "I wish I knew."

Nancy looked surprised. "She wasn't at her cousin's house?"

"She was," I said. "But that was the first time she disappeared. I don't know where she's gone."

"Aren't you trying to find her?"

I hesitated a moment, then nodded. "I thought you didn't want me to get involved?"

She picked at the eggs with her fork, her elbow on the table, chin in her hand. "I don't want you to get hurt," she said. "But what if something happened to her?"

I didn't respond.

Nancy didn't have many good feelings for Lily after what she did to me. But she wouldn't want to see something bad happen to Lily either.

She looked down at the article and saw where I'd underlined some of the names. "Who's Nora Hayden?"

"She worked at the motel. She was the one who found Michael Dempsey."

She looked up from the newspaper and pushed her coffee aside, her arms resting on the table. "Why do I get the feeling you're into this for more than just to find Lily?"

"I guess I'm trying to figure out what happened."

"So you're investigating the murder?"

I didn't know how to answer her. I was, and I wasn't. That was the truth. "If Lily's a suspect, and as long as she's missing, she's going to be, then I'm going to have to help her," I said. "It's as simple as that."

"Simple?" Nancy said, straightening in her chair. She looked down at the paper again. "So what's the story with this woman, Nora Hayden? Did you talk to her?"

"I haven't. Not yet."

Nancy sipped her coffee and stood from the table, her empty plate in her hand. "So, does this mean you're helping Lily, but... is she going to pay you?"

"I'm not sure," I said. "But you have to remember, Nance, not everything's about money."

She laughed. "I get that." She looked around the kitchen. "But what are you doing? Do you have any other clients? Or are you..." She closed her eyes and sat back down at the table, her lips tight together in a small grin. "I'm sorry. I just... I worry about you."

"You don't have to worry," I said. "I'm the one who's supposed to do all the worrying." I pointed to my chest and raised my voice a little more than I'd wanted to. "I'm the father, Nancy. You're the daughter. You have to remember that. We don't get to reverse roles."

Her eyes went toward the table before looking at me. "So I'm not supposed to worry about you?"

"I wish you wouldn't." I reached for her hand and gave it a squeeze.

She said, "You're not a suspect, are you?"

I got up and placed my dish in the sink and turned toward her, shaking my head. "Not really, no."

Her eyes opened wide. "'Not really'? What's that mean? Not *really*?"

The phone rang, and I hurried across the kitchen to answer it before Nancy could.

"Hello?"

"It's me."

It was Raymond.

I walked out of the kitchen and stood with the cord stretched around to the other side of the wall.

"Any luck?" I said.

"I don't think you'd call what I had to go through to get this, 'luck,'" Raymond said. "There was very little *luck* involved. Just old connections. It wasn't easy tracking this lady down, you know."

"I know. I owe you," I said. I took the Morrissey Motel card from my pocket, went back into the kitchen, and pulled a pen from one of the drawers.

Nancy was by the sink cleaning dishes and glanced back at me. I held the phone against my ear with my shoulder and pressed the card against the wall, ready with the pen. "Go ahead."

He read off the phone number, and I wrote it on the back of the card.

"It's an unlisted number with a hidden address," Raymond said. "If I were still in uniform, I would've had to get a warrant just to get the phone company to release it to me."

"I won't ask how you got it, then."

"Good. We'll leave it at that. I gotta run. Call me later."

I hung up the phone just as Corey walked down the stairs.

I stepped out toward the living room. "Good morning," I said.

"Morning, Mr. Horn," he said, stopping by the front door.

I gave up trying to get him to call me Jake. It didn't matter. I was just trying to help the kid relax.

Nancy walked out from the kitchen and stood in the doorway, looking at me. "What was the call?" she said.

I gave her a look, like I wanted to tell her it was none of her business, but didn't want to sound like a jerk in front of Corey.

"Uncle Raymond," I said. "Just doing me a favor."

She stared at me, like she was waiting for more, then took Corey's coat off the rack by the door. "You ready?" she said, handing it to him.

"Ready for *what*?" I said, watching her step past me and reach for her jacket. "You're leaving? Corey, don't you want something to eat?"

"We're going to meet up with some friends."

"Oh," I said, trying to hide the disappointment on my face.

"Is that okay?" she said, clearly picking up on my expression.

If I'd said I *wasn't* okay, I'm not sure it would have mattered.

"Yeah, of course. I just..." I stopped and thought for a moment. "No, that's cool. I have some things to do anyway."

"Please be careful," she said.

"You be careful," I said, leaning as I gave her a kiss on the forehead.

"I'll be here tonight. Corey's going into Boston to see a friend. So it'll be you and me tonight." She had a big smile on her face.

I wanted to ask him if it was the person I'd overheard him talking to on the phone, but it was none of my business. Maybe Nancy meant it when she said they were just friends. I asked him if he was sleeping at the house.

"No, sir," he said. "I'll be staying in Boston, come back tomorrow to pick up Nancy."

Nancy pulled open the front door. "I'll see you later this afternoon?" She walked out the door ahead of Corey.

"Thank you for putting me up," Corey said. "It's a nice bedroom."

A nice bedroom? "Anytime," I said, watching the door close behind them.

But the door opened again, and Nancy poked her head inside. "Can you move your car?"

***

I sat at the table with the phone in my hand and dialed Nora Hayden's number. I had her address and thought about going there first, without calling—the element of surprise—but decided to try calling.

After six rings, an answering machine came on. I had an answering machine at the office, for business, but not at the house. Not for all the money they cost.

A woman's voice came on the machine:

I'm not home right now, so please leave a message at the beep and I will call you back.

It beeped, and I hesitated a moment, unsure I wanted to leave a message or if she'd even return my call if I did. But I decided to go ahead and leave one. "Nora, hi, uh, my name is Jake Horn. I'm a private investigator in Boston and was hoping to have a word with you when you have a chance." I didn't leave more details on a voicemail than was necessary. "If you can call me back when you get this, my number is—"

The line beeped, and someone picked up the phone.

"Hello?" It was the same voice as the one on the answering machine.

"Nora?" I said.

There was a brief pause. "Yes, this is Nora. I'm sorry, what did you say your name was?"

"Jake Horn. I'm a private investigator and was hoping to—"

"What is this about?" she said. I could hear music in the background. It sounded like classical music, but I wasn't sure.

"I wanted to ask some questions about that night at the motel... I understand you were the one who was working the night, the night of Michael Dempsey's murder?"

The line went quiet for a moment. "I'm sorry, Mr. Horn. But I'm not interested in rehashing everything all over again. It's been hard enough trying to get what happened out of my mind. I haven't slept in days. It's really been—"

"I understand," I said. "And I'm sorry to bother you like this. But it would really be helpful if I could just come by. I promise I won't take a lot of your time."

"Can't you just ask me whatever it is over the—" She stopped, mid-sentence. "Can you give me a moment? Somebody's at my door."

"Uh, sure," I said.

The sound of the phone being placed on a hard surface came through the receiver. The music was louder, like she's placed the phone on top of the speaker.

I heard what I believed was her voice in the background but couldn't make out what she was saying, with the music coming through the phone.

A loud scream came over the music, followed by what I had no doubt were two gunshots being fired. My heart began to race, and I kept the phone up to my ear. "Hello? Nora? Hello?" I yelled. "Is anybody there? Hello?" I looked around the kitchen for my keys and grabbed them off the counter. I waited for Nora's voice to come back on the line, hoping what I'd heard was something else.

She didn't come back on the line. All I could hear was the classical music coming through the phone.

CHAPTER 19

BY THE TIME I arrived at Nora Hayden's house, the Quincy Police were already there, along with two rescue vehicles and a truck from the Quincy Fire Department.

I parked three houses down on the street, walking past Nora's neighbors, most standing at the edge of their driveways watching the scene, some huddled in groups whispering to each other.

One man in his driveway yelled to me as I walked past: "Hey, buddy, you know what happened?"

I kept walking without giving him a real answer, turning up the driveway of the small ranch with the green siding. The front door was held wide open, police and uniformed men walking in and out of the doorway.

A young cop built like a linebacker but with boyish looks stood at the bottom of the front steps. As I started past him, he put out his arms to block me. "Sir?" he said. "You can't go in there."

"I'm the guy who called it in. I was on the phone with her." I realized I had assumed the worst but didn't know for sure if Nora had been shot or whether she was dead or alive. "Is she okay?"

"Sorry, this is a crime scene, sir." He called out to one of the officers standing in the doorway. "Hey, Tommy, this is the guy who called in the shooting."

I took out my private investigator's license and showed it to both officers. "My name's Jake Horn."

A voice called out from behind me. "Horn? What are you doing here?"

Detective Moriarty, dressed in a red turtleneck under his made-for-TV detective's trench coat, walked up the driveway toward me. He had his wallet ready and held his badge up for the young officer, close enough to his face, he had to lean his body back to look at it. "Detective Jeffrey Moriarty, Boston Police. Bureau of Investigations."

The officer standing in the doorway looked confused. "Boston? Who the hell called *Boston*?"

Jeffrey put his hands on his hips from inside his coat and looked up at the officer. He nodded toward the house. "Nora Hayden had ties to an investigation in Boston. I'll be cooperating with your department." He walked up the steps and past the officer in the doorway without another word. He hadn't waited for me to answer why I was there.

I pointed up the stairs. "I'm with him."

The young officer held his treelike arm out to block me. "No, you're not."

I yelled toward the house, "Detective?"

The big cop stared at me, folding his arms in front of his chest.

I said, "Can you get him for me? Please? I have information I need to..."

Moriarty walked out from the house and down the steps. "Horn? You called this in? What the hell were you doing on the phone with Miss Hayden?"

"Is she dead?" I said.

"Very." He looked around at all the officers in the small yard, then said, "Horn, can you clear up some of my confusion, and please explain how you happened to be on the phone with her? And exactly what you heard?"

"I just wanted to talk to her about the night she found Dempsey's body."

He pulled off his sunglasses and stuck the end of the temple tip in his mouth, biting down with his teeth, like it was a pipe. "She had already been questioned. You needed to know something, maybe you should have just called me."

"Like you're going to tell me anything?" I said.

He looked past me and at the house, shaking his head. "Probably not."

Moriarty looked back and forth along the street. "Quite a crowd," he said. "Doesn't anybody around here have a job?" He slipped his sunglasses back over his eyes. "So what did she tell you?"

"Nora? Nothing at all. We barely spoke."

He didn't respond, his back to me, facing the street.

I said, "You think this is related? I mean, it has to be, don't you think?" I stepped around Moriarty to face him.

He was looking down at a small pad he held in his hand but lifted his head. "Did you say something?"

"I asked, I mean... I'm saying it's got to be related to Dempsey's murder. It has to be."

Jeffrey's eyes came over his sunglasses. "This is a homicide investigation. Quincy PD's going to handle it from here and share whatever they find with Boston. We'll work together to see if there's any connection." He pulled out a roll of mints from his pocket and popped one in his mouth. "They're going to want to talk to you." He flipped a page on his pad. "But while we're here, why don't you go ahead and tell me what happened during your call. What did you hear?"

"Someone knocked at her door. She'd just answered the phone and didn't sound like she wanted to talk. She sounded like she was afraid to talk, to be honest."

Moriarty said, "How do you know someone knocked on her door?"

"She told me."

Moriarty made a note on his pad, but I got the feeling he was just going through the motions. "Go ahead," he said.

"So she put the phone down. It sounded like she'd put it down on top of a speaker. There was music in the background. And it got a lot louder when she told me to wait, that someone was at the door."

He looked up from the pad. "Are you sure you heard this right?" He stopped to look at the house. "And there was no music playing, although I did see a turntable in there. But it wasn't on. Of course, perhaps one of the officers turned it off." He removed his sunglasses from his eyes and slid them into his inside coat pocket, moving the mint around his mouth.

I said, "Someone should check the answering machine, you'll hear my voice. Although she picked it up as I was in the middle of leaving a message. Maybe it was still recording..."

He paused a moment, then walked past the young officer and back up the steps, through the doorway into Nora Hayden's house.

I looked at the young officer with the thick neck and gave him a smile.

He stared back at me without a word.

Moriarty came out a few moments later and jogged down the steps. "No answering machine in there at all."

I thought for a moment, looking down toward the driveway. "Whoever killed her must've taken it. Which means they'll have my name on it."

Moriarty didn't have much else to add. "I let the investigators know what you said. If you can wait here, someone'll be out to talk to you." He started down the driveway but stopped and turned with his hand on his chin. "So how did you get Miss Hayden's number? I know for a fact it's an unlisted number."

I shrugged. "That's one of my specialities."

He nodded. "I hope you're not asking Maggie Donovan to do you any favors. She's a Boston police officer. It's not her job to assist a private detective in an ongoing investigation. Keep that in mind. I'd hate to see her get in trouble for something like—"

"She didn't get me the number. Maggie's a good cop, and you know that. But if you're afraid she's going to give me something to help find Dempsey's killer before you have a chance to, I don't think you should worry."

He pulled out his sunglasses and cleaned the lenses with a cloth he pulled from his pocket. He slipped the glasses over his eyes. "You think I'm afraid some hack private investigator's going to get in my way? You know how many cases I've solved in this city?"

"In Quincy?" I said.

"In Boston. And throughout Massachusetts."

I said, "No, and I don't care. This isn't a pissing contest, Detective. If that's what you're looking for, you've got the wrong idea of what I'm all about. You want the glory? So you brag about how many cases you solved? You can have it."

***

The ride back from Nora's house had my brain spinning in overdrive. There was plenty I hadn't shared with Moriarty. Maybe it was a little bit of a pissing match with him. I didn't like him. And he didn't like me. And although I'd rarely admit there was something about solving crimes that fed your ego, there was certainly some truth to it. The drive to get it right was hard to explain. No doubt, Moriarty had it. I did too. At least most of the time. And I knew it was the one thing we had in common that would have us bumping heads for the foreseeable future.

I didn't tell Moriarty anything about speaking with the owner of the Morrissey Motel. Maybe Nora would've still been alive if I'd gotten to talk to her sooner. That would've meant Adesh at least giving me her number when I'd asked for it. Or telling her to call me as I'd asked him to do.

Something wasn't right.

Especially since Adesh was the only person—other than Raymond and Nancy—who knew I was trying to track Nora down. Throw in the fact I was attacked in the motel parking lot while Adesh was allegedly out buying soda, and that he hadn't heard *anything* about a shot being fired... I couldn't help that my suspicions about him had started to grow.

By the time I made it back to the house, it was already evening. Although the days were getting longer, the sun had just about gone down. And when I pulled in the driveway, I saw nothing but total darkness through the windows inside the house.

I parked in front of the garage and stepped out onto the driveway. Something caught my eye on the other side of the window, in the kitchen. It could have been Nancy, I thought. But why would the lights be turned off?

I reached under my seat and pulled out the Smith & Wesson .357 Magnum. It was a gun my uncle had left me, but I never used it. I never had to shoot anyone with it and never wanted to. Although it came in handy more than once when the mere threat of it in my hand got me out of trouble.

I tucked it in my pants and knew enough not to even have it out by my side. Not if it was Nancy inside. In fact, when she was little, I almost never took a gun home from the office.

I stayed low along the house, stepping over the shrubs underneath the windows. I poked my head up and tried to look inside but saw nothing. I thought maybe I was just being paranoid.

But then I heard a noise and pulled the gun from my pants. I was almost certain Nancy would have no reason to be in there with the lights off. And I'd convinced myself someone else was.

I stayed close to the exterior of the house and walked around the side toward the backyard, stopping at the corner. I poked my head around to the back, enough to see the storm door on the back of the house was wide open. It appeared to be broken and almost hanging off the hinges. It was hard to see with the darkness, but the interior door appeared to be ajar.

Someone had broken into the house.

I had to think through my next move. The smart thing to do would be to go to the neighbor's house and call the cops. But then if someone was still inside, whoever it was would be gone. After seeing my car pull up the driveway, I assumed the person was either trying to find a way out or was waiting for me to make my move.

I wasn't about to let him, or her, slip away.

I stepped out from the side of the house with my .357 by my side, ducking under the windows until I made it to the back door.

In the few minutes since I'd pulled up the driveway, it had only gotten darker.

I started up the concrete stairs, trying to be quiet with each step.

I was right about the storm door, which I normally kept locked along with the interior door. Whoever broke in had torn it off the hinges.

I slowly pushed the interior door open, holding my .357 out in front of me. I stepped with one foot over the threshold and eased the door open. It creaked as I stepped inside and stood in the doorway. I had raised my free hand for the light switch when something hard came down and struck me on my arm. It came down again, this time knocking the gun from my hand. A large figure stood in the darkness, and I was struck in the head. I stumbled back and fell down the stairs, landing on the patio. My head cracked, hitting the cold, hard concrete.

I tried to get up, feeling the warmth of my own blood coming down my neck. But the man jumped down on top of me, driving his knee into my chest. He raised whatever object was in his hand and swung it toward my face. But I grabbed his wrist and stopped it before it struck.

He was too strong, and I needed both hands to hold his arm back.

A punch connected with my face, and my head whipped to the side.

I let go of his wrist and reached for a small ceramic pot next to my head on the bottom step and smashed it over his head. The pot exploded into pieces.

The man jumped off me, holding his head with both hands. It was still too dark to make out his face, although I could see he had a long, thick beard. He swung his boot at my head as I started to get up off the ground.

That's when I grabbed his boot with both hands and twisted his foot, trying to force him to the ground.

A light shone from around the side of the house and reflected off the trees. I knew they were headlights, followed by the sound of a vehicle's engine. "Back here!" I yelled, although I had no idea who it was.

Another punch landed on my head, followed by two more.

The man ripped his foot from my grasp and ran in the opposite direction of the headlights. I tried to get up, but he disappeared around the other side of the house.

It made it up and onto my feet, putting my hand to my face. I was covered in blood.

Raymond yelled for me. "Jake?"

"I'm in back," I said as loud as I could. But I didn't have enough energy in me to yell.

The beam from a flashlight bounced around the corner of the house and came toward me.

"Over here," I said, stumbling with my first step toward the light. I stopped and looked in the direction of where the man had disappeared.

Raymond stood in front of me. "What are you doing out here in the dark?" He leaned in closer and shined the flashlight on me. "Jesus Christ, Jake. What the... what the hell happened?"

CHAPTER 20

NANCY AND RAYMOND SAT looking at me from across the kitchen table. I had a towel over my eye, my wrist where I'd been hit, swollen but not broken. At least as far as I could tell.

If anything, I was just happy Corey hadn't dropped Nancy off any sooner than he had.

Raymond had my .357 in his hand and placed it down on the table. He got up from his chair and went to the fridge. "Mind if I have one of your beers?"

"Since when do you have to ask?" I said, wiggling what felt like a loose tooth in my mouth.

He opened the can and held it out toward me. "You only have a few left. You want one?"

I thought about it but decided against it.

Raymond walked to the window and took a sip from the can. He looked outside. "I know you don't want to call this in and get the boys involved but—"

"The 'boys'?" Nancy said, rolling her eyes. "Do you mean the *police*? It hasn't been 'boys' since before 1921."

Raymond looked at me, confused. I'm not sure he even knew what Nancy meant.

"She's right," I said, looking up at him. "Did you even know that the first woman joined the Boston Police Department then? In 1921."

Raymond looked back and forth from me to Nancy. "Oh. Uh, trust me... I wasn't trying to come across like that."

Nancy had her eyes on me. I knew she was scared but covered it up well. She said, "Shouldn't we at least call Maggie?"

I pushed myself up from the chair but felt the weight of my own throbbing head try to pull me back down. I leaned on the table with one hand and squeezed the front of my head with the other. "I feel like my head's in a vise."

Nancy stood up and grabbed me from behind, easing me back into the chair. She turned to Raymond. "You think we should take him to Beth Israel?"

Raymond shook his head. "You think he's going to let us take him to a doctor?" He tilted the top of the beer can toward me. "When was the last time you even walked into a doctor's office?"

I shrugged. "No idea. Ten years, maybe." I watched Raymond sip from the can. "You know what? I changed my mind. Grab me a beer."

Nancy went over to the sink and looked out the window into the night. "What if he's still out there?"

"I bet the guy's long gone," Raymond said, glancing at me out of the corner of his eye. But I could see in his expression he didn't believe a word of what he'd said.

But neither of us wanted Nancy to worry.

She stepped from the window. "Do you think this has to do with what happened to Lily's husband?"

"Can't say for sure," I said. Although I had a pretty good feeling it did.

Raymond sipped his beer and sat back down across from me at the table. "I checked both doors and examined all the windows. Your storm door was ripped off the hinge. I don't think that was necessary. But, and I'm just being honest here, I don't see how whoever got in here did it without a key. The only other way is if that back door was left open. But you said there was no way, right?"

I thought for a moment. "I guess the only thing is, when I took off out of here for Nora Hayden's house, I didn't waste any time getting over there." I looked at the door on the far side of the kitchen from the table. "I guess it's possible, I could've left it unlocked."

"That's not like you," Nancy said. "You'd never leave doors unlocked."

Raymond stood from the table and looked out the window toward the street. "Well? What do you want to do? If you don't want to involve the police, then..."

"I don't understand why you won't call Maggie?" Nancy said. She looked at Raymond with a smirk. "Unless you don't want a female cop involved?"

Raymond rolled his eyes.

She walked over to the phone and lifted it from the wall, handing it to me. "She always knows what to do."

"No. Hang it up. Maggie can't be involved in any of this. She was warned to stay clear of the Michael Dempsey case."

"Isn't this different?" Nancy said. "Shouldn't she be allowed to do her job?"

Raymond looked from me to Nancy. "I just want to make myself clear, that I have all the respect in the world for Maggie, and any other woman who wears the uniform. But it *is* true; there are men in that department—in departments across the country—who don't believe women have what it takes to be in law enforcement."

Nancy nodded. "I was just kidding. I don't think you're one of them. But I don't get why Maggie can't be involved?"

I said, "They fed her some BS, that it'd be a conflict of interest."

"But she didn't even know Michael, did she?" Nancy said. "And she never really liked Lily, so..."

"I think it's got to do with her relationship with me," I said. "At least I assume that's what it is."

Raymond said, "Maggie's the last person who'd let a personal conflict get in the way of doing her job. The captain knows that, so I guess I'm surprised..."

The phone rang, and I got up to answer it but Nancy beat me to it.

"Hello?" she said, then covered the mouthpiece with her hand, turning to me and Raymond. "It's Maggie!"

"Her ears must've been burning," Raymond said.

She put the phone up to her ear, listening. "Yeah, I'm okay. Uh-huh. I'm supposed to go back tomorrow." Nancy was quiet, listening. "Oh, okay. He's right here." She handed me the phone.

"Maggie?" I said. "Your ears must've been burning."

"They were," she said. "But I was just calling to... I heard the woman from the motel was killed today. Can you just tell me how you managed to get yourself involved again?"

"I wouldn't say I was involved. I mean, I was, of course. I just happened to be on the phone with her." I glanced over at Maggie, leaning against the counter watching me and knew I shouldn't go into details in front of her. She didn't need to hear them.

"But why were you on the phone with her?" Maggie said.

I pushed myself up from the chair so I could finally stand. The blood rushed to my feet, I'd been sitting for so long. Pain shot through my wrist. "Maybe we can talk about it later," I said.

I think Maggie understood why.

"Is everything all right over there?" she said. "You sound a little, I don't know, like you're..."

"I had a little problem at the house," I said.

Raymond let out a quick laugh, shaking his head at what I'd said and repeated it with a mumble. "'A little problem.'"

I waved him off and stepped through the doorway, standing on the other side of the wall. I kept my voice low. "I don't want Nancy to be concerned. She's already freaked out. Someone broke into the house and attacked me."

"Did you call the police?"

"Well, no. But I was going to call you once I—"

"I'm not a Milton officer, Jake. Why didn't you call them?"

"For *what*? The guy took off. Raymond's here."

The line was quiet for a moment.

"Listen, Jake," she said. "I'm actually calling because, well, I know you can't talk now, but I'm just wondering what you told the Quincy Police about what happened."

"What do you think I told them? I told them what happened."

"Well, apparently, they're not convinced you gave them the whole story. So it raised suspicions."

"There wasn't much more to it than what I told them. I don't know what part they wouldn't believe. The only part I left out is where I got her unlisted number."

"Where *did* you get it?"

"Raymond got it for me."

Raymond said, "Hey! I told you not to tell anyone I had anything to do with it."

I stepped to the doorway, shaking my head, pressing the phone against my chest. "Relax. You think Maggie's going to say anything?"

Raymond said, "I don't care. I told you, nobody needs to know I had anything to do with it. If I knew the lady'd end up dead, I would've never done it."

"I'm sure we all would've done things a little differently if we could all see the future." I put the phone back up to my ear and again stepped around to the other side of the wall. I said to Maggie,

"So what are you saying? Quincy Police think I had something to do with her being killed?" I took a deep breath with a long exhale. "Here we go again," I said.

"Is it too late for me to come down to the house?" she said. "We can talk a little more."

I nodded, stepping back into the kitchen. "Yeah, come down." I smiled at Nancy, but she looked more worried than she had before the call. "Nancy would love to see you. Raymond should be here, but I'm about to run out of beer."

"You want me to pick up a six?"

"It's up to you." I picked up my can off the table and realized it was almost empty. "I could use another one."

"Have you guys eaten?" she said.

"No, maybe we can run out, pick something up," I said.

"I'll grab something on my way down."

***

The four of us were seated at the kitchen table together, eating the Chinese food Maggie brought over.

Raymond leaned over his plate and took a bite of beef lo mein, looking at me. "You really don't think this guy was the one from Freeman's?"

I picked up my can of 'Gansett. "The guy from Freeman's was just your local drunk looking for trouble. And didn't have a beard. He made it clear when I was in there he didn't like me being in there, asking questions. The one tonight, he was here for a reason. Whether it had to do with what happened to Nora Hayden, or it's got to do with Dempsey..." I shrugged, sipping my beer. "I have no idea. He never even said a word."

Maggie had been quiet, trying to understand all we'd told her about my latest attacker. "Nothing?" she said. "No warning, or—"

"Not a word," I said. And we all knew, maybe with the exception of Nancy, when someone shows up like that, and no words are spoken, more often than not it means there was one purpose for the visit: to end me."

Nancy said, "It has to be related to that woman's murder, don't you think?"

I wasn't completely comfortable with Nancy being fully aware of the situation, but even if we spoke in tongues or left some of the grittier details out of the story, she had a way of piecing it all together.

Like her mother, she was rarely fooled.

"And her murder has to be connected to Michael's," Raymond said. "Right?"

Maggie and I both nodded, the four of us quiet for a couple of moments.

Raymond said to Maggie, "So who's taking charge? Boston?"

Maggie wiped her mouth with a napkin. "Quincy's heading up Nora Hayden's investigation, but from what I hear, Jeffrey's trying to push for Boston to take full control."

"Jeffrey?" Raymond said, giving Maggie a funny look. "You're on a first-name basis with the pretty boy?"

She gave him a crooked smile, slipping a piece of Hunan chicken into her mouth. "I got to know him over the last couple of years. Sorry if you don't like me using someone's first name, but—"

"I always thought of him as a last-name guy," Raymond said. "I don't even know much about him, but..."

"Either way," I said. "If it turns out the two forces are going to work together, it'll be double the red tape." I finished my beer. "Maybe it would be better they just hand it over to Moriarty, let him take charge. Otherwise, they'll never get anywhere."

Maggie gave me a look, like she didn't appreciate my lack of respect. "You say that like we never solve crimes."

"You have to admit," I said, "intercity investigations always get messy. At least, from what I've seen them do."

Nancy got up from the table and poured herself a Polar ginger ale from the refrigerator. "Can I ask a question?" she said. "How come none of you are talking about Lily? Isn't she the one who's missing?" She looked around the table at the three of us. "I would think you'd be worried. I mean, what if whoever killed this Nora lady…"

"What if it was Lily?" Maggie said, looking from me to Raymond.

I shook my head. "I don't see it." I pushed my plate aside and leaned with my arms folded in front of me on the table. "Are you going to tell me it's been brought up?"

"I haven't been in the station," she said. "Remember? I'm off for two days."

I had actually forgotten she hadn't been at work. "Then how'd you hear about Quincy, wondering if I—"

"I made a couple of calls when I heard about it. I have a friend, an acquaintance, works patrol for Quincy. He's the one who told me they were trying to poke holes in your story."

I looked at Nancy, staring at me from where she stood next to the refrigerator. I could tell her wheels were turning. They always were.

CHAPTER 21

NANCY WAS ALREADY AT the table in the kitchen when I came downstairs. "Did you sleep?" I said, knowing I hadn't closed my eyes through most of the night for more than a handful of minutes.

She looked up from her bowl of cereal and shrugged. "A little."

Maggie and Raymond had both offered to stay and keep an eye on the house so Nancy would feel safe.

But Nancy insisted she was fine.

I wasn't sure she was.

She had the *Boston Globe* in front of her. "How many of Lily's friends have you actually talked to?" she said.

I walked to the coffee maker and poured myself a coffee. "Most of her friends are back in New York," I said.

"How do you know she's not there? Maybe staying with a friend?"

I pulled up a chair across from her. "As far as I knew, Lily hadn't kept in touch with most of them. And she was so focused on her career once she moved to Boston, she didn't really have many friends here. I hate to say it, but..."

"Don't you have to find her?" she said. "Not only to make sure she's all right, but see if she can help *you*?"

"Help me in what way?"

Nancy shrugged. "Maybe there's something she hasn't told you. Maybe she knows there's more to what happened to Michael, then—"

"I think I'm at a point where I'm ready to let the police do their job." I didn't know what else to tell her. But after another restless night, I realized I was only putting my life, and Nancy's, of course, in danger.

She said, "What are you saying? You're just going to walk away?"

I looked around the kitchen. It was clean. Cleaner than it had been in a while. "Whoever was here was probably trying to scare me off."

"And you're going to *let* them scare you off?"

I let out a sigh and leaned back in my chair. I felt defeated, more than I had in a long time.

"Listen, Nance. I just need you to be safe. And I need to get my business moving again." I looked down into my coffee. "I didn't want to get into this with you, but I haven't had a lot of work lately. It's been months since I had a real client."

She held her spoon in her hand over the bowl of cereal but placed it down on the table. "Months?"

I nodded. "The work I've had, it's barely enough to pay the bills. And the more time I spend on what happened to Michael, and where Lily's gone, the harder it's going to be for me." I stared back at her across the table. "If I don't come up with some paying clients, I'm not sure how I'm going to pay your tuition for the fall semester."

Nancy swallowed hard, then looked down into her bowl. "I can get a job," she said, looking up at me. "I can pay for college myself."

"You think you're going to make eight grand waiting tables?" I shook my head. "I want you to focus on your schoolwork, keep those grades up, and get your degree."

Nancy played with her spoon in what looked like a soggy bowl of Cheerios. "So what happened? How come you don't have any clients?"

I rubbed my face with one hand, knowing I needed to shave, but the cuts and bruises from the night before meant I'd be better off waiting a few more days. "After Uncle Pat died, things just kind of dried up. He had a lot of connections. Even the Boston Police would turn to him. He had every attorney in the city calling. The phone would ring off the hook... five or six employees at any given time. But that was quite a few years ago. Right before he died, it was just me and him. Times changed."

"But you're good at what you do," Nancy said. "Everyone knows that."

I laughed. "Who's everyone? You? Cousin Raymond? There are some big private investigator firms out there now. They specialize. And they have the money to advertise. They're running full page ads in the Yellow Pages."

"I think you're afraid to toot your own horn," she said, then smiled. "Hey, maybe that could be a line in an ad: *Jake Horn, so good he doesn't have to toot his own horn.*"

I laughed.

"I'm serious," she said. "I'm kidding about the line, I mean, but maybe if you advertise, or—"

"It all costs money, Nance." The truth was, I didn't need to get into a deeper discussion with her about what really happened with the business. Nancy didn't know how much time I'd spent, almost every hour of every day, trying to find the truth behind what happened to her mother.

"What about Nonna's money?"

Nonna was what Nancy called my grandmother; her great-grandmother. "What makes you think she had money?"

Nancy shrugged. "I don't know. She had this house, and—"

"Times were different back then," I said. "Just because you have a house doesn't mean you have a lot of money."

Nancy sat, being quiet. I knew she was thinking.

"Maybe I need to take a semester off," she said. "I can get a job. Maybe I can work with you? Help you get the business moving again?"

"You're going to help get the business going?" I laughed. "Besides, if I can't afford to pay *me*, where do you think I'd get the money to pay *you*?" I reached out and put my hand on top of hers. "How about you just worry about school. Everything else'll work out."

Although I wasn't sure I believed it.

I reached for the sports section from the newspaper in front of her, hoping I could send the discussion in a different direction. Bruins center, Peter McNab, was on the front page, celebrating after scoring another goal. "Bruins beat the Blackhawks, seven nothing," I said. "This is the year they win the Cup."

Nancy looked up from her cereal but didn't respond. The look on her face told me her wheels were turning.

I flipped the sports page. Red Sox were a couple of weeks from opening day. There wasn't much football news, not in March, but Will McDonough's column caught my eye, with his inside scoop about the Patriots. According to what I read, Lawrence Martin was supposed to be in town with his agent to meet with the Patriots. It was reported he was staying at Copley Plaza in Boston.

Nancy said, "If you find whoever killed Michael Dempsey, and solve the crime, don't you think it would help the business?"

I looked up from the paper but didn't answer her.

She said, "And are you *really* going to just turn your back on Lily? I know you hate her, but..."

"Who said I hated her?"

Nancy rolled her eyes. "Well, okay, maybe hate's a strong word. But only *you* would help someone you couldn't care less about."

"I certainly don't want to see anything bad happen to her," I said. And I meant it.

"Then how can you say you're not going to do anything?"

I thought for a moment. "All I said was that it was time for me to let the police do their job. I have to trust they can get it right this time."

Nancy held her gaze on me. She knew what I meant, and why trusting them—the Boston Police—was just about impossible for me.

I closed over the sports section and pushed it aside. "What time did you say Corey was coming to pick you up this morning?"

She leaned back in her chair. Her eyes were somewhat narrowed as she stared back at me. "Don't treat me like that," she said.

"Treat you like *what*? All I asked was what time Corey was coming to get you. Didn't he say you were—"

"You're blowing me off. Trying to change the subject."

I couldn't help but smile, although only slightly. Once again, she reminded me of her mother. Accepting an answer other than the one she wanted was never an option. "Come on, Nance. There's a lot involved here. I know it all seems like it should be easy, like I can just figure it all out. But I don't have all the answers."

"I didn't say you did," she said, her eyes right on mine.

I got up and topped off my cup with coffee. I looked at my watch. "Will you at least answer my question?" I said. "What time are you going back to school?"

Nancy got up and walked to the sink, then washed out her bowl without answering.

"Nance?" I said, placing the carafe back on the coffee maker. "Did you hear me?"

She dried her bowl with the dishrag and placed it on the rack by the sink. "I thought maybe I could stay here for the rest of the week?"

"*What?* You mean, and not go to school? *Don't you have classes?*"

She shrugged. "I thought maybe you could use some help. Around here." She looked around the kitchen. "Didn't you notice I cleaned the kitchen this morning?"

"I did," I said, nodding. "Thank you for that. And believe me, I love having you around. But, I'm sorry. No. School is more important."

"I won't fall behind, if that's what you're worried about. I just thought, for a few days. It's not a big deal."

I sipped my coffee and looked out the window, facing the street in front of the house. "I'd like you to go back to school."

Up until that point I had decided before I got out of bed I'd underplay the danger I could be in. Of course, Nancy was smart enough to know what happened the night before could likely happen again, whether I backed away from the whole investigation or not. I was already involved, and there may not have been any turning back. And I couldn't risk it. She'd be better off, and safer, up in New Hampshire.

"I just think you're better off at school right now."

But Nancy was thickheaded, ever since the day she was born. Barbara used to say she inherited it from me.

Nancy said, "My grades are good. I'm not going to fall behind. My professors will—"

"Jesus Christ, Nancy!" I lost it. "I want you up at school. *End of discussion!*"

Nancy looked away, her eyes on the window over the sink.

"I'm sorry," I said, wishing I hadn't lost my cool. "There's just a lot going on here."

She had tears in her eyes. "Are you lying to me about not being involved anymore? Just so I'd go back to school and not worry about you?"

"No. Not exactly. I want to walk away from it, for more reasons than one. But I'm not sure I can. The truth is, until I'm sure everything is safe around here, I'm afraid you're better off up at school." I swallowed hard. "I'm sorry," I said.

"I'm sorry too," she said. "Because if you really want me to leave, I'm going to need a ride back. I called Corey at his friend's this morning, told him he could go back without me."

***

Nancy and I went out for a run, down and around the trail at Popes Pond. It had been a few days for me, and I could already feel it in my knees.

"So..." I said, trying to speak as though my lungs were holding up. "This guy, Corey," I said. "What's the story? Are you just afraid to tell me he's more than just a friend? Because he seems like a nice kid. You're old enough, if you—"

"You don't think I'd tell you if he was?" She laughed.

I looked straight ahead without saying another word, running another hundred yards or so until we stopped and looked toward the pond, catching our breath. I leaned over with my hands on my knees, trying to slow my breathing.

I straightened up and stretched my arms up over my head. "Is that a girlfriend he went to see in Boston?"

Nancy made a face. "A girlfriend? Why?"

I hesitated. "Well, I... I actually overheard him on the phone talking to someone and—"

"You were eavesdropping?" She had her hands on her hips, and I thought maybe she was half joking, but I wasn't sure.

"I just happened to hear him," I said. "And, well, whoever he was talking to... I heard him say 'I love you,' and I just thought, I don't want you to get caught up in something like that."

She looked at me, huffed out a laugh, and picked up her pace, running ahead of me.

"Wait up," I said, having to push myself to keep up with her young legs.

She stopped at the end of the path at LaFayette Street and waited for me. She looked somewhat annoyed. "Corey and I are just friends. I don't know who he said 'I love you' to, but it's none of my business. It's certainly none of yours." She shrugged. "How do you know if the call wasn't just with his mom? Or his dad? I tell you I love you, don't I?"

My breathing was labored again. And I felt like a jerk. "Yeah, I'm sorry about that. I shouldn't have been listening."

"Men and women can be friends, you know," she said. "Sorry if you're out of touch with the times. She laughed and started running along LaFayette."

But I caught up to her. "Well, if it ever turns into something," I said. "I'd approve. He's a nice kid."

She stopped and looked at me with her mother's crooked smile. "I'll let him know you said that."

***

Maggie was outside on the front steps in front of the door when Nancy and I got back from our run, her hands in her pockets. "I was wondering why you didn't answer," she said. She nodded toward my car. "I saw your car and…" Her gaze went to Nancy.

I reached past her and unlocked the door, letting the two in ahead of me. Maggie took off her coat and hung it up on the rack near the door and said to Nancy, "I thought you were going back to school this morning?"

"I'm going to stay another day. As long as Dad'll give me a ride back."

"I'm not sure we've agreed you were staying," I said.

Nancy glanced at Maggie. "He doesn't want me around."

Maggie smiled, giving me a quick look. "I know that's not true at all."

Nancy started for the stairs. "I'm going up to take shower."

I watched her jog up the stairs. "We'll talk about it when you're done." I went into the kitchen for a drink of water, standing over the sink as I guzzled every drop in the glass. I was still a little short of breath from the run, but it felt good.

Maggie stood in the doorway, and I could hear the water running through the pipes from upstairs. "You want some tea?" I said.

She didn't answer. "She's just worried about you," she said.

I tore off a piece of paper towel and wiped the sweat from my face. "I know. But I'm worried about her too." I knew Nancy was about to get in the shower but kept my voice low. "I don't know how safe it is here right now. She's better off at school."

Maggie stepped toward the table and leaned with both hands on the back of the chair. "She's such a smart kid. She's got so much of Barbara in her."

"You mean she's lucky she didn't get my brain?"

Maggie laughed. "You know that's not what I meant. She got a lot of you in her too. She's stubborn. And she cares about people."

I leaned with my back against the sink, looking toward the floor. "She sat here with us last night and probably heard more than I wanted her to. I never used to let her know anything about... I wanted to keep her away from it all."

"She's not a kid anymore," Maggie said. "She can handle anything."

"This morning I told her I was going to leave everything up to you guys... to the police."

"So you lied?"

I shrugged, looking across the kitchen at her. "I don't want her to worry."

Maggie stepped toward me and leaned back against the counter next to me. Her elbow brushed my arm. "You need to keep yourself safe, Jake. If not for you... for Nancy."

"Now you sound like..." I stopped, shaking my head. "Nothing's going to happen to me."

"Nothing? A man broke into your house and could have killed you. If Raymond didn't show up, you don't know *what* would've happened."

Maggie looked down toward the floor. "I actually came over here this morning because I got wind Moriarty's trying to get a warrant for Lily's arrest."

"*What?*" I said. "With what evidence? The judge isn't going to—"

"He has no power without one, Jake. At least now they can bring her in once they find her. It's just procedural, and now he can—"

"But what if she hasn't disappeared by choice? Why not put out a missing person? I just don't see what the hell a warrant's going to do." I walked across the floor and into the other room.

Maggie grabbed the tea kettle from the stove and took it to the sink, filling it with water. She placed it on the stove. "Can't you think of anywhere she would have gone?"

I shrugged, shaking my head. "Connecticut? New York? She could be anywhere at this point. And that's assuming she's not in some kind of trouble."

The water had stopped running through the pipes, although the quiet in the kitchen was replaced by the tea kettle starting to hiss.

"Let's just keep things quiet around Nancy. It's the only way I can get her back to school without worrying about me."

I'd pulled three mugs down from the cabinet when Nancy let out a bloodcurdling scream from upstairs. I dropped the mugs on the counter, one smashing on the floor, and ran through the doorway and up the stairs with half the steps it normally took. "Nancy!" I yelled, running down the hall toward our bedrooms.

She was crying hysterically, running toward me with a towel wrapped around her.

I put my hands on her arms and looked her in the eye. "Nancy! What is it? What happened?"

She seemed unable to speak, pointing toward my open bedroom door.

Maggie was right behind me and took Nancy into her arms.

I hurried into my bedroom and stopped, staring at my bedspread, turned down with the white sheets exposed.

On top, covered in blood, was an animal's severed head.

"Maggie?" I said, my voice raised while trying to remain calm.

She stepped into the room, had her gun drawn. "Oh my God," she said, closing her eyes and looking away. "What is it?" She eased her gun down by her side.

I stepped closer for a better look, glancing toward Nancy standing in the doorway. "A pig's head."

CHAPTER 22

MAGGIE WAS IN THE kitchen with a Milton police officer, Raymond out in the driveway talking with two Massachusetts state troopers I'd recognized but didn't know their names. There were a handful of cops upstairs and two or three in the areas around the house.

I stood by Nancy, seated on the couch with Mrs. Gallow, an older neighbor who had lived in the house next door for at least fifty years. She came over right away and asked if everything was all right soon after seeing the police arrive.

Another Milton officer came down the stairs holding a large black plastic bag. "I assume you don't own any pigs?" he said.

I followed him toward the door, stepping ahead to open it for him. The smell of exhaust seemed to fill the air outside, with well over a dozen vehicles, including a fire truck, a rescue, four Milton police cruisers, beacon lights on top flashing, and three state police vehicles—lights on also—all parked in the driveway and along the street.

The whole scene was like a repeat of a day earlier outside Nora Hayden's house. Except, luckily, there wasn't a dead woman involved.

I didn't even want to call the cops in the first place. But I was overruled. Both Maggie and Nancy insisted. And since Maggie picked up the phone and made the call herself, as an officer, we ended up with a much larger presence than one might expect.

Especially for a dead pig.

A group of neighbors, mostly older women, stood together in one of the driveways. I gave a quick wave but didn't dare approach them. Most were widowed and liked to chat. Answering all their questions would guarantee to take the rest of the morning.

I went back into the house, and Nancy, still seated on the couch with Mrs. Gallow, gave me a worried look. "Are you doing okay?" I said, walking toward them.

Nancy nodded, but I knew she was shaken.

Mrs. Gallow knew me as a kid, and as a teenager, and watched Nancy grow up in the same house. She looked up at me with a small grin. "Can I do anything to help, Jake?"

Before I could answer, Maggie called for me from the kitchen, waving me over.

I gave Nancy's shoulder a squeeze. "Give me a minute."

I walked into the kitchen, and Maggie introduced me to Officer Danny Green.

He sipped his coffee from the pot I'd made, then put the cup down on the counter. "I was just telling Maggie we're going to keep a car outside for the night, keep a watch on things. I assume you're okay with that?"

"I'm not sure it's necessary," I said. "I can't imagine whatever psycho did this'll come back tonight."

"You don't know that," Maggie said. She looked out toward Nancy on the couch with Mrs. Gallow. "I think it would at least make Nancy feel a little better. She'll know you're both safe."

After a brief pause, I nodded and rubbed the stubble on my cheek.

Officer Green shifted his stance. "I understand you didn't want to file a report, but if there's anything you want to tell me about the intruder you had here last night…"

I glanced at Maggie. She knew I'd hoped not to get the local cops involved any more than they had to be. But apparently it was too late.

Maggie looked back at me. "I'm sorry, Jake. I just thought it was something he should know."

I looked at them both. "The problem is, nobody *knows* the whole story. Nobody even knows part of the story. You've got Nora Hayden, which gets Quincy Police involved. A pig's head in my bed brings the Milton Police into it." I looked out the window where Raymond was still chatting with the two state cops. I said to Maggie, "Did you talk to Moriarty?"

"I'm going to call him," Maggie said. "When he finds out I was here and didn't call him…"

"Yeah, I get it."

The biggest regret I had right then was ignoring my initial instincts when Lily had first called me at my office. I should've hung up, like I wanted to. Although I knew myself better. I would've been sucked back into her problems one way or the other.

Danny said, "What was that you mentioned about Quincy?"

Before I answered, Maggie spoke up. "Nora Hayden was a woman shot and killed in her home yesterday. And Jake just happened to be on the phone with her when it happened."

The officer appeared confused. "You heard her get shot?"

"I heard her scream... the gunshots." I looked at the phone. "Standing right there, only spoke to her for a minute, called Quincy PD right away, went over to her house, but it was too late."

"And how do you know this woman?" Danny said.

"I'm sorry, but I'm not sure we have to get into this right now? Maybe Maggie will put you in touch with Detective Moriarty. He knows all about it."

Danny gave me a nod, like he understood, and started for the door. He stopped in the doorway and looked back. "We'll have an officer out there tonight, at least through the morning." He continued out the front door.

Raymond walked past him on his way into the house, went straight for the coffee maker and poured himself a cup. He leaned back against the counter and stood quiet for a moment. "I was just thinking," he said, his voice low. "Maybe Nancy can stay at our house tonight?"

Maggie looked at me, like she was waiting for my answer. "It's not a bad idea, Jake. Or she could always stay with me?"

"You both know her better than that," I said. "She's going to want to stay here."

Nancy stuck her head in the kitchen. "I'm going to walk Mrs. Gallow home," she said.

I stepped out from the kitchen, and Mrs. Gallow had already put her long wool coat on and pulled a hat down over her head. "I hope you catch the sicko who did this." She pulled on the doorknob and looked back at me. "I don't know what this world is coming to."

Maggie stepped from the kitchen and grabbed her coat from the rack. "I'll walk with you." She went out behind Nancy and Mrs. Gallow.

Raymond and I went back into the kitchen and sat at the table. "You want a beer?" I said.

He held up the cup of coffee. "Nah, this is good for now. I had a couple of beers earlier, was actually asleep on the couch when Maggie called." He sipped his coffee and placed the cup down. "So what do we do from here?"

"*We?*"

Raymond nodded. "Yeah, we. You think you're going to get through this on your own?" He said, "I know you don't trust cops, but maybe you're not too stubborn to be able to turn to a retired one." He put up his hands. "I'm just saying, if you need a hand, whatever it is, I hope you know I'm here for you. All right?"

"I appreciate it," I said. I leaned forward on the table. "Can't you see these police departments all tripping over each other? Trying to pull this together? It's a lot of red tape."

Raymond shrugged. "So what're you thinking?"

I looked out the window into the street. The last of the police vehicles pulled away from the curb in front of the house. "Who the hell would put a goddamn bloody pig's head in my bed?"

"Someone who watched *The Godfather* one too many times," Raymond said.

I was sure he was kidding. "Wasn't that a horse head?"

"Yeah, it was. But I'm just saying..."

Raymond stood up from the table, went over, and poured himself more coffee. "If you were a cop, it would make more sense."

"Because it's a pig?" I said.

Raymond sipped his coffee, watching me. "But you're not a cop."

I thought about it and got up from the table, standing in front of the window, looking out. "What if it's some kind of threat toward someone I'm close to? Like you? Or Maggie?"

"I guess it's possible," he said. "But it's kind of a wild guess. It's just as possible it's just a simple threat." He scratched his head. "No note or anything, huh?"

I was still staring outside. The grass was starting to show on the lawn, although there was still plenty of snow, especially the piles, that needed to melt. It couldn't happen soon enough.

"I wonder if a guy like Gautieri would be into this kind of theatrics," I said.

"All he asked was that you leave his daughter alone, right? And you haven't been down there since, so..."

"Maybe I should take a ride down, talk to him again."

Raymond said, "I think that'd be a mistake, Jake. He's the mayor for Christ's sake. You're going to go down to Providence, start pointing fingers? You do that, a pig's head in your bed would be the least of your worries."

We were both quiet for a couple of moments.

Raymond said, "Did you know that was a real horse head?"

"Huh?"

"In the movie. *The Godfather*. It was from a horse ready for slaughter at a dog food plant in New Jersey."

"Are you serious?" I said, feeling a little sick to my stomach just thinking about it. "I mean, it looked real on the screen, but..."

"I'm just telling you what I read," Raymond said.

I shrugged, walked from the kitchen and out the front door. Standing on the top step, I looked through the shrubs toward Mrs. Gallow's house. It was a two-story home made of brick, about the same size as my grandmother's but had a two-car garage to go with it. My grandmother's house only had one.

Raymond stepped out behind me.

"I've got to take a ride into Boston," I said.

"You want me to go with you?"

"No. Not now. I've got to make a few stops, go by the office... maybe run by Copley Plaza."

"Copley?"

"I saw it in the *Globe*, earlier, that Lawrence Martin was staying there today and tomorrow." I looked at my watch. "Maybe I can catch him."

"You really think he'd be hanging around the hotel in the middle of the afternoon?" Raymond said.

"I don't know. But like I said, I have to go by the office. I'll take a ride over."

"And tell me again why you want to talk to him? You think he has something to do with Dempsey's murder?"

"I don't know. He's got a solid alibi. But I still want to talk to him, see what he wants to tell me about Angela and Michael."

Raymond walked down the steps. "Weren't we just talking about the possibility Gautieri could've had something to do with that pig's head? And now you want to go talk to his daughter's ex-fiancé?"

"That's what made me think maybe I should. It's worth a shot."

I stepped out from the roof's shadow and onto the walkway. Even without my coat, the sun felt warmer than it had since the early fall.

"And you're sure you don't want me to go?" Raymond said.

I nodded toward the street as Maggie and Nancy walked from Mrs. Gallow's house and up the walkway. "If, like you said earlier, maybe you can take Nancy back to your house?" I tried to force a smile as the two walked up the driveway. "Everything all right with Mrs. Gallow?" I said. "She must be happy we're living here. Neighborhood's already falling apart now that I'm around."

Nancy cracked a slight smile. "She loves you," she said. "She was just telling us how many times you shoveled her walkway this winter." She walked toward me, and I opened my arms, wrapping her up in a hug.

I said, "I'm sorry this happened." I held her at arm's length so I could look her in the eye. "Listen, you don't have to go back to school. We'll talk about that later. But for tonight, I want you to stay with Maggie or Raymond. They both offered, so you can—"

"No, Dad," she said, on the verge of crying. "I want to stay here with you. I'm not afraid of anything."

"I just want you to be safe," I said. "All right? I'm just not sure this is a safe place to be right now. Not until we figure out who's responsible for what's happened."

"Then what about *you*? You're just going to stay here *alone*?"

I looked out at the quiet and empty street. "I'm fine," I said. "Nothing's going to happen to me."

"Then why can't I just stay here with you?"

Raymond stood behind me, next to Maggie. "Come on, Nance. You come home with me. Aunt Beth will be excited to hear you'll be sleeping over. She loves having you around. We all do."

Nancy looked at me, then glanced at Maggie as if looking for a perfect answer none of us had.

Maggie smiled at her. "You can stay with me next time you come home from school."

Nancy walked up the steps and stopped in front of the door. "I don't want to go back to college tomorrow either." She had tears in her eyes. "I can't. I won't be able to focus on *anything*." She looked down at the brick steps. "I don't know how I'm supposed to be two hours away, wondering if I'm going to lose you too."

Chapter 23

I saw the sign up ahead for the Morrissey Motel, turning down Conley Street and into Freeman's. I parked around on the side of the building and stepped out, looking over at the motel where only a couple of cars were parked in front of it.

I walked into a quiet Freeman's, not nearly as full as the first time I was there with the TV's volume up. I looked along the bar, recognizing a couple of the older men glancing at me but looking away once I made eye contact. The clown who jumped me outside wasn't there. At least not at the bar.

There was nobody behind the bar at first, until the kitchen door swung open. Sean walked out carrying a couple of plates in one hand, a bowl in the other. He walked from behind the bar and over to one of the tables where a man and woman, both older with white hair, sat quietly waiting for their lunch. Sean placed the food down between them and stepped back behind the bar, poured a beer from the tap, and grabbed a large bottle of wine from the cooler. He went back over to the couple's table, put down the beer and filled the woman's empty glass with white wine.

He didn't appear to have noticed me, until he stepped behind the bar again and walked my way, sticking an unlit cigarette in his mouth. He stopped in front of me, taking a lighter from his pocket as he lit up his smoke. "I'm surprised to see you back here," he said. "I'm real sorry about what happened the other day. By the time I realized what was going on..."

"You fired the gun?"

He looked toward the kitchen, shaking his head. "Bruce did. The cook. He shot it up in the air to scare him off before things got out of control."

"Out of control? Why the hell'd the guy come after me?"

Sean shrugged. "I've known him a long time, but he spent three years in Vietnam. Was a good guy before then too. It's just... it really screwed him up. Now, he has one too many beers, all he wants to do is fight someone. He doesn't care who." He gave me a nod. "You want a beer? It's on the house." He pointed with his thumb behind him, toward the kitchen. "You want some of that chowder, I'll get you a bowl. It'll be on me."

"So where is he now?" I said, catching two of the older men on the far side of the bar staring at me but turning away.

"Bruce won't let him in anymore. So you don't have to worry about nothing."

It wasn't that I was worried. But I wondered if Moriarty or anyone over there knew they had a loose cannon hanging around fifty yards from where Dempsey was murdered.

"Can of 'Gansett," I said, although I hadn't planned on having a drink. One wasn't going to kill me. I nodded. "I'll take you up on that chowder. But I don't need anyone to pay for my food."

Sean leaned down and slid the top open on the beer cooler, pulling out the can. He pulled off the top and put it down in front of me. "Glass?" he said, placing it on the bar before I answered. "What'd you say your name was again? Joe?"

I picked up the can and took a sip. It was ice cold, the way it should be. "Jake."

He reached out and shook my hand. "Like I said, I'm real sorry about everything." He walked through the swinging door into the kitchen.

I wanted to ask him the guy's name who jumped me but thought maybe it could wait. The thing was, I found it odd they let this guy hang around, putting back beers when they knew he was a ticking time bomb. Although that could be said for a lot of guys hanging in bars during the day. Especially the ones who came back from war, never the same.

***

I drove over to the motel and could see Adesh through the window, standing behind the service desk. As I stepped out of the Nova, I saw him look up, his eyes right on me. He immediately picked up the phone and had it up to his ear.

I had a funny feeling the call he was making was because of me. I continued inside, and he was still on the phone, turning from me with his voice hushed.

But even in a whisper, I managed to hear Detective Moriarty's name mentioned.

Adesh tried to get as far away from the counter as the cord would let him go. "Tell him it is Adesh Kahtri. Yes. From the Morrissey Motel."

I slapped the button on the silver bell on the counter and smiled at Adesh. "You don't have to call the detective, just because I'm here."

He kept his back to me, acting as if I wasn't there. "Yes, tell him it is important. He asked me to call him if—"

I reached over the service desk and put my finger on the switch, disconnecting the call.

Adesh kept his back to me, speaking into the phone. "Hello? Hello? Are you still there?"

I left my finger on the switch, holding it down until Adesh finally looked at me. "Ooops," I said.

His expression was a mix of fear and anger. "What do you think you're doing?"

"What do you think *you're* doing?" I said. "Did Moriarty tell you to call him if I showed up?"

Adesh still held the handset in his hand but slowly reached out and hung it up on the base. "You must go. Leave!" He picked up the phone again, like he was ready to dial. "Now, do you understand why I didn't want to tell you how to find Nora? Look what you've done!" He looked like he was going to cry.

I got the feeling there was something more to his relationship with Nora. At least, based on his reaction, she didn't appear to be a mere employee he no longer needed.

I looked past him on the wall where a handful of small, framed photos were hung. I recognized Adesh in each of them, posing with maybe friends or family, smiling for the camera. They all appeared to be taken right outside in front of the motel.

Adesh looked over his shoulder at the wall behind him. "What do you want?"

I nodded toward one of the photos. "Is that Nora?"

Adesh turned to the photos. The one I was looking at was of a woman with two other women, all three wearing uniforms. He nodded, pointing to it. "This is Nora. It was taken two years ago, when I bought this motel. She had worked for me since then."

"And you couldn't give her a day shift?" I said.

He stared back at me, looking over his glasses, but didn't answer.

I looked closer at the photo. Nora was short, no taller than Adesh, who was maybe five-and-a-half feet tall. Maybe less. "Who are the other two with her?"

"They clean the rooms."

"Do they still work here?"

He paused, then nodded.

"Are they here now?" I said, hoping I could talk to one or both.

Adesh's face seemed to swell, turning a dark shade of red. He raised his voice. "I am calling Detective Moriarty if you do not leave my motel!"

I put up my hands in front of me, palms facing him. "Okay, okay. Take it easy."

He lifted the phone and started to dial, lifting the base with his free hand and stepping out of my reach. He said into the phone. "Yes, my call was just disconnected. I need to speak with Detective Moriarty, right away."

I started for the door and pushed it open. On my way out, I said, "Tell the fine detective I was asking for him."

***

The woman behind the front desk of the Copley Plaza had her eyes on me, the phone up against her ear, waiting for Lawrence Martin to answer the phone in his room. She hung up. "I'm sorry, Mr. Martin's not answering."

She flipped through the book in front of her. "Oh, actually, you know what? He's scheduled to check out today."

209

"Is it possible he's already gone?" I said. But as the words left my mouth, I looked toward the elevator across the lobby when I heard a bell ding.

A towering man stepped off the elevator into the lobby, carrying a large suitcase that looked more like a purse the way it fit into his oversized hand.

I knew it was Lawrence Martin right away as he walked toward the front desk. He had a limp in his step, with his legs bowed like an old man's. He looked at me staring back at him, maybe assuming I was nothing more than an idolizing fan.

"Excuse me, sir," he said, stepping past me with a nod. He put his suitcase on the floor next to his boat-sized feet and leaned with his hands down on the front desk. "Lawrence Martin, checking out of room four oh three."

The woman gave me a quick glance as she smiled at him. "Was everything satisfactory in your room, Mr. Martin?"

He glanced back at me, pointing with his thumb toward the woman. "Did I just cut in front of you?" He had a slight Southern accent, but far from heavy.

"No," I said. "Go right ahead."

He turned back to the woman. "The room was good." He signed the paper she slid in front of him, then looked back at me again. "I'm sorry," he said. "You're staring at me. Are you looking for an autograph, or..."

"Actually," I said, "if you have a couple of minutes once you're done checking out, I'd like to—"

"I'm sorry," he said, folding the paper over and sticking it in his inside coat pocket. "I got a cab waiting for me." He stepped past me and continued for the door.

I followed after him. "Lawrence, wait."

But he kept going, clearly believing he was trying to escape a fan, or maybe a reporter.

"Where are you heading?" I said.

He stopped and looked at me. "Where am I *heading*?" He shrugged and didn't answer, moving toward the door as the doorman opened it for him.

"It's about Angela," I said.

He stopped as we stepped out onto the sidewalk. "How do you know Angela?"

"If you tell me where you're going, I can give you a ride so we can talk."

He nodded toward the cab parked on St. James Avenue. "That's my cab."

"Where are you heading? Foxborough?"

Lawrence shook his head. "I wish you'd please just tell me what's going on, man. Is Angela all right?"

"Lawrence?" the doorman said. "Your cab is waiting for you."

The sidewalks were somewhat busy, and someone pulled open the cab door and slipped inside.

"Hey!" Lawrence said, hurrying after the cab, but it took off down St. James. I could see in his face he wasn't happy about it. "You made me miss my cab!"

"The cab drivers around here aren't very patient." I gently slapped him in the arm with the back of my hand. "Come on. I told you, I'll drive you. Wherever you have to go, it's not a problem."

The doorman just stood, watching us, as Lawrence finally gave in. "Are you sure you can give me a ride? My flight leaves in an hour."

I waved him toward me and started toward the parking garage. "Come on, I'm parked around the corner, on Berkley."

He caught up with me and walked next to me, on my left. I reached across my body to shake his hand. "Jake Horn."

"Jake Horn, huh? Are you going to tell me what this is all about? Mr. Horn?"

I nodded, looking up at him and feeling smaller than I normally would. More often than not, I'm one of the bigger men in the room. But walking next to Lawrence was a different story.

"What are you?" I said, looking up at him. "Six six?"

"Six seven," he said.

"I saw you had a meeting with the Pats. Hope it went all right?"

"Nah, I'm all done. Knees are shot. It wasn't a meeting about playing again."

"Even with bad knees," I said, "you were twice as fast as any man on that field."

He didn't care for the compliment. "I don't really want to talk about it, if that's all right."

***

I pushed the seat back as far as it would go, but Lawrence still had to duck his head to keep it from rubbing against the headliner.

He glanced at me from the passenger seat. "I'd appreciate it if you'd tell me what this is all about? You sure Angela's all right?"

I took Stuart Street, nodding. "Well, I guess the first thing you should know is I'm a private investigator."

"Private investigator, huh?" Lawrence said. "This have something to do with Michael Dempsey?"

"So you know him?"

Lawrence nodded. "Yeah, I know him. And I had nothing to do with what happened, if that's what you're about to ask. Same thing I told the police."

"When did you talk to them?" I said. "Was it Detective Moriarty?"

"He showed up at the hotel. Said the same thing as you, saw my name in the paper. There's no privacy anymore. Not in this town, the way these reporters follow the athletes. Everything you do ends up in the paper."

"Were you around here, when Michael Dempsey was killed?" I said.

"Like I told the detective, I was in Florida." He looked out the passenger window.

"Angela said she hadn't heard from you," I said. "Does she know you're in town right now?"

He shook his head. "Nah, I wasn't in the mood for it. It's over between us, you know what I mean? That girl'll never leave Rhode Island. And, you know, I don't know how you people handle these winters. It's for the birds."

"Well, most of them fly south," I said.

"That's me. I'm a Florida man. Besides, once I got hurt, everything between me and Angela changed."

I took the ramp for the Mass Pike. "Changed? In what way?"

He didn't answer right away. "Well, I'll be honest, she got real mean. I'd never seen her act that way before. I mean, she was always condescending. It was like, when I told her I was done with football, she treated me different. Like I was nobody anymore."

"Are you serious?"

He nodded. "The thing is, I was kind of relieved when we broke it off."

I thought for a moment. "So, you didn't break off the engagement because you thought she was cheating on you?"

Lawrence looked at me, somewhat of a confused look on his face, shaking his head. "Who told you she was *cheating* on me?"

I followed the sign for Logan Airport and gave Lawrence a quick look as we approached the sign for Departures.

"Have you ever discussed anything with Angela about Michael Dempsey? They seemed to've had a relationship."

"But I don't believe she was cheating on me. I mean, I'm not really the type to get jealous like that. Especially if it's someone like him."

I pulled up in front of the doors for American Airlines. "What's that mean, 'someone like *him*?"

"Well, I don't know much about him. But it sounded to me he wasn't the most likable man."

I put the Nova in park. "But Angela liked him, didn't she?"

Lawrence shrugged. "I guess. As far as I knew, it was just business. I know for a fact her father didn't like him. Mr. Gautieri said he was a liar, and—"

"He said *who* was a liar? Michael Dempsey?"

"Yeah. I mean, I don't know the context or anything. But I remember, it's probably the only time I'd heard Michael Dempsey's name mentioned. Angela and I were at Mr. Gautieri's place, in Providence... Did you know he lives in a hotel?"

"Yes. But what exactly did you hear?"

"Oh yeah, well, Angela's father was in the other room. You could hear him yelling on the phone. And when he came out, he said something about Michael Dempsey, and that he was a liar. He was pretty upset. I didn't ask any questions."

"But you don't know who he was on the phone with? Or who he was yelling at?"

Lawrence said, "No, sir. I know there are rumors about her father being connected to the Mafia and all that, but I'm not sure it's true. Angela said it's just rumors, because they're Italian. The truth is, he treated me all right."

"You got along?"

Lawrence nodded. "Yeah, I'd say so."

"Sounded to me like Angela misses you," I said. "She seemed nice enough."

"She *is* nice," Lawrence said. "But she's got something inside her. She's a lot like her dad, you know? Real nice, but the littlest thing sets them off." He looked at his watch and stepped out from the car, reaching into the back seat for his suitcase. "Thank you for the ride, but I'm gonna have to hurry so I don't miss my flight."

CHAPTER 24

NANCY STOOD LOOKING OUT at me through the glass on the storm door, holding Raymond and Beth's fat orange cat, Max, in her arms. He jumped down when she opened the door and wrapped her arms around me, her voice cracking. "I was worried," she said, holding the door as I stepped into the house.

Beth walked out from the kitchen. "I wish I knew what time you'd show up," she said. "We just finished dinner."

The chowder from Freeman's was still sitting in the bottom of my stomach.

Beth walked back into the kitchen and opened the refrigerator and looked inside. "I made mac and cheese, if you want me to heat some up?"

Nancy gave me a look with a slight shake of her head.

I knew what she was telling me: Beth was good at a lot of things, but cooking wasn't one of them. It didn't even matter if dinner came in a box. *Stay away from the mac and cheese.*

"I'm not hungry," I said. "Raymond's not here?"

"He's upstairs," Beth said. "I think he's on the phone with Maggie. She just called when you pulled in."

I started for the stairs, and Nancy grabbed my arm. Her voice low, she said, "Did you find anything?"

"No. But I'm hoping Maggie did." I took three steps toward the stairs and looked back, expecting Nancy to follow. But she'd gone into the kitchen.

Raymond was in the spare bedroom he used as office ever since he retired. But I'm not sure what he did there, other than watch sports on the thirteen-inch he had up on the shelf. He just happened to have a leather recliner in the corner.

He was at the desk, his back to the doorway. With the phone up against his ear, he swiveled in the chair to face me. Into the phone, he said, "Here he is right now. Just walked in." He held the phone out toward me. "It's Maggie."

I took it from his hand and could see by the look on his face something wasn't good. "Hello?" There was noise, the sound of traffic, in the background.

"Detective Moriarty's looking for you," she said.

"Where are you?"

"At a pay phone."

"What's he want?"

"Apparently, the owner of the Morrissey Motel called him, said you were harassing him."

"I was there when he dialed the phone. But I certainly wasn't harassing him. Give me a break. For some reason, Moriarty's put it in the guy's head *I'm* the bad guy. The way he was acting, I swear he thinks I killed Nora Hayden."

"I can't imagine that's what Jeffrey told him," she said.

"Oh, I wouldn't be surprised," I said. "He'd love to get me out of the way, so he can go after Lily."

The line went quiet. "That's actually why I called, looking for you," Maggie said. "I hate to say it, but you're right about Lily. I don't know what it is, but he's trying to build the case against her."

"With what evidence? I still say he has nothing. So it just doesn't make sense." I said, "What about Angela Gautieri? Why isn't he even looking at her?"

"For one," Maggie said, "Angela's been cleared. And she didn't run away, like Lily has."

"But nobody knows for sure Lily disappeared on her own, or if—"

"Jake, Commissioner Kelly was contacted by Gautieri's attorneys who claim if they bother Angela, they'll bring lawsuits."

"Can they do that?" I said. "It's a murder investigation. I didn't know a suspect could get attorneys to force the cops off."

Maggie paused on the other end. "You know how things work around here."

Raymond sat in the chair in front of his desk, watching me.

I said, "I bet Tony Gautieri just wants to keep his name out of this. Maybe for political reasons."

Raymond got up from the chair and gestured for me to sit down. But I didn't.

Nancy showed up in the doorway, a look on her face like she wasn't sure she should be there.

"You can come in," Raymond said, pointing toward the yellow leather love seat pushed under the window. "Have a seat, Nance."

She sat down on the edge of the love seat.

"I gotta go," Maggie said.

"Okay. Hey, before you hang up, have you heard anything from Officer Green? Or anyone else at the Milton PD?"

"No. But I don't know if I have another dime to call him."

"Well, I haven't been home, so I'm not sure if anyone's called," I said. "I'd be curious to hear if they've gotten anywhere."

She was quiet for a moment, reaching into her pocket. "I found another dime. Let me see if I can get him on the phone. I'll call you right back."

I hung up the phone and sat on the couch next to Nancy.

When she was younger, I never discussed a case or anything that had to do with one of my investigations around her. Although she always had a way of knowing what was going on. She'd always have questions, and I knew she was at the age where there was no sense trying to keep it all from her.

I looked over at Raymond. "What'd she tell you?"

"Maggie?" he said. "That Moriarty won't take his eyes off Lily." He picked up a pen from the desk and twisted it between his fingers. "He must have something on her. And he's keeping it quiet, there's no doubt about that. But she said he has a warrant already. So he had to've shared something with the judge to get it."

"Depends who the judge was," I said. "You know as well as I do, plenty of judges in Boston need nothing more than their palm greased."

Nancy shot me a look. "What if he's right?"

"What if who's right?" I said.

"The detective. What if he really does know something you don't know. Maggie said he won't even tell her anything."

I shrugged. "I'm not sure what to think right now," I said.

The phone on the desk rang so loud, we all jumped.

Raymond grabbed it off the hook before it rang twice. "Hello?" He nodded. "Yeah, hang on." He stretched his arm toward me with the phone, ducking away from the cord running across the back of his neck. "It's Maggie."

"That was fast," I said, taking the phone.

"Jake, listen... I spoke to Danny. They found a headless pig down in Rhode Island, off Route Six out in a town called Foster. Danny said it's almost on the Connecticut border. Farmer out there not far from where they found it claims it's one of his."

"No shit," I said. "Moriarty know?"

"Not yet," she said. "He hasn't been in the office all day."

"Is he going out there?"

"Danny? No, I don't think so. Said it'd already been cleaned up. Farmer picked up the carcass, probably going to see if he can still sell the meat."

"That's disgusting," I said. "Who'd he say found it?"

"The Foster Police. It's a small department, only two officers running a shift at a time."

I thought for a moment. "Quite a coincidence the pig happens to be from Rhode Island?"

"You mean, because of Gautieri?"

"Yeah, is that what you were thinking?" I said.

Maggie was quiet. "I don't know what to think, Jake. I really don't. It's going to be hard for me to get involved," she said. "I hope you understand."

"Yeah, I get that. But I'm just saying. Think about it. Who would drive all the way down to Rhode Island for a pig's head from up here. I would think, whoever it was, was coming from Rhode Island. Tell me if I'm wrong, but—"

"I agree. But if you think you're going to somehow try and pin this on Gautieri, as the mayor of Providence, just because he lives there, I just don't see it. I mean, it's certainly plausible, but..." Maggie was quiet. "Jake, I'm sorry but I gotta run. I'll call you after my shift."

I got up from the couch and handed Raymond the phone to hang up.

"They found the pig?" he said.

I nodded. "You ever hear of Foster, Rhode Island?"

"It's all woods, out in the middle of nowhere, isn't it? Long way to go to put a pig in someone's bed in Milton."

Nancy stood up from the couch. "How could somebody do that to a pig? For what? Just to scare you?"

Raymond and I both looked at each other, but neither of us had the answer.

Nancy looked out the window, and I stepped behind her, resting my hand on her shoulder. "I know you don't want to hear this," I said. "But I think you're better off back at school."

She looked at the floor. "How do I know you're going to be all right?"

"You're going to have to trust me. But I'd feel better if you were back there, so I don't have to worry myself. Focus on your school-work. It'll be good for you."

She looked into my eyes. "And just pretend everything's normal? When you know it's *not*?"

***

There was a strong bleach odor in my bedroom. After trying to clean the mattress, it was inevitable I was going to need another new one.

Nancy walked into the room, sniffing the air, her bag hung over her shoulder. "Are you really going to sleep here tonight?"

"I don't think so. I give up."

The phone rang, and I stepped around to the other side of the bed to pick up the receiver. "Hello?"

"Jake?"

I was surprised, almost shocked, to hear the voice on the other end.

It was Lily.

"Where are you?" I glanced at Nancy, watching me. "The police are looking for you. They have a warrant out for your arrest."

"I know," she said.

"If you know, then why are you hiding? Why didn't you listen to me from the beginning? I told you how this was going to go. This has gone down just like I warned you; they're going to—"

"Jake, will you just shut up for a minute and listen to me?"

I grabbed the base of the phone and walked with it to the window.

"I haven't been honest with you."

"You think you're telling me something I don't know?" I said. "You've got to stop this. You can't keep hiding from the cops."

"That's not who I'm hiding from," she said.

I stood with the phone against my ear, quiet for a moment. I didn't trust Lily. But I knew she wasn't dumb. "Who are you hiding from?"

She was silent, at first. "I... I can't tell you. Not on the phone."

I stared out the window, into the darkness outside. I glanced at Nancy, still standing in the doorway.

"Dad? What is it?" Nancy said. "Is something wrong?"

"Who is that?" Lily said. "You're not alone?"

"It's Nancy," I said. "She's worried about you. We all are."

The line went quiet again.

Lilly said, "I find that hard to believe."

"Well, believe what you want. But you have to tell me what's going on, Lily. Or I can't help you. No more lies, or else you're on your own."

She didn't respond.

"Lily, tell me what Michael was involved in. Was it Angela? Did it have something to do with her father?"

"I can't answer that," Lily said.

"You can't answer? Are you kidding me? Or is it that you don't *want* to answer..."

The line was quiet.

"Lily? Are you there?" I thought for a moment. "Why did you really come to my office? Did you really believe Michael was cheating on you? Or was there something else to it?"

"Jake, no, listen, I—"

"What were you trying to get me to do?"

The line was quiet, and I wondered for a second if she'd hung up.

"Jake, please. I need your help. Please."

I didn't have to think about it for very long at all. "No, Lily. I'm done. The best thing you can do for all of us is go to the cops and come clean. Whatever it is you're not telling me... you have to tell them. In fact, you know what? I don't want to know what it is. Just do the right thing for once in your life."

"I don't trust them."

"You don't trust *who*?" I said.

"The police."

I took a deep breath and let out a sigh. "I don't know what to tell you, then. I really don't."

"Can you meet me?"

I looked at Nancy, being patient by the door, waiting to hear what Lily was telling me, which wasn't much.

I said to Lily, "Where have you been hiding? I assume somewhere in New England?"

"I can't tell you. But if you'll meet me in the morning..."

"Meet you where?"

"I'll call you at the house first thing."

I was quiet. I knew I had to help her. But I was also well aware it was a bad idea.

"Please, Jake. You have to just trust me."

"Trust you?" I laughed. "I'll wait for your call."

***

Nancy was quiet for most of the two-hour ride up to her school. She faced the passenger window for most of the ride along 93.

I had The Rolling Stones eight-track, *Hot Rocks*, playing on the stereo.

She reached for the console and lowered the volume. "I don't understand why you wouldn't just call the police, tell them where you're meeting her."

I gave her a quick glance, keeping my eyes on the dark highway as we crossed into New Hampshire. "She trusts that I won't."

"So what?" Nancy said. "She lies to you. That's all she's ever done. She lies. And I don't get why you'd risk your life to help her."

"Am I supposed to turn my back on her?"

I could feel Nancy's gaze. "She'd do it to you, so yeah. Kind of."

"I know you don't mean that," I said. "But I understand where you're coming from."

"Why wouldn't you at least take someone else with you? Cousin Raymond or Maggie?"

"I wish I could. But she won't meet me unless I'm alone. And Maggie's a police officer. No chance I'd let her get involved any more than she already is. In fact, I don't want either of them to know I'm meeting her."

Nancy shifted in her seat, tucking one leg up under the other, facing me. "You don't want to tell them because you know they'll tell you that you shouldn't. Just like I'm doing. But you're too stubborn to listen."

I didn't want to raise my voice, but even Nancy, who was as perfect a daughter as anyone could ask for, was more than capable of crossing the line with the way she spoke to me. "You may not agree with it. But it doesn't mean I'm wrong trying to help her."

I pulled up to her dorm and stopped in front of the glass doors. There were kids, or young adults, some bundled up in winter gear and a couple of boys in T-shirts, like it was summer. They were just hanging out on the steps of Nancy's building, watching us, waving once they saw it was Nancy being dropped off.

"See," I said. "This is where you belong. With your friends." She leaned over and gave me a hug.

"Do you need my help with anything?" I said.

Her bag was already on her lap as she pushed open the door. "No, this is good. But please, will you call me tomorrow? So I know you're all right?"

I nodded. "Don't worry about anything, okay?"

She pushed the door open and let the cold air in as she stepped out. "Love you, Dad."

CHAPTER 25

I WAS WIDE AWAKE and in the kitchen drinking coffee when the phone rang. I jumped from the table, almost knocking over my mug, and grabbed the phone off the wall on the first ring. I was pretty sure it would be Lily, and I was right.

She told me about a diner a little north of Worcester, where she wanted to meet me. She said, "I hope you don't mind the drive."

"I was expecting a two-hour drive. I'm surprised you're still in Massachusetts."

I wrote the address she gave me on a piece of paper and opened up a map on my table, holding the phone between my shoulder and ear. "The ride, I'd say, is about forty-five minutes. Are we meeting inside? Or..."

"Maybe we can get something to eat," she said. "I'm hungry."

I thought for a moment. I wasn't sure I was in the mood for having breakfast with Lily. "I'll meet you inside. Give me an hour."

We hung up, and I looked at the phone, wondering if I should take my own daughter's advice and at least let Raymond know where I was going. I felt safe enough meeting Lily, but at the same time, she didn't give me reason to trust her. But I also didn't want to put Raymond, as a retired Boston police officer, in a position where he'd be forced to withhold information the cops were after.

I thought maybe the less he knew, at least at that point, the better.

I didn't waste time getting on the road, and stopped at a Dunkin' Donuts to grab a coffee for the ride. As I pulled into the parking lot, I looked up in the rearview and noticed a gold Buick Skylark I was sure had been behind me since I left the house. But it didn't follow me into the parking lot, instead continuing with the rush-hour traffic on the road.

I parked and started toward the entrance, but the appliance shop next to the Dunkin' Donuts caught my eye. And what looked like the front end of the gold Buick appeared to be sticking out from the far side of the building. I couldn't see enough of the driver's-side door to make out the person behind the wheel.

I continued inside and wondered if Moriarty was having me followed, maybe hoping I'd lead him to Lily. It was a definite possibility I had to consider, especially if he assumed she would eventually reach out to me, as she already had.

There was, of course, a chance it was someone more dangerous, someone on the other side of the law. It would be unrealistic of me to believe whoever attacked me at the house and put the head of a dead pig in my bed likely hadn't just disappeared. It was very much a possibility that whoever it was still had their eye on me.

I ordered my coffee and got change for a dollar to use the pay phone outside. I had two calls to make. One to a college dorm, although I knew it was a little early since the pay phone in the hall would likely wake up all the girls.

But the more I thought about being followed, the more I started to worry about Nancy. I thought, at first, she was safer being away from me.

Was I wrong?

I dropped three quarters into the slot and pulled the paper from my wallet with Nancy's dorm number on it. I dialed, the phone ringing five times before one of Nancy's dorm mates answered.

The young woman's voice was quiet and raspy. She sounded like she'd sleep-walked to the phone. It was likely she had. "Hell... hello?" She cleared her throat.

"Hi, I'm sorry to call so early. This is Nancy Horn's dad. I'm sure she's asleep, but if you can get her on the phone..."

"Uh..." She paused on the other end of the phone, like her brain was still turning on. "Yeah, sure. I'll knock on her door."

The phone clanked, more than once, and I pictured the handset dangling from the cord, swinging into the wall.

Then it was quiet. I listened for the knock on Nancy's door or the sound of her voice but couldn't hear much of anything. Her room was, I believed, five doors from the phone.

A few moments went by, and the young woman picked up the phone. "Mr. Horn? Hi, I'm sorry... she's not answering her door. I'm sure she's asleep. We were all up late last night."

"Studying, I'm sure?" I said.

She let out a giggle. "Yeah, of course." She paused. "You want me to try again?"

"If you wouldn't mind. I'd just like to know she's there."

I didn't want to be overly concerned or paranoid about anything. I tried to convince myself Nancy was safe and there was no need to worry about her. But I couldn't help it. My mind had seen too much to stop itself from envisioning scenarios.

At least a minute passed, and the young woman was back on the phone. "Sorry," she said. "She's still not answering. I don't know her schedule, but it's possible she could've already left for an early class. Or, um, do you want me to tell her to call you? When I see her?"

I knew I wouldn't be home for at least a few hours. "You know what?" I said. "Don't worry about it. I'll call later; hopefully I can catch her. Thank you. And sorry again if I woke you up." I hung up and glanced at the gold Buick, without letting it seem obvious I knew someone was there, waiting for me. I held the phone up to my ear, acting as if I was still in conversation, sipping the hot coffee. I glanced over toward the appliance shop. The car hadn't moved. I still couldn't make out who was behind the wheel because of the way it was parked with the building blocking most of my view.

Was I just being paranoid? I thought of walking over to look inside the car, ask the driver right then, what his deal was. My other option was to get in my car and drive, seeing if whoever it was decided to follow me once again.

But what if it *was* a cop? I had two dimes in my pocket and dropped one in the slot. The last person I wanted to talk to, especially early in the morning, was Detective Moriarty. I dialed Boston Police and asked for Detective Moriarty.

I was put on hold, meanwhile telling myself not to slip up and mention anything Maggie told me that I wasn't supposed to know.

The phone clicked on the other end. "Detective Moriarty."

"Detective," I said. "It's Jake Horn."

"Mr. Horn. What a surprise to hear from you on such a lovely morning."

I looked up at the gray sky. "Is it?"

"To what do I owe the honor?" he said.

I wasn't going to waste either of our time. "Any chance you have one of your guys tailing me?"

He laughed. "Why would I have someone tailing you?"

I looked over at the other parking lot. The Buick hadn't moved, and I started to wonder if maybe whoever it was actually worked at the appliance store.

"You had someone outside my office the night Lily slept on the couch. And I don't see why you'd stop watching me, assuming at some point I might lead you to her," I said.

"Sorry, Jake. If I did have someone following you, well, for one, you wouldn't know it. And, secondly, I'd probably tell you if I was."

I wasn't sure if I could believe him. But something told me he was being straight with me. "So, you're not bullshitting me? You don't have a guy driving a gold Skylark on my tail?"

Moriarty was quiet for a brief moment. "Are you certain you're being followed?"

I looked toward the other parking lot. The Buick hadn't moved. "I guess, maybe, I'm *not* sure."

"Well... I'd hate to see you get yourself in any more trouble. So if you want to give me the make and model, maybe the plate, assuming you're smart enough to've gotten it, and—"

"I don't have a plate. But I'm looking right at it."

"Then give me the plate. I'm trying to help you, but you're not making it—"

"It's parked in a different lot," I said. "I can't see the plate from where I am."

Moriarty laughed. "So let me get this straight. You called me because you think you're being followed by a car parked in another parking lot... far enough from you, you can't even get the license plate?" He laughed again, his condescending arrogance beyond what I wanted to deal with.

"Never mind," I said. "I don't need your help."

"Oh, okay. If that's how you want to go about this..." he said.

The line was quiet. And I was ready to hang up.

"Listen," he said. "I know you have these negative feelings toward law enforcement officials, like myself. But if you feel like you're in danger, I hope you're not too much of a man to turn to the men in blue. We are, after all, here to serve and protect. And I guess that includes serving and protecting someone like you."

"Are you done?" I said. "It's a gold Buick Skylark. Probably a couple years old, maybe a seventy-six model. I'll go over and get the plate and call you back."

"Why don't you tell me where you are? I'll send a car over."

I didn't want to do that. "I'm not in Boston. Not your jurisdiction."

"But you're not going to tell me where you are? Are you serious, Jake? Is that how this is going to be?"

We were both playing the same game, and I wasn't going to be the one to give in. "Maybe it's nothing," I said. "I'll let you know. But, I guess, just forget I even called."

"So, now you don't want my help?" he said.

"No." I hung up the phone without another word and got back to my car. I left the Dunkin' Donuts parking lot, heading west, and drove slowly past the appliance store.

Sure enough, the Buick pulled out a couple of cars behind me.

***

I stayed within the speed limit on 93, the Skylark still in my view for most of the ride, although hanging a good handful of cars back. I took a quick turn for the exit onto the Pike and lost sight of him somewhere in the traffic, turning off behind me. I wondered if he knew I was onto him, and perhaps dropped back enough to stay out of sight.

I was on the fence of whether or not I could try and lose him, or lead him to a place where I could at least find out who he was.

I drove another five miles. By the time I jumped onto 290, the traffic had thinned, and I spotted the Buick still following. He'd gotten closer now, and I could just about make out the face of what looked to be a middle-aged man. His hair was slicked back, from what I could tell, and he was wearing dark sunglasses even though the sun was behind the thick, gray clouds.

I pushed the pedal down and let the Nova do its thing. I don't think my grandmother ever appreciated the power it had under the hood and probably never had reason to find out. But once I came off the ramp from the Pike, I was moving at a pretty good clip. I was going to give my tail a good ride, knowing I could probably lose him if I got far enough ahead and drove toward downtown Worcester.

But the Skylark didn't fall far behind. I was doing ninety, knowing the last thing I needed was a statie pulling me over.

There was no doubt at that point, my tail had a good idea I was trying to shake him. Although I was still debating in my head if I wanted to get face-to-face with him, or do what I could to cut him loose.

If I kept going on 290, I knew I was getting too close to Lily, and turning in another direction was my best option. The problem was, Lily wasn't going to hang around if I was a no-show. Even if I was ten minutes late—I rarely was—she'd be gone. That's just how she was.

I started to look for an exit. I couldn't just wing it and hope for the best either. And I started to wonder if I'd made a mistake not allowing Moriarty to help out.

But if I wanted to know who this guy was, and who sent him, I only had one choice: confront the guy.

Dangerous? Perhaps.

The Skylark stuck with me, never falling more than a car or two behind. I cut back and forth between lanes and blew by the exit I was supposed to take for the diner, continuing north on 290.

The traffic ahead was getting thicker, with the next exit a mile ahead. Looking in the rearview, I saw the Skylark had fallen two cars behind. I cut into the left lane to pass a couple of slow-moving vehicles, then slammed down the pedal, trying to jump into the right lane in front of an eighteen-wheeler. But I had overcompensated when I cut the wheel, skidding across and into the breakdown lane. I nearly hit the barrier to my right, jerking the wheel back, but I couldn't get back into the lane. So I slammed down the gas and stayed in the breakdown until I hit the next exit. I was moving at a high speed as I hit the exit's sharp curve, tires squealing when I straightened the wheel and saw a red light straight ahead. But I was going too fast. I took a quick glance in the rearview and saw the Skylark coming up behind me.

I had no choice but to go right through the light.

Tires screeched, and horns blew as I made it across the intersection. I looked in the rearview, and the Skylark had been stopped in the middle of the intersection.

I slammed down the pedal again and cut the wheel, turning into an industrial park with large brick buildings and warehouses and tractor-trailer trucks coming and going in all directions. Stuck behind an eighteen-wheeler, I tried to pass it on the left. But another truck was coming toward me, and I jerked the wheel back. Looking in the rearview mirror, the gold Skylark was right behind me. I got a better look at the driver than I had at any other point.

I yanked the steering wheel to the right and drove into the entrance to one of the warehouses, going as fast as I could along the side of the building. The Nova's engine screamed until I came to a road where a sign read DO NOT ENTER.

I ignored it and kept driving, turning a corner and heading straight toward a tractor trailer moving at a pretty good clip in my direction.

I threw my foot on the brake pedal, and the Skylark rammed into me from behind, sending me and the Nova forward, my head whipping back against the headrest before my face slapped against the steering wheel.

I felt the drips coming down my chin, the taste of my own blood in my mouth. I jumped out of the car and charged toward the Skylark.

The driver stepped out and stumbled with his first step, like he'd been shaken up by the collision. But he pulled a gun from inside his coat and pointed it right at me.

I stopped short and held my hands up to show him I was not armed.

"Where is she?" the man said. He, too, had blood coming down his face. His accent was not a local one. Far from it.

A Russian?

"Where is *who*?" I said, my hands still up where he could see them.

"Your girlfriend," he said, although he said it like gurla-frind."

"I don't *have* a girlfriend."

He pulled back the hammer on his revolver. "You know who I am speaking of. You tell me where is she, or I shoot you?"

"Where *is* she?" I spit blood toward the man's feet. "I think you mean, *where she is*." I couldn't see his eyes through the dark sunglasses but had a feeling he wasn't in a mood to play around. Not with his gun pointed my way. "What makes you think I know where she is?"

He gave the gun a shake. "You tell me where she is, and you will not be hurt." He gave me a nod with his chin, a smirk on his face. "And you will not have to worry for Nancy."

I stared back at him, my eyes squinted. "Why don't you put that gun away; let's do this like men?" I dropped my hands by my sides, had my right fist clenched, ready to take a swing if he came any closer.

He lifted what I believed was a .38 toward my face. "Tell me where she is, Mr. Horn. I will not ask for you to tell me again."

"Are you friggin' hard of hearing? Or is it the language barrier? I told you, I don't know where Lily is. Nobody does."

The man shrugged. "Okay, we will do it your way. We will see how fast you will talk."

I worried most about Nancy. What if someone had already gotten to her? Why did I make her go back to school? If I'd only gotten her on the phone when I called...

Without a second thought, I lunged at the man with my arms out and reached for the gun.

A shot fired, the sound exploding in my ear as I reached out in front of me, feeling the metal with the tips of my fingers, seeing the flash of bright white light.

I stumbled back and my body went numb. I felt nothing. At least for a moment. But then, there was a painful and slow burn inside me.

I felt a sudden weakness, dropping to my knees. I grabbed my side and watched the man back up and run away, toward his car. I tried to speak, but my mouth wouldn't do what I wanted it to. Looking down at my blood-soaked shirt, I heard a car door slam shut, the engine start, and tires squealing.

I collapsed onto the cold, damp asphalt, fighting to keep my eyes from closing. My face was on the ground, the pressure of sand and tiny bits of gravel pushing into my cheek.

I looked off in the distance for the man in the Skylark. Gone. My eyes went to a tractor-trailer truck stopped on the side of the road by one of the buildings, the driver's-side door wide open. A man walked toward me. I tried again to speak, to call for him, but I didn't have the strength. My ears were ringing so loud, I could hear nothing at all. It appeared the man, as he ran toward me, was yelling. All I could hear was the ringing in my head.

I was tired and closed my eyes. I wanted to open them. I tried. But I couldn't. And finally, the ringing stopped.

Chapter 26

It took me a moment, once I opened my eyes and looked up at Raymond with Maggie, to realize I was in a hospital room. Maggie was holding my hand and gave it a squeeze, smiling as I looked at her.

I tried to sit up, but my body didn't seem to want me to. I wondered if I was able to move at all, but I could feel Maggie's hand and looked at my toes under the blanket at the end of the bed. I felt better once I wiggled them.

"What hospital?" I said, my voice weak and my throat too dry for a full sentence.

"Worcester," Raymond said "Worcester Memorial." He put his hand on my shoulder. "Glad you're all right." He had a look of concern on his face, something I rarely saw.

My mind was going in too many different directions to focus, until I felt a sense of panic come over me. I pulled together whatever strength I had and pushed myself up in the bed, looking around the room, toward the bathroom, the other side of the bed... the empty chair in the corner by the window. "Nancy?" I said, looking at Raymond and Maggie. "Where is she?"

Maggie said, "She's on her way. Corey's driving her down."

I felt a sense of relief. "Are you..." I cleared my throat. "You're sure she's okay?"

"She's as okay as a daughter could be, hearing her old man's been shot," Raymond said.

I cleared my dry throat again. "He told me if I didn't tell him where Lily was, something would happen to Nancy."

Maggie looked at Raymond.

"They're already on the road," Raymond said, turning to Maggie. "You think maybe you can get someone out there? State police? Let them know what's going on?"

Maggie reached for my hand again and held it. "Don't worry," she said. "Any idea what kind of car he drives?"

"A BMW," I said, reaching for a cup of water on the tray on the side of the bed to my left. I took a sip, feeling relief as my throat opened up. I coughed and felt the tightness and pain on the side of my body. "It's white. A three-twenty model."

"Let me go make some calls," Maggie said, walking out the door.

Raymond stepped closer to the bed. "What the hell were you doing out here?"

I looked out the window. It was dark out, but I could see the streetlights and cars' lights on the road in the distance. I looked at my wrist, but my watch wasn't there. "What time is it?"

"Seven thirty."

"How long've I been in here?"

"You were in surgery for three-and-a-half hours," he said, appearing bigger and taller the way he towered over the bed. "Are you going to answer my question and tell me what you were doing?"

I looked toward the door and made a motion with my hand for Raymond to close it, which he did, then pulled a wooden chair up next to the bed and sat down, his hands on both knees.

"Lily called me," I said. I looked at the door again, making sure nobody walked in while I was talking. "She's in trouble, Raymond. I knew there was more to it. She's not hiding from the police or afraid to answer questions. Someone's after her. I'm not even sure any of this ever had to do with Michael having an affair." I looked toward the window. "I don't know *what* to believe."

"What did she tell you?"

I touched the bandage over my eye. "That's why I'm out here. She wanted me to meet her. I was on my way."

"When you were shot?"

I nodded. "I don't know what I was thinking. The guy followed me, maybe all the way from the house." I reached down, feeling the bandages on my side. "Anyone talk to Moriarty?"

Raymond shrugged. "I'm not sure. Why?"

"Because I called him. I thought maybe he had someone following me."

"You called Moriarty and asked him if he had a tail on you?" Raymond said. "Why wouldn't you call me? Or Maggie?"

I thought for a moment, looking at the IV needle taped into my hand. "I didn't want either of you to know I was going to see Lily."

"Are you serious?"

I shrugged, but it hurt my neck when I did. The pain was mostly on the side of my body, but there was soreness everywhere. I felt my lips and tried to wiggle my teeth. I smiled at Raymond with my teeth clenched. "Are you sure my teeth are all there?"

He leaned in and looked closer at my mouth, nodding. "Looks like it." He stood up from the chair. "So, will you tell me why you didn't at least call me, tell me what you were up to? Besides trying to be the hero?"

I looked down at the IV in my arm and sighed. "I guess I just thought you were better off not knowing. At least until I had a chance to talk to her. I never expected I'd end up with a bullet inside of me."

"Well, if it makes you feel any better, they removed it," he said. "The bullet tore a hole in your pancreas which, as far as I understand, was repaired during surgery. You were lucky."

I lifted my blanket and looked at the bandages covering a good part of my left side. "Any idea how long until I can get out of here?"

Raymond cracked one of his crooked smiles. "Do I look like a doctor?" He put his hand on my shoulder. "The doctor we talked to—the surgeon, Dr. Bourque—said you'd be here at least another few days."

"*A few days?*" I said, shaking my head. "I can't sit in a hospital bed for a few days! I gotta get out of here." I threw the blanket off me and looked down at my boxers, glad to see they hadn't left me naked. But what I didn't like was the clear tube with what looked like orange-colored liquid flowing through it, taped to my leg and coming out from under my shorts. "Oh shit," I said. "Is that a catheter?" I looked closer. "Why's it orange?"

Raymond took a quick glance but looked away, closing his eyes with a look of disgust on his face. "You can't feel it in there?"

"I don't feel much of anything. I'm kind of numb." I looked toward my toes and wiggled them again, just to be sure.

The door opened, and Maggie walked in, glancing toward my lower half. She, too, looked away. "Everything all right down there?" she said.

"It's still there." I pulled the blanket over me. "Can someone get the doctor in here? I gotta get out of here."

Raymond gestured for Maggie to sit in the chair but she shook him off. He pushed it back against the wall.

"I spoke to someone with the state police; highway patrol's on alert looking for a 1975, white BMW 320i. I assume they're coming down Ninety-Three out of New Hampshire, going to jump on the

Pike... so that's what I told them." She stepped around to the other side of the bed and had her eyes on the floor as she stepped around whatever was down there.

Raymond stayed on the other side, by the door.

"I spoke to Jeffrey," she said. "Moriarty. I thought he should know you were in here... and what's happened. He said you called him?"

I nodded. "I thought he had someone following me. I hope he doesn't feel guilty for what happened."

Maggie said, "Jeffrey? Guilty? He said you're reckless, and the best place for you to be right now is in a hospital bed to keep you out of trouble." She huffed out a small laugh and grinned.

A doctor walked into the room, and Raymond walked around to my left side, next to Maggie.

"I'm Dr. Bourque," the man said. "You're a lucky man. Bullet punctured your pancreas, but otherwise, the damage was fairly minimal. We removed the bullet."

"I thought I'd be in more pain," I said.

The doctor smiled, tight-lipped. "We gave you plenty for the pain." He looked across the bed at Raymond and Maggie. "As I told you, that truck driver who drove him here saved his life."

I hadn't even thought about how I ended up in the hospital. I had a vague memory of a man running toward me, although I didn't know if it was the man who shot me or someone else. "It was a truck driver?" I said. "He drove me here?"

The doctor nodded. "Saved your life."

To say I was surprised, and grateful, was an understatement. "Is he still around?"

"The driver?" Dr. Bourque shook his head. "I'm sorry, I don't believe so."

"You have his name?" I said.

"You'll have to check with the front desk downstairs. I was only concerned with keeping you alive. So, no, I didn't ask for his name."

Two police officers walked through the doorway and into the room, but both stopped when the doctor raised his hand to them, his palm out.

"I'm sorry, Officers," he said. "Not right now."

The older-looking one of the two officers looked down at me, then toward Raymond and Maggie, before looking back at the doctor. "We just need to ask Mr. Horn a few questions."

The doctor looked annoyed. "I just said, not right now. This man just came out of surgery and needs a few hours to recover. You'll have to come back later, or in the morning. I'm sorry."

The two officers looked at each other.

"I'm all right," I said. "I can talk."

The doctor looked at me like a parent about to chastise a child. "*You* are my patient, Mr. Horn. *I* am the doctor." He turned to the officers. "I'm sorry. Try again later."

The two officers looked at each other as if speechless and started for the door. The older officer—a gray-haired man who appeared to be tired and ready to hang up his badge—looked down at me. "Someone'll be back in the morning." They walked out of the room.

The doctor looked at Maggie. "I'm sorry, my priority is my patient's health. Not solving crimes."

***

I dozed off and opened my eyes to a strong antiseptic odor, feeling a hand on my shoulder. My eyes were blurry at first, but I blinked and focused enough to see Nancy's face, looking down at me from over my bed. I tried to sit up, feeling more pain than I had earlier.

Corey stood behind Nancy.

I tried to push out a smile, but even my mouth hurt more than it had.

Nancy leaned down to give me a hug, resting her head on my chest. I felt her tears soak through the gown. She straightened up and wiped her tears with both hands.

I reached out to shake Corey's hand. "Thank you for getting her down here," I said. "But I need you to be careful, all right? Anybody you don't know asks you about her—I mean, anyone around here or back at school—you need to let me know. And as far as you know, you don't even know who she is, if anyone asks." I looked him in the eye, looking for a response. "You got it?"

He slowly nodded, his mouth slightly open like he wanted to speak, but words didn't come out. He looked from me to Nancy, still nodding.

I looked toward the closet, where I believed my clothes were being kept. I assumed my wallet was still in my pocket. "I've got money for you, for gas," I said, looking at Corey. "It's up to sixty-five cents a gallon, so..."

"My dad pays for my gas," he said.

I guessed that made sense. But I didn't expect his dad to pay to drive Nancy back and forth from New Hampshire. I said to him, "You're not driving back tonight, are you?"

He looked at Nancy before he answered, then shrugged. "I hadn't really thought about it yet. I thought I'd wait around."

"I think you should stay around here tonight. I can't keep you from going back to school, but Nancy's not going back," I said. "Not tonight."

Corey nodded without asking any questions. I'm sure he didn't have a lot of friends whose dads had been shot, and doubted he knew what he was supposed to do or how to react. Either way, he seemed like a good friend to Nancy. If that was really all they were.

I reached for Nancy's hand. "I'm glad you're okay."

She cracked a smile through her tears, pushing a strand of hair from her face. "I didn't know if you were dead," she said, and choked back more tears.

"Didn't Maggie tell you I was okay?"

She nodded. "She did. But I could hear in her voice that she wasn't sure."

I nodded and pushed out a small grin. "Listen," I said. "Nance, I know I wanted you back at school. But, it turns out, I think you're going to have to stay out for a little while longer. I'm so sorry. I just—"

"It's okay," she said. "Is it bad?"

I didn't know how to answer, but I knew I couldn't hold everything back from her for long either. Sugarcoating the truth wasn't going to make things any better. "I just need you to be safe. Nothing's more important to me than that," I said, looking at Corey. "Can you help me with that? Keep her safe?"

He had his eyes on me, nodding. And I knew I'd just put a lot on a kid I hardly knew, but for some reason felt I could trust.

Nancy looked me over, under the blanket. "What about you? Are you going to be all right?"

I sat up a little straighter but felt a tinge of pain around my stomach. "I'm going to be fine. But I don't want you to worry about me."

She had a serious look on her face, her eyes right on mine. "You told me the same thing when you drove me back to school. How can you tell me that again and expect me to listen?"

I wasn't sure I had a good enough answer.

"You're going to stay at Raymond and Beth's tonight." I looked past her at Corey. "Both of you, if you're okay sticking around at least overnight." I squeezed Nancy's hand. "In the morning we'll figure everything out, where you can go."

"*Where I can go?*" she said. "You just said we'd stay at Raymond and Beth's."

"You are. Tonight. But, tomorrow... I don't want anyone to know where you are. I know how scary this all sounds, but I want to find a place you can go, away from me or Raymond or anyone who might know where to look."

Nancy wiped her tears, but they weren't stopping, even if she was trying hard to keep it all together.

Corey stepped closer to the bed. "Mr. Horn, we have a house out on the Cape. In Wellfleet. It's a small summer house, doesn't really have heat other than a wood-burning stove we can use. I can call my dad and see if—"

"Can you stay there without your parents knowing?" I said. "Would you get in trouble?"

He shrugged. "They're up in Vermont, so they won't even know. And there's a spare key, so..."

"Listen," I said, looking him right in the eye. "I don't want *anyone* to know the two of you will be there. That includes your parents. I'm not even sure, whoever did this to me... I don't know if anyone saw your car when you were at the house. So, you have to be careful. You can't tell anyone. Okay?" I shifted my eyes to Nancy. "If anything happens to her..."

CHAPTER 27

I HADN'T SLEPT MUCH through the night. On top of everything, the pain seemed to grow more intense as it got closer to morning. I'd refused more pain medication, although it likely would have at least helped me sleep through the noise from the machines and hallway outside my room.

I heard a voice out in the hall with arrogance and a condescending tone I recognized right away. I pushed myself up in the bed and stretched my eyes to look refreshed.

Moriarty walked in, looking me over with a slight smirk on his face. "Oh, there you are," he said. He looked around the room. "So, how do you feel about rejecting my offer to help you yesterday?" He was dressed in his usual made-for-TV trench coat, a red turtleneck underneath a V-neck sweater.

I shifted in the bed and felt more pain shoot up my side, although it was certainly something I could deal with. Sit-ups, I'd guessed, were out of the question. I had removed the sheet, exposed in my boxers with the catheter no longer running down my leg.

"Worcester PD been here yet?" Moriarty said.

"Last night. But the doctor told them to come back this morning." I looked past him, toward the door. "They haven't been back."

He nodded. "Good. I still need to talk to someone over there."

"You mean because it's connected to Dempsey's murder?"

He had his eyes on me. "You say that like you know it for a fact."

"Well, the man who shot me wanted to know where Lily was hiding."

"And what did you tell him?" He gave me a look, his eyebrows raised, like he was waiting for me to expose the big secret.

"I told him the same thing I've told you, at least a dozen times. I have 'no idea where Lily is.'"

He stared at me, his hands deep in his pants pockets, but not saying a word. "So you told him you didn't know, and he shot you? Just like that?"

"I don't know how it happened," I said.

Moriarty said, "I'm not sure I understand why you'd charge after a man holding a gun."

"How do you know I charged him?"

"I know the type," he said. "The way the doctor explained it, you were shot at very close range."

I nodded, rubbing my hands together. I felt a chill go through me and pulled the blanket up to cover my legs.

"Well, if I have to keep repeating myself to you. I don't know where Lily is. And at this point, I'd tell you if I did. That's the truth."

It *was* the truth. I *didn't* know where she was. Of course, I *did* know, the morning before. And unless she called me or somehow reached out, I wasn't sure I was going to hear from her again, any time soon.

Moriarty had his eyes on mine, with a slight squint. "Forgive me," he said, "But I'm having a hard time believing a word that comes out of your mouth. He walked to the open door, looking out toward the hall. "From the day we first met, I've had it in my mind that you're holding something back from me." He walked to the window and kept his back to me. "If you'd only been a little more honest with me from the beginning, neither of us would be here, stuck in this dirty, second-rate city."

There was a knock on the open door, and Raymond walked in.

Moriarty stepped from the window and looked Raymond over, up and down. "Raymond Horn," he said. "You really *are* as big as they've said." He stepped by the bed where Raymond stood and offered his hand. "I don't believe we've ever formally met... I'm Jeffrey Moriarty. *Detective* Jeffrey Moriarty."

Raymond reached out and shook his hand but didn't say a word, instead turning to me. "So how're you feeling?"

"I guess I'm all right." Although even that was pretty much a stretch. I looked toward the door. "Where's Nancy?"

"She's with Beth, had just gotten out of bed and wanted to come over here, but I told her to sit tight with the boyfriend."

"He's not her boyfriend," I said.

Raymond smirked. "Oh, okay."

I knew, even with Raymond with me at the hospital, Beth would keep Nancy safe with her own Smith & Wesson 9mm.

"As I told your cousin," Moriarty said, "if he'd only trusted me, I could've kept him out of this situation. But as I'm sure you're aware, he has some issues with the men who protect and serve our great country."

"I don't think you can make such a blanket statement," I said. "I don't distrust someone just because they wear the uniform. But, of course, especially in your city, there are plenty of bad apples."

Moriarty grinned at Raymond. "I hope he at least had a little more faith when you were a cop, being family and all."

Raymond had his eyes on Moriarty, and I could see by the way he looked at him, he didn't particularly like him. "Maybe if you'd listened to Jake when he told you Lily might not be as guilty as you'd like to believe."

Moriarty's eyebrows were raised, and I knew a condescending response was on its way. He looked from Raymond to me. "Oh goody. It looks like the two of you have already solved the murder case." He put his hand on his chin. "It's good to know... now maybe I can take that Florida vacation I've been thinking about." He laughed, shaking his head as he walked back to the window. He made a circle with his finger in the condensation on the glass. "You know what? I wouldn't be so quick to put your ex-girlfriend in the clear. Just because some random crazy person shot you doesn't all of a sudden mean Lily Dempsey had nothing to do with her husband's murder."

Raymond and I both remained quiet.

"Let me ask you something," Moriarty said. "Did she know where you were yesterday morning?" He walked to the foot of bed and stopped, staring down at me. "Because, if she did, then have you at least asked yourself if Mrs. Dempsey might've possibly had something to do with you being followed, and nearly killed?"

I stared back at him. "There was no way she knew where I was." Sure, I lied. But at that time, I had no choice. I chose to ignore the fact he may have had a point.

Moriarty's cocky smirk was back on his face. I knew he didn't buy what I'd said. "I haven't even asked you what you were doing out here in the first place. But I'm not going to waste my breath and expect a straight answer."

"You know I was being followed. What was I supposed to do? I just kept driving until I—"

"To Worcester? You expect me to believe that?" He reached into his inside coat pocket and pulled out a roll of mints, popping one in his mouth. He took a moment, moving the mint around his mouth. "So, what exactly did this man say to you?"

"I told you. He was looking for Lily. Maybe you should write it down, so you don't keep asking the same question."

Moriarty walked back to the window again, his own reflection coming back at him as he carefully adjusted his hair. "You know, if she hadn't disappeared in the first place, then perhaps—"

"What if she's dead?" Raymond said. Even though he already knew I was on my way to meet her.

Moriarty looked over his shoulder at him."Excuse me?"

Raymond took a step toward him. "I said, have you thought for even a moment that Lily could be dead? The woman was obviously scared and took off for a reason. And believe me, I'm the last one to want to believe a word that comes out of that woman's mouth. But clearly, this guy was after her. I mean, sure, maybe she took off at first because you made it painfully obvious she was your number-one suspect, before you even started your investigation."

The detective shrugged his shoulders, shaking his head. "I'm sorry, big guy. *What's* your point? You think maybe she's dead? It seems to me that's quite the wild assumption."

"He's right," I said. "It's a possibility."

"And you think, perhaps, this man who shot you somehow got to her already?"

I said, "If not him, then maybe someone else. Until you figure out why Michael Dempsey was killed, I don't see how you—"

"Please don't tell me how to do my job," Moriarty said, looking from me to Raymond. "I didn't come here to huddle up, see if we can act like we're some kind of team, trying to solve the case. All right?" He let out a sigh. "Listen, do me a favor, and tell me what you can about this man who shot you." He looked at his watch.

The two looked at me, but I had to think for a moment. I remembered getting a good enough look at the man, but it wasn't as clear as I'd hoped. "He was short," I said. "Older, hair slicked back." I had to think. I rubbed my face with both hands, running them straight back over my head. "I told you he had a Russian accent, didn't I?"

"Russian? No, you didn't say a word about the man being Russian. Are you sure about that?"

"You didn't mention he was Russian," Raymond said.

"Well, I mean, I don't know for sure he was Russian. But, the accent was—"

"Yeah, I get the point," Moriarty said. "So what else? You obviously got a good look at him?"

I nodded. "Sort of. He wore sunglasses, but otherwise, I'd say he was older, gray in his hair, slicked back on his head. He was short, maybe five six, give or take a couple of inches."

Moriarty pulled at his chin, his eyes toward the floor. "And you're sure of the accent... you don't think it was more of, maybe, an Italian accent?"

"I know the difference," I said. "Are you asking, because of Mayor Gautieri?"

Moriarty said, "No. I'm just making sure you know what you heard. You've been through quite a bit, and don't forget, you were unconscious when that trucker brought you in here."

"So now you don't believe me?"

Moriarty didn't answer, looked at his watch, and patted me gently on the shoulder. "All right, Horn. I think I'm done here. It'll be up to Worcester to track down your man. I would just make sure you've got your story straight, or it'll start sounding a bit far-fetched, chased down by a Russian man in a Buick Skylark."

"What's so far-fetched about that?" I said.

"Oh, I'm not saying it's far-fetched. I just recommend you get your story straight. Make sure you have it right." He gave me a nod. "Get well, Horn." And just as he started through the door, Maggie stepped in from the hall.

She said, "Oh... Jeffrey. I didn't know you'd—"

"Oh goody," he said. "Looks like the gang's all here." He let out a quick laugh and disappeared into the hall without another word.

Maggie let out a sigh. "I really wish I didn't bump into him."

"Why?" Raymond said. "You can't come visit a friend?"

She didn't answer, but stepped toward the bed and rested her hand on my shoulder. "Are you doing okay?"

I nodded just as the doctor walked into the room. He grabbed the clipboard from the foot of the bed and looked it over. "Your vitals are good," he said, his eyes still down on the paper. "But the nurse said you refused the pain medication?" He lifted his eyes to mine.

"Yeah, I don't need it," I said as convincingly as I could. "I feel fine."

The doctor hooked the clipboard on the bed. "You may feel fine, but your body's been through quite a bit of trauma," he said. "You're in good shape. You're healthy. A fair number of people wouldn't have survived it." He stepped next to me, lifted the blanket, and studied the bandage on my side. "The muscle around your midsection likely played a role in saving your life."

"Does that mean I can get out of here?" I said.

The doctor paused, slipped his hands in the pockets of his white coat. "If you promise me you'll take it easy, I'll see what I can do."

CHAPTER 28

"You heard the doctor," Maggie said, slipping behind the wheel of her Scamp. "No driving. Let's just get back to Raymond's."

It hurt to reach for the passenger door's handle, pulling it closed. "I'm fine," I said. "I mean, what's the big deal? It's not like it's a stick. I can handle it."

She let out a sigh, rolled her eyes, and backed out of the parking space outside the hospital.

"It's five minutes from here," I said.

Maggie pulled out of the parking lot and took a right onto Belmont, giving me a quick glance as she cut out into moving traffic. "You need to listen to the doctor."

"I need my car."

She leaned with her elbow on the inside of the door, her left hand supporting her head.

"You all right?" I said.

She straightened in her seat and glanced at me, nodding. "I'm worried about you."

"I appreciate that. But you don't have to worry."

She kept her eyes on the road, pulling up to the stoplight at Major Taylor Boulevard. "Listen," she said, her eyes still ahead, "I've been thinking maybe I can take a few days off. I have vacation time I haven't used, and—"

"Good for you," I said. "You could use the vacation. Where to? Florida? It's supposed to be nice this time of year, before it gets too hot."

The light turned green and she went left. "I'm not going anywhere. The truth is, I thought maybe you could use my help."

"Help with *what*?"

"The way my hands are tied at work right now, and probably even more so with Moriarty seeing me at the hospital, I just think I'd be able to help you more."

"But I don't understand. Do you mean—"

"Whatever you need. Protect Nancy. Keep an eye out while you get some sleep. Anything, Jake. I feel I owe it to you both to help."

I looked out the window as she turned onto Waldo Street and pulled up in front of Worcester Police headquarters. "You don't owe me anything," I said. "I don't know why you think you do."

"Okay, well, maybe that's the wrong word. I just, I can't help you when I'm on the clock, walking the streets of Boston. If something were to happen to either one of you, and I'm busy writing some jackass a parking ticket..." She shifted the Scamp into park. "I'm assuming asking for the time off on short notice won't be a problem. But if it is, then it'll be a different story."

I looked out the passenger window and up at the three-story brick building with the rounded-top windows that'd been headquarters to the Worcester Police, going back to 1918. I only knew that because I had another uncle who was a cop in Worcester last time the Red Sox won a World Series, in 1918. "You can't jeopardize your career," I said. "It's hard enough on you as it is, all you go through just to get the respect you deserve."

She shifted in her seat to face me. "Some things are more important than a job."

"Do you expect me to believe being a cop in Boston is just a job to you?" I said.

"No, that's not what I'm saying, but—"

"Can you imagine what'll happen if Moriarty gets wind you're helping me on your *own* time *after* they've made it clear they don't want you involved in anything that has to do with Dempsey's case? I mean, you have to keep in mind, it's not like I have any friends over there. I still can't help but wonder if Moriarty still believes I might've had something to do with the murder."

"Oh, I'm not sure that's true, Jake."

I reached into my pocket and took out the bottle of painkillers the doctor had given me. He said I might need them even though I said I wouldn't. But the thought crossed my mind with every pothole we hit on the short ride to the station.

I pushed open the door with a grunt and smelled smoke, looked and saw a cop walking past us with a cigarette hanging from his mouth.

Pain shot through my side as I slowly rotated my body in the seat. I eased both feet out onto the sidewalk and reached for the inside handle on the open door with my left hand, my right gripping the handle over my head, positioning myself to get up on both feet. I sat, my back to Maggie, and tried to look at her over my shoulder without turning more than I had to. "I won't let you put your career on the line like that," I said. "I appreciate it. I do. But, I can handle this myself."

With a quick burst that sent a sharp shooting pain through every part of my body, I made it up and stood outside the car. I took a deep breath and exhaled, thinking about the painkillers in my pocket. Maybe they weren't such a bad idea. I looked into the car at Maggie. "You mind waiting? I'm sure the car's all set, but—"

"I'm not going anywhere," she said with what looked like a forced smile. "I'd already planned to follow you all the way back to Raymond's anyway. Just in case."

***

Raymond's front door was closed when I pulled up into the driveway and expected Nancy to be on the other side of the storm door waiting for me with Max the cat in her arms.

Maggie pulled in behind me, and we both stepped out at the same time. She came up behind me and grabbed my arm, helping me.

But I pulled it away. "I'm fine. Really."

"You don't look fine," she said, placing her hand on my back. "Why're you so afraid to let someone help you?"

I laughed. But even that hurt.

The air felt cooler again. I loved New England but like everyone always said, you don't like the weather, just wait a day. Mother Nature, to me, seemed to like to play games. Just when you thought spring was around the corner, she shot another blast of cold air and threw in a few inches of snow. Just to keep us honest.

I stopped at the bottom stairs from the porch and looked up at the door, watching as someone opened it.

Raymond watched me, came out in a T-shirt and slippers and stepped down, reaching for my arm. "You all right?" he said.

I gripped the handrail and nodded, raising each leg like they were made of cement. "I got it," I said, brushing off his offer to help.

"You're so stubborn," he said, laughing, looking at Nancy.

I made it up the three steps, which seemed like I'd gone up twenty by the time I was at the front door, my breathing heavy.

Raymond opened the door, and I stopped to let Maggie go in ahead of me. "Go ahead," I said.

"No, you go." She kept her hand on my back, one arm out near my side, like she was waiting to catch my fall.

Raymond stayed outside and closed the door behind Maggie.

Nancy, Beth, and Corey were just inside waiting for us, and Nancy wrapped her arms around me without saying a word.

I winced but tried not to make it look that obvious I was in pain.

"Oh, I'm sorry," Nancy said, covering her mouth with both hands. She stepped back and looked me up and down. "Are you okay?"

I nodded and held up my thumb. "Good." I gave Corey a nod.

Beth came down the stairs and stepped in front of me, looked me in the eyes with concern, and put her hand flat on the side of my face. "I'm glad you're all right." She grabbed the hem of my peacoat. "Can I take this for you?"

I didn't tell her I was cold. Colder than I normally was. "I'm okay." I looked down at the holster on her hip, the same model .357 Magnum her father-in-law had gotten me, giving them out as gifts with the assumption everyone loved guns as much as he did. "Thanks for keeping everyone safe," I said.

She looked down at the gun and smiled. "I can't tell you the last time I wore this. Raymond thought it'd be a good idea."

Raymond walked in from outside and closed the door behind him. "I was just looking at the Nova," he said. "I didn't know you banged it up that much."

I nodded. "Just another expense to deal with."

Raymond looked at my side. "Let's catch the guy who did this to you, make him pay for it." And I could see he was dead serious. He had a look I hadn't seen since he wore the uniform. As a cop, he was the likable kind, treating everyone with a lot of respect. But he was also the type you didn't cross. As a kid he liked to fight, but they never lasted very long, being bigger than most kids by at least a foot, even then.

"The problem is, there's a good chance it's not a one-man show," I said. "I thought about it the whole ride here. I can't put these pieces together. The bearded guy, the pig's head... a Russian?" I looked around for a seat and made my way to the wingback chair by the fireplace. "Nothing makes any sense. And now, who knows if Lily's going to try and get in touch with me again."

"Well, someone tried to send a message the first couple of times. Shooting a guy in the gut, that's a different story."

I nodded as I slowly eased myself into the chair, trying not to make a noise that showed the pain I was feeling.

"Do you need a cane?" Beth said. "We still have Raymond's, from when he broke his foot."

I smiled, shaking my head. "I'm all right." Nancy and Corey stood next to each other watching me as if neither knew what to say. I said to Cory, "Where's your Beemer?"

Raymond said, "I had him move it behind the house, covered it with a tarp. Just to play it safe."

Always on top of things.

I nodded, looked around at everyone else standing, watching me like I was some poor soul that couldn't be helped. "Will everyone relax a little?" I said. "I'm fine. Really." I said to Cory, "You have a phone at that house in Wellfleet?"

He nodded. "I can write down the number."

Beth walked in the kitchen, came back with a pad and pencil she handed to Corey.

He sat on the bottom step of the stairs, rested the pad on his knee, and scribbled down the number. He got up and walked toward me, giving me the pad.

I looked it over and handed it back to him. "Go ahead and write down the address."

Corey got down on one knee, scribbled on the pad again and handed it back to me. I tore off the top sheet and stuck it in my inside coat pocket.

Nancy's and Corey's bags were already by the door.

I looked at Raymond and Maggie. "We should follow them out there."

Nancy shook her head. "You don't have to. I think we'll be okay."

I stopped myself from telling her *I* would be the one to make that decision. Instead, I agreed with her. I stood up from the chair and put my hand on Corey's shoulder, looking him in the eye. "You think for any reason someone might be following you, I want you to go in a different direction away from that house. Drive into a public place or straight to a police station, a fire station... anything."

Corey nodded with a smile on his face. "The car's wicked fast." The smile dropped from his face when he saw I didn't smile back.

"I'm not asking you to try and outrun anybody," I said. "I just want you to keep my daughter safe."

He nodded. "Yes, sir."

Corey and Nancy both picked up their bags by the door, and Raymond pointed toward the back of the house with his thumb over his shoulder. "Let's go out the back way. I already took the tarp off."

∗∗∗

Raymond stepped out onto the deck with me and Maggie, handing us each a mug of coffee. He went back inside, came out with his own cup and looked up at the sky. "Might snow tonight, you know."

I leaned against the railing, raising the mug up to my mouth, looking over the rim at Maggie. "Does he know what you were thinking of doing?"

Maggie nodded, turning to Raymond. "Jake doesn't want my help."

"Oh," Raymond said. "You mean about taking time off?"

"Yeah. It's a bad idea. I assume you agree."

Raymond shrugged. "Well, you could look at it a couple of ways," he said. "One is, you're going to get yourself killed, you try and keep trying to be a one-man band."

"It's not like the days your father ran the business, had people working for him," I said. "Hate to tell you this, but I don't have much of a choice."

"Well," Raymond said. "If she's willing to risk her career to help you, I'm not sure you're in a position to tell her she can't."

"Are you serious?" I said. "You honestly think she should take vacation from her job as a police officer so she can help me?" I said to Maggie, "I'm not even sure exactly what I'm looking for at this point."

Raymond said, "I kind of think finding Michael Dempsey's murderer is a pretty good option. Don't you?"

"Yeah, of course," I said. "I just mean, this all started with Lily claiming Michael was cheating on her. Now, it appears that may not even be the case. This is far beyond someone's infidelity."

"So, then why don't you want our help?" he said.

I looked at them both. "'Our' help? Are you saying..."

"I'm saying Maggie and I will do whatever it takes, Jake. You're in deep trouble here. And I know you have no plans of hiding while the police figure it out. So either you let us help you, and stop trying to be the hero... and let's get these sons of bitches."

CHAPTER 29

RAYMOND TOOK THE LEBARON down Washington Street and parked at a meter on the side of Providence City Hall. Maggie was in the passenger seat next to him, both wearing dark sunglasses and baseball caps pulled down low.

I said, "You really think someone's going to recognize either of you down here?"

Raymond looked back at me over his shoulder but didn't respond.

I decided the pain was too much to deal with and popped a couple of the pills the doctor had given me. And they absolutely helped. In fact, I felt more relaxed than I'd been in a long time. The feeling in my head was hard to describe. Somewhat off-center, I'd say. But certainly not drugged out, although maybe a little drowsy.

I got out from the back seat and stepped around to Maggie's window on the passenger side. She rolled it down, and I looked past her at Raymond. "Go around this block and park on Eddy Street. I'll meet you over there." I looked at my watch. "If I'm not out in an hour..."

"Try not to get yourself in too much trouble," Raymond said.

I started down the sidewalk, but Maggie called to me.

She said, "Are you sure you're all right, going in alone?"

I stared back at her without an answer but gave her a small grin. "Don't worry." I continued on Dorrance and along the granite sidewalk, looking up toward the granite-and-brick building's fifth floor.

Inside there were two police officers in the lobby: one seated at a desk and the other standing in front of the wide marble staircase that led to the Providence City Hall's main floor.

The officer behind the desk stared back at me, like he was already suspicious before I said a word. "Can I help you?"

I stepped to the desk. "I'm here to see the mayor."

"Do you have an appointment?" he said.

I glanced at the other one, watching me, shaking my head. "No, not really."

The one behind the desk squinted, staring back at me. "Not *really*? Is that a *no*? Sorry, but the mayor's a busy man. Too busy to see every Tom, Dick, and Harry that walks in from the street." He pulled a business card from the desk drawer and handed it to me. "Call this number. You'll have to make an appointment."

I looked at the card and slipped it into my inside pocket. "How about if you give him my name, tell him I'm downstairs? I'm sure he'd love to know I'm down here. In fact, he and I... I was just at his place at the Biltmore, having coffee. Actually, it was espresso. Which was pretty good."

I could see on the man's face it didn't make a difference.

I looked through the glass doors toward Kennedy Plaza. "Can't you just at least tell him I'm down here? Jake Horn. He won't be surprised when you tell him I'm down here."

The officer stood up from his desk and walked through a door behind him and into what looked like a closet, but there was a desk against the wall. He closed the door without a word before I could get a better look.

I glanced at the other officer by the stairs, but he just stared at me, expressionless.

The door behind the desk opened, and the officer walked out, pulling a pen from his shirt pocket. He picked up a clipboard from the desk and flipped it toward me, tapping the top sheet. "Sign your name, date it, and state the reason for your visit." He put out his hand. "I'll need to see some ID."

I pulled out my wallet and handed him my license, then signed my name on the clipboard. I looked up at the officer, then in the space wrote: *personal visit.*

He studied my license and handed it back, then stepped around the desk. "Follow me," he said, and walked toward the stairs but continued past them. We stopped at an elevator, and the door opened right away. He stepped in ahead of me, pressed the button for the third floor and stood without saying a word.

The elevator bell dinged, and the door opened. The officer walked out ahead and turned left down a long hall with marble flooring and offices on either side.

We continued to the end of the hall and through a set of double doors. Inside was an office space with a pretty young woman behind a desk. I could smell her strong perfume, although there was also a hint of men's cologne floating in the air.

"Have a seat," the officer said, pointing to the brown leather chairs all pushed up against the wall in a small waiting area.

She smiled when she looked up at the officer. "This is the guy who's here to see the mayor." He gave me a quick glance over his shoulder. "Jake Horn. From Boston." He walked out the door without another word to either of us.

The attractive younger woman stood and came around from behind her desk wearing a tight, short skirt with white stockings on her thighs tucked into black leather boots that went up above her knees. She opened a door and walked through, closing it behind her, returning a moment later. "Mr. Horn? The mayor will see you in a few minutes."

I was surprised, to say the least. I had gotten as far as I had and how cordial my visit had been to that point. I guessed Tony Gautieri recognized my name. If he hadn't, I might've been tossed out onto the street by the two officers at the door.

A young man with his hair slicked back, dressed in a pin-striped, double-breasted suit walked through the door and gave me a nod with his chin. "Mr. Horn?" He looked like a character out of *The Godfather*.

I stood from my seat with a nod.

"The mayor will see you now," he said.

I followed him through the door and immediately discovered the source of cologne. It was like the kid had taken a bath in it.

I followed him down a short hallway to a set of double doors, left wide open, and walked into a large office.

Tony Gautieri was behind a long and heavy-looking wooden desk with the phone up to his ear. He pointed toward the two chairs across from him and covered the mouthpiece on the handset. He looked me in the eye and with a nod, said, "You want a coffee?" But before I answered, he waved at the young man. "Get him a coffee, will you?"

The young man was almost at the door but stopped. "You want cream 'n sugar?"

"Black is good," I said, sitting in one of the chairs. I watched Gautieri, his eyes toward the tall and wide window, his hands moving all over the place as he spoke.

"I don't care if they won't approve it," he said, speaking with a loud voice into the phone. "I want it done. For Christ's sake... you can't make it happen? I'll find someone else who can." He slammed the phone down. "Goddamn bureaucracy with these friggin' regulations... they wonder why nothing ever gets done in this state."

The young man walked back into the mayor's office with a white mug, steam coming off the top. He placed it down on the table next to me, between the two chairs, then walked toward the doors and pulled them closed behind him as he left the mayor's office.

Gautieri got up from behind his desk and walked to the window. The view was similar to the one he had in his room at the Biltmore Hotel, although not as high from the ground. He had his back to me. "The people in this state are so close-minded. They have no idea what it takes to give this city what it needs, to play with the big boys." He turned from the window. "You gotta spend money to make money. Am I right? That's just how things work in this world today. You spend like a second-rate city, you're going to have a second-rate city." He stared back at me. "See? Boston knows what it takes. I'm not saying it's perfect, but Boston'll always put my city to shame unless people around here are willing to change."

I kept quiet at first and watched him sit back down behind his desk.

He had a mug in front of him, by the phone, picked it up and looked me over. "You don't look too good," he said. "Besides you look like you walked straight into a wall, you got no color in your face." He sipped whatever was in his cup. "I heard what happened to you, out there in Worcester?"

"Oh yeah?" I said. "What'd you hear?"

He looked at me like I was asking a dumb question. "I hear things, you know what I mean? I got friends all over. I know what goes on, all around me." He grinned. "Sometimes I even know before something happens."

"Are you trying to tell me you had something to do with it?"

He leaned back in his leather desk chair, shaking his head. "Not at all. But I had a funny feeling you were going to ask." He took a sip from his cup. "You think because I threatened you the other day at the hotel, I'd send someone all the way out to Worcester to shoot you?"

"I don't know. Maybe after the pig's head didn't scare me away, you—"

"A *pig's* head? What the hell's a pig's head got to do with anything?"

"You tell me." I looked toward the door behind me, looking for the two goons who delivered me to him at the hotel. "Where are your lap dogs?"

He smiled and huffed out a slight laugh. "This is the mayor's office. They work for *me*, not the city."

I lifted the mug of coffee from the table next to me and took a sip. "So, can you look me in the eye and tell me you had nothing to do with any of the trouble I've been running into?"

He ran his tongue inside his mouth like he was trying to work something stuck in his teeth. "Let me make myself clear, Mr. Horn. I send someone after you, or I got a message to deliver, you're going to know it came from me. I don't play games." He leaned back in the chair. "You mind telling me what the hell the pig's head has to do with anything?"

I'd always been good at reading people. I could pick out a liar a mile away, trusting my gut as much as anything else. And at that point I felt either Gautieri was an exceptional actor, or he was telling me the truth. He didn't appear to have even the slightest clue what I was talking about.

"Mr. Horn, you held up your end of the bargain. I asked you not to bother my daughter, and you did not. I appreciate that."

I took another sip of coffee, looked at him over the rim, and gently placed the cup down on the small table. "I wish I could say I don't believe you," I said. "But, for some reason..."

"I'm an honest man," he said.

I laughed. "Oh, okay."

Gautieri looked toward the window. "I love animals, you know. It sounds to me someone might have done something only a sicko would do."

"There was a bloody pig's head left in my bed. My daughter was the one who found it."

"In your bed, huh?" He cleared his throat. "Pigs are very intelligent animals, you know. Smarter than dogs. *Did you know that?*" He got up from his desk. "I hope you're not here because you think I had anything to do with it?"

"With me being shot?" I stared back at him. "I'd be lying if I said it hadn't crossed my mind."

"Like I told you, if it was me... you'd know it. And, I'll be honest with you, you wouldn't be sitting here right now, in my office, if I wanted you dead." He nodded his chin at me. "I hear the guy was Russian?"

"Going by his accent, he was." I said.

He shook his head as if in disgust. "Friggin' Russians... they come here from the Soviet Union trying to get a cut of everything they can get their hands on. These clowns are involved in all kinds of shit nowadays: drugs, guns... hookers. It's been a real problem. And not just here in New England either. They're spreading out up and down the East Coast." He gave me a quick nod with his chin. "You ever hear of the Potato Bag Gang?"

"Who?"

"The Potato Bag Gang." Gautieri nodded his head. "Yeah, down in New York, these Russians... they been posing as merchant sailors. And they claim to be selling antique gold rubles. They sell 'em by the thousands. But the poor suckers who give 'em thousands of dollars..." He laughed. "The *stunads* down there in New York pay all this money for these gold rubles, but you know what they're getting?

The poor suckers end up with nothing but potatoes stuffed into sacks they believed were filled with gold."

I said, "This have anything to do with the guy who shot me?"

Gautieri shrugged, his mouth with a downward curve on both sides. "Some of us, the mayors from around New England, we've tried to put a stop to it. But these Russians... they're everywhere now. Like ants. New York, New Jersey, here in Rhode Island, up in your neck of the woods and all the way down to the Central Eastern states like Maryland... Pennsylvania. If it's illegal, they got their stinkin' hands in it."

I thought for a moment, rubbing what had become a beard on my face. "You said guns? You mean, illegal trafficking?"

"You name it," he said.

"But isn't that what Angela and Michael Dempsey were involved in together?"

"What? No, no. Saying they were involved is a little strong. You know, Angela graduated from Rhode Island College with an art degree. She's a very good artist." He walked to a painting of a horse up on the wall by the door. "She painted this... it was a horse, used to be hers when she was a little girl."

I had no idea where he was going or if he had a point.

"So, my point being is, her involvement with Michael was more on the advertising side. Public relations, communications... that's the kind of stuff she does. And, well, between me and Mayor Bedford, we agreed to make it a priority to put a stop to the illegal gun trade. Dempsey was her direct contact up there at the mayor's office."

"To stop the Russians?" I said, knowing Gautieri, or at least his connections, had at one time been tied directly to the same gun-trafficking trade he claimed he wanted to stop.

"Not just them," he said. "We put on a whole event, hosted it right here at the civic center. Dempsey had a hand in pulling it together. He and Angela."

"So what exactly was his role?"

Gautieri shrugged. "I don't know. I saw him there; all he was doing was handing out pamphlets at the door."

Chapter 30

"Stop if you see a pay phone," I said, leaning with my arms on top of the backrest from the back seat of Raymond's car.

Maggie looked back at me from the passenger seat. "To call who?"

"Moriarty," I said.

Raymond said, "You're not going to tell him you just left Gautieri's office, are you?" As the words left his mouth, I spotted a phone on the corner lot of Casino's Pizza, but before I could say a word, Raymond took the ramp for Route 6 heading west.

I sat back and looked out the window.

Raymond glanced at Maggie. "How far did you say this farm is?"

"Supposed to be around twenty minutes," she said. "Stay on Route Six, the whole way." She turned to me. "You really think Michael Dempsey handing out flyers at a mayor's conference on illegal gun trafficking would get the Russians after him?" She faced the front. "It just doesn't make a lot of sense."

"Gautieri didn't come right out and say the Russians killed Dempsey. He was just, well, you put two and two together, including the fact the guy who shot me was Russian…"

Raymond glanced back at me. "If this is more than one or two men, I'm talking about the one who shot you and the guy who showed up at the house... and now you're trying to tell me this is much bigger, and you really believe the Russian Mafia's involved?" His eyes were in the rearview. "Maybe it is time to seriously consider backing away from this. You have no idea what you're up against, Jake. And if Lily is caught up in something, maybe she and the husband got in over their heads..."

He took the Olneyville exit and pulled into Wood's Gas station, parking by a phone booth on the corner of the lot.

I opened the door on the driver's side and stepped out, reaching into my pants pocket. But I only had one dime. I knocked on Raymond's window. "You got any change?"

He rolled down the window and reached for his ashtray. He handed me a few coins.

I picked up the handset and dropped three quarters in the slot, closing the bifold door behind me as I dialed the Boston Police. I waited for it to ring and watched a kid through the glass filling up his pickup truck with gas. The moron had a lit cigarette hanging from his mouth.

I couldn't help wondering how some people could be so stupid... do the dumbest things, put their lives at risk every minute of every day, and somehow make it through each day without a scratch. But then, on the other hand, you have honest people who do the right thing, eat the right food, don't drink, don't smoke at gas stations... and their lives are cut short. Sometimes for being in the wrong place at the wrong time. Sometimes, just bad luck.

The phone was answered on the fifth ring. "Boston Police," the male voice said.

"Detective Moriarty, please?" I said.

I was put on hold without another word and waited. I looked in the driver's-side window at Raymond and saw Maggie lean down and look over at me from the passenger seat.

I hadn't talked to her again about taking time from work to help me. She was the type of person who always put everyone around her ahead of herself. That's what made her a good cop, even though she got very little respect, being one of only a few female officers with the Boston Police.

I hadn't even thought much about our relationship. I guess I'd never given it much thought. It's like she was just *there*. Always. She was there for me when Barbara was killed. She was there for Nancy.

Had I taken her for granted?

The phone clicked. "Detective Moriarty."

"It's Jake," I said, without any of the insignificant salutations.

"I hear you got out early," he said.

"The hospital? Yeah, I'm out."

"You say it like you were just released from prison."

"It's not much better."

"Ha," he said. "Clearly you've never been to prison."

"Nope. Not yet."

The line went quiet.

"So, is there something I can do for you?" Moriarty said.

"I wanted to share some information with you. It has to do with Michael Dempsey and an initiative he was involved in, between Tony Gautieri and Mayor Bedford. I don't know how much you know about it, but apparently Angela Gautieri and Michael Dempsey took the lead in bringing the two cities together, trying to stop illegal gun trafficking. From what I understand, the Russian Mafia seems to be—"

"I hope you're not trying to tell me you think Michael Dempsey was assassinated by the Russian mob, are you?"

"Well, it's just that, because he was—"

"You think they'd go after a man because he was involved in coordinating a so-called conference? You really think an event like that actually has any impact? It's a show for those in public office, and nothing more. Just to make them feel like they're actually doing something. Christ, Horn. If all we had to do was put on a show, hand out some buttons and hats and brochures... we could put an end to crime for good. Don't you think?" He laughed on the other end.

"You don't even want to look into it?" I said.

"Into the Russian Mafia? No, I don't. Just because the hack who shot you had a Russian accent, doesn't mean the whole Soviet Union's out to get you."

"You're not even going to entertain the idea Dempsey could have been involved in something like—?"

"Of *course,* he was involved in *something.* People don't normally just get shot for doing *nothing.*" He paused, likely aware his condescending arrogance had pushed him across the line. "I'm sorry, I take that back."

I was quiet, tempted to slam down the phone. But I knew it wouldn't get me anywhere. "Why do I get the feeling you're not going to budge from your stance that Lily killed her husband."

"I can only look at the facts," he said.

"It seems to me you're ignoring most of them. And I'm not exactly sure why."

I heard Moriarty sigh into the phone.

He said, "I know you like to act like you have all the answers. But let me just make you aware that someone like you, a man who maybe deep down wishes he were a real detective, does not have all the answers. You know why? Because you don't have access to all the information an outsider like you would need to solve a crime such as this one."

"What the hell's that supposed to mean?" I said, the pain in my side starting to kick up again. I reached into my pocket, held the phone between my shoulder and ear, and twisted the top on the bottle of pain meds. I dropped three pills into the palm of my hand and put my head back, tossing them down my throat.

"It means you don't know how much of a lowlife Michael Dempsey really was. You don't know that he had cocaine in his system. You don't know how much alcohol was in his system. And on top of the fact he was a sloppy mess the night he was killed, it appears he may have hired a hooker to meet him at the motel. Is there anything I just said that isn't *news* to you?"

I held the phone up to my ear, still holding the bottle of medicine in my hand. "No." I felt like he'd just reached through the phone and slapped me in the face.

"See, that's what happens when someone who isn't a real cop tries to solve a crime. You're left picking up little pieces, or coming up with conspiracy theories that make no sense. The simple truth is, you don't have what it takes to solve even a simple crime in today's world. This isn't the nineteen sixties anymore, Horn. It's not like when your uncle was one of just a handful of private detectives out there... who got the respect from real law enforcement. The truth is, your days might just be over."

As much as I wanted to drive up to Boston and knock Moriarty on his ass, I was afraid he might not have been very far off base. Maybe my days as a private investigator *were* already over.

"And you know what else?" he continued. "Just in case you still think I'm full of it and want to pursue this so-called Russian man who shot you, the truck driver who saved your life never saw the man you described driving the Buick Skylark."

"Bullshit," I said.

"Yeah? You want to see the statement he gave to Worcester PD? He said he was on his way past the warehouse, saw you lying on the ground outside your car. They've yet to find any other witnesses who saw something. They're not even finding a witness who heard the gunshot."

I looked outside the booth at Raymond in the front seat, holding his wrist up so I could see it, tapping his watch. He mouthed something, and I could only assume we needed to go. I put up my index finger toward him and said into the phone, "So, what, you think I shot myself? This doesn't make any sense."

"I don't know what to tell you," Moriarty said. "Besides, well, maybe you can find something else to focus on. Because, here's the thing, Horn: I want you out of the way. Do us all a favor and just walk away from this investigation. If you can't do that, I'm afraid there are going to be some consequences you may not like."

"You can't..."

All I heard on the other end was a dial tone.

I slammed down the phone and kicked open the phone booth's door.

Raymond rolled down the window, he and Maggie looking out at me. "You all right?" he said.

"No. Not really," I said.

Maggie leaned her head down, looking up at me. "Moriarty?"

"Yeah. He's an ass."

As agitated as I was, my body felt calm. I was practically pain free. The pain meds, as much as I hated taking anything other than a six-pack to deal with both physical and mental pain, no doubt had an effect on me. "Give me a minute." I stepped back into the booth, reached into my pocket, and took out the paper with the number to Corey's parents' house on the Cape.

I dropped three quarters into the slot and dialed the number. It rang eight times. Nobody answered. I hung up and the coins dropped into the return. I picked them out and dropped them back into the slot, pulled the paper from my pocket, and dialed the number once again.

The phone on the other end rang another eight times. I let it keep ringing, maybe fifteen rings before I hung up.

I looked at the paper with the number and wondered if I read the numbers right. But it had been clearly written. And I couldn't imagine I'd gotten it wrong more than once. I stepped out from the booth and got back in the car. "No answer," I said.

"You want to try again?" Raymond said, turning the key in the ignition, knowing we were running short on time. I knew Maggie had to get to work.

***

Raymond went left off Route 6 out in Foster, in the northwestern part of Rhode Island, and continued up a long dirt driveway with large boulders lined up on either side of it. He stopped behind a black Ford pickup parked in front of a red barn the size of a two-story house.

I stepped out of the car and heard a tractor somewhere off in the distance. I started toward the barn and looked at least a dozen cows behind a wire fence. Closer to the side of the barn was a smaller pen with five or six large pigs inside it, with three small piglets running around like puppies, playing.

An older man driving a tractor, pulling a trailer behind it through the mud and patches of snow on the ground, turned the corner from behind the barn. He looked my way and shut off the engine, climbing down off the tractor. He started toward me. "Can I help you?" Maggie and Raymond walked up behind me, and his eyes went right to Maggie. He smiled at her with his stained teeth, showing off a wad of tobacco behind his lip.

"Are you Jed Roy?" I said.

He gave a quick nod, straightening his green John Deere hat. He looked at the three of us with suspicion. "Something I can help you with?"

"My name's Jake Horn," I said, reaching out to shake his hand. I introduced Raymond and Maggie behind me.

"Is there a problem?" he said. He spit tobacco juice into the mud where he stood.

My eyes went to the pigs in the pen. "I understand someone took one of your pigs?"

He nodded. "Sick sons of bitches. Just left her there on the side of the road. Couldn't even sell the meat, had been picked over by the coy-dogs. Lost me two hundred seventy dollars."

"Coy-dogs?" Raymond said. "What's a coy-dog?"

"Part coyote, part dog. They're all over the place out here now."

Maggie said, "Is that a real thing? A coy-dog?"

The farmer nodded. "See 'em at night once in a while, but not much different than a coyote."

I said, "Well, Jed, your pig's head ended up in my bed."

He removed his John Deere hat, ran his hand through his sweaty gray hair and placed the hat back on his head. "Your bed? Are you making a joke?"

"I wish I was."

He said, "Mind if I ask you why in the world someone would do such a thing?"

"I have a couple of ideas, but the reason we're here is I was hoping you could help me figure it out."

Jed looked at each of us. "Not sure how. If I knew who it was myself, I'd put a slug right in the bastard's ass." He looked toward the house, set back a ways from the barn and just before the woods. "Wife don't like to hear me talk like that. Says going to prison wouldn't be worth the money I lost on that pig. But I sure would like to know who stole her."

"So you never saw anything?" I said. "Or anyone?"

"Well, you know, I hadn't mentioned something to Bernie I realized after the fact. I probably should have, but—"

"Who's Bernie?" I said.

"Bernie? Are you not from around here?"

"Boston."

"Boston, huh?" He spit another stream of tobacco juice on the ground. "Bernie's chief of police here in Foster. He's the one came out when I first told him my pig had gone missing. Of course, he said he'd look around, but there wasn't much he could do. I'm not sure I understood why, but he came back a day later, told me they'd found her but didn't have any information."

"You said there was something you didn't tell him?" Maggie said.

"Oh, right." His eyes went past us again, toward the road. "A lot of people stop, pull in, and look at the animals. Some, I'm guessing, like, in the city, never seen a real farm before. Usually it's families, got little kids, take a drive out after church to see the animals. I don't mind, long as they don't come walking up toward the house or causing any kind of trouble."

I gave Raymond and Maggie a glance and assumed, like me, they wondered where Jed was going.

He continued. "One morning—sun was barely up—I was up at the house and could see a truck driving away. A small one, but..." He looked behind him toward his house. "Man got out, was over near the pigpen, just standing there. Soon as he looked up, must've seen me coming toward him, got back in his truck and was gone."

"Was your pig missing?"

"Not at the time. But it got me thinking just last night, I should've mentioned it to Bernie. Might be nothing at all, but..."

"Did you get a good look at the truck?" Raymond said.

Jed shrugged. "Well, like I said, it was still dawn. He'd parked it out by the road, walked up the driveway. Tractor trailer had gone by, headlights gave me a quick glimpse of it. I couldn't tell you what make or model exactly. One of those small Japanese makes. You know, a Datsun or Toyota. I couldn't make out what color it was. Maybe white or light blue." He looked at his truck. "You wouldn't catch me driving something like that. I don't even know how anyone can call it a *truck*. And if it ain't made in America..."

"So he saw you? And took off?" I said.

Jed nodded. "Ran down the driveway and jumped in the truck, was gone. I didn't get much of a look at him, but he was big." He looked at me, then up at Raymond. "I'd say he was your size. Honestly, too big for that little truck he was driving." He scratched the back of his neck. "Maybe I should go call Bernie."

CHAPTER 31

I HUNG UP THE phone at my desk and looked up at Raymond. "There's still no answer. Why aren't they answering the phone?" I was, without a doubt, concerned. "Why hasn't she called me?"

He had his back to me, looking at the photos on the wall of his father and some of his most famous clients. He said, "They probably went out somewhere."

"They're not supposed to be out. They're supposed to be in the house." I picked up the phone and dialed again. But this time, on the fifth ring, it was finally answered.

"Hello?"

"Corey? It's Jake Horn."

"Mr. Horn? Oh, hi, uh..."

"Are you two all right?" I said, maybe a slight hint of panic in my voice. "Where've you been? I've been calling you."

"Oh, yeah. Everything's good here. It's a little colder in the house than I'd expected. Nancy's right here, if you want to talk to her?"

"Yes. Please." I tried not to sound upset and probably had no reason to be. I waited a handful of seconds until Nancy finally got on the line.

"Dad?"

"Where have you been?" I said, not even asking how she was doing.

"Why do you sound mad?"

I swallowed and sat down in the chair at the desk. "I'm sorry. I'm not. I was just worried, that's all. I called you at least half a dozen times."

"Oh, sorry. We went out for pizza. We were both starving, and there's no food here."

One of my biggest problems was I could often let my imagination get the best of me. Although I'd seen enough in my lifetime to feed that imagination. "Is everything else okay? Corey said it's cold?"

"He's lighting the stove. They only have a little bit of wood, so..." She was quiet for a moment. "Are you sure this is even necessary?" she said.

"What, sending you out to the Cape?" I said, looking at Raymond as he sat down in one of the two chairs across from my desk. "For now, yes. Did you make sure nobody followed you?"

"Yes. We're good."

"Okay, well, just do me a favor and stick close to the house. And if you are going to be out for long, just give me a call at the house or the office and let me know. Or try Raymond's house if you can't reach me."

"Where are you now?"

"Raymond and I are at the office."

"Where's Maggie?" she said.

"She's at work. Although, she's got patrol around here, so she might drop in. Did you need her for something?"

Nancy paused on the other end. "No, not really. I was just…" She paused again. "I like when she's with you."

I didn't know how to respond or ask Nancy exactly what she meant. I guess I understood, because I knew how much Nancy loved Maggie. But she'd never said anything like that before. Not since she was little. "Don't worry," I said. "You want us to call you later, if she shows up?"

"Yeah. Okay. But, is it okay if we go down to the beach?"

"Isn't it a little cold?" I said.

"We're not going sunbathing," she said.

I laughed. "Don't go in the water. Your toes'll fall off."

"Okay. I'll talk to you later. Don't worry about me," she said. "We'll be okay."

I hung up the phone, got up, and walked over to the window, looking out toward West Broadway.

Raymond said, "Everything all right?"

I nodded, but kept my gaze outside the window. "I hope I didn't overreact, sending them off to hide in some house on the Cape."

"I don't know how you could think you're overreacting," he said. "The only thing I don't understand is why Moriarty seems to want to paint you as a liar. It makes no sense."

I nodded, agreeing with Raymond. "I'm not even sure exactly where to go from here." I walked back to the desk and looked at the phone. "It would be nice if Lily would call."

"We have to find her," Raymond said. "She's clearly got answers she's kept from you." He got up from the chair and sat back on the desk. "And what about the cousin?"

"Jill?" I said, shaking my head. "I don't know. I can't imagine she'd go there. I have a feeling at this point she'd be able to come up with a better place to hide. It's not like it's much of a secret at this point."

The pain was starting to kick in again, so I walked over to the coat rack by the door and pulled out the bottle of pain meds.

"Didn't you just take those?" Raymond said.

I read the label. "Well, it's kind of starting to hurt again." I lifted up my shirt and looked at the white bandage. There was a spot of blood coming through.

Raymond walked toward me, pulled the bottle from my hand and looked at the label. "Maybe you just oughta take it easy. You're not supposed to pop these like it's candy, you know."

I grabbed the bottle back from his hand. "I don't have time to take it easy." I popped the top, dropped three pills in the palm of my hand and tossed them down my throat. I grabbed my jacket off the rack. "You mind taking me back to your house to get my car?"

"The doctor said you're not supposed to drive."

"Yeah, I know. I heard him. Maggie already reminded me more than once. And now I've got you." I grinned. "I'm fine." I started toward the desk. "I need to go talk to Jimmy Ryan."

"The truck driver?"

"I want to talk to him ASAP, ask him why he lied to the cops about seeing the guy who shot me."

Raymond said, "But you don't even know where he lives."

I reached down, opened the lower right drawer of the desk, and pulled out the White Pages phone book.

Raymond laughed. "You know how many Jimmy Ryans there are in Massachusetts? I went to school with three of 'em."

I sat down in the desk chair and flipped through the phone book and stopped at the R's.

It turned out Raymond was right. There were a lot of Jimmy Ryans in Massachusetts. Including the last name Ryan with an initial J, and I counted eleven.

"I could make a call," he said, looking at his watch. "But it may have to wait until morning."

"It can't wait."

"What about Maggie?" he said.

"You heard her. She's on foot patrol all night. And I don't want her putting her career on the line for this, more than she already has."

He said, "She *wants* to help you."

I gave him a quick nod and looked back at the list of names in front of me. I ran my finger down and stopped at *James Ryan*.

The phone rang three times and a woman answered.

"Hello?" she said.

"Is Jimmy home?" I said, sounding cool and relaxed, like I was calling for a buddy.

She was quiet for a moment. "*Jimmy?* Who is this?"

"A friend of his, I—"

"Are you looking for James? Or Jimmy?"

"Uh, Jimmy?"

"Well, my husband, James, has been dead for three years. But, Jimmy, my son, I don't know why you're calling here looking for him."

"Maybe I have the wrong number," I said. "I drive a truck, and—"

"You must be looking for my son," she said. "He also drives a truck."

I'd clearly gotten lucky.

She continued, "Would you like his number?"

I smiled. "That would be great."

I wrote it down on the yellow legal pad and ran my finger down the other names in the phone book, stopping when I came to the number his mother had given me. "Thank you," I said, and hung up. *Easy enough*, I thought, running a line with my pen under the street address before the phone number.

***

GREGORY PAYETTE

Raymond drove me out to Shrewsbury to talk to Jimmy Ryan and pulled in the driveway of the small Cape Cod-style home with a small yard and trees around it. We parked behind a brown Ford Pinto with a Gerald Ford for President bumper sticker on the rear window. It had gotten darker since we left Boston, although the sun was hanging on longer than it had been all winter.

As soon as we stepped from Raymond's car, I heard the loud and whining sound of a gas-powered chainsaw. I could even smell the fresh-cut wood: a smell you rarely got in the city. I always found the smell of cut wood somewhat comforting, although I'm not sure why.

I didn't bother to knock on the front door, and walked with Raymond around the house toward the backyard. A man had his back to us, working the chainsaw through a downed oak tree laying across the mostly snow-covered yard, although there were spots where you could see the brown grass. The fence that enclosed the yard was broken, apparently where the tree he was cutting into pieces had fallen.

I didn't want to startle a man with a chainsaw in his hands, so I waited until he finally stopped and placed the saw down on top of the pile of wood. "Excuse me," I said. "Jimmy?"

He looked over at me and Raymond and calmly turned off the idling chainsaw. He wasn't the least bit startled.

I didn't recognize the man at all and wondered if we had the wrong guy. By the time he'd gotten to me after I was shot, I wasn't seeing very clearly. Most of the details of what happened after the gun was fired were unclear, to say the least.

"Who the hell are *you*?" he said, lifting his protective goggles from his eyes. To say he looked pissed to have two strangers in his backyard would be an understatement.

"You probably don't recognize me without all the blood," I said. "I'm the guy whose life you saved, over at the industrial park."

He removed his hat and wiped his forehead with the sleeve of his plaid flannel shirt, looking at Raymond, then back at me. "How'd you find me?"

"It wasn't that hard," I said. I didn't tell him his mother gave up his number without a question. "I thought I owed it to you, come out here and say thanks, face-to-face."

"No need. I did what anyone else would've done." He pulled the goggles down over his eyes and picked up the chainsaw. "If you don't mind, I gotta get this tree cut up before we lose what's left of the daylight." He went back to what was left of the fallen tree, pulled the cord and started the saw. He started cutting with his back to us once again.

I walked around so he could see me and yelled as loud as I could over the sound. "Do you mind giving me a minute?"

He looked up at me, kept the saw running for another moment until he finally turned it off, placing it back down on the pile. "I'm sorry, but I'd like you to leave."

Raymond walked around the cut-up tree and stood next to me.

"I just want to know why you told the police you didn't see the man who shot me?"

He pulled the goggles off his head and this time tossed them on the pile, next to the saw. He squinted his eyes a bit, stoic, without answering.

I said, "I was still conscious when the guy who shot me took off. I saw you get out of your truck. He drove a gold Buick Skylark right past you. I guess I'm just curious how you could say you didn't see it?"

Jimmy Ryan appeared to try to hide his swallow, but he had a thick Adam's apple, and it was like it had a life of its own the way it jumped in his throat.

He pulled work gloves off his hands and placed them on top of the saw, then stood quietly looking around the yard, like he was trying to come up with what he could say. He cleared his throat. "Listen, I'm glad to know you're all right. But I'm sorry. I can't help you from here. I got down from that truck; there was nobody else around. That's the truth. I saw you lying there on the asphalt, could see all the blood from a mile away. I knew there wasn't time for me to go find a phone, call the ambulance. I guessed you would've been dead." He gave me and Raymond a quick nod. "Now, if you'll both excuse me, I got somewhere I need to be."

I stepped toward him and grabbed his arm by the sleeve but he yanked it away. "Did someone threaten you? Tell you not to tell anyone what you saw?"

"I want you to get off my property. Don't make me call the police."

Raymond reached for my arm, pulling me back. "Come on, Jake. Let's go. He's not going to talk."

Jimmy picked up his saw and the gloves and goggles and started toward a door at the back of the garage.

I followed after him. "Hey, Jimmy. Any chance you happen to have any kids?"

He stopped at the door, his hand on the knob, turning to me. "I got a boy. A little boy. Lives with my ex though. Why?"

"You must miss him?" I said.

He took a step toward me, the saw in one hand, the goggles and gloves in the other. "You trying to make some kind of threat toward me?"

I put my hands up in front of me, palms toward him. "Not at all. What I'm trying to tell you is the man who shot me, the one you claim you didn't see? He threatened me. He threatened to harm *my* child, if I didn't give him what he was looking for. And by you saying you didn't see who shot me, or even see the damn car that drove right past you, you're putting my daughter's life in danger. Do you understand that?"

It was getting darker out at that point, but I could see Jimmy Ryan look past me toward the pile of wood he'd cut. He crouched down and placed the chainsaw on the ground in front of the door, dropped his gloves and goggles on top of it before straightening up. "They threatened me," he said. "It was two men, told me if I tell anyone I saw who shot you, I'd pay the price. They *knew* I had a kid." I could see in the light coming from inside the house that the man, shorter than me but by no means small, looked to have tears coming down his face. "I'm sorry, but I can't take the chance. I'm afraid... I know who these people are."

"You *know* who they are?" Raymond stepped next to me, staring Jimmy Ryan in the eye. "Did they come out here, to your house?"

"No. They followed me. Stopped me in my truck."

"But how do you know who they are?"

He took a moment before he answered. "I don't know if they're the Russian Mafia or got some other connection, but—"

"How do you know?" I said.

"That they're Russians?" He shrugged, looking around the dark yard as if someone could be listening. He kept his voice low. "Half the truckers I know are working for them."

"Is that true?" Raymond said, looking from Jimmy Ryan to me.

He put his hands together in front of him, like he was praying. "Please don't tell the cops. Don't tell anyone I told you. I don't know what they'll do to me... my little boy."

"Any chance you recognized the two men? Or seen them before?"

Jimmy cleared his throat. "One of 'em, the older one, I'm pretty sure he's the one who shot you. The way he talked about it, it was almost like he wanted me to know. Like he was proud. I think he thought you were dead."

"What about the other one?"

"He was a big guy. Bearded, twice the size of the Russian."

"Weren't they both Russian?"

Jimmy shrugged, shaking his head. "I don't know for sure. He looked more like a lumberjack than anything else. He didn't say much of anything, so I can't say."

Raymond said to him, "Are you serious, a lot of drivers you know work for these guys?"

He nodded. "They make an extra grand or two each delivery."

"Each delivery?" I said. "What are they delivering?"

"You mean the legal load or the illegal load?" he said.

"So they mix whatever it is in with their regular deliveries?"

"Of course. Yes. A normal run can be anywhere from as far north as Maine to any of the Middle Eastern states: Pennsylvania, Virginia, Maryland. If a driver goes all the way to Florida, he can make in a week what he'd normally make in a month."

"And what is it they're moving? Would I be right if I guessed they're running guns?"

Jimmy nodded. "How'd you know that?"

Chapter 32

Raymond turned off Route 44 into Woodstock and down the dirt road, not more than twenty minutes from Jimmy Ryan, in Shrewsbury. We were in the driveway, the headlights shining on a Ford Bronco that looked brand new. A sticker on the rear hatch said *Mayweather Ford*.

Smoke rose from the chimney.

Raymond nodded toward a long, tall pile of cut wood that ran maybe twenty feet in length, piled at least four or five feet high. "Must be nice, don't have to give all your money to the oil man."

I looked inside the Bronco as we walked up the driveway toward the house, but it was clean and empty inside. I could almost smell the rubber on the new tires.

Raymond stopped before the front door and looked up at the moonlit sky over the tall trees surrounding their property. "I could live out here, with all this quiet." He pointed at a house you could barely see through the empty trees, still weeks away from having any leaves. "Nice to not have neighbors who can see in your window."

I stepped around him and pressed the doorbell. "I thought you liked your neighbors?" There were lights on inside.

"I do," he said. "But I'd like them more if I couldn't see them from my driveway."

After a minute, the interior door finally opened, and Jill stood on the other side of the storm door's glass. She had tears in her eyes and appeared to be visibly shaken as she pushed open the door. Rather than ask us in, she stepped outside, looking down toward the stairs.

"Jill? What's wrong?" I said. I gave Raymond a quick glance.

She looked up and wiped the tears from her face with the sleeve of her heavy white sweater. She looked up and around the yard and out toward the road before she answered.

I glanced at Raymond, and before I could say another word, Jill flew into my arms, wrapped her arms around me, and cried.

"Jill, tell me what's wrong. What happened?"

She pulled herself off me and wiped both eyes with her hand, choking back her tears. "Someone was here... a man. He just left. He... he was here looking for Lily. He threatened me when I told him I didn't know where she was."

"Who?" I said. "What else did he say?"

She sniffled. "When I told him I didn't know where Lily was, he asked for Pete."

"Pete? He *knows* Pete?"

She shrugged. "I don't know. I was so scared, I couldn't even think. He threatened me, Jake. He went through my whole house." She looked back inside through the glass.

Raymond said, "Did you call the police?"

She stared back at him. "Who... who are *you*?"

I looked back and forth between the two, not realizing they'd never met. "Oh, I'm sorry. Jill, this is my cousin, Raymond."

She gave him a nod. "This man, he told me if I didn't want anything to happen to my kids, I wouldn't call the cops."

I looked back toward the road. "Can you tell me what he looked like?"

"He was short. An older man. I couldn't see his eyes, with his sunglasses on. He had a Russian accent."

I glanced at Raymond, then back at Jill. "You know what kind of car he was driving?"

"No. I didn't see a car. He came through the back door, waiting for me in the kitchen when I came downstairs."

I looked around the yard, glanced back at Raymond, and put my arms around Jill's shoulders. "Maybe we should go inside."

She nodded, grabbed the door, and walked in ahead of us.

I closed the door behind us and locked it.

It was warm inside. "Where are the kids?"

"Oh, they're in bed," Jill said.

I hadn't thought about how late it had gotten. I looked around the house and noticed how much different it looked from just a few days earlier. The plants and potted trees were still in every corner and on every window sill. But the old furniture was gone, at least in the main living area where we stood, replaced with a yellow leather couch and a matching love seat, arranged around a large wooden coffee table with bark around the rim of the tabletop, like it had been sliced from an old tree out back and placed on four legs.

Maybe it had been.

They'd had a small black-and-white TV on a metal stand before. But it, too, was gone, replaced with a large console TV, pushed up against the wall. It was a color TV, turned on, but with the volume down. There were more plants on top of it, vines hanging off the side, with small framed photos, and a set of rabbit ears.

I took off my coat and hung it over my arm. "Have you talked to Pete?" I said, looking toward the stairs. "He's not here, is he?"

"He's working. Driving. He called this morning, but that was the last time I spoke to him. I can't normally get in touch with him when he's on the road." Jill looked at the clock on the wall. "He usually calls by now." She blew her nose into a tissue and walked toward the kitchen, stopping and turning in the doorway. "He's been driving so much lately, he said sometimes he doesn't have time to stop and call me. He's not even home like he used to be." She crossed her arms and rubbed them up and down, like she was trying to break a chill even though it must've been eighty-five degrees in that house.

"I'm sorry for asking this," I said. "But is there... did you ever suspect there was something going on between Pete and Lily?"

A quick laugh broke through her tears. "Pete and Lily? Not a chance. Pete never even liked Lily very much."

"There's no way it's possible?"

"Is *what* possible?"

"That they were involved in something together?"

Jill's eyebrows tightened. "I'm sorry, Jake, but I don't think I like these questions. I don't know where you're coming up with any of this. But I can promise you, there was nothing between Lily and Pete."

"I don't mean just romantically," I said. "Anything. I'm just trying to—"

"I said there was nothing!" she snapped, walked past me, and sat down on the couch. She leaned forward, her elbows on her knees, balling her tissue between both hands.

I said, "Did he tell you I called last night?"

She looked up at me, wiping her nose with what was left of the tissue in her hand. "Pete?"

I grabbed a box of tissues from a small table in the corner and handed it to Jill.

She pulled one out and wiped her eyes with it. "Maybe he forgot to tell me," she said.

I gave Raymond a quick glance. "Maybe."

Jill took a deep breath and let out a sigh, looking toward the stairs. She whispered, "What am I supposed to do? I can't call the police."

"Well, I have a pretty good idea of who came here looking for Lily. But if he knows who Pete is, and he's looking for Lily..."

"How do you know who he is?" she said, almost like she didn't want me to finish my thought.

"I'm guessing you don't know this, but somebody shot me." I lifted my shirt and showed her the bandage."

Her eyes opened wide, and she covered her mouth with both hands. "You were shot? By the man who came here?"

"I believe so. I was on my way to meet Lily. She'd called me."

She looked me up and down. "Are you okay?"

Raymond looked at me, like he wanted to hear the answer too.

"I'm fine," I said.

"Do you know where she is?"

"That morning was the last I heard from her. I ended up in a hospital in Worcester."

I couldn't figure out if she was being honest with me or if she was just a better actor than I would have imagined.

Raymond said, "Where is your husband now?"

She looked up at him. "I already said, he's on the road."

"I heard that part," he said. "I mean, do you know what state he might be in? Or what his route is?"

I gave Raymond a look, almost to say there's no way she'd know that. But I had a feeling he was trying to get somewhere.

She shrugged. "I wouldn't know that."

"But you're certain he's actually on the road, right?" he said, then gave me a quick glance.

Jill looked confused. "Why... why wouldn't he be on the road?" She looked back and forth between me and Raymond. "I... I dropped him off at his truck last night."

"And you saw him drive off?"

Jill had a look on her face like she didn't like the questions. "I don't wait for him to drive away. Not anymore. I just drop him off and go, like he tells me to do."

Raymond and I exchanged a glance.

I said to Jill, "You mind if I ask you something somewhat personal?"

She stared back at me for a moment before she nodded. "I guess not."

"Well, it's just... you have all this new furniture. And that new Ford Bronco in the driveway's got to be at least six grand. You've got a big color TV I know costs quite a few dollars. But none of these things were here when I showed up looking for Lily." I glanced out the window. "I just find it kind of strange you'd go on a shopping spree like this when your cousin's missing."

"Pete's been working hard. We've never spent much money." She looked around the room. "Other than buying this house."

I said, "I don't know your financial situation, but I can't help but wonder about what all this stuff must've cost. I don't know how much Pete makes as a trucker, but..."

Jill got up from the couch and walked to the front of the room. She stood by the window to the right of the front door and looked outside. "Like I said, Pete's been working hard. He's put in quite a few extra miles the past couple of months."

"Enough to buy all this stuff? And a brand new vehicle?"

She stared back at me. "I don't know exactly what you're trying to imply, Jake, but I don't like it. If you think Pete—"

"I'm just trying to find some answers."

"Well, just because we had a little extra money to spend, doesn't mean there's something sinister going on. I don't like this at all."

"I'm not trying to get you upset, Jill. A lot has happened. And most of it doesn't make a lot of sense." I wasn't ready to tell her what Jimmy Ryan had told me about all the truckers out there, making money running guns up and down the coast. I had a feeling she wouldn't believe me if I told her or suggested Pete could've been somehow one of the drivers involved.

The three of us stood quiet for a couple of moments.

"Do you know what hotels he stays at when he's on the road?" I said. "I assume he has certain places he'll stay at, considering he must make the same run?"

Jill shrugged. "Sometimes he'll get some sleep right in the truck. Or he'll stay at hotels... usually the same places."

I thought for a moment. "You ever hear of a place called the Turnpike Inn, down in Pennsylvania."

She paused a moment before she answered. "Why?"

"It's just a place I heard something about."

She cracked a very slight smile, tilting her head, and placed her palm flat against her cheek. "Pete took me there once when he first started driving trucks. I went with him on a route, just to see what it was like. We stayed at the Turnpike Inn."

"Do you know if he still stays there?"

"I don't ask him much about his trips like I used to," she said. "Unless he has a story to tell me about something that happened along the way." She looked at Raymond, then back to me. The small smile on her face disappeared. "Can you tell me why you're asking?"

I thought maybe it was better that she didn't know every detail. But I thought if I was honest with her, she'd be the same with me. "I found a page from a phone bill in Lily's apartment. There were a handful of toll calls made there, to the Turnpike Inn."

Jill had a blank look on her face with a stare like she was trying to see right through me.

"I'm sorry," I said. "It's part of why I asked about Lily and Pete. I can't say for sure what it means, if anything. But, you'd have to admit, it seems to be more than just a coincidence."

She held her eyes closed for a moment, and when she opened them, they were filled with tears. "Lily and Pete?"

"We don't know what it means," I said. "But I'd be lying to you if I said it wasn't *something*."

She went back to the couch and sat down, tears coming down her face, but she looked to be in somewhat of a trance or shocked. In a soft, quiet voice, she said, "What am I supposed to do *now*?"

I sat down next to her. "I'm not sure if you and the kids should stay here. Is there somewhere else you can go?"

She shook her head. "I'm not leaving. I have to wait... I have to be here when Pete calls."

"But if this Russian guy comes back..." Raymond said. "Maybe you can just go to a hotel? Or a relative's house?"

Jill got up and disappeared into the kitchen. She walked back through the doorway within a moment holding a twelve-gauge shotgun with both hands. "If he comes back again, I'll be ready."

CHAPTER 33

JOHNNY CARSON WAS ON the TV, the volume low, when Maggie showed up at Raymond's house after her shift. Raymond and I were in the living room with a half-empty pizza box on the coffee table. She grabbed a slice and sat down in the wingback chair, leaning forward as she took a bite.

She knew most of what had happened when I spoke to her on the phone before she came over.

"But didn't you ask him, Jimmy Ryan, if he knew Jill's husband, Pete?"

Raymond and I both shook our heads. "I guess we could have. But I'm not sure it would've made much of a difference. I'm pretty certain he's in on something. You don't drive a truck—I mean, legally—and go out, drop six grand on a brand new Ford Bronco and a house full of leather furniture.

Maggie took a bite of pizza and nodded, her eyes on the TV. "And you really think Pete and Lily are in some kind of relationship? Did you ever suspect something could happen between them?"

"You mean, in the past? I didn't pay much attention to it. You know, I'm not the jealous type."

Raymond laughed. "So we'll ignore the time you broke Michael Dempsey's jaw?"

"You know what I'm saying. That was different. Either way, I don't know. They could've been flirting right in front of my face back then. I just wouldn't suspect it. If I'd been paying more attention..."

Raymond sipped from a can of Black Label. "We don't know anything about their relationship, so..."

Maggie and I both turned toward him.

He continued, "I'm just saying, without real proof, all we can do right now is make an assumption, mainly based on a phone call to a hotel. It's clearly not enough."

I looked at my watch and got up from the couch. "He's right. And whoever's after them—unless I've missed something—I don't believe it's got anything to do with them sleeping together."

Raymond said, "I'd be running for my life, too, if I had the Russian Mafia after me."

Maggie said, "But without any proof, you don't know how true that is either. Right?" She picked up her soda from the coffee table and took a sip, her eyes on mine. "Just because the man who shot you may be Russian doesn't necessarily mean he's part of the mob."

"Well, like I said, according to Jimmy Ryan, it looks like it's a pretty good chance the guy's connected. And the way Jill described him, it's the same man," I said.

"Still doesn't mean he's Mafia," Maggie said. "You know how many small-time crooks came over here from the Soviet Union?"

Raymond and I looked at each other.

I got up from the chair and had to catch my breath. The pain in my stomach was back. I looked toward my coat, hanging on the rack by the door. "But you take this illegal gun trafficking, you take

Pete driving a truck, throw in all the new things he and Jill just bought... it all seems to point toward something bigger than just some small-time crook making deliveries up and down the coast."

Maggie wiped her hands with a paper napkin and got up, headed toward the kitchen. "Mind if I grab a beer?"

Raymond pointed toward the doorway. "There's Black Label bottles, and a six of Narragansetts. Help yourself."

She walked back out, cracking the top on the 'Gansett. "This guy, the truck driver..."

"Jimmy Ryan?" I said.

"Yes. How do you know he's not driving for them? For the Russians?"

"I guess I don't. He said he's not."

Maggie took a sip from the can and sat back down in the same chair, next to me. "But they knew how to find him? Showed up at his house?"

I looked at Raymond, and he just shrugged, clearly neither of us having a good answer.

Maggie said, "Have you talked to Nancy?"

I nodded. "She seems good. I'm just not sure how much longer it makes sense to have her out there."

Raymond yawned.

"You could probably use some sleep," I said, getting up from the chair. I turned to Maggie. "Are you going home?"

She shrugged, shaking her head as she looked at her watch. "I'm wide awake. Why?"

"Well, I don't know if I feel like going home. I bleached the mattress, but..."

"You want to stay with me?" she said.

Raymond stood up, stretching his long arms with another yawn. "I told you, Beth fixed up the bed in the guest room. Clean sheets and everything." He grinned.

I thought for a moment, turning to Maggie. "You finish that beer, any chance you want to go grab one more?"

***

I parked behind Maggie's green Plymouth Scamp, and we both stepped out onto the street and over to the sidewalk at the same time. I pulled open the door to Gillian's Pub and looked back toward the street as Maggie walked in ahead of me. I watched a dark-colored sedan I couldn't quite see drive slowly past the building, but it sped up and disappeared down the street.

I tried not to be paranoid and didn't need to concern Maggie by mentioning a random, slow-driving vehicle that I assumed was nothing to worry about.

Gillian's Pub was mostly empty inside, other than an older man at the far end of the bar and the gray-haired bartender facing the other way, wiping down bottles from the shelves at the back of the bar. The customer wore a scally cap over his white hair, staring down into the glass before him. Smoke rose from a cigarette burning in the ashtray in front of him, but I wasn't sure he was even awake.

We pulled up two stools. The bartender glanced back at the clock on the wall behind him.

"Too late for a couple beers?" I said.

He scratched his forehead, pulled the towel off his shoulder, and wiped his hands. He placed two coasters down in front of us without a hint of a cordial welcome. "What'll it be?"

We ordered two Narragansett drafts and both sat quiet. The thirteen-inch TV on a shelf in the upper corner of the bar was turned off.

The bartender poured the two beers and placed them in front of us. I threw a five up on the bar and he cashed it out, placing three ones and a quarter in front of me.

"Listen, Maggie," I said, hesitant to say what I'd wanted to and thought it was the right moment. "I really appreciate all you've done for me. I don't mean just these past few days either. You've been around—helping out—for a long time. After Barbara was…" I picked up my beer and held it up in front of my chin. "I don't know if I would have made it very far without you."

She kept her eyes on her glass with a crooked smile on her face. "You would have been just fine."

I said, "I'm serious, Maggie. You did so much for us. For Nancy. And then"—I looked down into my beer—"after all that time you were around, for whatever foolish reason, I started dating Lily. And I think… I mean, I *know*, I sort of left you hanging. I kind of turned my back on you."

Her eyes were squinted, staring back at me as she slowly shook her head. "Why are you doing this? You never did anything wrong, Jake. I mean, it meant a lot to me, having Nancy—both of you—be a part of my life." She put her hand on top of mine. "Just because we kind of fell out of touch, it doesn't mean we're not a part of each other's lives."

I forced a smile, rubbing my unshaven face with my free hand. It was getting to a point it was almost a beard, but the bruises made it too much to shave. "I guess my point is, I'm not sure I ever actually thanked you. And now, here you are again. You've offered to practically put your career on the line to help not just me, but a woman I know you couldn't care less about."

Maggie took her hand back. "This has more to do with you and Nancy than it does helping Lily. That's just the truth, Jake. I'm not afraid to admit that. But, regardless of how I feel about her, it's my duty as a police officer to—"

"But they, your so-called superiors, don't want you involved. So this is more than you wearing the badge. And that's why I just think there's too much risk for you at this point. You can't risk your career like this."

"I'm a big girl," she said, putting her hand on mine once again. "You're a good guy, Jake." She got up and walked away without a word, continued past the old man, who finally lifted his head from his glass and looked over his shoulder at her as she headed for the restroom.

He looked at me. "That your lady?"

I smiled. "She's too good for me." I sipped my beer and saw the bartender walk through the swinging door from the kitchen. He stopped mid-step, and I watched his eyes widen as he looked past me in the direction of the front door.

I took a quick look over my shoulder as the door behind me creaked open. I jumped from my stool and almost stumbled, my eyes on the man who had just walked in.

The Russian, with his hair slicked back, sunglasses over his eyes—even though it was pitch black outside—stood in front of the door, facing me. He had his gun up, pointed right at me. "Unless you would like to have another bullet in your stomach, comrade, you are going to come with me."

I raised my hands up in front of me. "I'm not armed," I said. "And I'm not going anywhere with you."

He took another step toward me. "Would you like me to shoot you? Or do you want to tell me where she is?"

I looked behind the bar, but the bartender was gone. The old man down the other end had disappeared. I wanted to yell and warn Maggie, but I didn't want the Russian to know she was there. Although I guessed he already did.

I was afraid of what she was about to walk into. But before I'd even decided what to do, the door to the bathroom squeaked open.

Maggie stepped out around the bar and already had her gun raised, pointing it toward the Russian.

"Drop it!" she said.

But the man didn't flinch, facing me but looking out the corner of his eye, toward her. "You shoot me, pretty lady, and I shoot the boyfriend. Okay?"

I reached for my beer on the bar as he stepped closer, the gun out in front of him.

"I'm just getting a drink," I said, one hand up, palm out, the other holding the glass. I took a sip.

Maggie yelled, "Don't take another step toward him!"

"Shoot him," I said. I glanced at her, but I wasn't sure if she was ready to pull the trigger.

"The cops are probably on their way," I said, taking another quick glance behind me, hoping the bartender had at least made the call. "I can already hear the sirens."

The Russian man shook his head. "I do not hear anything. So why don't you put down your beer and come with me."

I saw a shadow through the window at the front of the place next to the entrance. I took a quick look at Maggie and saw her eyes go in the same direction.

Someone was standing outside the window. I didn't want to look to see who it was, drawing the Russian's attention to whoever it was.

But then I realized it was the bartender. He'd stepped back from the window and raised a shotgun up to the window.

I tossed my glass with the beer at the Russian at the same time a bright flash lit up the darkness outside the bar. The shot exploded, shattering the window as I dove out of the way.

The Russian's arms flew up in the air, his body thrust forward as he slipped on the wet floor and crashed into the stools right where Maggie and I had been seated moments before.

His gun dropped to the floor.

Maggie ran toward me, being careful not to slip in the beer I'd tossed. "Are you okay?"

I grabbed my side, nodding. "Are you?"

The bartender walked in the front door, looked down at the body, then nodded toward the old man, walking through the swinging door beside the back of the bar. "You call the cops?" he said to his friend.

The old man nodded without saying a word.

Maggie had her badge out. "I'm a Boston police officer." She crouched down next to the Russian's bloodied body and felt around his neck. She looked up at me. "He's dead."

***

I leaned against my Nova outside the bar, the old man from inside next to me but not saying much.

He looked toward the bar. "Did you know that man?" he said.

"A little."

He lit a cigarette and walked past the officer at the door and into the bar.

Moriarty showed up after the other officers but held court with them out in the street, along with Maggie. Boston squad cars were parked up and down both sides of the street. Moriarty pointed into the bar, animated with his hands as he talked, but I couldn't make out what he was saying.

The dead Russian was wheeled out on a stretcher, covered, and Moriarty walked up to it, lifted the sheet, and glanced at me. "You sure this is the same guy who shot you in Worcester?"

I nodded. "Yeah, I'm sure." He had his hands in the pockets of his trench coat, looked around, then stepped up to me. "Would've been nice if he was still alive to do some talking." He pulled a mint from his coat pocket and popped it in his mouth. "Didn't I ask you to stay out of all this?"

I was once again caught off guard by something Moriarty said, although I was getting used to it. "We were having a drink, minding our own business. This guy showed up with a gun in his hand, and you're talking like this was something I did? What the hell's your problem with me?"

Moriarty looked me right in the eye. "Because every time I get a call that there's a dead body, you're either already on the scene or somehow involved. You expect me to believe this is just some kind of coincidence?"

I wasn't sure how to respond. "You want the guy who's involved in everything?" I pointed toward the dead man on the stretcher. "Looks to me like you've got him."

CHAPTER 34

I SAT AT MY desk with the thick folders overflowing with articles and files and photos and copies of reports... a spiral-bound notebook filled with my own notes. Most of what I wrote included more questions than answers.

Everything in front of me had to do with my wife Barbara's death. It was the first time in a few months I'd even taken everything out from the locked metal filing cabinet behind my desk. I had the devil's ivy she bought for our Boston apartment on top of the cabinet and somehow kept it alive for all these years. Sometimes I wondered if I took better care of that plant than I did of myself.

Even before Lily showed up and occupied my mind with something else besides Barbara's murder, I'd slowly pulled back from trying to find the answer. I promised myself I'd never stop looking, but after more than a decade, I couldn't handle any more dead ends.

I pulled out the mugshot photo of Craig Parquet, the man convicted and charged with her murder. I thought back to the very first time she told me about him, and how he was a boyfriend from high school she'd only dated for a couple of months.

One day, out of the blue, he showed up at the flower shop where she worked in Back Bay. He bought flowers for his wife.

The first time, she admitted, she was almost excited to see him. We had an honest relationship, and I believed her when she said there was nothing to it.

But then he showed up again and waited for her outside the flower shop.

He asked her if she'd like to get a coffee. And when she called me to ask if I'd be okay if she went with him, I didn't like it. It wasn't that I was jealous. I wasn't worried she'd cheat on me. I just found it somewhat questionable.

But she was straight with me and assured me there was nothing to it. So I didn't make anything more out of it.

As it turned out, my concerns were warranted. Craig continued showing up after she got off work. And it soon got to a point she wanted him to stop.

I was forced to step in even though Barbara didn't want me to. I waited in my car across the street from the shop and saw him sitting on a bench along Newbury Street. I approached him, had a brief discussion—maybe including a slight threat or two—and it appeared to be over.

He apologized to me; we shook hands, and he swore he'd leave her alone.

Two weeks later, Barbara was found dead in her car at Franklin Park.

Within a week, Craig Parquet was arrested for her murder.

I studied his picture, then clipped it back inside the folder and swiveled in the chair and placed the folder back inside the filing cabinet. I got up and grabbed a paper cup, filled it with water from the bathroom, and poured it into the pot of devil's ivy.

There was a knock at the door and I stepped around the partition. Raymond's big head looked in at me through the window.

I unlocked the door and let him in. "Hey," I said, going back to the desk.

"You doing okay?" he said, closing the door behind him.

"I guess so," I said, lifting my mug from the desk. I walked to the coffee maker. "You want a cup?" I'd already had half the pot myself, and might've felt a little off-center with too much caffeine and maybe the extra painkillers I took when I first woke up on the couch.

I poured another cup anyway.

"I'm good," Raymond said. He sat down in one of the chairs in front of my desk.

I sipped the coffee, not exactly enjoying the burnt, stale flavor, and sat down with the files and folders in front of me.

"What's this?" Raymond said, picking up the folder with Barbara's photo inside it. He opened it, and looked over the contents. "I thought you were taking a break from all this?" He tossed the folder on the desk.

I nodded. "I was just looking at something."

"Yeah?" he said. "You don't have enough you're dealing with right now? It's been twelve years, Jake. I don't think putting it aside for a few months, taking a breather, was your worst idea."

I put down the mug and leaned back in the chair, nodding. "I guess you heard Vladimir Markov was in prison when Michael Dempsey was killed."

Raymond nodded. "Maggie told me."

"So that obviously shuts the door on him being the killer. Moriarty's eyes are back on Lily."

"If anyone can ever find her," he said.

I pulled out the folder with Craig Parquette's files inside it. "Can I share something with you, you're probably going to say is crazy?"

He nodded as he shifted in his seat. "It wouldn't be the first time." He grinned.

I looked toward the door and down at the phone on my desk, as if someone would hear what I was about to say, taking another sip of the coffee I didn't need, and placing the mug on the top of the desk. "What if there's some kind of connection between Michael Dempsey's murder and what happened to Barbara."

I would describe the look on Raymond's face as somewhat of a smirk, although I wasn't sure he knew exactly *how* he was supposed to react. But the look disappeared in a brief moment. He slowly shook his head. "I know you'll never believe Parquet is guilty, but this takes all your theories to another level," he said. "Honestly, it just doesn't make sense." He looked at the folders and files. "Come on, Jake. Put this stuff away. Give yourself a break."

He got up from his chair. "You want to tell me your theory?"

I stared up at him, shaking my head. "I want to go talk to Parquet."

Raymond's eyes sprung open. "Are you serious?"

I nodded. "I just... I'd rather do that than continue to speculate on what I'm—"

"Pulling out of your ass?" he said, leaning with both hands spread apart on the desk, staring down at me. "Maybe you just need to face the fact that Moriarty may not be as far off base as you'd like to think."

"What's that supposed to mean?" I said.

"You know what it means. Lily. Just like you refused to believe the man who was harassing your wife committed the unspeakable crime, you don't think Lily could do it either." He straightened up off the desk. "Let me guess, you didn't tell Moriarty about Lily and the cousin's husband?"

"Not yet. No."

"And you don't feel that's an important piece of information? Or are you afraid it'll make his case against Lily even stronger?" He started for the door and stopped, his hand on the knob. "I don't

314

know what to tell you, Jake. No matter what I say, you're always going to do what you feel you have to."

***

I sat in the private meeting room at Norfolk Prison, a vinyl-tiled floor with a rug-covered section in the corner with toys and books for the kids dragged by moms to see their convict daddies.

I stood still with my hands behind my back, looking out the window between the bars on the other side of the glass toward the yard. It was cloudy again, with a light drizzle coming down. Luckily, warm enough to avoid more snow.

The door opened.

Craig Parquet looked different. It had been a few years, but his hair was mostly gray on the sides and buzzed short. He'd put on a little weight, I thought. Last time I saw him he was thin as a rail.

The guard at the door gave me a nod. "I'll be right outside the door." He pulled the door closed.

Craig Parquet stood looking at me, in silence. "Why are you here?" He sat down at the brown wood laminate table pushed up against the wall. He wouldn't make eye contact with me.

I sat across from him, waiting to answer until I could look him in the eye. I paused, looking him over. "Will you look at me for a second?"

He raised his squinted eyes without a word.

"Did you kill my wife?"

He didn't give me an answer. Not right away, then slowly started to shake his head. "I may have done a lot of things I shouldn't have, and I know it doesn't matter what I say at this point. But I did *not* kill Barbara." He looked off, toward the white-painted cinder-block wall to his left. "I've already spent eleven years of my life in this place. And it won't be for another nine until I get my first shot at parole." He swallowed, shaking his head. "No matter how many times I say it, I'll never get the years back."

"Like you're the only one who's lost something?" I said.

"You asked me a question and I told you my answer. I don't know what else you want me to say." He looked down at his hands, rubbing them together before raising his eyes again to mine. "Do you still believe I did it?"

My heart pounded in my chest. No matter what I believed, I could see how one look at him, and you'd *think* he was guilty of something. He had a look about him. I don't know if I'd say it was a creepy look. But something was off. It still didn't make him a killer.

But it was more than just his looks that put him behind bars.

"That day you told me to leave her alone, I did that. I had no plans to ever even talk to her again."

I looked toward the door and the small windowpane with the back of the guard's neck the only thing in view. "Your attorney didn't do you any favors," I said.

He nodded and let out a deep sigh. "He was a moron," he said. "If I could've afforded my own defense attorney rather than a court-appointed idiot, maybe I wouldn't be here right now." He sat up straight and stretched his back. "I heard he's not even practicing law anymore. Got disbarred a couple of years ago." He snorted out a slight laugh. "Don't you think I should have been allowed a retrial?"

I said, "To walk in court and have your attorney say you were set up, but without an ounce of evidence to back it up..."

Parquet sighed again, nodding. "You're not telling me anything I haven't thought about for the past four thousand-plus days. Everyone knows how crooked the Boston Police have always been."

"But your lawyer never even mentioned he thought it could've been a cop."

Parquet nodded. "There was no chance of finding the evidence to say the gun was planted."

"You owned a lot of guns," I said.

He shrugged. "But that one, the one used to kill Barbara, it wasn't mine. All of my guns were registered but that one."

"Maybe if your wife hadn't taken the stand," I said.

Parquet stood up from the table. "Yeah, that backfired. I guess I didn't realize how pissed off she was about me bothering Barbara. Kind of put the nail in the coffin." He walked to the window and looked outside.

I got up from the table myself and stood ten feet behind him. "Just so I'm clear, I know the trial wasn't exactly fair. But I'm also not here to tell you I'm certain you're innocent. You were at that park. Someone saw you. And you left Barbara there."

He turned, staring back at me. "You were there. You heard me on that stand. I panicked. I knew how it looked. I knew someone set me up, and there was nothing I could do about it. I just wish I had the note."

"The note you destroyed?" I said. "Right about there is where I start to believe there's a good chance you're completely full of shit. And I should kill you right here, with my own two hands."

He put his hands up, palms out. "I didn't kill her. I know it's hard to believe. Nobody else believes me, why should you? But, you were at the trial. You heard the evidence."

"You say you've been in here, I don't know how many days you said, but you think a day hasn't gone by I haven't thought of what I lost? The mother my little girl lost?" I looked toward the door and saw the guard looking in at us through the small pane of glass.

"Can you tell me about the note?"

"You were there, in that courtroom. Why do you need me to—"

"Just tell me about the goddamn note," I said. "Everything you can."

"Why?"

I took a deep breath, trying not to grab this guy and put his head through the cinder-block wall. I closed my eyes and exhaled. "Please, Craig. Please, just tell me whatever you remember. It's important."

He swallowed, nodding as he sat back down at the table again. "Okay, well, the note... it was left on the front seat of my car. It was handwritten, so beautifully, on a piece of paper from what I'd assumed at the time was from the flower shop."

"But it wasn't," I said. "The owner testified you were bothering Barbara. And the prosecuting attorney asked him about the paper, which he denied having anything like what you described in his shop."

Parquet nodded and looked down at the floor. "I realize that now, but... I remember. I remember seeing the note. All it said was she wanted to meet me at Franklin Park. Her beautiful handwriting... it was so neat and—"

"Her beautiful handwriting? I don't remember you describing it that way on the stand. And, well, Barb had horrible penmanship."

Parquet said, "My attorney advised me to tone back the way I described it. He was afraid I would appear obsessed, describing it with any kind of emotion."

"Your lawyer was a buffoon," I said.

Parquet shrugged one shoulder. "What's it matter now?" He raised his eyes to mine. "The only person in that courtroom who, for some reason, seemed to be willing to believe I could be innocent... was you. Most people found that rather strange... the husband of the victim. Even Maggie—"

"Officer Donovan?"

"Yes. Sorry. Officer Donovan. I just... I remember when she took the stand; I knew right away her mind was already made up. To her, I was guilty before she ever knocked on my front door."

CHAPTER 35

I WENT STRAIGHT BACK to Milton from Norfolk Prison and pulled in the driveway behind the BMW I knew belonged to Corey. I hadn't heard from Nancy and wasn't exactly sure why they were back from the Cape.

The rain was coming down, and I ran up the driveway past the Beemer, straight up the steps with my keys in my hand. But Nancy was already at the door, holding it open for me.

"What are you doing here?" I said, somewhat upset she had, for some reason, decided to leave the Cape on her own without us discussing it. But I was also happy to see her, mixing my emotions.

She jumped into my arms, and we held each other.

"Maggie said the man who shot you was dead." She looked into my eyes, and all I could see was the little girl in her. "Is that true?"

I nodded, watching Raymond pull in the driveway in his Chrysler. I looked back at Nancy. "Yes, he's dead."

"But he's not the man who killed Lily's husband?" she said.

"No. He was in prison at the time. He'd only been out a few days when I ran into him." I stopped at the door and held it for Raymond running up the driveway in the rain.

"I didn't know you'd be back," he said. "Nancy called me."

The three of us walked into the house, Raymond making a beeline for the refrigerator. "You mind I take a beer?" he said.

"As long as you grab me one." I glanced through the doorway into the rest of the house. "Where's Corey?"

"He's changing," Nancy said. "We were outside in the rain for a little while, trying to get in the house."

I said, "Where's your key?"

"I must've left it at school. And the spare key wasn't under the rock."

I couldn't think of the last time anyone had to use it. "You sure?" I grabbed the umbrella and went outside toward the side of the house. I lifted the flat rock right at the corner before the backyard and crouched down, feeling the damp soil underneath. The key that had been there for as long as I could remember was gone. I ran back inside, and Raymond was waiting at the door.

"Didn't you look under there when the house was broken into?"

"I guess I didn't," I said. "Not very smart, huh?" We walked back into the kitchen. "But I don't know who even knew I kept it under there."

"Well, you might want to try and figure that out," Raymond said, staring back at me.

Nancy had a can of ginger ale and sat at the table.

I leaned against the counter in front of the sink. I said to Nancy, "So how'd you get in the house without a key?"

Nancy smiled. "The lockpick set."

"What *lockpick set*?"

"The one Uncle Pat gave me for my tenth birthday." She kept the smile on her face.

"You left your keys at school but remembered your lockpick set?"

"It's always in my backpack," she said. "You never know."

"I hope you don't get yourself in trouble with it," I said, somewhat proud of her for knowing how to use it.

Nancy took a sip from the can and looked at me over the top.

I walked into the living room and over to the coffee table. An uncovered shoebox I recognized was filled with Kodak envelopes with photos scattered around it.

Nancy walked in behind me. "I took it down to show Corey some photos of Mom."

I reached for one of the photos and looked at it, remembering the day I took it, like it was yesterday. Barbara was so young, holding Nancy dressed in her overalls with a Red Sox hat too big for her head. She had never been the girl wearing pink dresses and pigtails. I flipped over the photo. *October 1965* was scribbled on the back.

Barbara was gone a year later.

She had written something else on the back, but the ink had been smudged, and her handwriting was never what you'd consider legible. I couldn't read what she'd written.

Raymond walked in behind us. "What's this?" He reached into the box of photos and pulled out a large envelope. Out of it, another smaller envelope fell to the floor.

I bent over and picked it up, looking inside at what looked like nothing more than plain pieces of paper, folded in half. I pulled one from the envelope and saw it was a note Maggie had written to Nancy. I looked at the others, and they were all notes, written by Maggie.

Nancy took them from my hand and looked them over, smiling as she flipped through each note. She looked somewhat emotional enough, I wondered if she was going to cry. "I forgot about these," she said, looking up at me. "Remember, after Mom died? Maggie used to help me get ready for school? She used to put little notes in my lunch box." She looked down at the one in her hand, a note written on a small, plain piece of lined white paper. "I have to show these to her," she said. "I wonder if she'll remember."

"I'm sure she will," Raymond said.

Nancy pulled another note from the envelope, but this one was more colorful, on a pink piece of paper.

"I never knew she wrote you notes like this," I said, my eyes still on the one she was reading. I held out my hand. "Can I see that?"

She handed it to me, and I studied the floral artwork at the top. The note read *You are a special little girl. Your dad and I will always be there for you.* I stared at it and thought about all Maggie had done for us back then. Her handwriting was almost perfect. "Are there any others like this?"

Nancy nodded. "There are a whole bunch. There might even be more in the box. I saved each one she wrote."

I remembered how Maggie would come over early in the morning when we lived down the street from her in Boston, just to help Nancy get ready for school. At the time, Horn Investigations was still a busy place. Skipping out on all the active cases we had on our plates wasn't an option back then.

I held up the note. "I mean, is this the only note with the floral design on top?"

Nancy and Raymond looked at each other.

Raymond laughed. "I guess you like the flowers?"

Nancy looked through the envelope. "No, the rest are all on the same paper."

I handed the note back to Nancy. She placed it in the envelope, then put the envelope back in the shoebox.

I looked toward the stairs when I heard footsteps coming down.

It was Corey.

"Oh, hi, Mr. Horn," he said. He looked at Raymond and held up his hand with a motionless wave.

I reached out my hand to shake Corey's hand. "Thank you for taking care of her," I said. "If your parents find out you were out at your house, then tell them *thank you* for me."

Corey said, "No, they don't know. I'm not sure how they'd feel about me skipping classes. Or being caught up in, well..." He paused. "Whatever's going on around here."

The phone rang, and Nancy hurried toward the kitchen, reaching her hand around to the other side of the wall. She answered, "Hello?" She nodded, looking right at me. "Yeah, he's right here."

She reached out the phone. "Dad, it's for you."

I grabbed the phone from her hand and walked with it into the kitchen. "Hello?"

"Hey, Jakey. It's me, the mayor, Tony Gautieri. Listen, uh—"

"How'd you get my number?" I said.

"I don't know. I just got it. Don't worry about it. I just need to, we need to talk. All right?" he said.

"Yeah, isn't that what we're doing?"

"All right, you don't gotta be smart," Tony said. "I'm trying to help you here. I got wind of something, I think you oughta know about."

"Okay," I said. "What about?"

"Uh, no. Not gonna be able to get into it on the phone. You never know who's listening. You know what I'm saying?"

"You want me to come by city hall?" I looked over at Raymond, staring back at me.

"Meet me on the Hill, all right? We'll grab something to eat, at this place called Cardino's. My treat."

"The Hill?"

"Federal Hill." The mayor sighed into the phone. "I don't know about you Boston guys..."

Federal Hill was the Little Italy of Providence. I was familiar enough with it, although not enough to know the names of the

323

individual restaurants. The one I had heard of just happened to be Cardino's. Unless I had the wrong place, I was pretty sure there was a mob hit there a year or two ago.

"Well, my daughter's here now, and—"

"Home from college, right?"

"How'd you know that?" I said, turning to Nancy on the couch next to Corey, showing him more pictures.

She looked up at me in the doorway to the kitchen. "I thought you said we could go back to school?"

"Tony, hang on a second, please." I pressed the phone against my chest, shaking my head, still looking at Nancy. "I didn't tell you that."

"But it's safe now, isn't it?"

I looked at Raymond, and he shrugged, then nodded. "You might as well let her go back. I don't think you have to worry."

Nancy smiled. "Thanks, Raymond."

I put the phone back up to my ear. "What time are you talking?"

"Seven o'clock. I have my table for us already. Just ask for me when you get there."

I was about to respond, but all I had coming through the phone was a dial tone.

Tony had hung up.

I hung up the phone on the wall and went back into the living room. Nancy had turned the TV on, maybe to help me out so Corey didn't hear something he shouldn't. She was smart like that.

"How about you go back tomorrow?" I said. I reached in my pocket, pulled out my wallet, and held out a twenty toward Raymond. "Would you mind taking them back to your house? Buy a couple pizzas on the way?"

He waved off the cash I held out for him. "Of course. But the pizza'll be on me." He nodded for me to follow him into the kitchen, then stopped just inside the doorway on the other side of the wall by the phone. "What's this all about?" he said, his voice quiet.

"That was the mayor, Tony Gautieri. He said he has something to tell me." I shrugged with a slight smile. "Plus, he's going to buy me dinner. You know that restaurant, Cardino's?"

Raymond nodded. "Cardino's? Isn't that the place..." He pulled at his chin. "Oh, what was his name, something like Joey *The Barber* Colletti, right? Sat at the bar, someone walked in, and shot him right in the back of the head."

CHAPTER 36

THE MAÎTRE D' WALKED me past the bar and the patrons dining at the white, cloth-covered tables. The lighting was dim with short burning candles and a bottle of wine on just about every occupied table. The smell of real Italian food made me salivate.

Opera quietly played from tall speakers on shelves in the corners of the restaurant, although the loud voices in the place almost drowned it out. I was surprised at the volume of their conversations, especially for such a small place.

I glanced at a long table with five men in dark suits drinking and laughing like they owned the place. The bar was only half-full.

The maître d' continued toward another room with an archway over the entrance. Gautieri's two goons I'd already met, both stared at me as I followed the maître d' past them into what appeared to be a very private dining area, dimly lit with paintings on the light-colored plaster walls, and tall tropical plants in all four corners.

Tony sat at one of three cloth-covered tables, facing me. He had a glass of red wine in his hand, his elbow on the table, gesturing for me to sit across from him. "Please, have a seat." He sipped his wine and placed the glass down in front of him, folding his hands together under his chin. "You ever been here before?"

I looked around and pulled out the chair. "No." I took a quick glance over my shoulder at the two goons under the open doorway. Both still had their backs to us.

Tony had a black phone next to him on the table, the cord running along the floor and under a closed door with PRIVATE on a sign stuck to the front of it. A wicker basket was filled with bread in the middle of the table, a white cloth covering most of it. Tony had a small plate in front of him with crumbs on it.

Although the restaurant was busy, you couldn't quite hear the loud voices from where we sat. Not like you could on the other side of the wall. The opera music, on the other hand, seemed somewhat louder.

Tony said, "You like Raimondi?" He picked up the bread basket and lifted the cloth napkin to expose the bread.

"Who?"

"The music. Opera." He pointed up. "Ruggero Raimondi."

I nodded, reaching for a piece of bread from the basket he held toward me. "Yeah, he's all right."

I'd never heard of him.

Tony smiled. He grabbed a piece of bread for himself, tearing it in half. "I know you're a mick from Boston, but you gotta know good bread when you taste it." He stuck a piece in his mouth. "You won't find better bread anywhere."

"I'm only half Irish," I said. "My mother was actually Italian." I placed the bread on the small dish in front of me.

"Yeah?" Gautieri said, his eyebrows high on his head, a crooked smile on his face. "That's good, huh? You look more Irish, but I can see the Italian in you." He reached for a tall, dark bottle from the table and poured it into his dish, then reached across the table and poured it over my plate with the piece of bread on it. "Olive oil. For the bread." He dipped his piece into the oil on his plate, then stuck the piece in his mouth.

"So, what's the story?" I said. I wasn't there to get his take on the quality of the bread, although I tore it in half, dipped it in the olive oil and stuck it in my mouth. And he was right about how good it was. I shoved the other piece in my mouth and reached for another from the basket.

Tony waved over the waiter. "Ricky, bring my friend here a drink, will you?" He lifted the phone by the base and held it toward the waiter. "And put this back there in the office."

The middle-aged waiter, his dark hair greased back, dressed in a white buttoned-up shirt and black bow tie, stepped to the table. "What would you like?"

"I'll take a 'Gansett."

"I appreciate you like the Rhode Island beer, but maybe you want something stronger?" Gautieri said. "You drink bourbon?"

"Are you telling me I *need* something stronger to hear whatever it is you're about to tell me?"

He laughed and nodded toward the waiter. "All right, get the man a beer." Tony pointed at me with his pinkie while holding a piece of bread in the same hand. "You wanna glass?" He nodded at the waiter. "Bring him a clean glass."

The waiter walked away and Tony said, "We can order when he gets back." He was chewing his bread as he spoke. "The veal parmigiana is something I'd recommend. Although Mickey, the chef, makes an unbelievable veal marsala too." He narrowed his eyes and sipped his wine. "You all right? After that gunshot. You don't look too bad."

"I'm all right. Doesn't hurt right now." I didn't tell him, or anyone else, I'd been popping the pain meds like candy just to keep the pain at bay.

The waiter was back a couple of moments later, stood next to me, and poured the 'Gansett from the bottle into a short glass. He placed both down in front of me and faced Tony. "You want to order, Tony?"

Tony pointed at me with his pinkie. He pointed a lot. "You wanna try the veal parmigiana?"

I opened the menu but barely looked it over. I closed it and handed it back to the waiter. "I'll trust Tony's recommendation."

Tony held up two fingers. "Two veal poms."

The waiter walked away, and Tony pushed his bread dish and wine aside and leaned forward on the table with his elbows down in front of him.

"I know the man who shot you."

I was about to sip my beer but placed it back on the table.

He nodded. "Vladimir Markov. Just got out of prison."

"A day or two after Michael Dempsey's death," I said. "If the timing wasn't off, I would've guessed he's the one who killed him."

Tony stared back at me but didn't respond, like he was holding something back. Or thinking about what to say. "You know what he was in the can for?"

"Dealing drugs," I said.

Gautieri laughed out his nose. "Yeah, that's what the cops say when they bust a guy in his position."

"His position? What's that supposed to mean?"

Tony cleared his throat and picked up his glass of wine, looking down into it for a moment as he paused. "Vladimir Markov didn't deal drugs. I mean, maybe he did here and there. But that's not what he was busted for. He got pinched with a truckload of guns."

"How do you know that? And why would he get charged for dealing drugs if he was busted with guns? That makes no sense."

"It does if the cops're gonna keep the truck full of guns."

"Keep the guns?" I said. "The *cops* kept the guns? Why would they..."

"Vladimir Markov was involved with a group of them: the boys in blue. Half that department up there in Boston is crooked."

I sipped my beer, thinking it through. "I know the Boston cops aren't angels, but..."

"Well, a group of 'em were dealing the guns they'd take off these guys. What they'd do is they'd nail the small-time dealers, like Vladimir Markov. They had informants, you know? So they'd get a heads-up when a deal was about to go down. But they wouldn't run it through the department. It would be on the down-low. These crooked pigs would show up, drop a few grams of coke in the guy's trunk, and take him downtown for dealing. Then they'd take the guns and flip the whole truckload to another dealer they'd be working with." He looked past me toward the dining room. "That's why I thought it was important for me and Mayor Bedford to crack down on the illegal gun trade."

"*What's* why?" I said. "So you could cut down on the competition?"

He didn't seem to like that. "I don't know what kind of rumors you've heard, but they're mostly not true." He squinted his eyes. "I'm here trying to help you out. I don't think it's very wise of you to—"

"You're right," I said. "I'm sorry." I didn't exactly mean it, but I wanted to hear what else he had to say. I also didn't want to ruin the meal.

He sipped his wine and looked back at me over his glass.

"So why bust Vladimir Markov for drugs?" I said. "Why not just take the guns and let him go?"

"Sometimes they'd do that. Sometimes, a guy like Vladimir couldn't be trusted to just walk away. Plus, he probably knew there were worse things that can happen than going to jail." He looked toward his two watchdogs in the doorway behind me. "Sometimes a guy would just have to disappear. Especially one you know won't keep his mouth shut."

I picked up my glass and finally took a sip of beer. "So, is this what you wanted to talk about?"

He leaned back from the table and wiped the crumbs from the tablecloth into his hand, then rubbed both hands together above the carpet. "Angela told me something this morning I thought I'd share with you." He shrugged. "I like you, Jakey." He nodded his chin. "You okay I call you Jakey?"

I said, "I don't care what you call me."

He smiled. "You seem like a straight shooter. And I know you're caught up in something that's gotten a little messy. I think I may be able to help you get out of it."

I pushed the beer and bread plate aside and leaned with my elbows on the table. "What's the catch?"

He picked up his glass of wine and finished what was inside, turning toward the waiter standing far enough away so he couldn't hear, but close enough for when Tony needed something. Tony tapped the top of his glass, and within a moment the waiter walked over, took the cork from the bottle of wine, and filled Tony's glass three-quarters of the way.

Tony waited, watching the waiter leave the room. "There's no catch," he said. "But I've been told Michael Dempsey was nervous about Markov getting out of prison."

"How'd you know that?"

Gautieri gave me a look, and I knew I'd asked a stupid question. He wasn't going to tell me. "What I'm telling you, if you'd pay attention, is Dempsey was in on something with Vladimir. I can't say it's a fact, but from the people I talked to, it appears Michael Dempsey had a role in things when Vlad went down."

"Involved with who? The cops?" I said. "Or was he involved with Markov?"

Gautieri paused, staring back at me. "I believe he was in on the delivery. The one the cops busted up."

"Dempsey was dealing guns?"

Tony sipped his wine, looking back at me over the rim. "Again, this isn't exactly firsthand. But what I'm being told is, Michael Dempsey apparently arranged the delivery of the guns to the warehouse where Vladimir had set up the sale. But the cops showed up and nailed Vladimir."

"But if Vladimir was in prison when Dempsey was killed..."

"Right. I'm not telling you who killed him. I'm just letting you know I'd be surprised to hear it didn't have to do with Vladimir Markov being busted and whatever actually went down that day."

CHAPTER 37

I SAT WITH THE phone up to my ear, looking through the glass at Norfolk Prison as Craig Parquet took a seat on the other side.

He picked up the handset and stared at me through the glass, but didn't speak as I held up the note I took from the shoebox Nancy used to store photos.

I pressed the note against the glass. "Does this look anything like the note you said you found on the seat of your car? The one Barbara allegedly wrote to you?"

He stared at the note, his eyes moving back and forth, focusing on it until he looked me in the eye. "This is a note to Nancy? Your daughter?"

My blood boiled hearing him say her name. I didn't like it. "*Who* the note is written to is not the point," I said. "I just need you to answer the goddamn question."

He again studied the note for at least half a minute. He closed his eyes, his head tilted down until he raised his head and looked back at me. "I can see the exact note so clearly in my mind, like it's right here in front of me." He tried to lean back in the chair, but the length of the phone's cord wouldn't let him. Finally, he shook his head. "No, that's not the same handwriting."

An overwhelming sense of relief came over me. Although it was quickly replaced with guilt. "What about the paper? Is it the same paper?" I said, holding it up, pressed against the glass. "Does this look like the same paper the note was written on?"

Craig didn't hesitate. "It looked nothing like that."

I had heard enough. I hung up the handset and stuck the paper in my shirt pocket as I stood up from the chair. I turned for the door and didn't say another word to Craig Parquet, although I heard his faint, muffled voice from the other side of the glass.

The guard in front of the door stepped to the side and opened it for me.

I left Norfolk Prison and promised myself that would be the last time I'd talk to Craig Parquet.

***

Maggie was getting ready for her shift when I stopped at her apartment on Massachusetts Avenue. The apartment was less than two blocks from where Barbara and I had lived, the place where we'd raised Nancy when she was still a little girl.

It had been a long time since I'd been inside Maggie's place. Standing in the kitchen brought back a lot of memories as I looked around and out into the living room area with the same TV she always had, but I'm not sure she ever watched it.

Maggie always preferred a book over watching TV.

I walked into the room and stood over the green cloth recliner with the arms worn but otherwise in decent shape. I remembered her father sitting there when he lived with her.

It seemed like Maggie was always taking care of someone, or the first one to raise her hand when someone needed help. That's just who she was. It's why she became a cop, although I don't think the job turned out to be what she'd expected.

Nothing ever does.

Her cat, Max, who was bigger and fatter than I expected, rubbed up against my jeans. I crouched down to pet him and I could feel his purr. Right then, I was hit with the guilt I felt for allowing myself to think—even for a short time—that there was a chance the note Craig Parquet had received was going to match the note Maggie had written for Nancy.

She yelled down the hall from her bedroom.

"I'll be right there," she said.

My heart pounded in my chest. Normally, you could point a gun at my head, and I could still control my adrenaline. I even thought, at that moment, I would've *rather* had someone with a gun to my head than have to explain my actions—my baseless inquiry—to Maggie.

She stepped out from her bedroom dressed in her Boston Police uniform. Her hair looked damp and hung straight down past her shoulders. I wasn't sure of the last time I saw her with her hair down like that, but she looked different. As pretty as she was, it seemed she preferred to hide it.

Maggie ran her belt through the loops of her pants and adjusted her holster, her eyes on her cat, Max, still hanging around my feet. "He likes you," she said. "He doesn't usually like men." She cleared her throat and her face turned red. "I mean... not that I've had a lot of men in here, but..."

I forced a grin, although the only thought in my head was letting her know what I'd done.

But before I could say a word about it, Maggie gave me some critical news.

"The cop who busted Vladimir Markov is dead."

"He's dead?" I said. "What do you mean he's dead?"

Maggie cracked half a grin. "How many meanings could that have? I just found out about it, before I got in the shower."

"Did you know him? The arresting officer?"

"No."

"But wasn't there more than one cop? And nobody found that suspicious? That he was killed?" I said.

"It was a car accident," Maggie said. "It doesn't look like anything ever came of it. I'm not even sure I buy what your new mayor friend told you is true. Just because he told you a story about some bad cops over a plate of veal parmigiana, doesn't make it factual," she said.

I looked her in the eye. "What about Moriarty?" I said.

"What about him?"

"He's been acting like Vladimir Markov is just some random crook with a gun. But don't you think he'd look into it a little more?"

I could tell Maggie didn't like where I was going.

"First of all," she said, "you have no idea what he *is* and *isn't* looking into. He's a detective. He doesn't need to tell you anything. So, if you're trying to suggest Moriarty's not a good cop, because you don't like the idea he won't share his investigation details with a private investigator who..." She closed her eyes, shaking her head. "I'm sorry. I just..."

"All I'm saying is I can't help but wonder about him. Can't I ask the question?"

"I think what you need to do is be careful, Jake. You can't start pointing fingers because now you think everybody's a suspect. This is exactly what you did with Barbara's case. And look what it did to you. You can't keep doing this, Jake. You can't." She let out a sigh, her eyes on the clock over the stove. "I have to get to work," she said, grabbing her jacket from the small closet by the front door.

I pulled it open and stepped out into the hallway.

Maggie walked out behind me, turning to lock the door.

"Where are you going?" she said, heading toward the stairs.

"Right now? To Lily's," I said. "There's a picture of Pete on a shelf in her apartment I want to grab, show it around, see if anybody recognizes him."

She walked down the stairs ahead of me. "But even if this story Gautieri told you turns out to be true, do you really believe Pete was involved? Just because he happens to be a truck driver?"

"There's a little more to it," I said.

Maggie stopped as she stepped off the bottom step. "And before you accuse him, or anyone else, of killing Michael Dempsey, you'd better make sure you have a good enough motive."

***

I walked off the elevator in Lily's apartment building and down the hall toward her apartment, but stopped and peeked around the corner before I made it to her door. I wanted to make sure I could get into her apartment without any of her neighbors seeing me.

The coast appeared clear, and I hurried for her door. I opened my lockpick set and got to work, down on one knee, picking the lock. It didn't take me more than half a minute, standing as I turned the knob and opened the door, then slipped into the dark apartment. I started to close the door, but before the latch caught, I heard a voice from out in the hall behind me.

"Jake? Is that you?"

I knew it was Lily's neighbor, Marie, and for a moment thought about closing the door all the way and turning the lock. But I couldn't get myself to do it, dropping my shoulders as I opened the door.

"Hi, Marie," I said, standing in the doorway with a forced smile on my face.

Marie looked back at me with a frown on her face. "I hoped maybe you were Lily."

"Just me," I said. "But, hopefully she'll be back soon."

I could see how concerned she was by the look on her face. "Last time you were here, you said she was all right. But that's not what everyone around here's been saying." She lowered her voice into a whisper. "The rumor is something bad has happened to her."

I stared back at her without much of a response. "Well..."

"May I ask what you're doing here?" she said. "I know it's probably none of my business. I mean, you know I'm *not* one of those nosy neighbors..."

I wasn't sure that was as accurate as Marie herself wanted to believe.

"I wanted to take a look around her apartment," I said.

"You're looking for something?"

It was still dark inside Lily's apartment, so I finally reached inside with my hand, feeling for the switch on the wall. I thought I knew exactly where it was, but had to, instead, take a step into the apartment to look for it.

And just as I turned, Marie slipped past me and into the apartment. "Maybe I can help you find whatever you're looking for?" She reached for the wall herself and flipped the switch. The lights in the kitchen came on.

Marie gasped as we both saw what was an absolute mess inside Lily's apartment.

Furniture had been tipped and torn apart; storage boxes were turned over and dumped on the floor... clothes pulled from the closets... pages from magazines ripped and tossed all over.

"We need to call the police," Marie said, hurrying toward the phone. But the cord had been yanked from the wall. "I'm going to go call them from my apartment."

"Marie, wait. Not yet," I said.

"Not yet? But somebody made a mess of this place. Who knows what they took."

"Just let me look around, before you do," I said. "Please. It's the only way I can help Lily."

Marie stood still, staring at me with a look of suspicion. "My friend used to live here, before Lily. But she moved away, to Florida. Lily moved in a month later, but she's only invited me in once or twice."

"I thought you and Lily were pretty friendly?" I said.

Marie nodded. "We were. I'd invite her to my apartment for tea but..." She stopped with her eyes fixed on the framed photos. She stepped closer and picked up the one of Pete and Lily.

"Do you know them?" I said.

Marie studied the photo, then nodded as she looked toward me. "I don't know the woman, but this man... he certainly looks familiar."

"You mean you've seen him here, with Lily?" I said.

Marie had her eyes back on the picture. "I could be wrong, but I think I saw this man on the elevator. Just this week."

"I stood next to Marie, looking at the picture. I pointed to Jill. "That's Lily's cousin, Jill. The man with her is her husband." I asked her if she was sure it was him and she nodded.

"Yes, I know it was him. He's a good-looking man, and I remember him. He was friendly, said hello, and had a nice smile."

"Was he alone?"

"No, he wasn't," she said. "He was with another man who was much bigger. He was about your size, with a thick beard. He looked like a lumberjack. Not someone you'd see living around this part of town." She looked around the apartment.

341

"Did either one say anything else to you?"

Marie pointed to Pete in the photo. "He said hi to me, but that was it. The bigger one, he wouldn't even make eye contact. He acted very strange. Almost scary, the way he looked."

CHAPTER 38

THE LIGHTS WERE ON inside the office at the Morrissey Motel. With the darkness outside, I could see Adesh clearly behind the counter, flipping the pages of a magazine.

I pulled on the glass door and stepped to the counter. And as soon as he saw me, he reached for the phone and started to dial. But I reached over the counter and put my finger on the phone's switch.

"Wait," I said.

"I am calling Detective Moriarty," Adesh said.

I took my hand off the phone's base. "Please, I just want to show you something."

He paused, then hung up the handset.

I turned the framed photo toward him. "Have you ever seen this man?"

He gave the photo a quick glance. "I do not know that man."

"I didn't ask you if you know him," I said. "I asked if you've seen him. You barely looked at it."

Adesh gave the photo another look, this time shaking his head. "I am sorry, I have not. And I do not want to be involved in any of this."

"Well, you *are* involved," I said. "A man was killed in your motel."

He swallowed hard and reached for the handset. "If you do not leave, I am calling the police."

"Okay," I said. "But you would think you'd want to help find out what happened. No?"

"I just want to worry about my business. The rest, it is up to the police." He looked me over. "Private investigators are fictional characters. In books. And movies."

I didn't respond, instead leaving the office. I got in my car and started the engine, shaking my head. *What a jerk.* I shifted into reverse and squealed the tires backing out from the parking space and cut the wheel toward Freeman's Pub across the street.

I parked in front of the door and walked past two men coming out, both staring me down until I went inside. I sat on an empty stool on the right side of the bar.

The bartender, Sean, walked toward me.

"'Gansett?" He reached into the cooler before I answered and came up with a can, pulling the tab as he placed it down in front of me. He looked over his shoulder toward the other end of the bar.

I leaned a little to my left to look around him and saw the man who had jumped me the first time I'd been there. "Uh-oh," I said.

"Listen, man. We don't need any trouble today."

I nodded. "Yeah, no problem." I pulled a fin from my pocket and slid it across the bar. "Why don't you buy him a beer. On me."

Sean looked down at the bill. "He quit drinking. In fact, just so you know, he doesn't even remember going after you that day."

I grinned. "Threw a pretty good punch for being so drunk he forgot about it." I tapped the five-dollar bill on the bar. "Well then, give him another soda, or whatever he's drinking."

He walked away, poured a soda from the gun, and took the glass down the other end, placing it in front of the man. On his way back, he filled two empty glasses with beer for a couple of older men seated halfway down the bar.

"Sean?" I said, waving him over.

"You want a bowl of chowder?" he said.

"Not right now." I put the framed picture of Pete up on the bar. "You ever see this man in here before?"

Sean picked it up and didn't hesitate. "Yeah, he's been in here before." He shifted his eyes toward me. "I'm pretty sure he's been in with the guy you were asking about, who was killed at the motel."

"Michael Dempsey?"

Sean nodded. "It's been a while but I remember him. He was friendly."

He studied the picture again and pointed at Jill. "But, who's the woman he's with?"

"That's his wife."

Sean had a look on his face, staring at the picture. "Hang on a minute." He took the photo through the swinging door to the kitchen. I got up and tried to look through the round window, but I couldn't see what he was doing.

The door swung open, and the cook walked out, holding the framed photo. I remembered his name was Bruce, with his white T-shirt and stained smock hung from his tree-trunk neck. He stepped over and put the photo down in front of me. "We don't want any trouble in here," he said.

I picked up my beer and took a sip. "I'm not here looking for trouble. Just asked Sean if he'd seen the man in that photo."

Bruce pointed to Jill's face in the picture. "She's been here. Not with him, however."

Sean said, "I wanted to ask Bruce before I said anything, make sure she was the right one. But she was in here the evening before that guy was murdered."

"Jill? Are you sure?"

345

They both nodded, and Sean looked around the bar. "A good-looking broad like that comes in, you notice. She came in alone, had a drink, and left. Wasn't here more than fifteen minutes."

***

I swung by Raymond's to pick him up, went in to give Nancy a hug and told her not to worry. "We'll be back," I said. I gave Raymond a nod. "You ready?"

He nodded, and we both ran in the rain out to my car.

"Are you sure about this?" he said.

I started the car and thought for a moment. "Is it all right if I answer that when this is over?" I slapped the shifter into reverse and backed out of the driveway.

***

It took us forty minutes to make it out to the storage facility in Thompson, Connecticut, where Pete parked his eighteen wheeler when he wasn't on the road.

We pulled behind Maggie, sitting inside her Plymouth, parked along the chain-link fence surrounding the storage facility.

The rain had stopped. It was quiet all around us. Although, even for a place like Thompson, out in the middle of nowhere, it seemed almost *too* quiet.

The three of us stepped out from our cars and Maggie handed me a piece of paper. "Here," she said, pointing through the fence toward six parked trailers. "That's his, the third one from the right."

We all looked up at the barbed wire on top of the ten-foot-high fence.

"So how do we get in there?" Raymond said.

Maggie lifted the trunk lid and pulled out a pair of bolt cutters. "With these." She handed them to me, a slight grin on her face.

We walked along the fence and came to a gate kept closed with nothing more than a thick chain and lock. I used the bolt cutters on the lock and snapped it without much effort at all. I swung open the gate, and we walked through the opening into the open parking area on the other side. There were lights coming down from the top of the one-story brick building, reflecting off the wet pavement. The lighting was dim, especially in the fog-filled night.

I stood behind the trailer and checked the paper Maggie had given me, confirming the registration plate belonged to Peter.

The back of the trailer had a lock on it, but I snapped it with the bolt cutters, handing them to Maggie as I flipped open the heavy steel latch and climbed up onto the back of the trailer. I pulled up on the canvas strap, lifting the door open.

It was pitch black inside, with very little light shining from the lamps on top of the storage building. The inside of the trailer was filled with stacked wooden crates on either side, with a very narrow pathway between them.

Raymond handed me a flashlight, although I froze when I heard a muffled sound... a voice. I turned on the flashlight and shined it between the crates.

"Hello?" I started toward the back of the trailer, and again, heard the muffled voice. Taking one more step, I stopped, and almost dropped the flashlight. I was completely caught off guard and surprised by what I saw.

Lily was tied to a chair, with duct tape on her mouth, sitting in total darkness. I yelled over my shoulder, *"She's in here. It's Lily."*

Maggie and Raymond both stayed outside the trailer, looking in toward me.

"Is she all right?" Maggie said.

I didn't answer and had to turn my body to squeeze between the crates and get to her. The first thing I did was rip the duct tape off her mouth. I yelled, "She's okay!"

Tears ran down her face. "Oh, Jake. I've never been so happy to see you."

I pulled a knife from my back pocket and cut the rope from her feet, then did the same to the rope around her hands and whatever was used to tie her to the chair. I helped her to her feet. "I'm being honest, Lily. I wasn't actually expecting to find you here. I mean, it's not that I haven't been trying to find you, but..."

Lily wrapped her arms around me and kissed me right on the lips. "You could have lied for once in your life," she said.

"Lied?"

"At least pretend you're here for me."

"I was. I mean... I still saved you, right?" I took her by the hand and led her toward the opening.

"Raymond? Maggie?" Lily turned to Jake. "You all came here? To save me?"

"Not exactly," Maggie said, climbing up onto the back of the trailer. Raymond did the same, and they both started opening the lids on the wooden crates.

Raymond reached inside one of the crates and came up with a brick-sized white substance wrapped in clear plastic. He opened the top on another crate and found the same thing. "Where are the guns?"

I said to Lily. "What do you know about all of this?"

She shrugged, shaking her head. "Nothing at all. I swear."

Maggie held the same white brick, one she'd pulled from a crate. She looked at me and Raymond. "Even when you save her life she can't help but lie."

I looked into Lily's eyes. "You have to tell us the truth," I said. "You can't hide anymore."

Lily reached for my hand. "Why don't you believe me?"

"Do you really have to ask?" Maggie said.

I took the white plastic-wrapped brick from Raymond and looked it over. I said to Lily, "Was Michael involved with Pete, dealing drugs?"

"Why don't you believe me?" Lily said. "I don't know anything."

I heard what I knew, without a doubt, was the rack of a shotgun.

The four of us all turned to look outside the trailer. Pete was standing out there in the rain, a shotgun pointed toward us. "You couldn't have just left things alone?"

"What, and let Lily freeze to death in here?"

Pete shook his head. "We wouldn't let that happen," he said. "At least as long as she'd promised to keep her mouth shut."

I said to Lily, "So you knew?"

She shrugged. "He said he'd kill me if I told you anything."

I turned back to Pete. "So why'd you kill him?"

"Why'd I kill *who*?"

"Who do you *think*?" I pointed with my thumb at Lily. "Her husband. It was you. You and Jill. And I'm guessing that lumberjack freak who attacked me's a friend of yours?"

Pete smiled. "Oh, he wouldn't like you calling him a freak, so I'd be careful what you say."

"And the pig's head? Was that you?"

"Did you like that? I thought for sure you'd make the connection to your Italian mob friend down there in Providence."

Raymond said, "Where'd you get that from? Watching *The Godfather*?"

Pete nodded. "But I couldn't see killing a horse." He shifted his eyes back to me, pointing the gun my way. "But I didn't kill Michael."

"You expect us to believe that?" Maggie said.

I looked at the crates behind me. "The only thing here I wasn't expecting, other than finding Lily tied up in here, is that you're dealing drugs. I thought it was guns?"

"It was," Pete said. "But Vladimir was the one with the connections. We had to change course when he went to prison. Michael knew some people who needed a trucker to move some heroin, so..."

"But it was guns. Is that right? When Vladimir was busted, even though the cops say he had drugs... the deal that sent him to prison was guns. Correct?"

Pete looked hesitant to say much more, staring back at me with his eyes somewhat squinted. He finally nodded. "Something went wrong. Michael got wind there were a couple of crooked cops involved in the trade, nailing gun dealers but turning around and selling the goods themselves."

I looked at Raymond and Maggie. "You think that's true?"

Raymond nodded. "You know as well as I do, Boston PD has its problems with men in uniform who are dirty."

I said to Pete, "So, now what? You're going to kill all of us?"

Pete took a moment before he answered. "I didn't mean to get wrapped up in all of this, you know. Michael was the one who came to me, had a way for me to make some extra money."

"You have a truckload of heroin," Raymond said. "I'd hardly say you're innocent."

"I didn't say I was." He nodded. "This has just been sitting here. When Michael was killed... I don't even know where it's supposed to go. I never spoke to anyone. Michael was the one with the contacts, would call me at the motel, give me the drop-off location."

"The Turnpike Inn," I said.

Pete nodded. "How'd you know that?"

I didn't answer.

"So, why don't we make some kind of deal?" I said. "You let us all go, and we say nothing." I knew Maggie wasn't going to like that.

"I don't believe you," Pete said.

"Well," I said. "I don't believe you either. You're telling me you had nothing to do with Michael's death, but I know for a fact Jill was at that motel the evening before his body was found in that dumpster."

Out of the darkness, Jill stepped forward with her own shotgun in her hand, pointed up into the trailer. "Who told you that?"

Lily cried and said to Jill, "Did you kill Michael?"

"No! I did not!"

"Well then, why don't you explain why you were there? I have two witnesses who know you were there. You went to Freeman's for a drink."

"Sorry," she said. "But having a drink doesn't make me a murderer." She glanced at Pete, both their guns pointing at us inside the trailer.

"So you're not going to deny you were there," I said. "But you expect me to believe you didn't kill him?"

Pete said, "We went there to kill him, before he gave up my name. But we saw him leave in a car with someone."

"What kind of car?" I said.

Before either could answer, Raymond stepped past me with a brick of heroin in his hand, raised it up like he was throwing a football and tossed it hard and fast at Pete's head.

White powder exploded on Pete's face. He coughed and raised his gun, firing a shot into the air. But his eyes and mouth were covered in powder.

I jumped down off the trailer and landed on top of him, taking him down to the ground.

Jill had her gun pointed at me, but Maggie jumped off the trailer and took her down, too, dropping her body onto the wet asphalt.

Raymond climbed down off the trailer and picked both shotguns up off the ground. "Now what?" he said.

CHAPTER 39

MAGGIE WALKED OUT FROM the police station with her hand inside her coat, holding it closed in front of her. She opened the rear passenger door and slipped into the back seat of Raymond's car, closing the door. She reached toward the front and handed me the folder.

I looked ahead toward the station and saw Moriarty leaving in a hurry, turning down Berkley but in the opposite direction from where we were parked.

"There's nothing in there about Vladimir Markov's arrest," Maggie said.

"Nothing?" I opened the folder and flipped through the contents.

Raymond pulled away from the curb and did a U-turn, heading for 93.

"Hit and run, huh?" I said, skimming over the report. "Officer Denny Blake. He was pronounced dead at the scene. No sign of any other vehicle at the time. No witnesses. His patrol car was hit at high speed from behind, on Meridian Street, then crashed into the Meridian Street Library."

Raymond looked in the rearview at Maggie. "I remember when it happened," he said. "But I honestly don't remember the name Vladimir Markov."

"Nobody ever made any kind of connection?" I said.

"It was an accident," Maggie said.

"Or made to look like one," I said. I studied the report and anything else inside, although the folder was thin. "Open-and-shut. No questions asked."

Maggie said, "I can try the courts, see what else I can dig up on Markov's arrest and what really went down."

"We don't have time," I said. "And you asked about it?" I looked back at Maggie over my shoulder.

"I had started to ask the officer at the desk, but Moriarty walked by. He gave me a look, like he was wondering what I was up to, but didn't say a word. He kept walking."

"He left right after you," I said. "I saw him walk out of the station."

Maggie looked surprised. "*Moriarty?*"

I nodded as Raymond took the exit for 93 South.

We were all quiet for the next few miles, for the most part. Even the radio was off.

I looked out the passenger window as we cut left onto Route 3, the sign for Cape Cod overhead. "If there really was another officer there with Denny Blake, he took the guns off Vladimir to make a few bucks for himself; killing Officer Blake meant his identity would remain safe."

"What about the Russian?" Raymond said.

"Maybe they were in on it together," I said.

"Who? The so-called crooked cop and Vladimir Markov?" Maggie said. "You mean, maybe Vladimir was going to turn on Pete and Michael the whole time?"

A GOOD TIME FOR GOODBYE

I shrugged, glancing back at her. "I don't know. We may never know the answer."

"Well, hopefully the owner of the building where Pete delivered the guns will be willing to talk to us," Raymond said.

I looked out to my right at the sign for the Duxbury exit. "I guess we'll find out."

I thought for a moment. "I know we haven't seen the report, but obviously when Denny Blake arrested Vladimir Markov, it was within Boston's jurisdiction. I just hope Pete didn't steer us in the wrong direction, considering the guns were allegedly dropped off in Plymouth."

Raymond glanced at me but didn't respond.

***

We pulled into Cordage Park, the one-time home of the Cordage Rope Company, in Plymouth Mass, off Route 3A. The entire park was set on almost fifty acres with a large tower in the middle of a collection of brick buildings making up at least a few hundred thousand square feet. It had closed fifteen years earlier, in the early sixties, with space since made available for warehousing and, apparently, anyone involved in illegal activity.

Raymond continued around the back of the building and parked by a door no more than one hundred yards from Plymouth Bay.

I looked at the paper in my hand. "That's the one," I said.

The only other car parked anywhere within the vicinity of the building was a blue Chrysler New Yorker. It had an *Avi Nelson for Governor* sticker on the bumper.

Maggie stayed outside, just in case. She was the only one armed.

Raymond and I walked to the door and, as I reached for it, expected it to be locked. But I was surprised when I pulled it open, and we walked right in.

The interior of the building, like the outside, was mostly brick. The ceilings were at least twenty feet high with fans above our heads turning slowly to keep what felt like damp air moving. I could smell the mildew.

We walked down a long hall, through another set of glass doors, and stopped at an open door on the right. I could hear the sound of talk radio coming from somewhere inside, continued through a mostly empty office space, and stopped at another door. There didn't appear to be anyone around, but Raymond and I kept walking and continued past a small, open bathroom with nothing inside it but a toilet and sink. A string hung from the light on the ceiling.

We kept going, and the sound of the radio grew louder until we finally came to a door at the very end of the hall. It was cracked open no more than an inch.

I glanced back, and Raymond then gently knocked on the door. "Hello? Anybody here?" I waited, trying to peek in through the small opening, then knocked again. "Hello?"

Nobody answered, so I pushed the door open.

A gray-haired man was facedown in a pool of blood on a desk. The WBZ weather report came on the radio, sitting on top of the radiator behind him. The blood had dripped down the side of the desk.

Raymond stood over the man's body slouched over the desk. "You wanted to know if this guy knew anything?" He looked up at me. "I think my answer would have to be *yes*." He reached for the phone and lifted the handset to his ear.

"What are you doing?" I said.

"Calling Plymouth PD."

"It's not going to do him any good at this point. He's dead." I looked down at what looked like fresh blood. He hasn't been dead long at all."

Raymond touched the man's body. "He's still warm."

I looked toward a window facing the parking lot. I looked at Raymond's car, but Maggie wasn't standing outside it as she was when we walked inside the building. "Maggie!" I said, and without another word ran from the office and down the hall toward the exit.

I crashed open the first set of double doors, continued down the brick hall and through the next door, swinging it open as I made it outside. I looked back and forth.

Maggie yelled for me: "Jake!"

I looked toward the far end of the building and saw someone, a figure, pulling Maggie by her arm.

I ran toward them and got close enough to see who it was:

Jeffrey Moriarty.

He had his arm extended with a gun pointed at Maggie's head. They were headed toward his Dodge Monaco, parked at the far end of the parking lot by the docks along the bay.

I ran as fast as I could toward them. "Moriarty! *Let her go!*"

He stopped, glancing back at me, making sure I saw the gun pointed at her head. "Take another step," he said. "I *dare* you." He let out a sigh loud enough for me to hear from fifty feet away. "All the warning signs? And you couldn't just walk away?" He continued walking toward his car.

Maggie walked ahead of him, her hands up by her shoulders.

I had stopped running but kept walking after them. There was no way I was going to let him leave with Maggie. "What good is harming her going to do?" I said. "I know it was you. So why don't you kill *me*? Let Maggie go."

Moriarty turned again but kept the gun pointed at the back of Maggie's head. "Well, let me see how clear I can make this for you."

He pointed at the gun. "This just happens to be your gun, Jake. Combined with the evidence I've been able to pile against you at this point for Michael Dempsey's murder... the story will have to be that poor Officer Donovan tried to stop you. So you had no choice and killed her too." He laughed. "And there you have it! I've solved another crime."

"Don't do it," I said. "You don't have to. Take me in. I'll admit to killing Dempsey. Whatever you want. Just, please, don't hurt Maggie."

Moriarty said, "Well, you see, my plan doesn't work so well if I let her go. It's too late. And I can already see the headline." He made air quotes: "Love Triangle Gets Boston Mayor's Office Employee Killed by Wife's Ex-Lover... Boston Cop Killed Trying to Save Detective from Crazy Private Investigator." He shrugged. "I don't know. I was never much of a writer." He shoved her from behind and kept going past his car toward the docks.

"Where are you going?" I yelled. "What are you going to do with her?"

He kept walking but yelled to me over his shoulder, "You ask too many questions, Horn." He kept moving and stopped when he got to the dock. He pushed Maggie toward the edge of it with the muzzle of the gun—*my* gun—pressed up against her head. "I think I like the idea of Maggie being shot on the dock and falling into the water. Isn't that a good idea?"

"Please," I said. "You don't have to do this."

"You sound like a broken record, Horn. You think you're going to talk me out of this? And I'll just surrender to an unarmed private dick and his washed-up cousin?"

I looked behind me, and Raymond had stopped, a look on his face like he didn't know what we should do.

I continued toward Moriarty and Maggie.

"Please stop right there," Moriarty said. "Don't come another step closer." I was close enough to hear him say to Maggie, "You know, I'm really sorry about this. When I first met you, I thought maybe there could be something between us. Although the superiors frown against internal romantic relationships."

"You already killed three people," I said. "Isn't that enough?"

Moriarty grinned. "Oh, was that all?" He laughed. "Obviously, I'm doing my best to cover most of it up. Now, if you'd only stop talking for a minute, we could just get this over with." He leaned in and whispered something into Maggie's ear.

Maggie looked at me with fear and confusion in her eyes.

Moriarty laughed. "I wondered how she'd take the news you actually thought she could have killed your wife."

"Jake?" Maggie said, the gun now at her head. "Is that true?"

I stared back at her, shaking my head. "No," I said. "Please. Maggie... don't listen to him."

The detective turned her around so she faced him, pointing the gun toward her face.

"Stop!" I said. "We won't talk." I looked back at Raymond. "The three of us... we'll keep quiet." I knew Moriarty wouldn't buy it, but all I was trying to do was buy more time. "You can take me in... I'll confess. I'll tell them I killed Michael."

"You don't have to do me any favors," Moriarty said. "I told you. I've already got it figured out. You'll be surprised to see the evidence against you." He nodded toward the building. "The owner of the building was the only one left who might've known enough to get me in trouble. Too bad. I didn't want to have to kill the old man."

He kept his eyes on the building.

And it was enough for Maggie to try to knock the gun from his hand. She took a swing and hit him on the arm, then turned and drove her foot right between his legs.

Moriarty stumbled back, but got his footing and raised the gun toward her. Without hesitation, he pulled the trigger and fired a shot at Maggie from no more than four feet away.

Her shoulder kicked back, and she went off the dock, falling into the ice-cold water.

I was already running as fast as I could toward Moriarty, but he spun around and fired a shot in my direction. I ducked just as he turned, diving out of the way.

Somehow, he missed me. I rolled on the ground and was back up on my feet, running toward him again.

But Raymond screamed, "He got me!"

Raymond had been hit by the bullet.

My momentum took me into Moriarty with full force, driving my shoulder into his chest. I slammed him against a piling, and his body seemed to collapse with the impact.

We both went off the dock and crashed into the water.

Moriarty wasn't moving. His body was limp, floating, facedown.

I yelled for Maggie, looking for her, spinning in circles as I tried to tread in the frigid water. "Maggie!" I couldn't see her anywhere.

But then I heard a splash under the dock. Maggie's head popped up to the surface. "Jake," she said, choking, taking in water.

I reached for her and pulled her toward me. There was blood in the water all around her. I looked up and saw the bottom of Raymond's boots through the cracks in the dock's decking. A drop of blood came down onto the water from above.

"Jake!" he yelled. "Where are you!"

"We're under here!" I said, trying to keep Maggie from going under again, kicking my feet as hard as I could to keep us both afloat. Her eyes were closed, and I whispered into her ear, "Stay with me." I swam with her, so I could see Raymond reaching down with his hand.

He was bleeding. "Are you all right?" I said.

"Like a papercut," he said, grabbing Maggie and lifting her out of the water.

I did what I could to push her up with him, then swam toward Moriarty once Raymond had Maggie up on the dock.

The detective was going under when I got to him. I dragged him with one hand and swam toward a ladder.

Raymond reached down and pulled him up out of the water, then reached down with one hand and helped me climb up the dock.

I ran to Maggie lying flat on her back on the dock. She had blood coming up around her neck from under her coat. I pulled off my wet coat and rolled it up, placing it under her head like a pillow. "Maggie?" I said. "Can you hear me?"

She opened her eyes.

"Is she all right?" Raymond said, standing over my shoulder.

She coughed, nodding, and lifted her head as she unbuttoned her coat to show me the bulletproof vest she had on underneath. She cracked a crooked smile. "It hurts. But I think I'm okay." She leaned her head back and closed her eyes.

I unbuckled the vest. There was a lot of blood coming through her shirt. Being at close range when Moriarty pulled the trigger, the bullet appeared to have gone through the vest.

"You'll be all right," I said, wiping the hair from her face. Sirens screamed in the distance, and I glanced over at Moriarty. He was trying to get to his feet. "Raymond!" I said, "Don't let him up!"

Raymond hurried over to Moriarty and punched him in the face. Moriarty's head smacked against the deck beneath him. "He's not going anywhere," Raymond said.

Maggie raised her head, looked down at her bloodied shirt, and grabbed her chest. "Oh, this really hurts."

CHAPTER 40

MAGGIE SAT UP IN her bed at Jordan Hospital when Nancy and I walked in. She smiled when she looked down at the flowers in my hand. "That's sweet of you," she said, and reached out and grabbed Nancy by the hand, pulling her in for a hug.

"I love you," Nancy said.

They held each other for a moment, and Maggie looked up at me over Nancy's shoulder with tears in her eyes.

Nancy looked at Maggie. "If I go back to school, can you both at least promise me you'll try not to get shot ever again?"

I put my arm around her shoulders. "I'll do my best." I handed the flowers to Maggie. "I'm glad you're all right."

She reached for my hand and put hers on top of it. She said to Nancy, "Would you mind if I talk to your dad alone for a minute?"

Nancy nodded with a slight smile on her face, although I knew she had no idea what it was about. "Sure." She put her hand out toward me. "Can I buy a soda?"

I reached into my pocket and pulled out some change. I handed her two quarters. "Don't forget to get the change."

Nancy left the room.

Maggie looked back toward the door. "Can you close that?"

I knew what it was going to be about and closed the door, then stepped by her side. She placed the flowers down on the table next to her. "How could you think I had anything to do with Barbara's death?"

The lump in my throat made it hard to breathe. I swallowed, although I tried not to. "I... I didn't. I mean, I knew you had nothing to do with it. I thought, maybe... I don't know. Maybe you wanted to set him up. Or..." I thought the more I said, the worse it would all look. "I'm just so sorry."

"But you couldn't help yourself?" she said. "You don't know me well enough to just ask me? Or tell me what you were thinking?"

I tried to force out a smile, but it just didn't work. "I worked through this conversation in my head knowing we'd have it. And I wished I could explain myself. But I can't. I just... all I could hear was my uncle telling me when I'd first started with him, 'Don't ever leave a stone unturned. Even if you have a personal reason to let it stay as it is.'"

"Your uncle was ruthless," she said. "You're not like him."

I shrugged. "But that's what made him a good detective."

"You're a good detective, Jake. And you're a good person. You can be both, you know."

I couldn't tell you the last time I cried. At least in front of anyone. But my eyes filled with tears. "I'm sorry," I said.

She put her hand flat over her heart. "I know you are. But it still hurts that you—"

"I never knew you put those notes in Nancy's lunch box. You never told me." I reached for her hand and held it.

"I didn't tell you a lot of things, Jake. You had enough on your plate. That's why I did what I could to try to fill the void in Nancy's life."

"But you had your own life, your own career."

She shrugged. "You and Barbara were my family. I lost my best friend when she died. You lost the love of your life. And Nancy lost her mom. I did what I thought I had to."

I squeezed her hand and looked into her eyes. I guess I'd never paid enough attention to see how crystal blue they were.

But she pulled her hand back, squinting as she stared back at me. "What is it?" she said. "Is there something else?"

I was hesitant to mention what I hadn't been able to stop thinking about. "I don't understand how Moriarty knew I took the note to show Craig Parquette."

We were both quiet.

There was a knock at the door.

Raymond walked in with three Dunkin' Donuts coffees. He handed one to me and walked around to the other side of the bed, placing one down on the tray for Maggie. "I don't know if you're supposed to have coffee now, but..." He looked from me to Maggie. "Did I interrupt something?"

Maggie and I both smiled and didn't exactly answer.

"Everything's good," Maggie said, giving me a quick glance.

"Are you sure?" I said, looking down at her as if having my doubts.

She smiled, nodding. "Yeah, I'm sure."

Nancy walked in the room behind Raymond. She had a bottle of RC Cola in her hand. "Can I come back now?"

Maggie laughed, stretched out her hand, and patted the top of the bed beside her.

Nancy stepped around Raymond and sat on the bed with Maggie.

Raymond said, "So they got the bullet out?"

"The vest stopped it from hitting my heart. If I didn't wear it, I'd be dead."

Raymond pulled off his jacket. "You're smart like that." He showed us the bandage on the back of his arm where he'd been shot, just above the elbow. "All those years on the force, and I never once even came close to being shot. Here I am, retired..."

I looked at his arm. "I thought you said it barely hit you?"

He nodded. "Well, they had to stitch it up. Twelve stitches, I think. Bullet went right through the muscle."

"So now we can all say we've been shot," I laughed.

Nancy said, "Can you explain to me what's funny about that?" But she still had a slight smile on her face. "I hope I don't need to do that to be part of your gang."

"A gang, huh?" Raymond laughed. "Is that what this is?" He turned back to Maggie. "So where'd you get the vest?"

She paused. "My father was friends with a guy who started a body armor company. The police don't have the budget for them now, but he gave me one to wear. I guess I should call him, tell him it worked."

Raymond put his hand on my shoulder. "So when were you going to tell us you knew it was Moriarty?"

I walked over to the window and looked down at the parking lot. "I didn't like the way he was trying to get a hook in me from the beginning. I just knew... I knew something was off with the guy. And I'm not just talking about the way he dressed." I stepped to the foot of Maggie's bed. "It didn't really click until I saw him leaving the station after Maggie grabbed those files. He must have known we were getting close. He knew he had to get ahead of us and into Plymouth in time to make sure the landlord wouldn't talk."

Maggie said, "Did you talk to the owner of the motel?"

"Adesh?" I nodded. "I stopped by before I picked up Nancy and came out here. I told him everything. He said as long as it's all true, he's willing to testify that Moriarty strong-armed him and threatened if he talked to me or anyone else, he'd have his family deported."

"I wonder why Moriarty didn't kill him?" Nancy said.

The three of us looked at each other.

Nobody had an answer.

The doctor walked in the room, and I stepped out of his way so he could grab the clipboard from the foot of Maggie's bed. He held it in front of him and looked it over, then looked up at Maggie. "Your vitals are all good. You can probably go home in a couple of days." He looked around at the rest of us. "Is this your family?"

She smiled, and I saw her eyes fill with tears. She nodded. "Yeah, I guess it is."

***

I was back in my office with my yellow legal pad filled with notes from all the calls I'd gotten over the past two weeks since we helped bring Moriarty down. Word traveled fast, and my phone was ringing off the hook, not only from regular citizens, but also police departments looking to have me work as a consultant.

That's the way my Uncle Pat did it when he first started Horn Investigations.

Six other cops were on trial along with Moriarty for being involved in illegal gun and drug trafficking. I was publicly credited with knocking over the first domino. I had a feeling the six officers were just the beginning.

I hadn't spoken to Lily, back living in her apartment, but I'd heard she was maybe going to move into her cousin's house in Connecticut to take care of their kids. She was cleared of any wrongdoing, but the same couldn't be said for Pete and Jill.

I looked at the legal pad. There was no way I could take every potential case, even if I wanted to. I knew who I could turn to if I needed to bring someone else on board to help.

Either way, I was excited about Horn Investigation's next chapter.

I stood from the desk and sipped my coffee. After a week of cold rain, the sun was shining. The temperature jumped forty degrees overnight, although the weatherman said it would be down to freezing by the weekend. New England weather...

I walked to the file cabinet behind my desk and pulled out the latest folder with *Barbara, April 1978* written on the tab. The only thing inside was the note Maggie had written to Nancy. I took it out, put the folder back in the drawer and closed it. I looked at the note... at Maggie's beautiful handwriting, and folded it in half. I stuck it in my shirt pocket so I could put it back where it belonged, in Nancy's shoebox.

The folder for April 1978, at that point, would remain empty.

***

Thank you for reading *A Good Time for Goodbye*. It genuinely means a lot.

If you enjoyed the mystery, I'd love to stay in touch. Head over to GregoryPayette.com to sign up for my newsletter — you'll get some fun free stories just for joining.

And if you have a minute, an honest review on the store where you purchased *A Good Time for Goodbye* makes a real difference for an author. Even a line or two helps other readers find the series.

Jake is back for his next case in *The Silence of the Sand* — the second book in the Jake Horn mysteries.

Learn more at GregoryPayette.com

Visit GregoryPayette.com for more stories

HENRY WALSH MYSTERIES

Dead at Third

The Last Ride

The Crystal Pelican

The Night the Music Died

Dead Men Don't Smile

Dead in the Creek

Dropped Dead

Dead Luck

A Shot in the Dark

Dead or a Lie

JAKE HORN MYSTERIES

A Ring and a Prayer (Series prequel)

A Good Time for Goodbye

The Silence of the Sand

When the Smoke Clears

U.S. MARSHAL CHARLIE HARLOW

Shake the Trees

Trackdown

Half Moon Rising

JOE SHELDON SERIES

Play It Cool

Play It Again

Play It Down

STANDALONES

Bicayne Boogie

Drag the Man Down

Half Cocked

Danny's Womack's .38

We're Not Down (summer 2026)